Thirteen Weeks On The Last Mile Bus

C.A. Caldwell

BookLocker
Trenton, Georgia

Copyright © 2025 C.A. Caldwell

Print ISBN: 978-1-959620-60-0
Ebook ISBN: 979-8-88531-807-5

All rights reserved. No part of this publication may be reproduced, stored in a retrieval system, or transmitted in any form or by any means, electronic, mechanical, recording or otherwise, without the prior written permission of the author.

Published by BookLocker.com, Inc., Trenton, Georgia.

The characters and events in this book are fictitious. Any similarity to real persons, living or dead, is coincidental and not intended by the author.

BookLocker.com, Inc.
2025

First Edition

Scripture references from Jeremiah 29:11 (NIV).

Library of Congress Cataloging in Publication Data
Caldwell, C.A.
Thirteen Weeks On The Last Mile Bus by C.A. Caldwell
Library of Congress Control Number: 2025911673

THIS BOOK IS
DEDICATED TO
THE SPECIAL
NEEDS CHILDREN
OF THE WORLD

eSPECIALly

AARON

OLIVER

&

BEN

NONE OF THE CHARACTERS OR EVENTS IN THIS NOVEL ARE BASED ON AN INDIVIDUAL CHILD OR FAMILY. RATHER, IT STRIVES TO REFLECT COMMON CHARACTERISTICS OF THE VARIOUS CHALLENGES FACED BY CHILDREN ON THE AUTISM SPECTRUM AND THOSE WITH SIMILAR DISABILITIES, AS WELL AS PAY HOMAGE TO THE BIG-HEARTED, SELF-SACRIFICING PEOPLE WHO HELP CARE FOR THEM.

ANY SIMILARITY TO REAL PERSONS, LIVING OR DEAD, IS STRICTLY COINCIDENTAL AND NOT INTENDED BY THE AUTHOR.

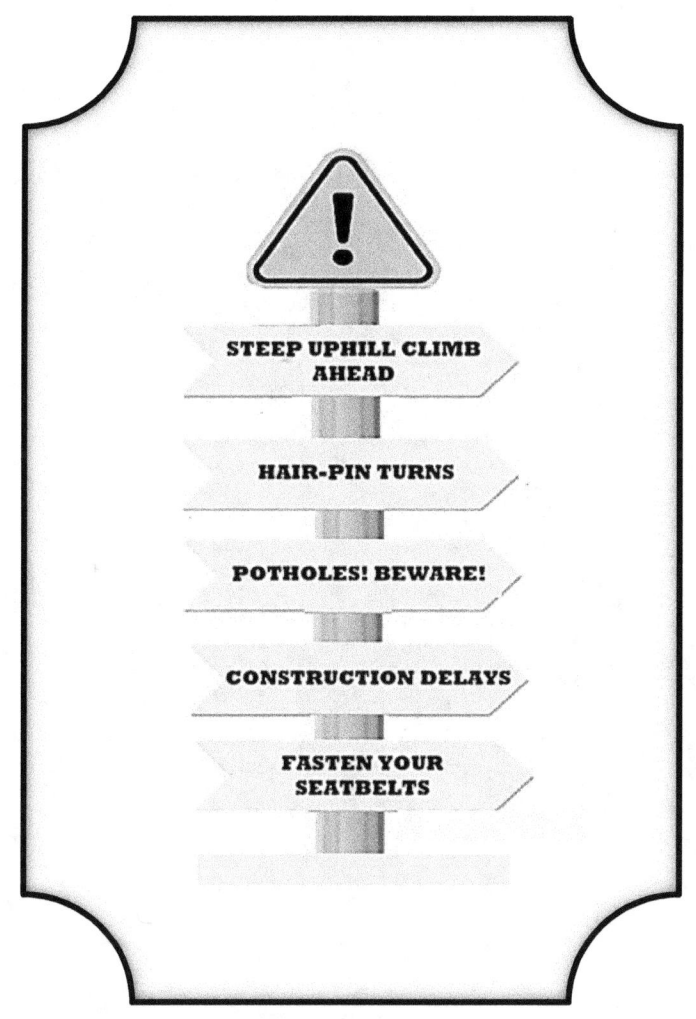

IT'S A BUMPY BUS RIDE,

BUT THE TRIP *IS* WORTH IT.

WEEK ONE

MONDAY
January 07, 2019-Afternoon

Grady Redwine had been on a first-name basis with trouble for most of his life. So, when the dispatcher told him to report to HR directly after his high school bus route that morning, he figured he was probably in for it even if he wasn't sure why.

What could they possibly want this time?

He parked; hot-footed it across the parking lot and approached the receptionist with the enthusiasm of a dental patient facing a root canal. "I'm here to see Margaret Sorenson, Director of...."

Margaret's voice shot down the hall. "Come on in, Mister Redwine."

Grady cringed. His twenty-nine-year relationship with Margaret had seen its highs and lows, but she had never addressed him as "Mister," not even the day she sat in the meeting while the School Board fired him as their Head Basketball Coach.

He decided to try casual charm. "Hey there! How're ya doin'?"

She motioned him toward a chair across from her. "Not now, Grady. This isn't a social visit."

He sat as directed and watched as she slid a form toward him across the desk. He tried to make the swipe of his palm along his pants look coincidental, but the form still stuck to damp fingers when he picked it up.

"I didn't want to have this meeting, Grady. I really didn't. But after all we've been through, you've let me down again and here we are."

"Wait. What? How did I let you down? There's obviously been a mis..."

"There's no mistake, Grady. You've been notified in writing about this on several occasions and you've chosen to ignore it. So here we are for the second time in six months having a formal discussion about your performance."

She pointed toward the paper in his hand. "Please read the second paragraph aloud."

Grady cleared his throat. "Is this really necessary, Margaret? Can't we just talk? I…"

Her hand jerked upward. "Second paragraph. Please."

He fished his glasses out of a breast pocket, perched them on the tip of his nose, and began to scan through the print.

"Read. Aloud. Please."

He blew out his breath then squinted back down at the page. "All employees are required to attend certain mandatory meetings and/or training sessions based on his or her job responsibilities. Failure to meet this requirement will result in disciplinary action, up to and including dismissal."

He looked up.

She nodded toward the paper. "Please continue."

He searched for and re-found his place. "I understand that I am considered an *employee at will* and my employment can be terminated for any reason, without notice or establishment of *just cause*, with the exception of infractions involving age, creed, religion, gender, or any other protected category under Title Vee-Eye-Eye, oh—uh—I guess that's a *seven—Title Seven.*"

"Is that your signature at the bottom?"

He puffed out his cheeks and exhaled. "Yes it is."

Margaret let the message soak in a minute. She continued: "Performance expectations for bus drivers are waaay different from those of being a coach, Grady. You don't just climb on a bus in the morning, drive around picking up kids for an hour, then go home. You have to attend meetings. You have to arrive at your stops the way they're scheduled. You have to fill out reports on things that may not mean much to you but are important to the school system, so you do them…correctly…and turn them in on time."

After an awkward pause, Grady leaned forward and spoke: "Margaret. I've showed up on time. I've run my route on time. I haven't dented or broken anything. I've done my paperwork right. I've passed every surprise drug test. I haven't taken any days off. I've smiled at parents even when I wanted to slug them. I don't even have beers with the boys anymore. And you're going to fire me? Over *this*? Over *meetings*?"

"Over three missed *mandatory* meetings."

"But…"

She held up a hand to silence him. "You were already on thin ice when you came to *Transportation*, Grady. Most people would have been fired for your last infraction, but everyone bent over backwards to give you a second chance because of what you've done for the school system in the past…"

"And I'm very grateful for that."

"...yet here you are a-gain." She removed her glasses and looked him straight in the eyes. "The ice is melting fast for you, Grady. These latest rule infractions are real...and serious...and actionable."

"Margaret...I swear. I check my mailbox every day. I didn't get any notice about any meetings."

"The notices were sent by email, Grady."

"I didn't get the emails."

"This is ridiculous. Are you trying to convince me your dog ate your homework?"

"No. I'm trying to tell you I don't know how to do email."

"Grady. We've been sending you emails for two years. You've answered them all."

"I didn't answer them. My *wife* answered them."

"You posted on *Facebook*. You've texted, used *Twitter* and *Instagram*."

He reached into his pocket, pulled out a banged-up flip phone and raised his right hand. "I swear. I answer the phone. That's all I know how to do."

He watched her eyebrows leap toward her hairline. "Texting has been around since nineteen-ninety-*two*, Grady. It's **Two-Thou-sand-Nine-Teen**. What planet have you been liv-*ving* on?"

He took a deep breath and managed to reply in a civil tone. "It's never been a problem...until now."

"Well, it's time-to-get-on-board."

Her eyes bore into him, then she shook her head slowly and took on a look of surrender. "I swear, Grady Redwine, anyone who hadn't worked with you and Mary all these years would call BS on all of this and kick your butt out of here. But I've watched you together. Admired you two. I know you were a team."

All he could manage was an appreciative shrug.

"I don't want to seem harsh, Grady. We all loved Mary. Her death was an absolute tragedy. Everyone misses her like crazy and we know how much she meant to you. But she's been gone nearly eight months."

Grady looked off into space and silently corrected her. *Eight months and two days.*

She continued: "And there comes a time after a loss like yours that you have to find a way to move on. The hard facts are that you have responsibilities. You know the policy. Everything is high-tech now. Every report has to be filled out and filed online. Payroll is reported online. Every notice comes through email. You have known this for a long time. You had to have a plan of some sort."

A voice inside Grady shouted, *"I had a plan to win the State championship again. I had a plan to team up with the girl of my dreams and grow old with her. I had plans to retire and travel to Tuscany. But it never, ever, occurred to me that I needed a plan for dealing with what would happen in my life after watching my dreams die of cancer."*

He forced the voice down and swallowed hard. "Nope. No plan."

"Well, all I can say is you better get one, Grady."

He didn't reply.

"Grady?"

He shifted in his chair. "I'll get one."

"Okay then. Fasten your seat belt. I'm about to give you some things to get you started."

He sighed.

"I've got good news and bad news. The bad news is that I was supposed to let you go today and your route has already been assigned to someone else. The good news is that the Board left the final decision about *how* to let you go up to me and I've decided to put you on a *Performance Improvement Plan.*"

"Thank you."

"You are to be suspended for two weeks without pay, but you can use sick leave if you have any left," she paused.

"I spent it all taking Mary to doctors."

She took a hitched breath and moved on. "Your plan is based on four criteria. One, you have to get onboard with texting and email. Two, you must buy a smartphone and know how to use it when you report back to duty. Three, to save your insurance and pension, you have to maintain a spotless record with no infractions for one full year. At that time, your status will be reviewed, and we will determine your future with this organization."

Grady stared at her, dumbstruck.

"I'm presenting this decision at the Board meeting on Friday afternoon, and I feel certain they will approve it." She paused and looked him straight in the eyes. "This is your only chance to resolve these issues, Grady. You have a full fourteen days to get your act together. Use the time well. If you mess up, you will be terminated immediately. Is that clear?"

"Yes. It's clear." He shifted in his seat. "Uh, you said four. What's the fourth cri...the fourth one."

"You are to be transferred to our *Special Needs* team. Fortunately for you, Ellen Parsons is starting a new program over there and she has an opening, so you will begin to drive for them upon your return." She handed him a slip of paper. "Call this number. Ask for Eddy. He will give you details." She slid a document across the desk and pointed to a line at the bottom. "Sign here."

He picked up a pen. "A handicapped bus? You're assigning me to a *handicapped* bus?"

"After all this, you're *com-plain-ing*?"

"No, uh, no." He signed his name.

"And it's a *Special Needs* Bus, Grady. Not a *handicapped* bus, a *gimp* bus, a *short* bus, or any other kind of derogatory bus. Not ever. Got that?"

"Got it." He hesitated for a moment. "How about if I can work a trade with the guy who got my old route?"

She slid her glasses down her nose and stared over the top of the frames. "No, Grady. No."

"But I don't know anything about driving a handi-...uh *Special Needs* Bus."

She pushed her glasses back into place. "Learn."

Late Afternoon

Grady was in a daze when he walked back to the bus to pick up his personal things, mumbling to himself: "Don't people **talk** to each other anymore? Why didn't someone just *call* me—leave a message? Or have a plain ol' conversation in the hall to find out why I was missing meetings—what a *con*cept!" He stopped to snatch a couple of heavy-duty trash bags from a box beside a bin, unfolded them and shook some air inside to inflate them.

"Margaret knew Mary was the business arm of our marriage. If she had just picked up the phone and called me, we could have straightened this out in five minutes.

"So now what have they got? They've got a bunch of little kids riding around on a bus with a driver who doesn't know a *thing* about handi...-uh-*Special Needs*. Great solution, guys. **Great** solution."

He climbed aboard the bus and stuffed his gear into the bags. When finished, he tightly twisted the tops and tied them in knots. Then after a short, sad, last look around, he hauled the trash bags across the lot to his old pickup and tossed them into the truck-bed over the tailgate.

After settling in behind the wheel, he rolled down his window to check out some dark clouds rolling in and inhaled deeply. "Ozone. It's gonna rain."

He inhaled again, exhaled slowly, and cast another quick glance at the sky. "Looks like we could get lucky, Mary my dear. This might mean an early Spring."

He managed a smile. Mary would've loved this moment—learning her garden could come back to life soon. She'd be sitting in the seat next to him searching for the trumpets of daffodils in yards all the way home.

Grady grew a little wistful when he turned the key in the ignition, wishing God had kept daffodils in mind when he designed humans—let them rest for a while in the winters of their lives, then when Spring rolled around, return them fully restored to those who love them and allow them to bloom again.

###

While driving home, Grady felt dread building up in his body as his thoughts returned to his meeting with Margaret and her list of technology demands. *I need a plan.*

This was a new experience for him—needing a plan for something and not already having one because Mary was a planner by nature. She had plans for potential vacations, schedules for maintenance and improvements to the house. She had diagrams drawn for what she wanted to plant in her garden, when to plant it and where. She had evacuation plans if the house caught on fire; *bug-out bags* packed and ready to go if they had to escape a tornado; and a stash of pre-packaged MRE meals if a storm-front trapped them at home.

Who'd ever guess in light of Mary's meticulous planning, that the thing he would need most right now was a plan!"

It wasn't as if Grady wasn't capable of planning. He could scan through a scouting report and come up with a helluva good game plan in no time. But when it came to technology and managing the daily logistics of life, he had to admit that he was pretty much clueless. Thank Heavens Margaret gave him two weeks to deal with it.

Oh, he'd miss the money, for sure, but he never would have been able to meet the requirements for his return to work if he had to do everything on her list by Monday. He felt certain if she knew that two weeks off was actually a bonus, she wouldn't have done it, so that was a secret he'd take to his grave.

Grady usually did his shopping on Friday, but since his workweek was officially finished by Margaret today, he decided to stop off at *Qwik Pick* and stock up for the weekend, just to get it out of the way. That decision would have been considered a good one if the little Spring shower he thought he spotted an hour ago hadn't become a torrential downpour by the time he pulled into his driveway.

He switched on the dome light and sized up the passenger side of the seat piled high with groceries and some burgers he picked up at a drive-thru, then he scanned down to the half-case of beer jammed into the footwell with two ten-pound, *buy-one-get-one-free* bags of ice.

How the Hell am I gonna get all that stuff inside?

Most people would just drive into their garage and make several trips back and forth to the pantry. But life wasn't that simple for Grady.

After six months of driving home soaked in sweat every day, filled with dread over having to face Mary's empty kitchen, he finally came to what he believed was a logical conclusion that the only way he would be able to heal from her loss was to stop going in there.

Even though that decision meant eating out every meal and chilling all his drinks in a cooler, he believed inconvenience was a small price to pay for peace of mind. Unfortunately, he hadn't carefully considered what a big pain in the butt camping out in the den could become until he was faced with this spell of bad weather.

He turned his attention away from the groceries, searching for a possible break in the storm, but all he saw were dark clouds stretching for miles. So, he sat and stared at the garage door in his headlights while weighing his options and trying to ignore the incessant voice in his head that kept offering its unwelcome opinion.

This is an emergency, Grady. Just make an exception. Go on in through the garage.

To almost anyone else, making an exception would be a no-brainer, but Grady was a coach to the core who reluctantly strayed from a game plan. He knew that if he took the easy way out he could start over again, but he'd also hate himself in the morning. So, he shifted his eyes toward the only option left open to him: the main entry to the house, barely visible down a flooding dirt pathway, almost a full block away.

Ugh.

He noodled the issue around in his mind while he wolfed down the burgers and fries so he'd have fewer things to carry, and decided just to take bare necessities in now, then come back for the rest sometime later.

He tucked a roll of toilet paper down the front of his shirt; stuffed as many cans of beer as he could inside his jacket, then while cursing himself for packing his gloves with the stuff from the bus, managed to lift a bag of ice with each arm, grab his keys, and make a mad dash for the front door.

He slogged through ankle-deep muddy water, fighting sharp, sleet-filled headwinds and bushes whipping around in the path, growing increasingly grateful for the bags of ice that helped anchor him down. He clinched and unclenched his hands as he walked, attempting to coax feeling back into fingers growing numb from the cold.

Don't drop the keys, Grady. Don't drop the keys.

Fumbling around with the lock in the dark at the front door with half-frozen fingers was a challenge, but he miraculously managed to make it inside just moments before the elastic gave way in the waist of his jacket and a couple of cans fell to the floor. He dropped the ice in a panic and clutched at the load left in his jacket.

Oh please. Oh please. Not now. Not today.

He sank to the stone floor by sliding his back down the door jamb, hoping to reduce the distance any more loose cans could fall. Then he sat in the doorway while holding his breath and listened for soft sounds of hissing. When satisfied that he had managed to escape a disaster, Grady gingerly unloaded the rest of his cans, lined them all upright along the wall and left them there to let the beer settle.

Soaked to the skin and shivering, Grady stripped to his skivvies, dropped his clothes in a soggy heap on the floor and wiped himself dry with the throw-rug. After a quick stop in the john, he pulled on heavy warm-ups, settled into the recliner wrapped up in a blanket and scanned through the *TV schedule* to start plugging into his weekend.

What a day. What a day.

With the exception of *Michigan at Illinois* starting at eight, tonight's college schedule looked pretty lame. *Michigan is still undefeated...the Illini have lost four games straight.* He wasn't as big a pro fan as he was of college, but the *Thunder-Spurs* game at 9:30 had some promise. He could toggle.

He checked the clock. *Five-thirty—two and a half hours to tip-off.* Marjorie's image flashed through his mind—maybe he should...

The voice in his head interrupted his thought: *You can start dealing with the phone and email tomorrow. It's been a hard day. Take a nap. Relax. You have two weeks to get that stuff done.*

He was tired, but he was also wound up. And since he wasn't a big fan of the unknown, he decided to work on his technology issues for a couple of hours and determine an approach for his plan.

Grady had been able to dodge his kitchen heartache all day today, but there was no getting around the grief that washed over him when Mary's grandfather clock chimed six as he passed by on the way to her office, evoking wave after wave of memories.

The clock face was a true work of art fit with polished brass weights and a graceful brass pendulum; all housed in a finely crafted walnut and glass case. It had been Mary's most prized possession.

*Grady always smiled when he saw it, remembering how adamant she was that this was **the** clock...the **only** clock in the entire world that would do.*

They couldn't afford it, but they bought it anyway, and on the day that it was delivered, he spotted her in the hall with one hand on the clock and the other on her chest, smiling.

"Come here for a second," she said when she saw him. "I have something to show you."

She reached out, took his right hand and placed it across her breastbone.

He raised his eyebrows. "Ooooo. I like this already."

"This is serious. Put your other hand on the clock."—He did— "Now be really quiet and listen."

It was an amazing experience to learn that the tick of the clock was in perfect sync with her heartbeat. "Wow."

"Isn't that wild?"

"Magic."

She tilted her head to the side and smiled. "Meant to be."

As he often did since Mary's passing, Grady placed his hand on the clock and stood there awhile, feeling her soothing presence nearby.

"I gotta go through your stuff tonight, honey. Please forgive me." In his heart, he heard her voice whisper while the pendulum swayed, "It's okay-it's okay-it's okay."

Eventually, he managed to tear himself away and head for her office door but hesitated with his hand hovering over the doorknob. He took a deep breath, straightened his back, then opened the door and stepped inside.

Even when Mary was alive, Grady didn't go into that room much. It was *her* office – filled with her photo albums and books, her handwriting and files; a place for everything and everything in its place. Since the funeral, he mostly just kept the door closed.

He flipped on the light, sat down in her chair and began to survey the situation. He wasn't exactly sure what was what, so he followed the various cords from the computer to where they led. One went to an oversized monitor on the right. A split-cord tracked to a set of speakers—one right, one on the left. Yet another cord ran to what he proudly recognized to be a mouse sitting on a little cushion. Another led to a printer. And the last one was plugged into the wall.

He spent some time gingerly tilting the laptop, searching for a way to get in. After five minutes of poking, prodding and pushing, he was embarrassed to learn that *getting in* just meant lifting a hinged cover. The next struggle was finding a lever, or some kind of button marked "on." All he saw was an alphabetic keyboard with a bunch of symbols in the top row that he didn't understand, so he resorted to a random pressing of buttons. Finally, he heard fans whirring, felt a slight vibration, and saw four little colored balls whirl around on the screen above the words:

Starting Up. Hang Tight.

So far so good.

He wiped his sweaty hands on his shirt and waited for the machine to do whatever came next.

Grady would never have guessed that **next** was the monitor flashing on and projecting a home movie of Mary and him enjoying a long, slow dance on the beach.

His eyes flashed to the keyboard— *How do I stop this*—He felt around for an *off* button on the monitor's frame—*a volume control—something.*

Stop. Please. Stop! He found nothing.

Finally, defeated, he closed his eyes and let the music play on, as the images of them dancing at the wedding of friends replayed in his mind.

They were scheduled to leave that week-long event a day early because they had a long drive to the airport; an even longer flight home; and Mary didn't want to risk missing her annual dental appointment that Wednesday.

But after some light-hearted ribbing about jinxing the marriage and jokes about choosing a root canal over being with friends, they gave in and tried to reschedule their departure date. Fortunately, all the flights were full, so they continued home as originally planned.

It turned out to be the last carefree fun they had as a couple before Mary Louise Redwine locked her eyes onto his and mouthed, *I love you*. Then with his name on her lips, gripped his hand and slipped away, taking what Grady believed was the best of himself with her.

He reached out and gently touched her face frozen in place on the monitor. She wasn't a strikingly beautiful woman, but to him, she was lovely.

So Lovely.

More hazy memories began to rise in his mind: *falling in love during a blind date neither of them wanted to go on in college; watching her walk toward him down the aisle at their wedding; crying in each other's arms when she learned she couldn't have children; renewing their vows while she still had ability to say them; watching orderlies wheel her away to remove the tumor under her tongue; kissing her for the very last time.*

Brutal memories.

But priceless.

The ring of his phone in the living room shocked Grady back to reality. He raced down the hall to answer the call but whoever it was just left a message.

Grady ignored it—watched the game. He couldn't face going back to the office.

The phone rang again. He ignored that call too.

Damn telemarketers...never give up.

FRIDAY
January 11, 2019-Morning

Grady slept in late…the first time that happened in ages. The *Thunder-Spurs* game the night before was an unexpected thriller—a whopping 154 to 147 —a mind-boggling 301 points total! *Unheard of.*

After coffee and fetching the paper, Grady probably would have walked down the hall to the electric chair faster than he walked to Mary's office to continue his quest to meet Margaret's demands. He'd spent most of the week after his meeting with Margaret avoiding going back in there, but decided he'd better quit procrastinating. He only had ten days left to get everything done. In order to do that effectively, however, he knew his number one priority had to be figuring out how to stop that video from playing again.

After he found the cord to the monitor and disconnected it, he opened the computer and studied the keyboard. He didn't waste any time trying to decipher the symbols. He just redid what worked the last time: randomly pressing keys until he heard a whirring. It worked again, and the screen lit up with the familiar:

Starting Up. Hang Tight.

An oblong box containing a photo of Mary's garden in full bloom flashed on above a new prompt:

User Name

Grady stared at the screen. *Time to man up, Redwine.*
Hmmmmm. Username. He tried *Redwine. No.* He tried *MRedwine. Yes!*
Maybe this wouldn't be so bad after all.
Up popped another request:

Password

He counted six empty dots to be filled in. *Hmmmmm what could be six.* He tried her birthday. *No.* He tried his birthday. *No.*

As if the computer was reading his mind, a small question underlined in blue appeared at the bottom of the screen.

Having trouble signing in?

He took a risk and clicked on it.

*Tell us one of the following to get started:
Sign-in email address or mobile number
Recovery phone number
Recovery email address*

Grady studied his choices. Thought a minute. Then the world slammed to a halt, and he slapped himself on the *head. Mary's phone. Mary had a smartphone!* He didn't have to buy one—he could use hers—if he could get it going again.

He returned his attention to the screen and entered Mary's mobile number. He got nearly an instant response.

Accepted

Yesss! He joyfully rubbed his hands together. *We're cooking with gas, people.*

*We have sent a temporary password to that number.
Please note that this password will expire in fifteen minutes.
If you have not logged in at that time,
you must resubmit the password reset request.*

Oh my God! Where **is** *her phone?* He checked the time. *Eight fifteen.*

Grady listened for a ring. *Nothing—it should be ringing. If they sent me a password, it should be ringing—but no.* He didn't even hear a chime from the clock.

Maybe it was a ding. He strained for a ding. *Something. Anything...dinging.*

Finally, a weak little beep beckoned from down the hall.

Her bag. The bag from the Hospice. He'd left it on the bed in the guest room.

Grady rushed to the bed. Snapped open the locks. Threw open the lid of the suitcase.

Please have the phone. Please have the phone.

He plunged his hands in the middle of the clothes. Squeezed. Felt around the edges. Nothing.

Desperate, he dumped the lot on the floor. Rummaged through the contents.

Still nothing.

*Where **is** it? Where could it be? It **has** to be here.*

He sank to the edge of the mattress feeling slightly light-headed from the antiseptic fumes rising out of the bag.

Grady checked his watch. *Eight twenty. Please God, help me find this phone.*

He rose and began to return to the office but was called back by another sad little beep rising mysteriously from the empty suitcase. Grady grabbed it. Tipped it over.

Swinging from the lid of the bag was a heavy lump encased in a hidden silk zipper compartment. There it was.

Thank you, Lord. Thank you, Lord.

He ripped the phone out of the compartment and searched for the *on* button. He located two bumps on the left side—pushed the top one—nothing happened—pushed the bottom one—nothing—found another on the right side and pushed in—still nothing. The phone was obviously dead.

Charger. I need the charger.

Grady searched the suitcase for another zipper compartment. *Nope.*

He ran down a list of possibilities. *Maybe the office. Maybe the bedroom.*

He sprinted to their bedroom, searched Mary's side of the bed. *No!* He raced back to the office and checked the outlets around her desk. *No!*

Damn!

Think, Grady. Think.

The ladies of the Hospice mercifully packed Mary's things for him when she passed. It might have been left there.

Where else? What else?

He'd about concluded that he'd have to buy a new charger the next day, when his gaze shifted momentarily out the window to Mary's car resting in a ring of light in the side yard. *Car charger!*

He searched madly through the jumble in their junk drawer. *Keys, keys, keys. Bingo!*

He rushed to the yard; climbed in behind the wheel and opened the glove compartment.

The charger burst out like a jail break.

Yes! Oh Jesus! Yes!

Grady jammed the charger into the cigarette lighter. Cranked the engine. Got nothing but a high-pitched whine.

He pumped the accelerator. *Come on. Come on.*

He cranked again. Still no.

Please! Please!

He cranked again and double pumped. The engine sputtered to a start. *Finally.*

Grady jammed the cord into the bottom of the phone; pressed each of the three buttons one at a time—*nothing*—desperate and frustrated, he just strangled the damn thing. It took a minute, and he didn't know why, but the screen finally decided to light up.

Yesss!

Grady expected to see a list of missed calls or messages, but the screen was filled with nine circled numbers arranged like a calculator. Across the top were six dots and the command:

Enter Passcode.

Noooo. Noooo! Another **code***?!*

He tried their anniversary. Didn't work. He tried 1,2,3,4,5,6. Didn't work. He took a shot with the last six digits of her social security number. A notice appeared:

The device has been locked for security reasons.
Call the number below to talk to an agent.

Grady's head dropped back against the headrest. He didn't have to check his watch to know his fifteen minutes were up.

He crawled out of the car and dragged one foot after the other back to the house. If he only had five more minutes…just five. He might have had the code. Or at least know what he should do next.

He rounded the corner and stopped dead in his tracks at the top of the driveway where his truck was parked. *You Dumb Ass.*

He slammed his fist on the hood and kicked a tire. *You. Are. An. Effin'.* **Dumb. Ass.**

You knew you hadn't started Mary's car for over a year. Why didn't you just take the charger out of the glove compartment and use it in your **truck***? You'd have had your five minutes!*

He stomped into the house and sprawled in his chair. *You've got to turn your brain on, son. This is ridiculous.*

After several more minutes of sulking, he noticed a flashing light on his home phone reminding him that he had received two phone calls the night before. *Probably should check and see who it was or delete them to stop the flashing.* He dialed into voicemail and listened.

> *It's Margaret Sorenson, Grady. I'm calling to let you know that today has been your lucky day! This afternoon, the Board decided to overturn your week of suspension because the Special Needs team needs you to start driving on Monday. Please keep in mind that the rest of the terms set forth in our meeting remain as written.*
>
> *Eddy will be calling you soon with more details about your bus number and route. Good luck on your new assignment, Grady. If you have additional questions, please give me a call.*

Grady slumped down on the couch. **Holy Hell!** He pushed the *play* button for the second message.

> *Hello, Mister Redwine. This is Eddy. Margaret Sorenson asked me to remind you that you are scheduled to start your new route on Monday. You're assigned to Bus Fourteen Eighty-Six. It's parked somewhere on the lot at the school. The keys to your old bus will work on your new one. Report for work at six A.M.. Use your old time-fob. You'll be met by Clara Foster, your Bus Monitor. She will fill you in on everything. Oh, and Margaret said to remind you not to forget your smartphone. She will text you sometime later in the day just to check with you. Have a good weekend. Goodbye.*

Grady dropped the receiver onto the cushion beside him. *Please. Someone. Shoot me.*

He popped open a beer and ripped open some chips. S*martphone. By Monday. You're gonna need a better plan.*

SATURDAY
January 12, 2019

Grady slept fitfully all night and dragged out of bed around Noon. He plugged the car charger into the cigarette lighter of his truck and attached Mary's smartphone before he took off to fuel himself up for the day, hoping the caffeine in his coffee would kick in before reality took hold.

He drove around listening to Notre Dame battle it out with North Carolina, letting the phone charge up a little, then headed for home at half-time.

About ten minutes from his house, the sign for an electronics store that he drove past but ignored every day finally drew his attention.

Let's face it, Grady. If you charge that thing and finally reach someone, they're just gonna ask questions you can't answer. If you're not careful, you're gonna spend your last business day running in circles, getting nowhere.

You only have until Monday to sort all this out. Just say to Hell with it all, get some professional help, and start over.

Good point. He'd go in there and give it a try. He had absolutely nothing to lose.

###

Grady parked and wandered into the store. A man in a suit with a name tag on his lapel that identified him as Jack McMullen, Store Manager, joined them. "Welcome, sir. What brings you here to see us today?"

Grady glanced around at the aisles of refrigerators and TVs. "I need some help with my computer and cell phone. Do you do that here?"

"Absolutely. How can we help you?"

Grady took a breath and began to rattle off his problem.

"I got locked out of my computer because my wife passed away and I don't know the password and I guessed wrong too many times and I finally got them to send me a code to my wife's phone." He held the phone up for all to see. "The code came to unlock it, but I've never used a phone like this one before and I don't know how to work it."

Grady watched McMullen's eyes squint while he absorbed what he had just been told. "Sooo if I understand you correctly, you're having trouble changing the password on your wife's phone, which you need so you can get a code to unlock your computer. Is that correct?"

"Uh," Grady mulled over what McMullen just said a moment and settled on, "Pretty much. I think so. Yeah."

McMullen glanced around the lobby and gestured toward the rear of the store. "Let's go back to the service desk, sir. It's a little more private there."

Grady trailed along behind McMullen, and after the Manager stepped behind the counter, he said, "In order to get started, since it was your wife's phone, all we need for security purposes is a little legal documentation. Did you bring a copy of your wife's *Death Certificate* with you?"

Grady shook his head. "A court order?" *Court order?* McMullen seemed to take the expression on his face as a *no*. "How about a copy of a *Will* leaving her property to you."

He finally managed, "We only had each other. Everything is just mine automatically."

"*Marriage Certificate?*"

Grady held up the hand with his time-worn wedding band and said, "Just this."

"Hmmmm. Well then, let's try it another way. If you give me her *APPLE I.D.*, I can..."

Grady foraged around in his brain for a few seconds—came up empty. "The only thing I know about apples is I like them."

McMullen chuckled. "Good one." He pulled out a pen; prepared to write. "Sooo...?"

Grady shrugged. "Haven't got a clue.*"*

"How about email—maybe we can start with that. *Google*? *iCloud*? *AOL*?"

He shrugged an apologetic, *Sorry.*

"Hmmm. Was she the only person using the phone?"

"Yes. Yes, she was."

"How about a phone bill. Did you bring one?"

"We have everything on autopay. I've never seen a bill."

Grady saw frustration flash through the man's eyes and realized it was time just to swallow his pride and explain.

"When I was in college, high-tech was an electric typewriter, Mister McMullen. After that, I was a basketball coach for twenty-five years, and the only technical skills I needed for that job, were dribbling, passing and shooting. When our department went through its first big technology upgrade, I got a whiteboard with erasable markers.

"My wife was the computer genius in our family, so there was never any *need* for me to know how to use one."

Grady paused—took a breath—rushed on. "No one expected my wife to die young, Mister McMullen, but...she did. And I never thought the day would come when I wasn't coaching a team, but...I'm not. I'm driving a school bus for a living so I can have medical benefits. And I have been told that if I'm not able to get phone calls, text messages and emails by Monday, I'm not going to be a bus driver either."

There was an awkward pause between them while Grady watched the man take a nervous glance around the increasingly busy store. Finally, after an obvious struggle with his conscience, McMullen took a long, deep breath and nodded toward the smartphone. "Does that one work?"

Grady shrugged a shoulder. "It seemed to work when I came in here. I hooked it up to the car charger in my truck this morning, but it wasn't plugged in for long."

"I have a charger at the other end of the desk," said McMullen. He reached out for the phone and Grady handed it over. "Let's go down there and see what we can do."

When there, McMullen plugged it in, slid his thumb over the screen a couple of times then smiled. "It works. We've got a good start."

He tapped his fingers around the keyboard of a computer for a while then looked back at Grady. "May I see your *Driver's License*?"

Grady fished it out and handed it over.

McMullen studied it a minute—compared it with the screen. "Great. This is good. Your name is on the bill. I see you've been a customer a long time."

"Yes."

He stood and looked Grady straight in the eyes. "Here's the honest truth, Mister Redwine. I'm going to try hard to help you with your computer and phone, but there's no guarantee that I can."

"Whatever you can do, I'll be grateful for. Just thank you for trying, Mister McMullen."

McMullen reached out a hand. "Jack. Please. Call me Jack."

Grady took Jack's hand in his and shook it. "And I'm Grady. You have no idea how much this means to me."

Jack smiled. "I've needed help a few times in my life. I understand." He headed for the door to a back room then turned back toward Grady. "This may take a while. We have a waiting room around to your right. They have coffee—sodas—a TV—uncomfortable chairs..." Grady laughed. "Why don't you go back there and wait while I check out what I can do."

"Thank you. Will do."

Half an hour later, Jack came into the waiting room with the phone and a small stack of paper. He joined him at his table, handed the phone to him and smiled. "Congratulations. You're unlocked and loaded and ready to go."

Grady's arms shot into the air. "Yessssss! Wow. **Thank** you! How did you *do* it?"

Jack waggled his eyebrows; flashed him a benevolent smile. "Don't ask." He picked up the papers he brought with him and slid them across the table.

"I was able to find your wife's email address because she had to use it as her APPLE ID, then I took a wild guess and tried using her birth date for her PIN and it worked. With those two things, you should be able to unlock everything else and begin to send and receive messages right away."

Grady felt goosebumps rise on his arms. "Wow. That's wonderful."

"Unfortunately, I can't do anything to help with your computer today, so I built you a little cheat sheet."

"Ohhhh Kaaaayyyy."

Jack pointed at the first item and worked his way down the page.
- "If you're given four empty circles, enter one-nine-five-nine.
- "Five circles almost always mean they want the last five of your Social. Try your wife's first. If that doesn't work, try yours. You only get three tries, so if neither one works, click on *forgot.*"

Grady's brain started to spin
- "Six circles usually mean they're going to send you a code."
- "Any time something says *APPLE and you're given a lot of room to write, they probably want your wife's email address. I've written it right here for you.*"

Grady squinted at the notation. "Thank you."
- "Just remember, **her** email address is **your** APPLE ID, and if they ask for a phone number, use hers.
- "These are the steps to write an email, and this is how you open and answer one."
- "This list shows the steps to answer a text and what to do when you get one. "

Jack handed him two more pages. "Make a couple copies of this page and keep one of them with you somewhere safe. I've printed out the process to do everything I think you need to get started. Here's a consolidated list of your passwords. If you just stay calm and take everything one step at a time, you'll be fine."

Grady stared at Jack in wonder. "How do you know all this stuff?"

"Worked for several high-tech companies in Silicon Valley over the years then retired and opened this store." He paused; looked Grady straight in the eyes and obviously observed fear.

"You can't do this, can you."

Grady gave a weak smile. "No. Not by Monday."

Jack's voice took on a confidential tone. "I'm not exactly advising you to lie, my friend, but if nobody *directly asks* if you know how to open an email or send a text, you don't *have to just volunteer* the fact that you *don't*. My advice is, *fake it 'till you make it*, Grady. You're a smart man. You'll be fine.

He handed him a cord. "Oh! Almost forgot. I had an old wall charger. Thought you could use one."

"Thank you."

"Try practicing a little the rest of today and you have all day tomorrow. You won't be an expert by Monday, but you can look your boss in the eye and honestly say you have met the requirements."

"Thank you, Jack. Thank you. If there's anything I can ever do for you, just ask."

"Just tell your friends about us."

"Count on it."

Jack walked with him to the door; opened it for him and held it. "You may not like your smartphone for a while, Grady, but there will come a time when you wonder how you ever lived without one."

Grady smiled and didn't say it but thought, *In Your Dreams*.

SUNDAY
January 13, 2019

Grady was up early after another restless night worrying about his phone. He didn't try to turn it off but remembered to plug it in, so he figured he had a full charge when he took it off the nightstand.

He carried it into the living room; arranged the sheets of paper Jack had given him on the couch beside him; prepared to read the instructions and practice.

When he picked up the phone, the date and time were displayed at the top of the screen. At the bottom were two circles, one around what was obviously a flashlight, and the other around what looked like a camera. The rest of the screen was blank. Eventually, several small letters appeared along the bottom. He squinted at them, reached for his readers and adjusted the phone to a better position to read it. *Who **does** this? Make the print so small?*

He looked sadly at his flip phone lying on the side table. It was so simple: *You open it; you dial, you talk for a while. You close it, and you're done.* He wanted it back. He had lifelong friends whose loss didn't hurt as much as losing that phone.

After a few more minutes of mourning, Grady swiped up on the screen again and found himself back at *Contacts* with five random symbols along the bottom. At least *these* five were labeled: *Favorites, Recents, Contacts, Keypad and Voicemail.*

He aimed with his thumb at *Keypad,* but *Contacts* returned. Grady didn't blame this one on the phone, though. He knew he had fingers the size of cigars.

After two hours of failure and frustration, he finally gave up.

It is what it is, Redwine. You did your best. You've got no choice. Just do what Jack told you to do and fake it.

WEEK TWO

MONDAY
January 14, 2019-Morning

Grady was wide awake when the alarm went off at 4:30, because he'd spent most of the night pacing around in the den. It wasn't worry about driving a new route that weighed heavy on him…he'd been doing that job for a year…it was guilt over being deceitful.

He tried hard to be a dependable guy; someone people knew they could count on. And even though he wasn't above stretching the truth for a good cause or bending a few facts now and then, doing something as self-serving as this, just wasn't in him.

Maybe it's time to admit that driving a school bus isn't for you and find a way to go back to coaching. There are hundreds of guys out there who failed in one place and found success in another.

He gazed at Mary's picture for a moment or two. *That's true. But I'd have to move to another town to start over, and everything I love or care about is here.*

He unplugged the smartphone from the wall and watched it tally up time like a bomb until the snooze alarm went off down the hall and forced him to make a decision.

You've got no choice, Redwine. Your back is against the wall. Just go do what you gotta do.

###

Grady's feelings of guilt grew worse when he found frost on his old pickup. He knew he should be parking her in the garage, but when the weather was bad, using the entrance through the kitchen became too enticing, so he started leaving her out on the driveway.

The door to the truck stuck a little when he first pulled it open and the springs groaned when he climbed aboard, so he held his breath when he turned the key in the ignition. The reliable ol' gal fired up without hesitation, which was an enormous relief and a welcome good omen.

"Try to quit winding yourself up over this, Grady. All you're expected to do is pick up some kids and drive them to school; then take them home in the

afternoon. The main difference between this route and your old one is that you'll have a monitor there to handle the children, and that's a good thing. Just relax; settle into your normal routine and go get your coffee."

When he pulled into the drive-thru at the truck stop café' Grady was greeted by a smiley-faced server so short she had to step on a stool to see through the window. The name on her shirt identified her as Minnie, but in Grady's mind, it should have been: Mini.

"Wow! Mister Redwine! What a surprise to see you so early! Want your usual large Chicory Dark Roast today?"—"Yep! Extra cream. And throw in a couple shots of that…uh…that ex-presso." — She got a kind look in her eyes. "Jet fuel for a difficult day?"

"'Fraid so."

Minnie stepped down and disappeared for a while, then popped up again like toast from a toaster. "That will be seven dollars today, please."

He winced a little but opened his wallet, counted out a five and four one-dollar bills then handed them over. "Keep two for you." — She smiled and tucked them into her pocket. "Why thank you!"

It took two hands for Minnie to deliver his coffee. "Hope you enjoy your *ES*-presso today…" — She got a softer tone in her voice. — "…and everything turns out okay."

"Thank you."

He stopped for a sip at the end of the drive then pushed the speed limit all the way to the bus barn to try and find Bus Eighty-Six.

Grady entered the main gate expecting the worst. Big buses were assigned permanent spots in numerical order, but everyone else parked wherever they could without rhyme or reason. His bus could be anywhere on a dark twenty acres, and there was no time to spare. He had a list of ten things to get done before he could start driving…five of them non-negotiable.

When the beams of his headlights revealed a *Special Needs* Bus parked at the front of the Service Line straight ahead, Grady didn't hold out much hope that it was his. He wasn't usually that lucky, but he flipped on his brights anyway.

"Well, I'll be damned. Fourteen Eight-Six. Good Old Eighty-Six. Wow. Thank you, whoever you are, for making this changeover easy."

Life was good...actually, too good. It was beginning to make him nervous.

He checked the clock—5:45. He had to hurry. He parked with his headlights shining into the bus to make it easier to locate the lights and idle the engine. That way, he could be sure to have heat when he began driving.

He unlocked the bus and opened the door. Then he hurried back to his truck; stacked his jacket, the clock, Mary's phone, and his coffee on top of a clipboard; picked up his backpack; and bumped the door closed with his butt.

He did a fairly good job of juggling the stack on the clipboard one-handed by keeping it high and holding it steady using his chin. But disaster struck at the foot of the stairs, and he tripped on a sleeve hanging down from his jacket. Grady stumbled his way up a couple of steps, then everything in both hands went flying.

*"Noooooooo! ARE YOU KID-**DING** me?!!"* Far more painful for him than the gash in his knee and the burn from the spill on his hand, was watching Mary's phone skitter face down on the sheet metal floor and disappear into the dark under the seat of the driver.

"Son of a..." He glanced toward the onboard cameras and quickly searched for a school-appropriate word. He settled on, "...gun."

After all that he'd gone through over the weekend, the prospect of having to face this day without coffee was almost more than Grady could stand. He stared at the puddle he'd made on the floor to assess how much might be saved, but he'd been a school bus driver long enough to know what can end up on the floor and decided he'd have to chalk it all up to experience.

He licked what coffee he could off his hand then groped around for Mary's phone in the dark and finally located it lodged in some greasy goo lurking underneath the accelerator.

"I hate you, you effin' piece of..."

He was searching for an appropriate adjective when a woman's voice drifted his way from the open door behind him. "I take it now may not be a good time..."

Grady froze for a moment then came to his senses. "Uh no. No!" He managed to drag himself to his feet. "I was just looking for my cell phone. I...I dropped it."

"I noticed." She walked up a couple of steps and looked down at the puddle of coffee. "I suppose it's safe to assume that you're not naturally a *morning* person."

She climbed aboard then reached down to pick up the safety lid and examined the logo on the empty cup.

"Ooof, expensive. Major loss on a Monday."

Grady sort of shrugged. He set down the phone and dusted dirt off his knees. "Life's too short to drink cheap coffee."

She reached for a roll of paper towels and laid down a bunch to soak up the puddle. "Truer words were never said. If this had happened to me, I'd be sucking it out of my shirt sleeve."

She held out her hand. "I'm Clara Foster, your Bus Monitor."

He awkwardly shook it. "Uh, I'm Grady...Grady Redwine. Nice to meet you. Eddy told me you'd be here. Said you'd catch me up on things." He turned up the lights in the back of the bus and looked around. "So, this is a handi...uh, *Special Needs* Bus."

"Yep."

"I see the wheelchair lift over there. What else is special?"

She leaned against one of the vertical poles and crossed her arms. "There are lots of special things about this bus, Mister Redwine, but most of them are not mechanical."

"Why don't you just call me Coach."

"Would love to, but protocol is Mister and Miss."

He glanced down at her hand. "But you're married."

"Miss. It's still Miss. Miss Clara." She glanced at his left hand. "And you're married, too, I see."

Grady missed a beat before answering, "Yes. Yes, I am."

She reached across him, ripped a plastic folio off a strip of Velcro on the wall of the stairwell and handed it to him. "Here's the route information, data about the children, the evacuation plan, and the signed release papers from their parents."

"Release papers for what?"

"Field trips. We're participating in a new series of experimental programs. The children in our category attend academic classes in the mornings, then in the afternoon, we take them on field trips and work on their practical living skills."

"*We*...as in..."

"You and I."

"*Work on*...as in..."

"Teach."

"Shouldn't a teacher come with us?"

"Normally that's the case, but this program gives us leeway to use common sense." She smiled. "I know. What a concept."

He smiled back.

"Anyhow, they're short-handed right now, so wouldn't it kind of make sense to have you drive the bus and teach P.E. too? After all, we already have coaches in our *District* who drive their teams to games and no one objects."

"Well, with all due respect for using common sense, I know for a fact those coaches drive because they get double pay to do it."

"Good luck on that one."

"Oh, I wasn't thinking about asking for more money. My point was that there's a big difference between that situation and this one. The reason those coaches get double pay is because they are *certified* P.E. teachers who are *also certified* to drive a school bus. I would be a *certified* bus driver who is *not certified* to teach P.E.— *teaching* P.E.. I don't think that would fly."

"What do you mean, not certified? You were a coach. You taught P.E. too, right?"

"Well yeah, but I'm just a bus driver now, so that idea, however great it seems on the surface, probably won't work."

Clara shifted her weight on her feet. "I have to warn you up front that Ellen Parsons, the Director of our program, tends to beg for forgiveness, not ask permission. Flexibility is a big deal to her. I think she's expecting you to drive *and* teach."

Margaret Sorenson's face flashed through Grady's mind and one thing seemed certain. If their success rested on the remainder of his quota of forgiveness for breaking rules, it was going to be a tough year.

He sat down and tried to digest it all. "So, we teach living skills, like what? Like handling money and stuff?"

"Money is a big part of it, but we also address things like personal hygiene…both of us; exercise…that'll probably be you; cooking…probably me; shopping…mostly teachers, I think; and some higher level things like reading newspapers, using maps and working on the internet…person to be determined."

Grady broke out in a cold sweat. "The internet?"

"I take it nobody told you about this."

"My transfer here has been kind of a whirlwind. My entire orientation session with Eddy was: "Y*ou're assigned to Bus Fourteen Eighty-Six. It's parked somewhere on the lot at the school. The keys to your old bus will work on your new one. Report for work at six A.M.. Use your old time-fob. You'll be met by Clara Foster, your Bus Monitor. She will fill you in on everything."*

"Well, I'll be up front with you, Mister Redwine. Working in *Special Needs* is not for everyone, and I hate it that you've just been thrown into the deep end. But here we are. It is what it is. All I can do is assure you that we're a team and you won't be flying alone. The afternoon programs are already planned and scheduled for this week, so you don't have to do anything but drive and observe. By next week, you should be fine." She held up a high-five. "So, are you in?"

He hesitated, thinking, I *have no* **choice** *but to be in.*

She wobbled her high-five. "Well?"

He slapped her hand with the sincerity of a losing coach after the game. "I'm in."

"Good. I'm glad. Then let's get started, shall we? What questions can I answer?"

He removed some well-worn cushions from the driver's seat and plunked them behind it on the floor. "Well, for starters, what happened to the last bus driver?"

"Miss Martha had an opportunity to go on a mission to Venezuela for her church and decided she should do it…in her words…*before she was too old to haul lumber around.*"

"Lucky for Venezuela and lucky for me, I guess." He glanced through the paperwork. "How many kids on the route?"

"Five. All middle schoolers."

He puffed up a little. "My last route had sixty-four kids and thirty-two of them were in pre-school. This is practically a vacation."

She chuckled. "I hope so, Mister Redwine. I truly do."

She rolled up the coffee-soaked paper towels and tossed them into the trash, then turned toward a pile of blankets and started to fold them. "We better get going. You do your pre-check, and I'll get set in here. I'm sure you're anxious to meet the kids. We can discuss them as we pick them up."

Grady's route sheet directed them to their first stop at *The Hamilton Children's Shelter*, a sprawling private institution built on the grounds of a hilly, walled estate on the outskirts of town. He pulled up to an ornate gated entrance, framed by lush, meticulously manicured hedges and he turned toward Clara when she walked up beside him. "Wow. I didn't know all this was here."

"Beautiful, isn't it?"

"You can say that again."— He looked at the metal arm extending into the drive. — "What do I do now? Is there a card or a code?"

She reached down and pointed to five numbers after the address on the route sheet.

"Oh! I thought that was the zip code."

"It is. That's how they keep it a secret."

He opened the side window and punched in the numbers.

When the gates began to swing open, Grady stretched up and studied a surprisingly large complex of tall, neat brick buildings surrounding a manicured lawn.

As they drove down the wide, winding driveway, Clara pointed out the various pick-up locations. "We make four stops on the *Shelter* property in the morning: one on the main level at the medical facility up there on the left, one on the ground level at the residential treatment center in the lower level of the same building, and one at a group home over there on the right."

"Where's the fourth one?"

"We go to the Hamiltons' home on the other side of the property. Their son, Bennie, is one of our kids."

"Hamilton? *THE* Victor Hamilton, as in Victor Hamilton, owner of the *Comets* and half the other pro teams in the State?"

"Uh huh. *And* founder of *The Hamilton Children's Shelter* where we are now."

"My skin always gets a little crawly when I hear the word, *Shelter*."

"There's no Charles Dickens here, Mister Redwine. This *Shelter's* the best around."

"That's a *good* thing. Where's pick-up number five?"

"Halim lives outside the property in a private home."

Clara motioned to the right. "Pull over here. The first one is a wheelchair, so line up the front of the bus with that white stake by the driveway."

He examined the route sheet. "Prissy Milcamp."

Clara chuckled. "Hold on to your hat."

As if on cue, a door opened at the top of the drive, sending light streaming down the pavement. A tiny wheelchair powered by the arms of a joyful, smiling redhead raced their direction. She was trailed by a man in white medical scrubs, pumping his legs hard, but with no chance of keeping up.

"Wow. Look at her go," Grady said. "I've never seen a wheelchair like that one."

Clara headed down the stairs to greet them. "Athletic Model. Prissy runs 4Ks."

Grady did a double take. *Wow.*

In his mirror, he saw Clara open the side door and pin it back, then reach for the lift controls. He heard muffled voices and the sound of the lift grinding downward then up. Before he knew it, Prissy zipped into position behind him like a racecar driver parking in the pits.

"Miss Miller caught Marcell stealing Sonti's c*innamon toast* again this morning. She said he was going to Hell the big fat bastard."

Grady stopped what he was doing mid-motion, wide-eyed. He focused on Clara in the mirror, mouthing, "Am I supposed to say something?"

She started attaching safety straps to Prissy's wheelchair and mouthed back, "I'll explain later."

In the big mirror above his head, he watched Prissy settle back in her seat. "*Cinnamon toast* is all Sonti will eat for breakfast. Miss Miller says it was the last serving and Sonti probably won't have a bite to eat the rest of the day unless they have a pear at school, which they probably won't. They never do."

He saw Prissy's eyes finally focus on his in the mirror. "Who are *you*?"

Clara darkened the view between them as she tucked a blanket around Prissy's legs. "This is Mister Redwine, Prissy."

"Where is Miss Martha?"

"She is taking a little vacation. Mister Redwine is filling in for her."

"Oh. Okay." Prissy plunked some pink, feathered headphones on her head. "Where's our music?"

Clara glanced at Grady. "Miss Martha played the radio while she drove."

Grady turned back to the directions for his route. "Okay. Maybe later."

Prissy piped up. "But Miss Martha…"

Grady released the brake. "We're running a little late, Prissy. I'm sorry but we'll have to discuss it later."

Grady pulled around the corner as directed but had to maneuver a little to park correctly between the markers of a security driveway. *I hate picking up kids in the dark.*

He turned on the interior light and rustled through his route sheets. "Okaaayyyy. Sontiago Smith."

Clara leaned toward him. "We call him Sonti."

He glanced up from the sheaf of paper. "Anything I need to know besides cinnamon toast?"

She took a breath to answer, but Prissy blurted out, "Miss Miller says Sonti is like a box of chocolates, but Marcell says he's a King Size Nut Roll." She paused while she adjusted her book bag. "I think Marcell is fixin' to get his ass fired like that Jackie Mason the gardener did for talking bad about us kids. Miss Miller says Mister Hamilton won't stand for it. No sir. And good riddance to bad rubbish."

Grady's sense of duty took over. "We don't use words like that on this bus, Prissy."

"I didn't use those words, Miss Miller did."

"Maybe so, but you could choose to use nicer words when you tell us what she said."

"But that would be a lie. Everyone would know Miss Miller didn't say it if I took out those words. I'm not allowed to lie." Her voice grew louder, higher, faster. "Before she went to live with Jesus and they gave me up to the State, my mother said, 'We don't lie in our family.' She made me promise never to lie, because if I did, I would go to Hell and never see her again." Prissy smoothed out her blankets. "So, I don't lie, Mister Redwine. Ever."

Grady looked at Clara and said under his breath, "I guess *I* got told."

"Guess so."

"Perhaps I better pay more attention when you tell me you'll explain something later."

Clara smiled. "Perhaps."

"And maybe someone should talk to Miss Miller."

Clara laughed. "You're a large muscular man, Mister Redwine, but, trust me, Miss Miller could take you."

Grady checked his clock and frowned. "Sonti is making us late."

"He tends to take some time to get on board. We just have to roll with it and make up time later."

Grady rustled through the papers again. "Anything more I need to know about Sonti?"

"We almost always pick him up here in the morning. Afternoons vary too. Sometimes we take him home. Sometimes we bring him here. It depends on his mother's work schedule and what's going on with his sisters and brother."

"I'm confused."

"Sonti eats and sleeps here at the *Shelter* because he's too big for his mother to handle and, because of Workfare, she is required to have a job. On days when she works an early shift, she likes to have him home with her after school so he can have some family time. She usually brings him back to the *Shelter* around bedtime."

"How do we know which place to take him?"

"She sends us an email…usually around Noon."

Grady's heart sank. *Email.*

He squinted up the driveway. "Are they expecting a flood or something? Those have got to be twelve-foot walls."

As if on cue, the door opened at the back of a brick portico at the top of the drive and a large man in white appeared. "I think you're about to find out why now," she said.

The first man was followed by another one, struggling with a young man wearing what Grady recognized as a safety harness over his clothes.

Prissy's voice popped up behind him. "Here we go again."

Shouting and screams drifted their way as the melee at the top of the drive continued. Grady looked at Clara. She mouthed back, *later.*

The young man broke away and bolted down the drive, jumping and clawing up the walls trying to escape.

Grady watched with recruiting eyes. *Man! Look at that wingspan! What a vertical jump!*

He looked over at Clara. "I take it, he's not a big fan of school."

Prissy answered for her. "Sonti hates school. He likes to be home with his Mama."

After several minutes of ducking and dodging, Sonti raced for the door of the bus. Grady opened the door, and the boy leaped aboard, ending on the landing face-to-face with him. They froze eye-to-eye like two boxers at a weigh-in.

What the Hell!

Grady mentally prepared himself for an attack, but Sonti's eyes suddenly filled with fear. As if someone had pulled a plug, he dead-dropped onto his belly on the floor and peered around, obviously lost.

Clara motioned for Grady to stay where he was. "He thinks he's on the wrong bus." She stepped aside so the Aides could come on board. They lifted Sonti respectfully and walked him toward his seat. On the way, Sonti reached into Clara's stack of blankets, picked the purple one with a cartoon theme and plunked it on top of his head. The men placed him in his seat, snapped the restraining clips into the rings on his safety harness and left, looking exhausted.

Sonti burst into tears, howling his discontent. "Ahhhhhhhh! Ahhhhhhhh! Ahhhhhhhh!"

Prissy's hands shot up to cover the ear cushions of her headset. "Try the music, Mister Redwine. He's used to the music."

Grady looked at Sonti. "What kind of music would you like, Sonti?"

Sonti struggled against his restraints. "Ahhhhhhhh! Ahhhhhhhh!"

Clara leaned toward Grady and whispered, "Sonti is non-verbal, Mister Redwine."

All red-faced, Grady turned on the radio. The wail of organ music burst into the bus.

*You have **got** to be kidding.*

Grady stared at Clara.

"Miss Martha found it soothing."

He switched the radio off.

Sonti kicked the seat in front of him. BAM! BAM! BAM!

Grady turned toward Clara and mouthed, "Does this happen every day?"

"I'll explain later," she said, still close. "Leave him alone. He'll settle down soon. Mondays are hard because he's had two days off." She checked the clock. "We're late. Let's go get J.D. He's on the grounds, just around the corner to the left."

"Ahhhhhhhh! Ahhhhhhhh!"

Grady felt a nervous tremor in his hands as he gripped the wheel and pulled into the curb outside a dormitory. He checked his sheet. It read, "J.D. Parker."

They watched a young African American emerge unaccompanied through the front door of the dorm and run pigeon-toed their direction. He had a black hoodie hanging loosely on the back of his head, flapping along behind him like a cape.

Prissy leaned into the aisle. "J.D. has a crush on a girl. Her name is Nikkie. He's going to ask her to the dance on Friday. He says it's a secret but everyone I told about it already knew."

Sonti kicked the seat again. BAM! BAM! BAM!

Clara raised her voice above the din as J.D. entered the bus. "Good morning J.D."

"Mow-ning," J.D. shouted back, then looked at Sonti, still crying. "Don't be sad, Sonti. It's going to be okay."

"This is Mister Redwine, J.D."

"Oh."

As J.D. made his way to his seat, Sonti finally pulled a corner of his blanket over his eyes and wound down to a stop.

J.D. slid onto his seat and hurriedly pulled a thin rectangular electronic something out of his backpack and turned it on. Then he placed a smartphone on top of it and began using the devices simultaneously, right hand on one and left on the other.

Clara spoke up. "Don't forget your seatbelt, J.D."

"Oh. Sah-wee."

He fastened his belt then flipped the hoodie around to cover his face and draped the rest of it across his lap.

Grady looked at Clara and mouthed, "Is that real?"

She nodded enthusiastically then announced loudly and proudly, "J.D. is first in his computer science class, Mister Redwine."

"J.D. can do the many-task?"

She blinked and swallowed hard.

J.D.'s voice drifted out from under the hoodie. "Mistoe Wedwine. It's m*ulti*-tasking, not ***the minny***-task. You have to wook on you toominology."

Clara smiled and shrugged. "There isn't a lot of beating around the bush here. We pretty much just tell it like it is."

"I guess soooo."

Clara took over. "Let's go get Bennie." She directed them away from the dormitories at the *Children's Shelter*. Half a mile later, they turned left into a winding, glorious, tree-lined driveway.

"Hamiltons'?"

"Uh huh. This is another wheelchair, so line up the front of the bus with that white stake over there."

Shortly after Grady set the brakes and turned on the hazard lights, one of the doors in the four-car garage lifted and a figure began to roll toward them.

Grady blinked. "Nooooooo. Really? Is that…?" He looked at Clara. "You're enjoying this, aren't you?"

"You've got to admit it's entertaining."

Grady watched what looked like a miniature version of a robot from some 'sixties TV space show, zip smoothly down the driveway, propelled by a wide track of treads like a snowmobile. A transparent bubblehead with a TV screen for a face swept side-to-side above a cylindrical body containing blinking components and two accordion-like arms with claw hands holding a tray under a long, sideways slot in its belly.

Prissy's voice drifted his way from behind him. "We call him BennieBot." He glanced over at Clara. "Why the tray?"

"Feeder device for his fax machine."

Grady continued to watch, fascinated as it entered the lift and eventually settled in behind Prissy. Moments later, a small blond boy's face appeared on the TV screen in its head.

"This is Bennie Hamilton," Clara said. "Bennie, this is Mister Redwine."

Grady expected to hear the usual measured, monotonal tin-can voice from the movies, but a normal human, child-like voice emerged from the speakers. "Nice to meet you, Mister Redwine. I'm looking forward to riding on your bus."

"I'm looking forward to *having* you on my bus, Bennie."

Clara began strapping the robot in like she did Prissy.

Grady watched. "I've never heard of anything like this before. How is it even possible?"

Clara stopped attaching straps to rub her thumb over the tips of her index and middle fingers, indicating *Big Bucks*….

Of course. Silly me.

…But her official response was, "Bennie is part of a pilot program that's exploring the feasibility of robotic assistance in the classroom. BennieBot operates on a battery pack and runs two-way video via the net through the GPS system of the bus. Same thing at school. Cool, huh?"

Grady didn't really understand much of what she was saying but faked an answer anyway. "Yes! Really cool."

"Normally they would just leave the BOT at school, but Bennie likes to ride the bus like the other kids, so we pick him up every day." She patted BennieBot on the head. "We're all set, Mister Redwine. Let's go get Halim."

Halim Kalimantan was standing alone outside a small, neat house not far from the Hamilton compound. He seemed tall for his age and had a deliberate, elegant swagger in his walk.

Grady smiled.

Halim wore khaki trousers with razor sharp creases just slightly off in alignment which made it obvious his Mom had ironed them. His striped shirt was a little worn at the collar, but the whites in it sparkled and the colors were still bright. He carried a fashionable backpack over one shoulder and an instrument case in his hand. He never looked down and never stepped on any cracks in the driveway but simply adjusted his stride as he walked.

Miss Clara greeted him as he climbed up the stairs. "Good morning, Halim."

Halim didn't look at her or answer. He just bent down and grabbed a red blanket from the stack, exposing a wide, ugly scar along the top of his head.

Clara mouthed, "Drunk Driver."

Halim sat down in his seat with his backpack and instrument case beside him. He finally noticed Grady's reflection in the mirror and frowned.

"This is Mister Redwine," Clara said.

Halim didn't respond. He just silently used the blanket to form a tent between his seat and the one in front of him.

They watched as the bump of his head beneath the blanket traveled toward the window and settled in.

Miss Clara peeked under the blanket. "Don't forget your seatbelt, Halim."

When Grady heard the seatbelt click, he turned out the lights and released the brake. Moments later, a hideous animalistic growl rolled through the blackness from under the red blanket and settled behind the drivers' seat.

The hair stood up on the back of Grady's neck.

"That's Halim's monster," Prissy said. "Halim loves monsters."

Bennie piped up. "Halim's a gamer."

"And he can do all kinds of voices," Prissy added. "Even the girls. Sometimes he plays games all night—or watches old movies."

Grady glanced at Clara. She had a sheepish look on her face. "Kinda forgot to mention that."

Thanks.

###

As he navigated through traffic on the way to the school, Grady ran through the Administration's mandatory Safety-First speech in his head then pulled over and parked outside the bus loop. He picked up the microphone and cleared some phlegm in his throat.

Loud cries of anguish bounced off the walls of the bus.

Miss Clara said, "It's a small space Mister Redwine. Why don't you just stand and speak softly."

Grady sighed, dragged himself to his feet and turned around to face what looked like the cast of a cartoon, all rocking forward-back, forward-back, forward-back, with their hands clapped over their ears.

*What is **that**?* He swallowed and said, "Now listen up."

J.D.'s voice drifted towards him. "Why do we have to look at the ceiling to listen?"

Clara explained. "We're a very literal group, Mister Redwine."

He motioned downward. "It's okay. It's okay. You can just look up here at me."

Heads rotated back down, but bodies rocked even faster: forwardback-forwardback-forwardback…

Why the Hell are they rocking?

"Welcome to Bus Eighty-Six, everyone. My name is Mister Redwine. I am your driver, and I have some safety rules you need to be aware of while you're on the bus. First of all, you must keep your back to the back of your seat and your bottom to the, uh…"

Clara shook her head.

"Actually, just keep the aisle clear at all times. For example, that box sticking out from under Halim's tent…what is it, a horn?"

Halim collapsed the blanket. "It's a trumpet, not a horn."

"Uh, Well, uh, thank you for the explanation, Halim. Just be sure to keep it out of the aisle, okay?"

Halim adjusted the case inward.

J.D. raised his hand. "Could we please hoo-wee? My tablet is going to wun out of chahge."

"Okay. Sure! Of course we can. Just one other important thing." Grady looked toward Prissy. "No listening to music during announcements, please."

Prissy looked stricken. "I'm not listening to music." She turned to Clara. "Tell him, Miss Clara. I *never* listen to music."

"We know you don't, Prissy. He's just new. I'll explain it to him."

Prissy got a little misty-eyed. "I don't listen to music with these, Mister Redwine. *Ever*. These are my *quiet ears*. They are *sound suppressors*. I **need** them. **All the time**."

Clara sighed. "There's the warning bell. We better let them off."

Grady mentally threw up his hands and surrendered. "Uh, just remember to be safe out there, everybody, okay?"

Grady sat back down, started the bus up again, circled around to the designated drop-off area and pulled into the curb. Clara leaned toward him. "We drop Sonti off first. They come out to get him."

A tall, muscular bald man wearing purple surgeon's gloves taped at the wrist walked toward the bus. pushing an empty wheelchair.

"That's Mister Wilson," Prissy said. "He's Sonti's teacher."

Mister Wilson came on board and unsnapped Sonti's restraints. He looked at Clara. "Rough morning?"

"Afraid so. He hasn't eaten today."

"I have cookies inside. I'll give him some."

Prissy piped up. "C*innamon toast!* Sonti wants c*innamon toast!*"

Mister Wilson put a firm grip on Sonti's upper arm. "How are ya doin' today, buddy? Ready for school?"

Sonti repositioned the blanket above his eyes and allowed his teacher to lead him off the bus. He put up no fuss when strapped into the chair.

Grady turned to Clara. "Why the wheelchair?"

"Sonti can run like the wind, Mister Redwine. He got loose inside the school one day. It took the fire department and the football team three hours to catch him." She headed for the stairs. "Just between you and me, it's a big school and a long walk to his classroom. I think Sonti gets a kick out of making Mister Wilson push him."

She waved the rest of the kids off the bus then lowered Prissy and BennieBot to the pavement. "Have a great day, y'all. We'll see you this afternoon."

Grady wiped sweat off his forehead with the sleeve of his shirt. "***That*** went well."

Clara leaned against the front seat. "Welcome to *Special Needs*, Mister Redwine. Enjoying your vacation?"

Afternoon

Grady didn't eat what he usually had for lunch; there was way too much acid in his stomach. He swallowed a couple of antacid tablets, downed a thick chocolate shake and knew better, but decided to buy another coffee anyway. There was a long line of cars ahead of him, giving him time to reflect on the morning.

Maybe this is a nightmare. I hope I wake up soon.

He never saw the line at this place move so slowly. He would park, get out and just walk inside, but he was blocked in by a retention wall and he was a prisoner.

By the time he arrived at the window he didn't have time to pick up his order. He was going to be late getting back on time, and they knew him there, so he just shouted through the delivery window that he'd be back to pay them later and took off down the road.

###

Clara was leaning against the bus with J.D. when he arrived. She raised her arm to take a long, disapproving look at her watch when she saw him.

'Sorry," he said, and began to say more, but she interrupted. "Teachers let their classes out early on Monday. The kids go to assembly and then work off energy running laps on the track. J.D. is exempted from the running part so sometimes he hangs out with me."

Grady remembered J.D.'s awkward pigeon-toed run and understood. "That's great!"

He sent a weak smile Clara's direction as he unlocked the door. "Betcha thought I went on vacation for real."

"I don't think it's in the stars for *either* of us to be that lucky today."

"You're probably right."

He looked around for a spot on his console to place his phone. "What do they *do* with these things? Where do they keep them? They're too big for a breast pocket. Too heavy for your pants."

"I keep mine in my purse."

"Thanks, but I don't think a man purse is in my future." He settled for a small flat place in the middle and set his phone there. "I hate this thing."

Clara got J.D. all settled in then joined him at the front of the bus. "Have you received the email from Sonti's mother yet?"

Grady's stomach clenched. "No. I have not."

"Well, it should come soon."

"I have a work-around in case it doesn't."

"Oh?"

"We'll take Sonti to the *Shelter* first. If no one comes out to get him, we take him home."

"That's one approach, but it will mess up the timing for the other kids. How about sending his Mom an email introducing yourself, and ask her where he should go today?"

Grady rubbed at a dull, deep throb in his temples. "Unfortunately, I can't. My personal email isn't exactly up and running on this phone yet. And on top of that, she'll be sending it to my work email, and I still can't get it to forward to this phone."

"Oh."

"I sweated blood all weekend trying to make this thing work. I ended up locked out of everything, so I just gave up and started over. Do you know how many things you need to start this stuff from scratch?"

J.D.'s voice drifted from behind the hoodie. "Fo-tee-thwee."— Grady jerked to attention. J.D. continued. — "You need seven IDs, seven passwoods, twenty-one seek-wet questions…"— Grady's headache grew,— "…an employee numbuh, a Social Se-cu-wi-tee numbuh, two intoe-net addwesses…"

Clara was obviously used to this and kept on problem-solving. "So how about a text? We have her phone number."

"…a cwedit cod numbuh, an expi-wation date, …"

Grady perked up. "Really?..."

"…a CVC numbuh, a telephone numbuh…"

"I can do that. I can do the text. Sort of. I, for sure, can't do the emailing. I did manage to download three of those app things, though."

"… And don't foget to keep weceipts for ev-wee-thing."

"Sometimes I push and push the numbers, and they won't appear. I move my thumb and the page just…disappears."

J.D. threw his hoodie aside and walked to the front of the bus. "Nev-uh-mind."

He held out his hand and nodded toward Grady's phone. Grady hesitated. J.D. pumped his palm toward him as if to say, "C'mon. Give it to me."

Grady gingerly laid the phone in J.D.'s hand.

J.D. squinted at the screen and pointed. "This you email?"

Grady pulled out the list Jack had given him and nodded.

J.D. scrolled down a little. "This one fwom the school?"

Grady checked the list. He nodded again then handed the list to J.D.

"Okay, I see you passwoods."

J.D. talked as his fingers flew across the screen. "It doesn't take a wocket scientist to email, Mistow Wedwine...." He finished and handed the phone back. "...but don't feel bad about you disability. Evewybody has one."

Grady's heart melted a little. "Thank you, J.D. Thank you very much. You *really* helped me."

J.D. was already headed for his seat. "I know."

Halfway down the aisle J.D. turned back. "It was pwobably because you *typed*. You got to get caught up with the times, Mistow Wedwine. You *inputting data*. Touch the scween like you love it not like you mad."

Clara shrugged and smiled.

Grady heard a ding on his phone and a message miraculously appeared in a box on the screen.

J.D. smiled. "Now *that* is wocket science."

Grady fished out his reading glasses and read.

> *"Please bring Sonti home after school today.*
> *Thank you. Catalina Smith."*

J.D. settled into his seat and looked out the window. "Uh Oh."

Grady and Clara followed his gaze and watched as Sonti burst through the doors of the school and began racing toward them, pursued by a breathless, frazzled Teacher's Aide.

Grady leaped to his feet. "He's loose."

Clara pushed past him and rushed down the stairs, racing, reaching for Sonti's hand. Sonti swiped at her, resisting. Grady prepared to pounce.

Eyes on Clara, Grady spoke over his shoulder. "Scoot over close to the window J.D. and stay there unless I tell you to move, okay?"

"Okay...but..."

"No buts, J.D."

"But my shoes."

"Just please, J.D. Do what I say."

Grady couldn't hear what Clara was saying. Whatever it was, it worked, because Sonti finally slowed down and allowed her to guide him toward the bus.

Grady moved down the aisle and positioned himself between Sonti's seat and J.D. He tensed as Clara led Sonti up the stairs.

Clara brushed some wayward hair off her forehead with the back of her wrist. "He hates to *go* to school. Fortunately, he *loves* to go home." She paused to take a deep breath. "This happens occasionally. The hardest part is making sure he gets on the right bus."

Grady stepped aside to let Sonti grab his purple blanket and plop it on his head. He positioned himself between Sonti and J.D. until he'd settled in peacefully and let Clara clip him into the safety harness.

Far too late, the Director of the *Special Needs Department* appeared in the doorway obviously distraught. "Sorry for the confusion, folks. Sonti's Aide, uh, *fell ill* today and we're short-handed. Please just bear with us."

As she and Grady watched him walk away, Clara scrunched up her mouth. "Not good. That's really not good. This is the second Aide he's had this year. Hope this one comes back."

J.D. hemmed and hawed and made a big racket as he moved his stuff back to where it belonged. Clara went to help him.

Grady returned to his seat and observed the two of them getting organized in his mirror. He was surprised to see J.D. stick his feet into the aisle, sneaker laces dangling. Clara tied them.

What?!

She looked toward Grady and mouthed, "He doesn't know how."

Grady was digesting the magnitude of what he'd just seen when he was startled by Halim leaping into the stairwell, landing loudly beside him. The boy spread his arms exposing an impressive wingspan, and announced in a haunting full-toned bass, *"MY NAME IS DEMISE. I AM **NOT** A DRAGON."* He posed in the aisle a few moments, imaginary wings unfurled, then sort of floated to his seat where he casually constructed his blanket tent and climbed in.

Prissy's voice drifted in their direction from the bottom of the lift. "I think Halim got a new game."

BennieBot chimed in from behind her. "He's been doing that all day."

Halim wasn't quite finished. He cleared his throat and practiced saying his name twice more. "DE-MISE. MY NAME IS DE-MISE."

Clara got everyone lifted aboard, strapped in and ship-shape then turned to Sonti. "You're going to see your Mama today, honey."

He beamed and bounced a little in his seat.

She turned toward Grady. "We take Sonti home first. Head back to the *Shelter* but turn right at the stop light instead of left."

Grady followed Clara's instructions. After the turn at the light, she pointed down the street. It's the third house on the right. Grady pulled up beside three overflowing trash cans waiting for collection and a sad, banged-up mailbox leaning at an angle on its base.

Sonti screamed with joy and fought against his restraints. "Ahhh-Ahhhh-Ahhh."

"Here comes Mama, Sonti. Settle down for her, okay?"

Grady immediately noticed that there was no car parked beside the clapboard house half-hidden on the heavily forested lot where Sonti's family lived. There were no tread marks in the carpet of leaves on the cracked and sunken asphalt of the driveway and no sign of children playing in the yard other than a rusty old basketball hoop with no net standing beside a tool shed.

Grady expected them to have a large dog, considering the length and girth of the tie-out cable attached to the base of the pole, not to mention the conditions in the neighborhood. Grady thought you could tell a lot about a family by their dog…big fluffy vs pit bull or yippy little ankle-biter. Generally, the family dog was the first to greet the bus, but theirs must have been in the house.

A woman wearing a turtleneck sweater under the baggy uniform of a restaurant of some sort, emerged from a side door and trotted toward the bus, arms wide in greeting.

He turned toward Clara. "Who's *that*?"

"It's Sonti's mother…Catalina."

Grady watched Catalina as she approached them. She had honey-colored, flawless skin framed by rich brown hair that swung side-to-side as she ran. It was obvious she had been quite beautiful once and still would be, were it not for what must have begun as a perky straight nose that was now somewhat flat at the bridge with the off-side slant Grady generally identified with boxers. Her eyes had a little sparkle and shine to them but were ruined by the serious bags and dark circles below. She was trailed by an older girl carrying a toddler on one arm and holding the hand of another. They joined her at the curb and looked at the door of the bus expectantly.

Grady studied the children gathered around her. The toddler-in-arms faced backward over his sister's shoulder. Grady assumed it was a boy because he wore pull-up diapers with cars on them. The older girl in charge was a perfect reflection of her mother with fine features and lively brown eyes. But, to his dismay, the one whose hand she held had close-set button eyes full of the dull, dead look of illness.

Sonti pounded on the window in greeting, drawing everyone's attention. The toddler whipped around and searched for the source of the noise with the same dull look of his sister.

Grady pressed a hand to his chest, and his breathing turned slightly shallow. She had two. Two! Two more disabled children. They were obviously hers…they looked just like her. Sonti alone would be a handful for anyone. Grady just couldn't imagine what life must be like for her.

As soon as Clara unclipped his restraints, Sonti leaped to his feet. He tossed aside the purple blanket and rushed for the stairs, making wild wringing gestures with his hands. Clara trailed behind, hauling his heavy backpack.

His mother stood on the curb reaching out for him while his siblings chanted, "Sonti! Sonti! Sonti!"

Grady studied Sonti's mother…worn-out, exhausted, and old before her time, but obviously crazy about her son.

When Sonti reached the top of the stairs, his mother stretched into the stairwell to retrieve his backpack from Clara, and Grady spotted the tip of an ugly scar peeking out of the turtleneck directly under her ear.

Sonti made his way down the stairs and leaned a little toward his mother's arms, but instead of an embrace, he pulled a quick head-fake and ran for the house, leaving her standing there, arms opened wide. She was obviously disappointed but not surprised.

Clara stood beside Grady. "Hugs are hard for some of our kids. They experience them as pain."

Grady and Clara rode back to school in silence, each one lost in private thoughts. To Grady, that half hour felt like a luxury vacation…silence…especially since he felt so rattled.

Driving had always been second nature to Grady. It was automatic, like walking or breathing. He could eat while he drove, sip on his coffee, follow a map, adjust the radio, talk politics, or even mentally plan a vacation. After the day they just had, he possessed the concentration of a kid taking his driver's test. All he could manage was to grip the wheel, hit the brake and steer.

He tried to relax and pull in as much air as he could—two, three, four times—but he felt so emotionally drained, he barely remembered taking the other kids home.

You have to get a grip on yourself, Redwine. This is not good,

When they reached the bus barn, Clara paused at the top of the stairs. "Well, congratulations, Mister Redwine. You made it through your first day. Do you have any questions?"

Grady wiped his brow with his elbow. "Would you say this day was fairly…typical?"

"Let's just say there's hardly ever a dull moment on *Bus Eighty-Six*, and I wouldn't call any of it…typical."

Grady gathered his belongings, then leaned back in his seat and hesitated for a moment. "Miss Clara, I'm sorry but I have to ask. Is there a cure for... this?"

She took a deep breath. "No, Mister Redwine. I'm afraid there's no cure for any of the children on our bus -- no operation, no medication, no therapy that will make it go away."

"Will they ever get better?"

"Better is *our* job."

TUESDAY
January 15, 2019-Morning

Grady was used to his alarm going off at 5 a.m., but getting a text that early was a whole new experience. It took him a few minutes to figure out where the ding was coming from, and it was possible he might never have done so if his phone hadn't lit up in the dark when the text arrived from Sonti's Aide at the *Shelter*.

Sonti isn't riding today.

He placed the phone back on the night table. *Well, good. One less thing to worry about.* Maybe this texting stuff wasn't going to be as bad as he thought it was.

###

Grady stopped to get coffee on the way to Transportation. "I'll take two cups today, Minnie."—She looked surprised. — "It's a thank you for my new Monitor." —She smiled. "I guess everything turned out okay!" — "It did."— "That's so great! Want espresso today?" — "No. Just the usual."

It felt good to get two of something again. He'd always brewed a cup for Mary in the morning, and he missed it.

As Grady pulled up to the impound, Clara was waiting beside the bus as usual. He handed her the cup. "Breakfast."

"This is a nice surprise. Thank you." She took a sip. "How are you doin'?"

"Hanging in there."

"Any questions?"

"Yes! What's with all that rocking…everyone,,, rocking?"

She chuckled. "Repetitive motion like that is comforting to them. They do it instinctively when they're upset or nervous. I forgot the professional term for it…don't like it much anyway. I'm sure that's why new mothers buy rockers."

She put her purse down on the seat and smiled. "I have a couple of surprises for *you, too*. Bennie is only riding this afternoon AND, we don't have to plan *Life Skills* on Tuesday afternoons for the next two months because they're starting the new *Wizard* series."

He took a sip from his cup. "Ah yes. The *District*'s much anticipated deep dive into *American literature*."

She laughed. "I guess they've decided to include some *English Lit.* this year."

"My wife, Mary taught *American Lit.* for a while. She thought it was hilarious…Steinbeck, Styron, Robert Frost and Frog Warts."

Clara laughed again. "Shame on you." She seemed to mull the topic over a while. "Why all the fascination with frog warts, I wonder."

"Mary said the Wizards use toxins that frog warts secrete to enhance the power of spells."

He placed his coffee in the cup holder. "Got a text this morning. Sonti isn't riding."

"Oooo texting. I'm impressed."

He smiled and prepared for his pre-check inspection. *Actually, so am I.*

Clara was checking seat belts when Grady returned inside and cranked the bus. "I'm not surprised about Sonti," she said. "He's almost always difficult in the morning. But it's really hard to get him going after he's spent time at home. He loves it there."

As on the previous day, Prissy jetted down the driveway full of news. "Sonti isn't riding this morning, and he wasn't at breakfast either."

Miss Clara responded. "He might have stayed at home with his family."

"Nuuh uuuh. His mother brought him back to the *Shelter* last night. He and Marcell got into it in the shower room this morning. Nobody is talking about what happened, but you could hear them fighting all over the house. Sonti was screaming his head off but that's not unusual.

"They had to put Sonti in the quiet room when it was over. That's why he's staying home today."

Qui-et room?

Clara mouthed into the mirror, *"Later."*

Grady put the bus in gear and headed for J.D.'s dorm. "Did they put Marcell in a quiet room too?"

"Nope. Miss Miller marched him out to the front porch right then and there and fired his ass. She said he crossed the line this time and told him never to come back."

J.D. was waiting for the bus at the curb when they turned the corner. He was wearing his usual hoodie. But today, he had on a black pointed hat covered with stars, held in place by a rubber band under his chin, and was waving what appeared to be a stray yellow stick from a game.

He climbed on board and announced, "*Amewican Lit.* today."

Prissy piped up. "We get to start learning about Wizards…"

J.D. walked past her, still waving his wand, interrupting. "I'm weddy. Bwought my equipment."

"…Mister Carter says we're going to watch eight Wizard movies this year"

Grady rolled his eyes. Sounded kind of lazy to him.

###

Halim's house looked like a cheap road-side carnival when they turned onto his street in the complex. Sirens were screaming; strobe lights were flashing; all the bedroom lamps in the neighborhood were switched on with worried faces peering out through the curtains.

Oh Lord.

A robotic voice from the driveway security speaker blared into the bus when Grady opened the door. "Alarm! Alarm! Back Door is Open! Back Door is Open! Alarm! Alarm!"

Clara pressed against the window. "I hope everyone's okay."

Prissy stretched up and surveyed the action. "Halim probably ex-scaped again."

J.D. commented from under his hood. "Halim isn't in pwisen, Pwissie. He didn't ex-cape, he pwobably just wunned away."

Grady got a huge rush of adrenaline when Halim emerged from the darkness and dashed in their direction.

I can't close the door. He'll run into it.

Halim made a wild-eyed leap onto the stairs, rocking the bus sideways. After a heavy-footed charge to the top step, he hunched over and pointed to his friends in a rage. "Get **DOWN** you blue-eyed monsters."

Grady got locked and loaded, prepared for a fight, but Prissy leaned back in her chair and calmly pulled on her quiet ears. "*The Monster? A-gain?*"

Grady nervously glanced around, a little embarrassed. *What am I missing here?*

The security system finally shut down and a dark, bandy-legged Asian woman no bigger than a minute emerged from the shadows in her nightgown, dragging a heavy backpack. She handed it up to Clara.

"He broke the door. I *tried* to catch him. He's been up all night." She turned toward the boy still standing on the stairs. "What do you have to say to these people, young man?"

Grady expected an apology, but Halim shouted, "**Pain**. I predict... *pain*!"

Grady felt goosebumps erupt on his arms.

Obviously embarrassed, the woman gazed up at them and shrugged with regret. "I'm so sorry. He seems to be stuck today. I'll call the nurse and have her give him meds at ten."

Clara stood between Halim and the others as he stomped toward his seat snarling, "*GET **DOWN**— GET **DOWN**— GET **DOWN**. WE'RE GOING TO CRAAAASSSSH.*"

Prissy yawned again as he passed by her. J.D. waved his wand. "Weally Halim? *Weally*? Can you watch something *else* tomahwoe?"

At his seat, Halim stretched and yawned then curled up on the floor in front of him and promptly fell asleep.

Clara reached for a blanket...

Grady mentally gasped.

"I'll sit here with him."

"Whatever you do, don't wake him up."

###

Grady drove with clammy hands all the way to the school. After the kids were unloaded and headed for the doors, he sort of peeled his fingers off the wheel and turned to Clara. "What was *that*?"

"*That* was Echolalia. It's generally an affliction associated with Autism, but Halim's comes from a brain injury."

"Okaay—but what *is* it?"

"Well, the only way I can think of to explain it, is that it's sort of like standing on the edge of a canyon shouting *hello* and hearing echoes bounce it back."

Grady scratched nervously at his beard, trying to relate what he'd witnessed to what she described. He finally cleared his throat and looked in her direction. "I've been to a lot of canyons in my day, Miss Clara, but, as my Uncle Ernie would say, *I ain't never seen nobody climb up on a boulder and shout, 'pain' into a canyon.*"

"Well, I think Uncle Ernie might be thinking about it backwards. Halim *ain't* the shouter. *He's* the echo. Much of what you hear Halim say is something he heard somewhere else."

"But what made him so *angry today?*"

"I know he *seemed* angry, but he wasn't. He was probably just acting out lines from the movie he was watching while he waited for the bus. Halim seems to be absolutely awestruck by monsters and gore."

"No teddy bears? Little deer? No talking fish in the sea?"

She chuckled. "Afraid not. *The Monster* is Halim's main man. He can't recite the letters in the alphabet, but he has an uncanny ability to repeat every scene in a two-hour movie without missing a word."

"Is it something he can control?"

She mulled it over in her mind for a minute. "It doesn't appear to be something that turns on and off like a lightbulb. It's more like when he gets over-excited, or stressed, or feels helpless in a situation, he just sort of goes somewhere else for a while and leaves it up to *The Monster* to handle."

She folded up a couple of blankets. "Halim is a sweet-natured little boy who wouldn't hurt a fly, but *The Monster* gets him in big trouble sometimes."

She stowed the blankets away. "It feels a little creepy at first, but you'll get used to it..."

Grady wasn't quite as sure about that as she was.

"...Just be glad he didn't fall in love with something destructive, full of weapons, fights to the death, and doom."

Afternoon

Prissy was full of excitement when she got on the bus that afternoon. "We started learning about Wizards today. One little Wizard boy named Willy is an orphan like us kids. His stepbrother is a big bully and picks on him all the time, but Willy outsmarts him and hides in a cloak that makes him invisible. He inherited it from his mother."

She paused a moment, reflecting. "I wish I could have a cloak that makes things invisible."

Grady turned her way. "Prissy. You're a pretty girl. Why would you want to be invisible?"

"Oh, not for me. For my chair. I'd take that cloak and wrap it around the wheels. And then people would only see *me*—Prissy Milcamp—a regular ol' person just sitting down—and I wouldn't have to explain to anyone why."

She thought for a while longer. "Or maybe I could ride on a broomstick instead of my chair. It would be nice to be able to fly."

Grady watched the river of kids flowing out of the building, but his eyes were drawn to the flash of a face darting in and out of the bushes in the side yard.

"Clara. Look over there. Is that J.D.?"

Clara glanced out the window. "Yep."

"What's he doing over there?"

"J.D. takes computer science in a *regular* classroom. The school lets our kids out first, so sometimes he goes out the side door and waits for the second bell so he can blend in with the *regular* crowd."

Prissy stretched to look outside. "J.D. doesn't want anyone to see him get on a short bus. They make fun of him."

BennieBot usually came to the bus with Halim, but this time, he showed up with Sonti and Mister Wilson who delivered a message while he got Sonti settled in: "Halim won't be riding home with you today. He checked out early."

BennieBot added more details. "He kept walking around in class shouting, 'CRASH' and breaking everyone's pencils."

About that time, J.D. left the bushes and arrived at the door in a big lather. He bounded up the stairs and squeezed past Mister Wilson in the aisle, staying all ducked down and bent over.

Mister Wilson sent a mystified shrug Grady's way.

J.D. was fastened in and hiding behind his hoodie by the time Mister Wilson was leaving the bus. "Let's go. Huwwy. I'm weddy to go."

Grady scanned the yard for what might be a problem but saw nothing out of the ordinary.

He shrugged at Clara who took over from there. "Where are your hat and wand, honey?"

"They ah safe. I put them in my lockuh." Grady watched in the mirror as J.D. slouched low in his seat. "Evwybody is on the bus, Miss Clawa. We ah weady to go. We should be moving by now, not talking."

###

Driving everyone home was uneventful until they reached J.D.'s dorm and Grady bid his standard farewell. "Good night, J.D. See you in the morning."

J.D. stopped at the top of the stairs. "Why do you always say that Mistow Wedwine? It's the aftuhnoon. I am not going to bed. I have to have dinnuh."

Grady smiled. "Just habit, I guess."

"Well, you need to get you time stwaight. I go to bed at eight o'clock" He took a couple of steps farther. "And you might not see me in the mowning. I could be sick oh something sometimes."

"How about, 'Have a good rest of the day'?"

J.D. paused to consider the suggestion. "I don't west much the west of the day."

"Well, how about, 'so long'?"

"'So long' sounds like 'goodbye foe-evuh.' This is just goodbye foe one night."

Grady took a glance at his clock. "What would you *like* me to say, J.D.?"

"I will think about it and tell you tomahwoe."

Grady watched J.D. walk up the path for a moment then closed the door and turned to Clara. "Well, *he's* been a little edgy today."

She nodded in agreement. "About everything. Can't wait to see what he comes up with to say goodbye."

"What did his last bus driver say?"

"I think she just opened the door and let him walk off."

"Smart lady."

###

Back at the bus barn, Clara began gathering her things. "I hope Sonti is okay."

"I'm sure he is, or we would have heard about it by now."

"True." She scanned out of the timeclock and started down the stairs. "Oh. Before I forget. Tomorrow is service day for the bus. You know the drill."

"Yep. Check in our bus; check out a substitute bus for the day; and print the number on the magnetic sign."

She picked up the stack of blankets. "We'll need these. I'll write in the bus number when you pick me up in the morning."

"Great. Thanks. Anything I need to know about the kids?"

"That's an unknown at the moment. This is our first time through the process with them this year, so it should be interesting. They're not fond of change."

She headed down the stairs and began to walk away. He shouted at her back, "I'd say good night but I'm afraid to."

She laughed and turned back. "Don't worry. You're safe. I *am* going to bed now."

Evening

Grady closed down the bus and headed home on autopilot, stopping first at *Qwick Pick* to buy some chips and a Lottery ticket.

He loved *Quick Pick*...especially on days like today when he was this tired. Everyone in there was focused strictly on getting you in and out of there fast, and that included the customers.

He hadn't won anything more from the Lottery than a free ticket for years, but for five minutes or so every day, he managed to feel hopeful, so he kept on.

He let the machine choose the numbers, then paused beside the trash can outside the front door because he knew it wouldn't be long before he would need it. He placed his new ticket in his money clip, compared the winning numbers for the day with those on the worthless ticket he'd bought the night before, then crumpled it up and tossed it.

As he approached his truck and reached up to unlock the door, he heard a voice calling his name from behind him.

"Woo hoo! Mis-ter Red-wine! Mis-ter Red-wine! Is that you?"

He turned around and saw a petite elderly woman with a slight stoop toddling toward him, waving a hanky. "Woo hoo! Woo hoo!"

Oh please, Lord. Not here. Not now.

She approached him, rather breathless. "Oh, I'm so glad I caught you, Mister Redwine...Grady...Can I call you Grady?"— She didn't wait for an answer. — "I'm Lila Harper. I was in prayer group with Mary, and I've been meaning to call you to express my condolences."

Grady had never met Lila Harper in person, but he didn't have to. Her reputation as a gossip preceded her. "Thank you, Miss Lila. I appreciate the thought very much."

He intended to let it go at that and leave, but she rattled on.

"We all miss Mary so much at church. We were talking about how sad it was at bridge club last week; and the girls in our garden club — ugh. Don't get me started."—She paused to inhale. — "It all happened so fast...so unexpected at her age...what was it again, cancer?"

Grady made a mental eyeroll and took a deep breath. "Yes. Cancer."

"That's what I thought...I heard that it was her dentist that found it quite by accident...a lump under to tongue, is that right?"

He swallowed hard. "Yes. A lump."

She shook her head. "So many surgeries...so awful...so sad, poor thing...and she never smoked a day in her life, they say, did she?"

Everything within him wanted to shout, "Go Away!" but instead he politely replied, "No. She never did."

Lila kept talking. "Everyone thinks it's so sad you two didn't have children...such a nice couple..." —Her voice dropped half an octave and filled up with pity. —"...and now here you are...all alone."

He glanced around. People were staring. *Enough.* He'd had enough, so he reached up and unlocked the door. "I'm sorry, Miss Lila, but I'm late for an appointment. I've gotta go."

She stepped back. "Well, if you need anything, don't hesitate to call someone. Just know our thoughts and prayers are with you."

He stepped inside, started the truck, backed out and drove away. *Thoughts and prayers. Everyone has thoughts and prayers. Where were you all when she needed you.*

###

After Grady left *Qwick Pick*, he stopped at the drive-through next door to pay the tab for the order he skipped out on last time and picked up dinner for tonight, then continued home to eat while he searched around for something to watch on TV. Halfway through the first burger, he fell asleep in his chair.

WEDNESDAY
January 16, 2019-Morning

It was always a good sign to Grady when he was able to sail through the process of turning in his bus for its monthly maintenance routine and signing out a substitute to drive in the meantime. He was especially pleased that the Maintenance Manager had slotted his bus in for service early so he could return it to him by Noon.

Good feelings about the success of the day grew even greater when he swung around to pick up Clara and saw her already standing there with a stack of blankets and two double lattes.

She handed him the coffee and smiled, but the smile died when she discovered that the restraining equipment they used for Sonti was positioned at the back of the bus on the opposite side of the aisle. "Oh brother. This is not good."

Grady got up and assessed the situation. "Can't we move it?"

She tried to squeeze between the seat and the rear wall so she could undo the clasp, but the space was far too small. She tried feeding the strap from the rear to the front so she could reach the clasp, but it was too tight to move.

Grady tried. Failed.

She reached down behind the seat and tried to undo the clasp that way. "We need tools."

"Do we have another belt?"

Clara quickly searched through the equipment bins. "Nope."

"Can we get one?"

"*Special Needs* would bring us one, but we pick him up too early in the route. They couldn't get to us in time."

Grady felt his heartbeat rising. "Maybe he won't ride today."

"Oh, he'll ride. He's missed too much school already. We'll just have to deal with it."

He felt drops of sweat forming around his collar. "Hope you remembered his purple blanket."

"Oh yes. Never leave home without it." She slid into her seat. "Oh, by the way. No BennieBot today. Wrong technology on sub-buses."

Grady checked his watch and crawled behind the wheel. "That's good because we're late. We've gotta go get Prissy. She'll tell us what's going on."

Grady sipped on his luke-warm latte while Clara was on the curb loading Prissy. He could hear her at the bottom of the lift. "It's *Citizenship Day*, Miss Clara. We get to work and earn some money!"

"Yep, you sure do."

"Morning, Mister Redwine! We get to work today and earn some money. We're going to the *Food Bank*. You get to watch us sort cans."

"I know. That's very exciting."

"Last time we did beans. I wonder what we'll get this week."

He looked at her in the mirror. "Have you seen Sonti today?"

"Nope. Haven't seen him. Haven't heard him."

Grady released the brake and headed around to the back of the building. Sonti was standing peacefully between two attendants, waiting for them.

This is new.

Grady pulled into the curb and opened the door. When the attendants helped Sonti up the stairs, he looked around, obviously disoriented and confused.

Miss Clara took him by the hand and placed his blanket on his shoulder. "We have a different bus today, Sonti. It's going to be an adventure." She led him to the back, guided him down into the seat and clipped him in without any effort. He looked around a little, then covered his head with his blanket and went to sleep.

The orderly leaned into the bus. "New medication."

Grady breathed a big sigh of relief and headed for J.D.'s dorm. J.D. was pacing along the sidewalk when they pulled up. "You late, Mistow Wedwine. You thwee minutes late. Ah we going to be late fo school?"

"No, J.D., you're going to have plenty of time to get to class."

"Thwee minutes. You wasted thwee minutes." He looked at Sonti. "Why is he sitting in the back? Is that why we late? Because of Sonti?"

Grady shifted into gear. Miss Clara said, "No, it isn't because of Sonti. Please sit down, J.D., or we *will* be late."

J.D. looked at the time on his phone. "I think you wong, Miss Clawa. We alweady late. Will we have to go to *Attendance*?"

"No J.D., you won't have to go there. Just go right to class."

"But we supposed to go to *Attendance* when we late."

"We'll look at the time when we get to school and decide then if you have to go, okay?"

"Okay. But I know we going to be late. You have to tell them we on a diffwent bus."

"Let's go get Halim, okay?"

"Okay. I'll tell him about being late."

Halim emerged from the garage door and walked down the driveway as he always did. Rather than make his usual little run up the stairs, he stopped and stared at the magnetic sign with the hand-written bus number on the side. "This is not our bus."

Miss Clara smiled. "Our bus is getting worked on today, so we're going to use this one."

"What's wrong with our bus?"

"Nothing is wrong. It just needs to be serviced."

"I can't ride on a bus with something wrong."

"There isn't anything wrong. It's like going to the dentist to have your teeth cleaned. It's just to make sure you don't get any cavities."

"The bus has cavities?"

"No. No cavities."

Halim climbed aboard reluctantly and headed for where he usually sat. A foot away, he stopped in his tracks. "Attention, Attention, A-tten-tion, Halim Kalimantan cannot ride this bus. Halim Kalimantan cannot ride this bus."

Clara looked around him to see what the problem was. "What's wrong, Halim?"

"Halim Kalimantan cannot ride this bus."

"Why not?"

"He cannot fasten his seat belt. No seat belts, no riding."

Grady saw Clara check out the belt. "There's nothing wrong, Halim. The seat belt is okay."

"No. Red to red, blue to blue. This seat is one red one blue."

Clara lifted the seat bottom and searched through the belts lying on the floor below. She located a blue strap and pulled it up. "Here you go. Blue to blue."

"No! I have red. I always have red. This isn't our bus. I want our bus."

Halim lifted the seat bottom and dropped to his knees; fished through the pile for a red seat belt.

Grady cleared his throat and pointed at his watch.

Clara shrugged helplessly. "Halim. We have to use blue today."

"No."

She patted the seat across the aisle. "There are two red ones on this seat. You can sit here today."

Halim backed away. "No. That's not my seat."

A voice from the sidewalk drifted into the bus. "Is there a problem?"

Halim's head popped up like a startled deer.

Grady stretched to look out at the sidewalk. The same tiny woman from the day before was standing beside the trash can at the curb.

Clara went to the door to talk with her. "Halim's upset, Mrs. Kalimantan. This isn't our regular bus and where he usually sits doesn't have the right color belt. He wants red. It only has blue."

Mrs. Kalimantan climbed to the top of the stairs and pushed up the sleeves of her bathrobe. "Blue is a *good* color, Halim. Blue is *good*. Are you going to school? Or are you coming back in the house with *me*."

Halim was in the seat with the seatbelt fastened in a millisecond.

Grady gulped a little. He would have chosen school too.

Halim's grandmother glanced from Grady to Miss Clara. "I apologize for the delay. Unexpected change is hard for Halim."

Grady's heart went out to the woman as he leaned toward her. "Don't worry, Ma'am. You don't have to apologize. They told me our regular bus would be finished in time for the field trip, so everything should be back to normal soon."

Clara's eyes shot wide. She had the look of a mother whose toddler just stepped onto a highwire.

Mrs. Kalimantan shouted toward the back of the bus. "Did you hear that, Halim? You will have your bus this afternoon. Everything is going to be fine."

He saw Clara grow a little pale.

J.D.'s voice cut off the conversation. "We up to **ten** minutes. We ah **late**. Definitely **late**. I can't believe we wasted eight moe minutes."

All the way to school, Halim practiced the voice of his grandmother. "Blue is a good color." He cleared his throat and tried again. "Blue is…" He changed the pitch. "Blue is…" He changed again and got it right. "Blue is a good color, Halim. You will have your bus this afternoon."

J.D. reported the time again when they pulled into the bus loop at the school. "Fifteen **minutes**, Mistoe Wedwine. You should call *Attendance*. Tell them we going to be late."

Afternoon

Grady decided to nap in his truck for a while instead of going home for lunch. Cutting out commute time would give him some extra wiggle room in case there were glitches in getting the sub-bus checked in and the other one fueled up for the field trip. He set the alarm on his phone, leaned his head back, and dozed off.

Unfortunately, the sound of a text arriving jolted him awake before it was time for the alarm to go off. He scrambled around to retrieve his phone, rolling his eyes skyward a moment before he read. *Please. Please. Make this a text from Sonti's Mom.*

He fished his readers out of his pocket and zeroed in on the screen. It was from the mechanic in Transportation.

> *Had a major emergency this morning.*
> *Can't get your bus ready until after 5.*

###

Grady grew tense all over when he saw Clara pull up in her car with a frown on her face. *Uh oh.*

He attempted to appear relaxed when he opened the door. "Hey there!"

"I take it the bus wasn't ready."

"They had an emergency." He waited until she climbed on board. "What should we do about Halim?"

"Well, he made it to school this morning. It probably won't be pretty, but I believe he can make it to the *Food Bank* too."

"I suppose if I have to, I could carry him on."

"Picture trying to put a cat in bathwater. Talk is definitely better."

She stowed her things in her seat and turned back toward him. "I think you've already learned this today, but I feel obligated to say it, anyway: You should never make a promise to one of these children unless you, and you alone, are the one with the power to make it happen. Because if it *doesn't* happen, the kids won't trust you and you'll hear about it forever—and I do mean, for-*ever*."

"I understand."

"Good. Okay. Change of subject. They had some excitement at school this morning. Apparently, Sonti fell asleep in class, and they had such a hard time waking him up, the nurse rushed him off to the doctor…"

Grady vacillated between genuine concern for Sonti and feelings of guilt over how happy he was to not have to worry about him that afternoon.

"…They're pretty sure he just needs his medication adjusted."

Grady relaxed a little. "That's good. Hope they're right."

"Actually, I came back early because I think we should strategize a little about what we need to do at the *Food Bank*. Have you ever been there?"

"No. Never have."

"Well, then, I think you're in for a big surprise."

"Oh yeah? Why."

"We're not going to one of those places you see in the news all the time where people pop open their trunk and load up groceries. This location is where all the charities go to *get* those groceries."

"And I'm going to be surprised becaaauuse..."

"Because almost everyone who works there is either part of the prison work-release program or doing community service."

Grady's eyebrows shot up his forehead. "Well, that's where I'd want to send *my* child to sort cans."

"I know—sounds awful, but it makes perfect sense if you think about it. When you're open twenty-four-seven and there are that many people depending on you, you have to know your help is going to show up. Volunteers are good people, but sometimes they aren't reliable. Convicts have no choice."

Grady cocked his head and absorbed it all while Clara prattled on.

"It's actually very safe there. They don't allow any violent offenders or anyone you have to worry about around children in the program. But they still have tight security, and that means *lots* of rules."

Grady lifted a hand. "Been in the military—understand rules. Don't like 'em but do 'em when I have to."

"Good. Glad to hear it." She sat down across from him. "The building is enormous—and chaotic—and noisy. They have eighty-five miles of conveyor belts in there."

"Okay. Soooo, keep calm. Bring the headsets."

"More like, keep calm. Forget the headsets."

Grady chuckled. "I feel like I'm in a scene from a mob movie." He lowered his voice an octave: "Don't take the guns. Take the cannoli."

"Funny."

"Really, though, what's the deal? You'd think headsets would be standard equipment where it's noisy."

"It's dangerous to have people rockin' out while they're working around heavy equipment, and they have lots of it there. They tell me that the only rule everyone hates more than not wearing headsets is having to ask permission to use the bathroom. So, when Prissy rolls in wearing her quiet ears, it causes all sorts of uproar."

"Prissy is in a wheelchair."

"I know."

"There are laws..."

"I know. But unfortunately, there's a big group of *vol-un-teers* who would rather protest about wearing headsets than work, so the staff ends up spending all day dealing with that issue instead of being able to concentrate on feeding people. We've discussed it and they have given us three choices: have Prissy wear earplugs until we get to the room, leave Prissy behind, or withdraw from the program altogether."

"Whoa. Okay, so keep calm. Bring the ear plugs."

"Unfortunately, that's a challenge too. Prissy can't wear them for very long. Her ear canals are so narrow the pressure of the plugs make her feel like she's drowning, and she gets too frightened to breathe."

"You're making this up."

"Nope. It's a real thing—called labyrinthitis."

"So, we're supposed to put her through all that pain just to get her a proper check in the *can sorting* box? Couldn't we just not do it and say we did?"

Clara opened her mouth and began to speak but he held up a hand to stop her. "No! Really! Listen! I've-got-a-plan. You take everyone else inside—there are people who'll help you in there, right?" He didn't wait for her answer. "And I'll take her home then come back to get you. No harm. No foul."

"That would be a great plan if we were talking about a different child, but Prissy and her mother were living in a car before she went to the *Shelter*. She knows hunger first-hand, so there's no way you're going to talk her out of doing this, regardless of the pain. So, all I've got to say is, drink your latte, get prepared and roll with it."

When they reached the school, J.D. and Prissy took their places on the bus animated and excited. Halim, however, examined the hand-written bus number and dug in his heels. "This is the blue bus. I don't *like* the blue bus. You **said** you would have our bus back. My seat belt is red. I want red."

Clara appeared in Grady's mirror; eyebrows raised. She didn't say it, but he read *"forever"* in her eyes.

Grady lowered his gaze then turned toward Halim. "Remember what your grandma said? Blue is a good color, Halim. You don't have to worry about blue."

J.D. leaned into the aisle. "Blue is a good culuh, Halim."

Prissy leaned in too. "Halim! Halim! Blue is *good*. Let's go sort cans!"

Halim dragged his feet but gave in and sat down. "You ***prom-ised***. You ***promised*** our real bus."

All the way to the *Food Bank*, Halim practiced the voice of his grandmother again. "Blue is a good color." He cleared his throat and tried again. "Blue is…" He changed the pitch. "Blue is…" He changed again and got it right. "Blue is a good color, Halim."

Grady pulled into the *Food Bank* shortly after one o'clock. He'd anticipated something like a large garage or a hangar, but Clara was right, it was enormous—more the size of a terminal.

Clara stood up and leaned over the dashboard to point the way for him. "So, here's the drill. We park over there in the *Blue Zone* by the loading docks. As you can see, it's quite a hike, so we unload everyone at the end of the main sidewalk over there and walk up to the door. Just park as close as you can. Be sure to take anything metal out of your pockets and leave it on the bus. We'll meet you at the main door and go from there."

Grady had to dodge in and around several loaded eighteen wheelers to get to the *Blue Zone* but managed to find a fairly convenient parking spot beside a high-security fence surrounding the loading docks. He dumped the change out of his pockets then hoofed it around the corner to the entrance where Clara and the kids were waiting.

Clara picked up where she left off. "The hardest part is getting through security, but most of them know us and try to make it as fast as possible."

When he noticed that Prissy was still wearing her quiet ears, Grady sent Clara a questioning look. She leaned toward him. "We always leave them on until the Officer tells us we have to take them off. She gets to wear them longer that way."

Once inside the building, Grady looked with awe at what was at least three acres of space filled with row upon row of shelved boxes overflowing with fruits, vegetables, and canned goods, all connected by conveyor belts and forklifts racing around like ants foraging for food at a picnic.

Clara was right when she told him how loud it was in there. Even J.D. and Halim looked agitated and uncomfortable when they joined the line to go through the metal detector in security.

An Officer assisted by two large men wearing bright orange jump suits with INMATE printed on the left shoulder checked Grady's and Clara's IDs then walked around from behind the desk to pass a wand in and around Prissy's chair. Then when satisfied, they filled out and handed each of them an ID card to place in a pocket.

He pointed to a box on the counter. "Be sure to place them in this box when you leave the building."

Prissy put her ID away, then looked up at Grady and said, "Now comes the part where I pretend I'm a mermaid and try to breathe under water."

Grady's voice grew soft. "We can always take you home, Prissy, if you don't want to do this. Everyone will understand."

Her eyes met his with a steady gaze. "There are little kids out there without enough food, Mister Redwine. I want to do my share."

Her expression softened after she made her point, and she refocused on him a little misty-eyed. "Just push me fast, okay?"

"I promise."

Halim's voice drifted up from the back of the line. "Are you making a **bus** promise or a **real** promise?"

Grady saw J.D. elbow his friend in the ribs. "Stop making twoble, Halim. This is sewious."

Clara opened the package containing the ear plugs, compacted them with her fingers as much as possible, and began inserting the first one into Prissy's ear. "Hold on, honey. Try to remember there is no water—keep thinking, *there is no water*—keep breathing even if you don't think it's safe."

Clara pointed to a corner half a football field across the room and focused on Grady, "We go through that door over there. When you get there and see that she's okay, push her to the girls' room at the back...we have permission. She likes to splash some water on her face. Walk fast. Do not run, understand?"

Grady nodded nervously, sweat beading up on his forehead. He knew sprains and gashes, bloody noses and concussions. He didn't know a thing about stuff like this.

Clara bent over to Prissy. "Ready, honey?"

Prissy put a death grip on the arms of her chair. "Ready."

"Okay, then. Ready—set—deep breath—"

Prissy breathed in. Clara pressed the second plug into its canal.

Grady watched Prissy's eyes glaze over.

Clara quickly stepped away from the chair and shouted, "**Go... Go! GO!**"

Grady immediately forgot everything he was told except where to go. He grabbed Prissy's chair; took off like a shot and raced across the floor, breathing in and out hard as if it would somehow help her breathe too.

After dodging around equipment like a running back, he burst through the door of the designated room like a man on fire, frightening the bejesus out of a guy in there arranging tables.

The man side-stepped past him toward an exit at the back of the room. "Are you *crazeeee*, man?!? Running in a place full of felons and guards with guns?"

Heart knocking inside his chest, Grady mumbled an apology and pulled out Prissy's plugs. "Come on, honey. Breathe. **Breathe.** You can breathe now. " He held her hand and kept watch until her skin turned its usual color again.

When she was finally taking normal breaths, he pushed her back to the girls' room as instructed. "Take your time, honey. I'll be right out here. Call me if you need anything."

When the door closed behind her, Grady's knees went weak. He slumped into a chair and swiped at his forehead with his shirtsleeve, half wishing he *had* been shot.

This just seemed wrong on so many levels.

###

It wasn't long before the table guy reappeared, pushing a box on a dolly. About halfway back into the room, he stopped in his tracks and gawked at Grady. "Hey! I know you. Didn't you used to be Coach Redwine?"

About that time, a voice came from across the room. "Still is as far as I'm concerned."

Grady glanced up and saw a cheerful-looking elderly gentleman coming through the exit door. The man looked in the direction of the table guy. "Thank you, Cordel. Just park the box by the table. I'll take it from here."

The man walked toward Grady and extended his hand. "I'm George Roberts, Coach. You and I never met, but my grandson, Robbie, attended a couple of the workshops you taught for the JCs a couple years ago."

Grady stood and shook the man's hand as he fished around in his memory for a kid named Robbie. "Oh! Sure! Little guy? Freckles?"

"Yep! That's him. You remember!"

"I never forget a kid who tries, Mister Roberts."

"Robbie is a little challenged as an athlete, but he's big on brains—huge basketball fan. Thinks you hung the moon, by the way."

Grady had begun to reply when the restroom door opened, and Prissy emerged. Her face lit up when she saw who was there with them. "Mister Roberts! You're helping us again today?"

"Sure am."

Just then, the rest of the crew arrived, all as glad to see Mister Roberts as Prissy had been.

J.D. joined in. "You helped us last time."

"That's right. And we'll be working together again today." Everybody clapped.

"I have some special things for you this time as a thank you for helping us put together food packages for people who are having a hard time right now," He reached into the box, pulled out *Food Bank Volunteer* t-shirts and passed them around to collective *Oohs* and *Ahhhs*.

"Sometimes the cans are dirty, and we want to protect your clothes, so go ahead and pull them on."

He dug back in. "I have name tags here. Let's see if I remember. Prissy, here's yours. Halim—and J.D., right?"

J.D. grinned. "Wight."

Mister Roberts looked around for the owners of the other two tags.

Clara spoke up. "Sonti and Bennie couldn't make it today, so Mister Redwine and I will fill in."

"That's great. Thank you. We have a lot to do today." He herded them all over to the tables in the middle of the room. "I have just a couple of reminders before we get started. First of all, no bare feet…"

Clara leaned toward Grady and said out of the side of her mouth. "Sonti took his shoes off last time."

Bet that went over big.

"And the most important thing to remember is safety first." Mister Roberts smiled and shifted gears. "We're going to be sorting cans again today."

Prissy clapped. "Yay!"

"You did such a great job last time sorting by *type* of can, we're going to step it up a level. This time, we're going to check for *quality* and put together a *Variety Pack*."

He reached into the box on the dolly, lifted out a smaller one and set it down beside Prissy. "This is your box. You are in charge of green beans."

"Great! I know green beans. I did them last time."

He gave a box to J.D. "You are in charge of black beans."

"Okay."

He did the same for Halim. "You are in charge of white beans."

"Can I have red beans? I like red beans better."

Mister Roberts smiled. "Of course! Clara, would you mind trading?"

"Not at all. I'll be glad to do white beans."

He placed the last box next to Grady. "That makes you in charge of mixed beans."

"Good! I'm a mixed beans kinda guy."

"And **I** am in charge of making sure that everyone has put one of their cans in the *Variety Pack*.

"So, let's get started." Mister Roberts held up a can. "If you get any cans that look like this one with a dent in it, do not put it in the box. Just set it on the table and pick out another one."

Halim raised his hand. "Does the dent have to be that big? What if it is just a little dent?"

"That's a very good question, Halim. If you have a can with any kind of dent, any size, just set it on the table and get a new one." He held up a rusted can. "If you get any cans that look like this one, do the same thing. Place it on the table and pick up another one."

J.D. raised his hand. "Does that mean any wust at all?"

"Yes. Any rust at all." He picked up a can without a label. Can anybody tell me why you wouldn't want to put this in the box?"

J.D. spoke up. "Because you don't know If it is weely beans. It could be peaches oh something."

"Exactly. Very good, J.D." Mister Roberts walked over to the end of the table. "This is going to work like musical chairs. Do you all know musical chairs?"

Everyone nodded.

Mister Roberts demonstrated as he talked. "You will walk in a big circle. As you pass by your box, you pick up one of your cans, check it over, then continue walking and place that can in this box." He rotated the can toward the front of the box, "Make sure the label faces this way," he said. The kids stretched their necks to see what he meant. "Then you travel back to pick up another one of your cans, and we keep going until all the cans are in these new boxes." He looked mainly at J.D. "Do you have any other questions?"

"Nope."

He appeared relieved. "Okay, then. Shall we begin?"

Everyone picked up a can. J.D. rolled his around in his hands several times, frowning. He looked at Mister Roberts and pointed to a small nick. "Is this a dent?"

"No, that's a nick."

"Do nicks go in the box?"

"Nicks are okay."

"So, when does a nick become a dent?"

"I tell you what. If there is either a nick *or* a dent, just put it on the table and pick out another can, okay?"

"Okay."

J.D. picked up another can, rolled it around in his hands and set it on the table. Nine cans later, he still didn't have one that passed inspection.

Prissy grew impatient, picked up one of J.D.'s table cans and examined it. "This can is okay, J.D. You can use this one."

J.D. pointed to a spot on the label. "It has a nick. That's a nick."

"That's not a nick. That's a scratch. Scratches don't count, do they Mister Roberts."

"Scratches are okay. They can go in the box."

J.D. raised his hand. "When does a scwatch tuhn into a nick, Mistow Wobets?"

Grady pulled Mister Roberts aside. "Do you have any donations that come directly from the factory?"

"I think so, yes."

"Why don't we take a little break while you find some black beans new from the factory and bring a carton in for J.D. to sort."

"Excellent, excellent idea."

Clara gathered the gang around the table. "Let's have some lemonade and a treat. Whaddaya say?"

The room filled with enthusiasm. "Yes!"

She pulled sippy-cups and a box of donuts out of her bag and set them on the table. Everyone chowed down until Mister Roberts brought in the new box of beans, and they began sorting again.

Grady and the children marched around the table depositing cans in the box quite efficiently. After a while, Miss Clara playfully began to sing: *All around the mulberry bush, The monkey chased the weasel, The monkey thought 'twas all in fun*—then she pointed toward the rest of the group, and they joyfully finished with: ***Pop!*** *goes the Weasel!*

As natural as it was for the other kids to sing, Halim began making trumpet sounds with his mouth to accompany them.

Grady felt a little flabbergasted. It was like sorting cans in a grade school jazz club—a ***good*** jazz club.

Eventually, everyone just naturally fell into a pattern of coordinating their sorting with the song. They'd pick up a can and examine it, then march around the table in step with the music and wait for ***pop!*** to put their can in the box. Within an hour, thanks to their little unplanned system, every can had been efficiently sorted and re-packed.

Soon, short horn blasts and a voice on the public address system announced the end of the work shift.

Mister Roberts gave them all a big smile. "Well kids! That's about it! You have done a wonderful job today—and right on time."

There were grins all around when he reached into his pocket, pulled out a wallet and presented each child with a crisp new five-dollar bill. "Your pay today comes from the Indiana JCs."

Clara took over. "What do you say, everybody?"

"Thaaaank youuu Misssterrr Robberrrts."

Mister Roberts smiled. "No! Thank all of *you.*"

Beaming, they turned and handed their five dollars to Miss Clara to keep for them until Friday. After Clara collected the money, she waved the bills around and said, "Tell me what this is called."

There was a chorus of voices. "It's a salary."

"Right! And who earned it?"

"WEEE DIIID!"

"Right. YOU did."

"And who did we help?"

Prissy answered for everyone. "Little kids who don't have enough to eat."

"Right. And we're *very* proud of you. Now let's straighten up around here and get ready to go home."

Grady heard the equipment gearing down out on the floor and walked to a window at the far end of the room to watch—tensing up as he anticipated Prissy's ear plug challenge again.

Mister Roberts wandered over and stood beside him. "Shift change."

The two of them watched the flood of people heading for the loading dock doors for a minute or two. "Those are great kids you've got there, Coach."

"Yeah. They tried hard, didn't they?"

"They did great. That Prissy sure has come a long way. Gonna be a stunner like her mother."

"You knew Prissy's mother? How do you know Prissy's mother?"

"I was a volunteer at the *JC Food Bank* for several years. She came in there all the time. Prissy doesn't remember me. She was too little. But I remember her and her Mom—hard to forget that red hair. Drove a battered up old station wagon held together with duct tape—barest tires I've ever seen—cord showing through cracks in the rubber. There was no doubt they lived in the thing."

"What was her story? How did she get in that condition?"

"Don't know. We were cordial but not friends. She was very skittish—always looking over her shoulder. I learned just to give her a smile and load up the groceries—sneak in some extra diapers and cookies when I could.

"I saw a lot of sad things when I worked there, but those two ripped my heart out. She obviously had nothing—all skin and bones— but she kept them both really neat. Real clean. She was obviously nuts about Prissy—carried her everywhere.

"Every once in a while, I'd see her car parked in the lot of the shopping center down the road and drive by real slow just to check on them. The stores there are pretty generous that way. They're open 24 hours—have security on hand—let people use the restrooms."

"Why do you suppose she didn't go to a *Shelter*?"

"I assumed it was because she was afraid they'd take her little girl away—Prissy being challenged and all."

"What happened to her? Do you know?"

"Don't have a clue. She came in every Wednesday like clockwork for two years, then one day she just didn't show up—never saw her again." He paused for a minute, reflecting. "Still can't drive by that shopping center without looking for her car."

"Does Prissy know all this?"

"No. She didn't recognize me when she first saw me—probably too young back then to remember. I have nothing new to tell her—don't want to bring back any bad memories or anything.

Prissy's paperwork said she had issues with noise, but I had no idea how serious it was until I saw what happened when they put those ear plugs in last time."

Grady scrunched up his mouth. "Tough to watch."

Roberts continued. "Fortunately, getting out of here is easier on her than getting her in. You leave during a shift change so the equipment is shut down and it's not nearly as noisy." He lifted the lanyard away from his chest. "These cards have a chip in them. The computer checks you all in, then tracks you around the complex all day."

Grady watched Clara and the kids pack up their things. Prissy stopped mid-motion and flashed him a smile. Clara began to usher the kids out the door and shouted toward Grady, "You go through that door over there. It leads to the dock. Scan yourself out and pick up the bus. "I'll get us all checked out and we'll meet you up front where you dropped us off."

Mr. Roberts leaned sideways toward him. "I have to return that dolly over there to the Supply Room today, so why don't I walk both you and Prissy out to the dock. There's a little box out there that works like an ATM. You put in your card, it pulls it inside and scans it, checks you out and lifts the barrier. Put the cards in the box at the end of the row, and you're free to go home." He smiled. "Don't forget to return the ID cards. If you don't, men with guns will follow you home and arrest you."

"The gate will automatically let you and the bus out of the yard. Need help with anything else?"

Grady smiled. "Can't think of anything but thank you. You've done more than enough."–He offered his hand and Roberts shook it. – "We're all very grateful."

"You're more than welcome. Glad to be helpful." He picked up the dolly. "Well, I'd better hustle this thing back to the equipment room." He jogged a few steps then turned around and waved. "See ya in a week or two. Look forward to doing it again."

When Grady drove back to the front of the building, he spotted the gang on the sidewalk. Clara was concentrating on Halim who had obviously started lagging behind. Ultimately, he came to a halt at the bottom of the steps and examined the hand-written bus number.

"This is still the blue bus. Where is the *real* bus? You said it would be back today."

Grady felt acid burning in his stomach. "They had an emergency in the service department, Halim. They couldn't get our bus finished on time."

"I don't like the blue bus. My seat belt is red. I want the red one."

"Remember what your grandma said? Blue is a good color, Halim. You don't have to worry about blue."

J.D. leaned into the aisle. "Blue is a good culuh, Halim."

Prissy leaned in too. "Halim! Halim! Blue is good."

Halim dragged his feet but gave in and sat down. "He promised. He *promised* we would get our real bus back."

Grady sat silently behind the wheel and concentrated on the road, feeling like he'd been hit by a truck. In minutes, a heavenly hush fell on the kids and all three of them were out like a light. They rode in silence for about thirty minutes, grateful to have the kids quietly napping in the natural rocking of the bus—until they rounded a corner and hit an unexpected pothole.

Bam!

Halim literally leaped from sleep and started struggling with his seat belt, screaming, "I have to get off of this bus. I have to get off of this bus. I HAVE TO GET OFF OF THIS BUS…"

Grady gripped the wheel and glanced in the mirror. *What the* **Hell** *is going on!?*

Clara jumped out of her seat and rushed toward him down the aisle. "Halim, honey. You're almost home…"

Grady gripped tighter. Tried to concentrate. Pushed the speed governor to the limit.

Halim pounded on his knees and the seat in front of him. *"...CRAAAAAASH! SMAAAAAASH!..."*

Prissy covered her ears. "Take him home, Mister Redwine! Take him home first. Pleeeasse. Pleeasse take him home. It hurts! It hurts!"

Grady picked up the mic to the radio. "Fourteen Eighty-Six to base. I have a Ten-Eighteen. Please call the *Hamilton Shelter* and tell them we will be returning late."

"... **I HAVE TO GET OFF OF THIS BUS!** *I HAVE TO GET OFF OF THIS BUS!*..."

Grady shouted over his shoulder. "Hold on. Making U-turn. Passing the *Shelter* now."

"Base to eighty-six. Will do. Do you need assistance?"

"Will advise. Eighty-six out."

"...CRAAAAAASH! SMAAAAAASH!..."

"...You're almost home, honey. We're going home." Clara offered Halim a blanket. He side-armed it back.

J.D. reached across the aisle. "Halim stop. Evwything will be Okay. STOP!"

"...TIME TO CRAAAAAASH! CRAAAAAASH!..."

Clara rushed back to her seat and grabbed her cell phone. "I'm texting his grandmother to meet us at the curb. How long, Mister Redwine?"

"Ten minutes away."

She pushed the message onto the screen. "I hope she's home."

"...SMAAAAAASH!"

"Hurry, Mister Redwine. Take him home. It hurts! *It hurts!*"

Clara reached over to Prissy. "Try to calm down, Prissy. It won't be long."

"...SMAAAAAASH! TIME TO CRAAAAAASH! SMAAAAAASH!..."

"Got an okay from his grandmother." She turned toward Haim. "Grandma's coming, Halim. It won't be long, honey."

Grady gave a sigh of relief; made a left turn into Halim's complex. "Two minutes."

"...CRAAAAAASH!"

Clara glanced out the windshield. "She's there. I see her." She turned toward Halim. "Here's Grandma, honey. Here she comes."

Grady pulled over to the curb and opened the doors. Halim's grandmother climbed aboard. "Was he asleep?"

"Yes. And then we hit a pothole and..."

"I'm so sorry," she said. "I thought you knew. Sudden loud noises give him flashbacks of the wreck he was in with his mother."

She turned to Grady and mouthed, "His mother died."

Clara followed his grandmother down the aisle and stepped aside as she reached to unclasp Halim's seat belt.

Halim stopped struggling. "Hulk says get off of this bus."

"I know," she said.

Grady watched the old woman take Halim's hand and silently lead him off the bus, walking like she carried the weight of the world, "I'll let you know if he's riding tomorrow."

Clara thanked her then sadly shook her head. "That old woman is only fifty-five years old."

Grady's eyes followed the woman to the door. *Wow.*

J.D. leaned into the aisle and announced, "I think Halim was upset."

Grady and Clara exchanged a wide-eyed look— *'Ya think?'*

Prissy piped up. "Halim misses his mother. She's living with Jesus like mine, you know." She paused as if mulling things over. "I wonder if they know each other. Wouldn't that be great?"

Clara reached over and patted Prissy's arm. "Yes, it would. It would be really great."

Grady checked on J.D. in the mirror. He was rocking in his seat, forward-back, forward-back, forward-back. "Please don't worry, J.D. You're almost home."

"I am twenty-thwee minutes late, Mistow Wedwine. Will I get in twoble?"

"No, J.D., you won't get in trouble. Miss Miller won't be mad."

"I don't want huh to wowwy."

They drove in silence again after that until Grady pulled into the curb and parked. "Aaaannd, here we are, J.D. Hope you have a good..."

J.D. interrupted. "I think it would be okay to say, *'So long'* evwy day, Mistow Wedwine."

Grady smiled. "Okay, J.D. *'So long'* is just fine with me too."

Prissy shifted into high excitement when Clara rolled her onto the lift to get off the bus. "Tonight's our party to celebrate Marcell is gone." As she was lowered to the ground, she shouted back at Grady, "We get cake! Chocolate with chocolate frosting...and sprinkles."

###

Grady had to work hard to find enough strength in his legs to work the brakes by the time they pulled onto the bus lot. He managed to open the door for Clara but quickly returned his hands to the wheel so she wouldn't notice them shaking.

"What a horrible day this was. Whoever has such a horrible day?"

Clara packed up her things and prepared to leave but paused at the top of the stairs and turned toward him to answer. "We do."

She shut him up again as she went down a couple of steps and looked at the darkening sky. "The Weather Service is forecasting black ice."

She stepped down two more. "Go home, Mister Redwine. Get some rest. Hope for a snow day tomorrow."

He already had.

Grady watched Clara walk to her car, filled with a deep longing to return to the days when his biggest problem was finding a wad of gum under a seat.

He peeled his hands off the wheel then locked the door, making a mental note to add an antacid to his list for the Qwick Pick.

By the time Grady reached his truck and climbed in, he considered adding some more hard stuff to the list too, then nixed it. He had a pint and a case of *Tall Boys* at home...that's all he needed.

THURSDAY
January 17, 2019-Morning

Grady hadn't woken up with a beer in his hand since college. In his twenties, his ability to toss down shots with chasers all night and still be able to function the next day was legendary. But after he managed to pry his fingers off the can and add it to the debris on the table beside his recliner, it became painfully obvious that those days were long gone.

As he struggled his way to consciousness, Grady grew aware of an unrelenting sound in his room that he knew was a small ding, but right now, was banging in his brain like a gong.

What is that? Where is it coming from?

He wanted it to stop. He needed it to stop.

It wasn't until the screen of his phone flashed on, that it dawned on him he was getting an email. He glanced at the clock.

Four-thirty. *What the Hell! Who does that*?

Grady groped around in the recliner for his glasses and squinted at the screen. His anger flipped immediately to feeling the gratitude of a drowning man just tossed a float ring.

The National Weather Service has issued a severe storm warning for Thursday, January 17
All schools will be closed today.

Thank you, Lord. Thank you! Thank you! Thank you!

Eventually, he managed to turn his attention to the pile of debris that surrounded him from the night before.

The coffee table in front of his chair overflowed with crushed *tall boy* cans and a shot glass resting on the neck of a half-empty bottle of whisky. At his feet lay a large plastic bar-b-que bag full of chicken wing bones and an open box of extra-large pizza that he had only a vague memory of ordering. Sharing space in the box with a single left-over slice, were two crumpled taco chip bags, a few wadded-up dollar bills, and a scattering of small change.

He felt deep waves of shame at the scene. *Grady. Grady. Grady.*

###

After spending a couple of hours nursing his headache from Hell, Grady's attention refocused on the coffee table. How had he managed to do all that? He had the distinct memory of taking a shot when he got home. And then two more with a couple of beers. What happened next was mostly a mystery.

One thing was obvious—he got royally hammered.

It wasn't until he leaned on the arm of the chair that he noticed a rug burn on his elbow. Had he fallen?

Most likely. His whole body was sore.

Threading together clues to his drunken behavior wasn't a new skill for Grady. He learned in college that being able to function after a night of party-hardy didn't necessarily mean he could remember much about it.

He faded in and out for a couple of hours, but eventually fell into a deep, dead sleep, only to be startled awake half an hour later, by the persistent ring of his phone.

Still in a fog, he floundered around, trying frantically to find the right thing to push. Don't-be-the-school-don't-be-the-school-pleeeese-don't-be-the-school.

Finally successful, he managed, "Huh-low?"

It was a woman's voice. "Mister Redwine?"

"Yes."

"This is Sister Mary Mercy in Monsignor Ryan Goodman's office. I'm calling in response to the message you left His Eminence last night."

Ryan? I called Ryan last night? Oh, my Lord—who else did I call?

"His Eminence says he can work you into his schedule during his lunch hour today. Can you come in at twelve-thirty?"

"I—uh—I—" He ran out of words.

"Hello? Are you still there, Mister Redwine?"

"Uh, yes! Yes! Thank you for calling me...back. Tell him...Tell him... *"What should I tell him? I don't want to drive through an ice storm all the way to Indy.*

"Mister Redwine?"

Oh, what the Hell. I haven't seen him in months. "Please tell him, 'Thank you.' I'll be there at twelve-thirty."

"We'll look forward to seeing you then."

Afternoon

Grady sidled past a man painting a simple gold frame on the glass in the door of the local diocese office. He paused and smiled to see Ryan's name and title in the middle of the oval. Who would have guessed that his old college roommate would reach such lofty heights.

He approached a desk adjacent to Ryan's office that displayed the name plate of Sister Mary Mercy. "Go right in, Mister Redwine. He's expecting you."

Grady smiled. "Thank you so much for your help today."

She smiled back. "Any time."

Grady gave no warning knock, just walked directly into the office. A sandy-haired man sat behind a mahogany desk, concentrating hard on a leather-bound book.

Grady walked toward him across the oriental carpet. "So, they finally pulled the trigger on your promotion, I see."

The man stood and smiled. "It's good to see you again, Grady."

They shared the hearty handshake and back-slapping man-hug of great, long-time friends, then Ryan stepped back and looked into Grady's eyes as if seriously searching for something. "Why are you here?"

Good question.

Grady fished around to find an answer. "Well, uh, we haven't been able to talk in months. And you got this promotion. And I, uh, just thought we should get together—is all."

"So let me get this straight. After all this time, you started missing me so much at two in the morning on a Wednesday, that it brought you to tears?"

I was crying?

"So, you called me?"

"Something like that."

"For an appointment to make a confession?"

Con-fess-ion? "Uh—"

"First of all, I can't hear your confession, Grady. You're a...sort of Baptist. And second of all, I only have an hour, not a weekend."

"Funny."

The cleric shrugged a shoulder." So, what's really going on?"

"Could you just take off that collar and talk to me, Ryan? I need to pick your brain."

The cleric waved him toward an armchair across from his desk and reached for the white plastic tab in his collar. "I can 'just talk' with this in, you know."

"Yeah, but I can't."

Ryan sighed good-naturedly, pulled out the tab and settled into his own chair. "Okay, pick away."

Grady hesitated, trying to figure out how to begin.

Ryan spread his hands. "Just dump it all on the floor, Redwine. We'll sort it out as we go."

"Okay..." Grady cleared his throat. "Okay." He slid closer to the edge of his chair, "My life is a mess, Ryan. I'm in a really bad place."

"Tell me more."

"You might have heard I got fired from my coaching job."

"Everybody heard. I was in Italy and heard. You took on Bill Hader?! Really!? In public? The guy's got more power than Putin."

"He may be President of the Board of Education and the richest guy around, but that doesn't mean what he was doing was right."

"What, exactly, was he doing?"

"Messing with my kids' heads in the middle of a game."

"It's basketball. People shout things. You know that."

"Yeah, but he was coming down on the sideline to shout during the State Basketball Playoffs. Who in the Hell does he think he is? He's not the coach. And the bastard kept calling my point guard—his very own son, by the way—an effing loser. I couldn't let him get away with that. It was affecting the whole team."

Ryan screwed up his mouth.

Grady plowed on. "I didn't hit him or anything. Just invited him off the team sideline a little loudly."

"For that they let you go?"

"Well, that and calling him an arrogant ignorant asshole, I guess. He seemed to take offense at that too."

"Yeah, but still...you brought three consecutive championships to that school...five of your kids are in the NBA! Couldn't you just buy him a beer and talk it out?"

"Tried that the first time. Didn't work."

"The *first* time? So, this happened before?"

"Only once. He said he didn't like being humiliated in front of everyone in the gym. Threatened the *Board*. Said he'd shut down the donation train if they didn't get rid of me."

Grady shifted in his seat. "I know I probably shouldn't have done what I did, but I was under so much pressure, Ryan, with what was going on with Mary. She was so sick, and we didn't know what was wrong."

"I remember."

"I just had a really short fuse and..."

"They let you go."

"Yeah...sort of. After some of the parents threw a fit, the *County* offered me a job driving a school bus so I could keep my benefits. Called it a lateral move."

"Yeah. Lateral. How did you feel about that?"

"It hurt. But to tell you the truth, it turned into a blessing. Coaching a team is twenty-four-seven and I needed to be home. Toward the end, Mary didn't know who I was most of the time, but she was terrified when I wasn't there. And then when she...when she passed away—it was kind of a relief just to have to drive a couple of hours, take a nap, then drive a couple hours more."

"You keep saying was."

"Well, yeah, I got fired again."

"What?!"

"It's a long, stupid story, but we worked it out. They gave me probation and let me keep driving."

"I'm waiting for the 'why you're upset' part. Did they cut your pay?"

"No."

"Take away your benefits?"

"No."

"Change your hours?"

"No, Ryan."

"So, you're still driving. What's the problem?"

"They assigned me to a *Special Needs* Bus."

"And..."

"And I have absolutely no business driving one. I have zero training. Every time I turn around, I'm doing something stupid or saying the wrong thing.

"These are good kids, Ryan. They deserve the best and, That. Definitely. Isn't. Me."

"Come on. You're great with kids, Grady. You've been building champions for years."

"That's the whole point, Ryan. I build champions. What you do to build a champion is choose the best of the ones with the most potential and send the rest to the minors. That makes my skills completely wrong for this job. You can't turn around to a busload of children with physical or mental challenges and say, 'Sit down and shut the Hell up or you'll be sitting on the bench.' They're already on the bench. You can't threaten to kick them off the team. They'd never get picked for a team. You can't say, 'no pain no gain' to children whose lives are already filled with pain. And saying, 'Okay, smart ass, get down and give me twenty,' or 'That'll be ten laps.' is just ridiculous and completely inappropriate."

Ryan shrugged a shoulder. "So, you've got a problem. You need some training. You're smart. Get some. Do what you always told your kids: Learn, adjust and move forward."

"It's not just training I need, Ryan. My instincts are completely out of whack. Used to be, going with my gut never failed me. But here—doing this—it's useless. I'm in trouble all the time. You have to have a calling to do this job and I. Just. Don't. I go through every day feeling guilty and selfish and…well…to be honest with you, a little afraid. Those children deserve better."

Ryan leaned back in his chair. "I hate to point out the obvious, my friend, but it seems to me you do have a calling. If you quit your job, the bank will be calling, *Amex* will be calling, and who knows who else…will be calling."

"Yes. You're right. I have bills. But I can tell you one thing for sure. If you're only in it for the money, this ain't the job for you."

Grady took a deep breath and exhaled hard. "I'm going to fail, Ryan. It's absolutely inevitable. And the truth is, while I'm busy failing, I could accidentally do something wrong and seriously hurt someone."

There was a long pause before Grady noticed Ryan's silence. "You're staring at me."

Ryan appeared somewhat bewildered. "Your eyes are bloodshot. You reek of alcohol. Who are you and what-have-you-done with my friend?"

"Why? What do you mean?"

"When did you start taking the easy way out, Redwine? When did you start ducking a fight or caring what other people thought?"

Grady winced.

Ryan forged on. "You were always a pain in the butt, my friend, but one thing you weren't was a quitter."

"This isn't quitting. I'm just trying to stop doing something that might be dangerous to others…little children…little *Special Needs* children. There's a difference."

"And that difference is…"

"Well...stopping is using common sense to make a decision to do something. Quitting is chickening out."

"Oh. Sorry. Here. Let me rephrase my question. Grady, when did you apply common sense and decide it was time to start chickening out?"

Grady clenched his jaw. *Chicken out? Chicken out! I've spent four days in Hell trying to make this work.*

Ryan proceeded in earnest. "Before you decide anything, I suggest you spend a minute thinking about how you're going to feel when you hear that those jerks are sitting around in the Booster Club laughing because they've stuck you with a busload of losers and you, *Mister I Build Champions,* don't have a clue what to do with them."

Grady took a breath; started to speak. Ryan held up a hand to stop him. "But you know what ticks me off the most about all this?"

"What."

"The four years of college I wasted bailing you out of jail for taking on some jerk in a bar because he was picking on a little guy."

Grady shifted in his seat. "Up yours, Ryan."

"That's up yours, *Your Eminence.* And...you're welcome." Ryan checked his watch. "I know you're not a particularly religious person..."

Grady spread his arms. "Hey! I always made sure we had a prayer before the game."

Ryan chuckled. "Impressive."

Grady watched him reach into the top middle drawer of his desk and take out an envelope. Although he knew all along that it was probably unrealistic to go to a Cathedral and hope there was no discussion about religion, Grady still hoped a little.

Oh man. Here it comes.

Ryan laid the envelope on his desk. "This is something I give everyone who comes to me."

Grady groaned inwardly. He knew Ryan meant well and was only doing his job, but it was just too awkward. How do you tell an Archbishop not to bother because you're fed up with his boss?

Ryan pulled out a blank piece of paper, wrote something brief, then folded it, added it to a document already in the envelope and handed it his direction. "If some day you have nothing else to do, you might find it helpful too."

Grady faked a smile. "Thanks."

"Sometimes events in our lives bewilder us. But God has a divine plan. I believe there must be a reason you are where you are, Redwine. The longer I'm in this job, the more convinced I am that nothing occurs by chance."

Ryan looked at his watch. "Sorry, buddy, I'm late. Gotta go."

Grady walked toward the door and turned back, intending to say something. Ryan was already halfway out the back door. He held up a hand and slid the tab back into his collar. "Text me, Grady. Or leave a voicemail. Our machine takes long messages. Let me know what you **decide** to do."

Prissy's determined little face flashed through his mind. "My kids aren't losers, Ryan."

Ryan shouted back at him over his shoulder. "Neither are you."

Evening

By the time he got home, the temperature had dropped, and the slush was turning to ice. The storm was here. Grady pulled into the driveway and slogged around to the passenger side to gather his stuff. No sooner had he opened the door than a bitter gust of wind swept into the cab, sending papers swirling onto the sidewalk. He grabbed for them, missed, and stomped his foot along the ground trying to stop them from escaping, but they ended up half soaked in a puddle before he was able to corral them.

Swell. Just swell.

He stood in the storm and stared at the puddle, tempted just to leave it all there. But for some inexplicable reason, Grady picked everything up, shook off what wetness he could, and carried the whole mess inside.

He tossed the receipts and miscellaneous stuff into the trash but hesitated with the envelope from Ryan. Writings about God didn't seem to be something to be thrown away, even if you had no intention of reading them or only took them in the first place to be polite.

Grady made a one-shoulder shrug; laid Ryan's envelope on top of the bills on the table; then promptly put it out of his mind.

FRIDAY
January 18, 2019-Morning

Grady knew it might feel a little awkward between him and Clara when they met at the bus that morning, so he stopped to buy a couple of lattes as a peace offering.

He held hers out to her when she entered the bus, but she hesitated and said, "You look tired. Are you okay?"

"Yeah. I'm okay."

She tilted her head slightly and got a concerned look in her eyes. "Is there something you want to ask me, Grady?"

"No. Not really, why?"

She shrugged and finally took the cup from his hand. "Well, when I saw that you called at two in the morning Wednesday, I thought you might have something on your mind."

I called her too?!

"Uh, no—it must have been—"

"A butt-dial?"

"Yeah. One of those."

She opened her latte and took a sip. "Good. Oh, by the way, No Halim today."

###

Prissy was a little subdued when she got on the bus that morning. She wheeled into her place and stared sadly at Halim's empty seat. "Is he coming today?"

"No honey. Halim's staying home."

"I hope he's okay."

Clara set about buckling her in. "So do we, honey. So do we."

Grady thought it was a good time to try cheering things up a bit. "How was your *Marcell's Gone--Chocolate Cake-with-Sprinkles-- Party* on Wednesday?"

Prissy answered with a sad tone in her voice. "Oh…it was good."

He watched her turn her attention away from Halim's place on the bus and lean back in her chair. "I thought you *loved* chocolate cake with sprinkles."

She gave a weak answer: "I do," and left it at that.

###

Grady took a deep breath as he headed for the dorm to get Sonti, trying hard to convince the butterflies in his belly to fly in some sort of formation.

He was so nervous; he lost concentration and clipped the curb with a back tire when he rounded a corner too soon.

He saw Prissy grab the arms of her wheelchair "Whaoh!"

Clara's face soon appeared in the mirror. "That isn't like you. What's going on?"

"Sonti's had three days out of school."

Prissy piped up. "And he will probably be a mess." Clara seemed somewhat apprehensive too. "I think when he's been away this long, he starts to think its summertime or something, and he doesn't have to go back to school. Let's just hope the new medication is still working well."

Her phone dinged. She checked her messages. "Bennie has a doctor's appointment, so he won't be on the bus. At least we have some extra time."

Grady looked up the driveway. "Well, it appears that we'll need it. No such luck on the medication."

They watched the usual hassle at the top of the driveway as the Aides herded Sonti down to the bus screaming and struggling all the way.

When he was finally aboard, Sonti reached into Clara's stack of blankets as he always did, picked the purple one and plunked it on his head.

As soon as he hit the seat, he burst into tears. "Ahhhhhhhh! Ahhhhhhhh! Ahhhhhhhh!"

Prissy's hands shot up to cover the ear cushions of her headset. "Oh brother."

"Ahhhhhhhh!"

Clara sat in a seat beside Prissy. "It's best just to leave him alone when he gets like this."

Sonti flailed his arms; kicked the seat in front of him. BAM! BAM! BAM! He screamed some more and then began trembling.

Grady saw Clara leap to attention and hurry to check on him. *Oh-Lord. I hope he isn't having a seizure.*

Grady gripped the wheel and tried to concentrate, alternating between the road and his mirror. "You okay? Do I need to pull over?"

Clara's voice behind him said, "He's just upset. I think he's fine. He's stopped shaking. I'll just leave him alone—give him time to calm down."

Grady breathed a mental sigh of relief and headed for J.D.'s dorm. He'd no sooner relaxed his grip and settled into the seat, than Sonti let out a shriek.

From nowhere, two sneakers and a pair of dirty gym socks hit him on the back of the head. *WHAT THE HELL?*

Prissy fell back against her headrest and smacked her forehead with her hand. "Oh no. Not a-gain!"

Clara sighed. "Oh, Sonti. Not today." She left her seat, picked up the shoes and collected the socks resting on the back of Grady's shoulder.

Grady pulled into the driveway of J.D.'s dorm and stared at Clara in his mirror. "What's going on?"

"Well, either Sonti has decided clothes are optional today, or he's mad and wants to make sure we've noticed."

J.D. appeared at the door. "Mowning."

Grady answered. "Good morning, J.D."

J.D. looked at Clara. "Shoe day?"

Clara turned toward him. "Yep."

"Oh." J.D. sidled around her, settled in his seat and took his normal position underneath his backward hoodie.

When he heard the click of J.D.'s seat belt, Grady released the brake and headed for the school. As he drove, he said to Clara, "Does this shoe thing happen often?"

J.D.'s voice drifted out from behind his hoodie. "Not often, Mistow Wedwine. Moe like fweequently."

Grady laughed and pulled into the bus loop.

As she was preparing to unload the children, Clara said, "What day is it everybody?"

"Chicken Nugget Day!"

"That's right! You have a great morning, be good, and we'll meet over Nuggets this afternoon."

After they all paraded off, Clara walked to Sonti's seat to tackle his shoes. She kneeled down next to him. "Sonti, we're going to have to put these back on, honey. You need them for school."

Grady watched as Clara began to slide one of the socks onto his foot. Sonti sat peacefully and looked casually at his surroundings as his ankle waggled around in the aisle. Clara's first attempt was foiled when his toenails caught on a thread. "Someone's got to cut this child's nails."

She unsnagged the thread; readjusted the sock; tried again. Sonti let his leg go completely limp, offering no leverage for Clara to push against. When she pushed, his leg bent sideways at the knee and wobbled around like a noodle.

She tried again, but his leg still bounced up and down from his hip. It was like trying to put a sock on a string of spaghetti.

Clara looked back at Grady. "I could use some help."

He climbed out of his seat and stood in front of Sonti, preparing to take directions.

Clara moved aside to give him some room. "I think it will work best if you pull his feet out over the edge of the seat and hold his ankles. I'll have something to push against that way."

Grady did as she wished, watching as Sonti's eyes turned from black and fathomless to alert and amused.

Soon, Clara threw up both hands Nixon style. "Success!"

The face of Sonti's teacher appeared at the top of the stairs. "Not another shoe day."

Clara answered. "Afraid so."

He groaned. "Need some help?"

"I think we've got it, Mister Wilson. He'll be ready for class soon." She picked up a sneaker and began unlacing it. "Got the socks on. Now for the hardest part."

Grady frowned. "High-top sneakers? Who puts a kid who hates shoes in these if they have to go through this to put them on?"

"It might be it's because they want him to fit in. Or maybe they think if they lace them tightly it would be harder for him to get them off."

Mister Wilson's voice drifted from the stairs. "Actually, it's quite possible that these were the only shoes in the church's charity donation bin that fit."

Grady felt a pang of guilt as he waited for Clara to stretch the sneaker wide at the laces and prepare to slip them on. "Do like we did with the socks," she said. "You push down on his knee and hold his leg straight. I'll do the rest."

Ten minutes later, Grady watched Mister Wilson push Sonti to the door of the school. *He might think twice before he kicked them off again if he had to walk up there barefoot.*

The voice inside his head answered back. *Yeah, but your butt would be in jail for child abuse before you could even say shoe.*

As if she'd read his thoughts, Clara said, "Sonti's a little bit like a puppy. You can't punish puppies when you get home from work if they wet on the floor that morning. They don't put the two together. That's the way it is with Sonti's shoes."

Grady respected her expertise but didn't really buy her premise. He'd seen the light of intelligence in Sonti's eyes. There was more in there than people gave him credit for. If you asked him, kicking off the shoes was just another *teacher and the wheelchair* thing. Sonti said, *up yours*, then got a kick out of making them try to put the shoes back on.

Clara talked as she folded the purple blanket. "It's important to remember that just because Sonti can't say anything, it doesn't mean he doesn't have anything to say. He just uses shoes and socks to say it."

Grady mentally rested his case.

Afternoon

When Grady and Clara pulled into the bus loop to pick up the kids for the afternoon, they were met with a rousing cheer. Prissy led the charge down the sidewalk from the school toward them, bellowing, "Indy Chick'n Day! Chicken Nugget Day! Best day of the week."

Mr. Wilson brought Sonti down in a wheelchair and they loaded him onto the bus using the lift.

Clara looked Grady's direction as she anchored Sonti's chair behind Prissy. "He'll need it inside the restaurant."

While Clara finished, Grady surveyed the school. "Where's the teacher? Isn't one supposed to be here?"

"Miss Grundel takes her own car to these things. She's not comfortable on the bus."

In a conspiratorial tone, Prissy said, "I think we drive Miss Grundel crazy."

"Unfortunately, so do I," Clara said under her breath.

###

Grady drove the short distance from the school to *Indy Chick'n*, a popular local restaurant, and pulled into their lot, grateful to be able to park in one of their Van Accessible Spaces.

Clara handed each child the five-dollar bill that they earned at the *Food Bank* so they would be able to pay for their lunch.

###

When Miss Grundel finally arrived at the restaurant, Grady watched how she worked with the children, intending to learn the proper process to use in case he and Clara were alone with them one day.

She approached the kids already arranged around a table in the middle of the room and snatched Sonti's bill from his hand. "We all know what you want, don't we? Chicken Nuggets are your favorite."

She moved on to Prissy. "What would you like for lunch, my dear?"

Prissy produced her five-dollar bill and recited, "Six-Chicken-Nuggets-French fries-chocolate-shake-Four-dollars-eighty-cents."

Miss Grundel flashed a plastic smile. "Excellent."

Miss Grundel took J.D.'s money. "And what would you like for lunch, dear?"

"Six-Chicken-Nuggets-Fwench-fwies-chocolate-shake-¬Fo-dollahs-eighty-cents."

That smile again. "Very good."—She turned to BennieBot. "Did you get your order, Bennie?"

At home, Bennie focused the camera on his tray. "Yes. Six chicken strips, Sweet Potato fries and a banana yogurt."

Miss Grundel managed a genuine smile. — "That's great, honey."—then she left the room and walked to the register.

Grady leaned across the table to Clara. "The only one that doesn't sound like a robot is the robot." Clara chuckled.

Miss Grundel returned to the table with the change in her hand. "Here's your money, everyone." She made the rounds of everyone again, asking what they should get back from their order and everyone answered, "two monies," with the exception of Bennie, who remained silent.

Grady looked at Clara. "Monies?"

She mouthed, *Later*.

After that, Miss Grundel counted out eight dimes…two for each child. Together, everyone counted, "one, two," as she placed the coins in someone's hand. When the dimes had all been distributed, she circled back around so everyone could dump them back into her palm. She turned to the table, said, "Excellent," then retrieved her purse, dumped in the dimes, and headed for the ladies' room.

Clara said quickly in an undertone, "Don't let her get to you, Mister Redwine. Most *Special Needs* teachers are angels on Earth. She's supposed to retire at the end of the semester and she's just biding her…shhh here-she-comes."

In a flurry of activity, Miss Grundel, trailed by two employees carrying trays, delivered everyone's lunch and the children gleefully chowed down.

Afterward, Miss Grundel joined Grady and Clara in their booth and whispered confidentially, "We always come here because they have this private room. It's a great win/win. We don't hold up the line and the children aren't exposed to stares."

Grady took a sip of his shake and asked her why she was teaching the children to say monies.

Clara kicked him under the table.

"Oh that. Very simple. It's because yesterday, these children knew the difference between a penny and a dime. Today most of them don't. And even the ones who remember today, will have forgotten again by Monday. So, I always say, *I've got your money* and that queues them to use the term *money* as well…only they tend to use the plural version of—she made quotation marks with her fingers—*monies* because they're getting more than one dime back."

She took a bite of her double burger and chewed for a moment. "Same thing goes with other concepts. Yesterday they knew the difference between a number and a letter. But when they got to school this morning, they had forgotten so we had to start over."

She sucked on the straw to her coke and chewed some more. "You're new, but you'll eventually find some techniques too." She sucked again. "And, actually, people tell me they find *monies* somewhat endearing.

"Ultimately, with these children, what we're aiming for is behavioral correction rather than actual learning as you and I understand it."

Grady couldn't finish his lunch.

At the end of the outing, the children paraded onto the bus. When Grady reached out a hand to help Sonti up the stairs, he did a double take. Sonti had the swollen face of a chipmunk with its cheeks packed full of nuts. "Clara. Have you seen his face?"

Clara bent over and whispered to him, "Yes, I have. I've tried to stop him, but there's nothing I can do about it. He tries to bite my fingers if I try to take them out."

Grady whispered back. "He could choke."

Clara whispered some more. "I know. But he never does. Let's talk about it later."

Later. Grady was getting really sick of that word.

Clara fastened Sonti into his seat. There were cheers when she said, "It's a three-day weekend everybody. What day is Monday?"

"*Martin Luther King* Day."

"And do we go to school that day?"

"No!"

"Then let's go home and enjoy it!"

###

Grady' heart pounded hard in his chest as he drove. He kept one eye on the road, the other in the mirror on Sonti, and sent up a small word of thanks when he managed to deliver him into the arms of his family alive.

He saw Sonti's Mom cup her son's face and look concerned when he got off the bus, but she did nothing that indicated alarm over the bulge in his cheeks.

Surely she sees it. How could she not notice?

He watched her usher her son to the sidewalk where his sisters and brother waited, then join with them as they gleefully danced around shouting his name.

"Sonti! Sonti! Sonti!"

The family had nearly reached the back door of the house when he noticed Sonti start dragging his feet. Then without any obvious reason, he suddenly turned back toward the bus and shot them a look filled with fear.

Grady felt goosebumps rise on his arms.

He gave Clara a quizzical look in the mirror. She answered with a gentle shake of her head and made a sweeping hand movement that clearly conveyed, "I know this is sad, but it isn't our business. There are three other children here we're responsible to care for. We have no choice but to move on."

Grady lowered his head in compliance and started checking the side mirrors so he could safely pull away from the curb, but he couldn't resist taking one final glance up the hill.

As his eyes swept the property, he noticed an old car with a dented front fender hanging askew, parked on the grass next to a tool shed. It was missing a license plate; a headlight was cracked; and it was covered with patches of ugly gray primer. *That's new.* Still feeling alarmed, Grady continued to watch guardedly until everyone disappeared into the house, then he took a more meticulous look at the car. It had a heavy-duty dog barrier across the back seat and more primer paint on the trunk, but nothing else to take note of other than the considerable effort the driver had made to maneuver it around the basketball hoop and position it under the tie-out line in such a small space.

He heard Clara approaching then felt her standing beside him. "What are you doing? What's the hold-up?"

He kept his eyes trained on the yard but responded, "I was wondering how Sonti's mother can justify having a dog that big when she can't feed her children."

"I've never seen a big dog there. What makes you think they have one?"

"There's a heavy-weight tie-out line attached to the basketball hoop and a dog barrier across the back seat of the car."

She squinted out the window. "Oh yeaaah. I never noticed. Maybe the tie-line belonged to a previous renter..."

"Maybe."

"Or maybe she keeps the dog in the house, so it won't chase the bus."

"Could be."

He paused a moment longer to examine the tie-out line before shifting into gear. *Those things are expensive. You'd think they'd roll it up and store it or something if they weren't using it.*

Back at the bus barn, Grady turned to Clara. "What's up with the *Chicken Nuggets?*"

"Awful, isn't it? I pray all the way home every Friday.."

"Have you asked Miss Grundel about it? Surely by now, she's come up with a—he held up quotation fingers—*technique.*"

She laughed. "I wish. His teachers think he must have had to fight for his food at some point in his life, so he gets defensive if he thinks you're trying to take it from him. It's sort of another puppy thing."

"Can't we just get him to spit them out and save some for him in a box?"

"You'd think so, but Miss Grundel warned me not to put my fingers in his mouth. They can't find a dentist who'll take him, so even if he doesn't bite your fingers off, you could end up with tetanus."

Clara picked up Sonti's purple blanket and began to fold it. "Prissy told me Miss Miller thinks either Sonti is trying to save something for someone or he's afraid there isn't going to be any food at his mother's."

The vision of Sonti's chipmunk cheeks and fearful eyes flashed back through his mind. This just didn't feel right...didn't feel right at all.

SATURDAY
January 19, 2019

Grady's favorite thing to do was sit around in his underwear, drink beer and channel surf. His favorite month to do it was January when college football was over, and Saturdays became filled with NFL playoffs leading up to the Super Bowl. He was especially excited about the weekend ahead of him because the NBA was also raging, and, miracle of miracles, the *Comets* were scheduled to play both Saturday afternoon and late on Monday, *Martin Luther King Day*.

Grady was back in his element and stoked. He spent the morning pulling together his favorite tailgate: wings, coleslaw, hotdogs, chips, salsa, and a dozen *Tall Boys* buried in a cooler of ice. Satisfied with the setup, he turned his attention to the schedule and meticulously mapped out his day, planning to watch the *Comets* first then surf over to a sequence of NFL games following the post-game analysis.

Everything in place, he plunked into his recliner wearing his lucky flannel boxer briefs in official *Comet* red and black. He placed the remote on his chest and settled in for a fun, uninterrupted day. It felt heavenly…like coming home to family.

In this setting, Grady was king. Ask a question, he knew the answer. He could coach the offense. He could coach the defense. He knew how to win a game.

For four intense, unpredictable quarters, he watched both teams rock. Offense switched to defense and back within seconds, trading score for score. Down one at half-time, the *Comets* battled their way through triple-overtime and with ten nail-biting seconds left, Grady came unhinged: "Duncan! Give it to Duncan!"

Their shooting guard, Duncan Chase, hit a twenty-footer to win the game.

Grady leaped to his feet, throwing wild fist pumps in the air.

"I knew it! I knew it all along!"

He threw open the cooler, pulled out a *tall boy* and chugged it.

"Wow. Effin' WOW."

He pulled out another beer and a handful of chips, then leaned back in his chair to enjoy the commentary.

This was his world.

It was where he belonged.

He felt alive.

###

Grady's problems didn't begin until the post-game recap of the *Nuggets* and the *Spurs*. For some unknown reason, he began to be haunted by flashes of fear in Sonti's eyes and those chipmunk cheeks packed full of chicken. Every time the commentators said *Nuggets*, the memory of that poor kid dragging his feet up the driveway toward that junky old car ran through his mind.

He hated not knowing what to do about that situation. When he was a coach, he always knew what to do…how to fix a shot…how to beat another team…how to fix a bad attitude. Now, he knew nothing. It was as if this job cut out his brain…cut off his balls. He felt like he was stumbling around all the time like some brainless eunuch.

Grady closed his eyes trying to force the vision away. Couldn't he, please, please, for just one day, have his life back?

Damn that job.

Damn that bus.

Damn the whole lousy situation.

Grady ended up just dumping his whole viewing schedule and surfed over to the NFL early, feeling frustrated and deeply resentful.

He spent his time toggling around among football games sucking down beer and yelling play suggestions at the TV.

Grady knew no one was listening.

Probably wouldn't ever listen again.

But why…why? He was still the man he was before…still knew what he had always known.

Nothing you say is going to matter, Redwine. Nobody wants to hear what a washed-up Coach has to say.

Grady longed to be back in it.

Would give anything to be back in it.

Hell, he'd even apologize to that arrogant ignorant asshole.

In front of the whole auditorium.

Twice.

SUNDAY
January 20, 2019

Grady purposely left the TV off all morning because he knew the only programs to watch were bad news or church and the last thing he needed right now was fire and brimstone on top of a horrendous hangover.

He drank a beer in the shower to take off the edge; had another after dropping the towel on the floor; then spent the rest of the morning moping around in his robe, searching for some food to settle his stomach or something to snack on.

He came up empty after checking the cooler, so he wolfed down a few stale bread sticks he found on the floor while he flipped through the TV viewing guide and passed some time by planning the lineup for his pre-game shows and viewing.

There was basketball *and* great football today—the NFL Conference Championship games.

*Why do they **do** that to us?*

After some careful consideration and one more beer, he decided to watch as much as he could of all of them –starting with the Raptors and Grizzles at 1:00; tuning into the Rams and the Saints at 3:05; then beginning at 6:00, he'd toggle between the Bucks and the Thunder and the Pats and the Chiefs; then watch the final quarter of the Lakers and Rockets.

When it finally came time to order his pizza, he was sprawled out in his chair sloppy drunk, just trying to make it through the weekend.

And when he finally switched on the TV at one o'clock prepared to watch the first tip-off, he discovered that for some inexplicable reason, every fast-food restaurant in the world was running advertisements for Chicken Nuggets that day…basketball …football…early or late…it didn't matter.

It was like water torture to Grady…death one drop at a time.

A-gain? A-gain?

Why? Why? Why to-day?

He pushed the mute button, but the sound was still in his head…and the memory of the fearful look in Sonti's eyes haunted him.

Let it go, Redwine! He was twenty feet away. It could have been your imagination. It's obvious that his family adores him. Let it go!

He couldn't.

WEEK THREE

MONDAY
January 21, 2019

Martin Luther King Holiday

Grady woke up to a *Martin Luther King Memorial Day Special* blasting from his TV He loved to watch sports with the volume on high, but news specials, not so much…especially with a dull pounding behind his eyes.

He located his remote buried in the ruins of the weekend and surveyed the evidence of his wasted days. He lowered the volume and thought, *Well, you only drank beer, no hard stuff. You only ordered medium pizzas, and you DID leave a slice for breakfast. That's something, anyway.*

Grady chomped on the extra slice as he shuffled into the bathroom; leaned on the sink as he chewed and looked in the mirror. Staring back at him was a face flushed and blotchy with dark circles under puffy, bloodshot eyes.

He took a sharp indrawn breath and looked away.

Mary would be so proud of you today, Redwine. So very proud.

He cleared his throat, producing a long, phlegmy cough, ran his tongue over fuzzy teeth, then threw back a couple of pain pills with a handful of water, and swallowed.

Returning his attention to the mirror, he rubbed his hands over his face and scratched the scruff along his jaw. He would shave tomorrow. Maybe grow a beard.

He caught his reflection in the shower door when he opened it to turn on the water; sucked in his gut; heaved a sigh and stepped inside. Surges of sadness and shame flowed along with the stream cascading down his body.

Twice, Redwine. Twice in a month you've done this. It's time to put a full stop to it all and face the music.

###

In their lives together, when something went awry with him, Mary would expect repentance and an act of contrition, which to Grady, meant apologize and then do something nice to make up for it. He learned early on that the apology had to be *sincere*, and *something nice* did not mean "go buy flowers." In order to be forgiven and for the *something nice* to count, you had to do something *hard*...something that required *sacrifice*.

Grady knew just taking a shower and cleaning the house wasn't nearly *nice* enough to make up for his irresponsible weekend. He had to do something *genuinely hard*.

Hardest would be not watching the *Comets* game that afternoon. He thought about the situation awhile and decided he wasn't quite that sorry, so if he gave up watching such a crucial game, he'd automatically be disqualified for being insincere. He decided it would be best to just stick to the basics: *sincere* and *hard*.

He'd start with cleaning the house and figure out the *hard* part as he worked.

After he showered, Grady went ahead and added shave to the *nice* list, then began the cleaning process. He gathered up all the empty beer cans and old fast-food wrappers circling the trash basket in the corner and tossed them into a garbage bag along with the chicken bones and leftover salsa.

He then tackled the table beside the front door, jamming the junk mail in with the other trash and neatly stacking his bills. When he came across Ryan's envelope again, he hesitated and turned it around in his hands for a while, thinking.

On the one hand, he'd accepted the note from Ryan, but never really intended to read it. On the other hand, it felt incredibly wrong just to throw it away.

I thought your mission was contrition, Redwine.
Contrition for Mary. Not contrition for Ryan.
How about contrition for you?

He struggled with his conscience a little longer and finally surrendered.
Well, Hell.

He sat on the couch, opened the envelope and flattened out two water-stained pages. The first was an easy read:

> *Weep not for what you have lost, fight for what you have.*
> *Weep not for what is dead, fight for what was born in you.*
> *Weep not for the one who abandoned you, fight for who is with you.*
> *Weep not for those who hate you, fight for those who want you.*
> *Weep not for your past, fight for your present struggle.*
> *Weep not for your suffering, fight for your happiness.*

With things that are happening to us, we begin to learn that nothing is impossible to solve, just MOVE FORWARD

– Pope Francis

Grady read it twice, gave it some consideration and resolved to *try* as he turned his attention to the other page. Written in Ryan's familiar scrawl was what he recognized as a Bible passage: Jeremiah 29:11 ESV.

You couldn't just write it out? You're making me look it up?

His mind shifted to the empty box on Mary's desk.

Grady realized he should have returned her Bible to its rightful place a long time ago. Mary believed in its lessons. She loved them and lived them. He should have respected it more.

He walked down the hall, placed his hand on the grandfather clock and closed his eyes. "Please forgive me for this weekend, my darling. I'm sorry. I truly am." He lingered awhile; feeling its gentle ticking, then took a deep breath and headed for the guest room.

Looking at Mary's Bible tossed carelessly on the bed sent his mind back ten years to the day he bought it while on a surprise weekend trip to New York City he gave her for their twenty-fifth wedding anniversary. For the most part, Grady was not prone to making grand gestures, but this was an important event for them, and he was determined to make it special.

He and Mary lived a teacher's life on a teacher's income, so there was never much excess cash in the bank, but Grady loved a challenge and had a plan.

His most prized possession was a 1927 Babe Ruth baseball card that his great-grandfather saved as a memento of his grandfather's birth. He always thought of the card as his security blanket...something he could use in case of a dire emergency. But he didn't hesitate for a minute when he sold it to a collector he met at a trade show for fifty-five hundred dollars so he could pay for the trip: first-class tickets, three nights in a suite at an uptown hotel, a spa day for Mary, two dinners in four-star restaurants, and Central Orchestra seats for *Lion King* and *Hamilton*, row six.

When Mary was on her spa day, Grady decided to kill some time in *Rockefeller Center*. Out of sheer curiosity, he wandered into *Christie's Auction House* and discovered a beautifully worn mahogany box with a simple gold cross carved in the cover. It had become somewhat hidden in the back corner of a display containing elegant coffee table books and was completely ignored because of a rare First Edition of *Alice in Wonderland* valued at five-million-dollars in a case at the front.

Even though the estimated price on the box was five thousand dollars, in that particular setting, it had become no more than a rich person's version of an orphan sock in the clearance jumble of a discount store.

Grady remembered feeling a little weak in the knees when he got nerve enough to open the box. In his wildest dreams, he never would have imagined that he'd discover violet velvet lining and a white calf-skin Bible inside.

Inside, the book was just as beautiful as the binding. The paper was thin and sort of glowed. He leafed through it a little and discovered that the first letter of every chapter began with a large, colored capital surrounded by artistic swirls and delicate illustrations of birds.

When he turned it over, he found an elegant engraving of a frame surrounding letters of gold quoting what he thought was probably a Bible passage, but he wasn't sure:

The mind, which knows not where to fly, flies to God.

He looked at the price tag again. Five thousand dollars. Grady didn't have two extra dollars to rub together, but he knew a rare opportunity when he saw one and grabbed it. He offered *Christie's* twenty-five hundred dollars as a down-payment for the box and Bible. To actually pay for it, he commissioned them to sell the game-worn, autographed, Michael Jordan jersey presented to him by the Booster Club back when he was Head Coach of the winningest basketball team in the Southern Conference.

He didn't know then that the day he was honored by the Boosters would be the pinnacle of his coaching career. But even if he had anticipated what was going to happen to him, he would still have sold the jersey without a moment of hesitation just to be able to give something that special to her. He knew he'd never be rich, but Grady took great comfort in the fact that Mary went to her grave knowing how much she was valued and loved by him, and that she owned one fabulous thing.

###

Grady gently lifted the Bible off the bed; carried it to the living room; sat down in his chair and held the book against his chest a while.

Eventually, he swiped his eyes with the back of his forearm and forced himself to refer back to Ryan's note. *Jeremiah Twenty-Nine: Eleven ESV whatever that is. Whoever heard of Jeremiah? Mathew, Mark, Luke and John. That's the Bible. That's it.*

He fanned through the pages. *Maybe there's a Table of Contents or something.*

A sheaf of folded papers fell out of the back as he searched. He picked it up, absent-mindedly placed it on the table and returned to the book.

Jeremiah, Jeremiah, Jeremiah. Ah. Jeremiah. Let's see if I remember. Chapter then verse, so Chap-ter-twenty-nine and verse, verse, there you are, verse eleven.

He read aloud:

For I know the plans I have for you, declares the Lord, thoughts of peace, and not of evil, to give you a future and a hope.

He closed the book and slumped back in his chair. *I hope you're right, buddy. I really do.*

He reached over for the sheaf of papers thinking they were class notes from Mary's Bible study or something. He'd been a little careless with them when they fell out and he was in the process of getting them organized again when he took a casual glance at the item on top and found himself suddenly, utterly stupefied.

No.

He looked at it again, only this time more closely.

Nooooo. You have got to be kidding.

He had just discovered that what he held in his hand was a note to him from Mary.

His fingers shook as he unfolded the paper, and his eyes misted over when he saw her deteriorated handwriting. It was a weak, ragged scrawl, but still legible.

My Darling Grady,

As sad as I am that God has decided my time has come, I am grateful to Him for the years he has given me with you.

I want you to know that my happiest moments have been spent in your arms, my love. I didn't know there could be so much love in a marriage. We have been blessed beyond belief.

Until the day we are together again, I want you to know that my greatest wish is for you to find a way to live a happy life without me. Remember that my total love for you is everlasting, but there is room in everyone's heart to love more than once.

Try hard to have more Faith in God and his goodness, honey. It will sustain you.

I love you more than life.

Grady clutched the letter to his chest and came undone.

When he finally got a grip on himself, Grady returned to putting Mary's notes back in the Bible, but in the process found a listing of passwords and online accounts along with a record of their bills, how much they owed, and how they got paid.
Oh. My. Lord.
After a few more minutes of reflection, he carried the Bible to her office and placed it gently back in the safety of the violet velvet along with her final letter to him, knowing she must be sleeping more quietly now. "Rest peacefully, Mary, my love. Rest in peace."

###

In time, Grady returned to the task he had started that morning: setting the house in order. After it sparkled—after he was personally squeaky clean and his conscience was clear—Grady relaxed in his chair with a cooler of energy drinks, and watched the *Comets* crush it!

TUESDAY
January 22, 2019-Morning

Grady got two texts before his alarm went off that morning:

*Bennie has a doctor's appointment today.
He won't be riding. See you tomorrow.*

And later:

Please pick Sonti up at home today. Thank you.

Grady thought, *Hmmm. That's a really good sign. Sonti's mother would have taken him back to the Shelter if things had gone wrong.*

He felt a lot of built-up tension leave his body as he stood under the water in the shower. The week was starting well.

Grady's route called for him to pick up the other kids first when Sonti was at his Mom's house, so he and Clara headed for Prissy's place with high hopes that the long weekend Sonti had with his family had a calming effect on him.

Prissy was her usual jovial self when she wheeled in behind him wearing her sorcerer's hat. Grady greeted her in the mirror. "Let me guess. It's *Wizard Day* again in History class."

"*The Vault with the Book of Spells.*" She took a conspiratorial tone. "I cheated and read ahead."

"Well, fun things were meant to be read more than once, anyway." He headed for J.D.'s dorm. "Did you like it?"

"Oh yes. I liked it a lot. There is a little boy Wizard in the book named Willy. It was about his twelfth birthday. We're almost the same age now."

"Wow."

"He was riding his broom to Frogwarts when a big wind came along, and he crashed."— "Oh no! What happened next?"—"He broke his arm."— "Ouch!"— "But here's the best part. He went to the hospital, and they put a secret formula called *LikeNew* on his arm and the very next day it was all better."

"That's pretty wonderful."

Her voice took on a wistful tone. "Mister Redwine, do you think *LikeNew* is real? Or do you think it's just made up?"

"I could be wrong, but I'm pretty sure it was made up. Why do you ask?"

"I was sorta hoping maybe we could buy some for my back."

Grady had to swallow hard before he could answer. "I wish we could, honey. I really do."

They fell into silence until they rounded the corner to the dormitory area of the complex.

Prissy rose up in her chair. "Oh look! J.D.'s waiting at the curb this morning. I wonder why."

Grady pulled over and opened the door. "Let's find out."

J.D. hurried to hop aboard. "The Wizuhds ah going to open the Vault with the Book of Spells in it today. I can hawdly wait. We need to get to school fast Mistoe Wedwine. I have to get my hat and wand out of my loccuh befoe class stahts."

"We're on our way now. Have to pick Sonti up first."

"Ohh maaan. You always get Sonti befoe me. Why is he last to-day?"

Prissy piped up. "Because he spent the weekend with his Mom and we're picking him up at home."

"Does that mean we going to be late, Mistoe Wedwine?"

"We should be right on time, J.D. We don't have to pick up Bennie."

J.D. let out a long sigh of relief as he draped his hoodie over his face. "Thank goodness."

After being tormented by Sonti's situation all weekend, Grady felt increasing degrees of dread as they drove through the faded subdivision where Sonti and his family lived. Grady held his breath a little as he searched the dimly lit side yard for the Junker he'd spotted the week before, only to see a blue metallic sports car backed into that spot instead.

Wow.

Before Grady could digest what he saw, Sonti literally exploded out the door, hell-bent on escape. He leaped blindly off the porch; stumbled; scrambled to his feet; ran helter-skelter around the yard, shrieking, clawing, ducking, dodging and ripping his clothes from the grasp of three screaming females trying to stop him. "¡Ayudame!" "¡Ayudame!"

God he's fast.

The kids started rocking. The bus began bouncing.

Grady snapped out of his seatbelt. "I'm gonna help."

Clara leaped up. "No!" She blocked him. "Our duty is the kids on the bus."

"But you'll be here."

"I can't drive this bus!"

"I have to do some-thing." His eyes shot back up the hill. Can I call the police?"

Grady whirled back to Clara, wanting an answer.

"We can wait five minutes. If it isn't under control, we have to leave."

Five minutes? Grady's instincts nagged at him. *Go up there anyway. Go!*

He faked a move to the left; got stiff-armed.

Whoah!

She shot him a death-stare. "Five minutes. Then we go."

Grady knew he could get past her, but he wasn't going to hurt someone to help someone, so he hung there in a state of helpless misery watching Sonti frantically barricade himself in the shed beside the basketball hoop.

Two women wedged themselves against the door while his mother fought to lock it. She slumped against the shed for a moment, obviously exhausted, then turned and limped barefoot toward the bus, trailed by banging and shrieks and sounds of shattering wood.

She clutched her nightclothes high around her throat and kept her head down, face hidden by her hair as she talked. "Sonti will not be comeeng to school today, Meester Bus Driver. I am very sorry you had to wait."

Grady glanced up the hill and watched the shed rock on its foundation as Sonti threw himself around inside. "Is…is there anything I can do to help?"

She shook her head. "No. Thank you. There is notheeng anyone can do right now. We will just let him stay in the shed until it is over. I will have the Shelter come and get him when it is time."

J.D.'s voice arose behind him. "We late, Mistow Wedwine. We going to be mahcked taah-dee."

Grady closed the door and released the brake, feeling jittery. "We're leaving now, J.D., don't worry. They won't mark you tardy."

"We thwee minutes late. We will have to go to a-ten-dense."

Grady gripped the wheel and glanced back at the sad vision of Sonti's mother limping up the drive. "It'll be okay, J.D. Miss Clara will call the school and explain."

"But we going to be mocked tah-dee."

Grady took a deep breath and let it out slowly while he prayed for patience. "Not if we call, J.D. Don't worry."

"Five minutes now. I still have to get my hat and wand out of my loccuh."

Grady looked in the mirror. "Miss Clara, would you please call the school and explain?"

She picked up her phone and dialed.

"Seven minutes. We have nevuh been this late. We going to miss the staht of Willy Wizzud. And it's his boofday, too."

Grady pushed the speed limit all the way to the school but slowed to enter the bus loop.

"You sloowwing down! Why ah you sloowwing dowwn, Mistoe Wedwine? Don't. Slowww. Dowwn."

Grady opened the door and spoke as calmly as he could over his shoulder. "We're here, J.D. Time to go to class."

"Ten. Minutes. Late. We missing Pledge Allegiance and evewything. And I still have to go to my loccuh."

Prissy sounded fed up. "Willy falls off his broom, J.D. But everything turns out okay."

J.D. packed up and pushed past her toward the door. "Willy falls off his bwoom! On his boofday? I need my wand foe shoo."

Clara intervened. "Slow down you guys. Take turns. Safety first."

Prissy adjusted her wheelchair and headed for the lift, obviously disgusted. "Boys."

Clara took charge of the chair. "Come on, honey. Let's get you to class. I'll push."

Grady watched the kids bicker about something all the way to the door. When Clara returned and gave a giant sigh of relief, he said, "Was there a full moon last night or something? What's with this *day*?!"

Mid-Morning

As Grady pulled into the driveway of his home during his lunch break, what he witnessed at Sonti's house was like jet fuel poured on the embers of his troubled weekend. *Bwoom!* The memory of the events of that morning filled his entire body with anxiety. He was still an emotional wreck. He didn't get it. He just couldn't understand a world where getting involved was considered the wrong thing to do. What kind of man just stands by and does nothing when three women are screaming for help? And what kind of school system makes him do it?

After going inside, Grady tossed his keys on the table by the door, closed his eyes, took a deep breath and released it. Normally, on a nerve-wracking day like this one, he'd scarf down a couple of triple bacon cheeseburgers, top them off with a milk shake, and sleep it all off in his chair. He came home intending to do just that, but today, the burger tasted like sawdust and his chair felt hard.

He wandered through an archway leading to his den and stood in front of what Mary always called her *Hero Wall* when she showed people around the house. From ceiling to floor, that side of the room was covered with memorabilia from Grady and his family.

He went to his grandparents' section and focused on a picture of his pregnant grandmother leaning back in the protective arms of his grandfather the day before he left for duty in World War II. Then he moved on to a framed, folded flag hanging above three display cases containing his grandfather's purple hearts—one from World War II, two from Korea—and the Medal of Valor presented at his funeral for saving a man's life under fire, encased with the Army's hallowed words, *Duty, Honor, Country*.

Grady wondered what his grandfather would think of him that day, standing idly by and merely watching what happened at Sonti's house.

He already knew what his grandmother thought. She gave him her opinion when he was seven years old as they left the principal's office after he got in a fight in the playground: "You may be in trouble for fighting, today, but I'm proud of you, Grady. You saw someone being bullied and did something about it." She took him by the hand and walked him to her car. "I don't care what they tell you at school. You can look yourself in the mirror tonight and know you did right today. That's all that matters to me."

When they got home, she took him into her bedroom and pointed to pictures of his grandfather and an uncle he never knew, who died in a fire while rescuing a child. "You're a Redwine, Grady. Redwine men run toward trouble, not away. It's in their DNA." Then she pointed to a needle point she had sewn, that now hung with the heroes:

To whom much is given, much will be required. (Luke 12:48)

Grady then studied his section of the wall. It contained plaques from his charitable work. He found it embarrassing that there were so many and wanted Mary just to hang one or two—the ones he was most proud of— but she was proud of them all. "Besides," she'd say, "It would be wrong to throw them away, and we don't have enough storage space to keep them in the house."

People would take a look at the wall and ask Mary if she ever saw him. She'd smile and shrug. "What can I say? The man isn't capable of saying no to a good cause."

Conversation nearly always turned to how a person from such a military family ended up a coach.

"There wasn't a war," he'd reply. "I was in the National Guard when I was in college, but I had to quit when I became a Head Coach. I couldn't serve the mandatory one weekend a month, and it really wasn't in me to be a peacetime military man anyway."

He wouldn't mention how happy his grandmother was when he was forced to quit. "I'd never ask you to leave the service," she said, "But I've given a husband and two children to this country. I couldn't bear losing you too."

As he took his trip down memory lane he wondered what he'd see in the mirror that night. Was Ryan right? Did he chicken out today? Did he do what was easy instead of what was right?

The only skill he had that aligned with the needs of this job was his ability to drive the bus. He found it pitiful. Pit-i-ful. The kids deserved better than that.

Afternoon

Grady was already behind the wheel preparing to begin the afternoon route when Clara arrived. She was late and that wasn't like her. He watched her get out of the car and hurry toward the bus, obviously upset about something. She started talking before she got up the stairs. "I just got some really sad news."

"What happened?"

"Halim's therapist has advised them to take him out of the program."

Grady felt mixed emotions. "Why?!"

"They say he just isn't ready. The good news is, they're willing to let him try again next year."

"Well, let's hope for the best, and welcome him back with open arms when he returns." He agreed with the therapist, but even with all the mayhem Halim caused, Grady knew he would miss him.

He and Clara were both deep in thought while they headed over to pick up the kids at the school. Finally, Grady broke the silence and changed the subject, hoping to find a glimmer of light in the ruins of their dreadful morning. "That's some big stiff-arm you've got there, lady. Where'd that come from?"

She smiled and tucked a few papers into a briefcase. "Four brothers, two sons."

"And the death-stare?"

"Duuubya, duuubya, Eeee."

"W.W.E.? You're into wrestling?"

"You know what they say about taking the country out of the girl... CAN'T..." she suddenly froze mid-motion. "Oh. My. Goodness."

"What?" Grady followed her gaze up the sidewalk and could hardly believe his eyes. "Wow."

There was Sonti, completely calm and composed, walking toward them with his teacher. He had his elbow draped across his forehead to shade his eyes and his blanket piled on his head as it usually was. It could be any normal day. You would never know it had begun with so much violence.

Grady felt compelled to say it again. "Wow."

Mister Wilson handed Sonti up the stairs. "There you go, buddy. Have a good rest of the day."

Clara took charge of him, and Mister Wilson motioned Grady toward the sidewalk next to the bus with a lift of his chin.

Grady climbed off and walked toward him. "I sure didn't expect to see him today. When did he get here?"

"They brought him in around Noon. He was really banged-up and tired. Pretty much slept all day, but he seems fine now."

Grady shifted on his feet. "Do we know what happened? Can he tell you?"

"No. Sonti can sign a little...'hungry' and 'thank you', basic things like that, but he can only say a few things, mostly at the toddler level. We're trying to expand his vocabulary, but it's very slow. He can say 'Mama' and 'bye-bye'. He'll occasionally say 'wa-wa' when he's thirsty. We're working on 'shoe' right now, but he struggles." He chuckled and showed Grady two ugly bruises on his neck. "He's pretty good at saying no, though. His poor mother comes in looking the worse for wear sometimes."

"How do you communicate with him in the classroom?"

"We have a little book for him to use that has pictures of his Mom, the bathroom, items he likes to eat, stuff like that. He points to what he wants. And sometimes we just have to guess until we get it right. The problem with guessing is how frustrated he gets when we get it wrong. All he knows is that he wants what he wants *now*, so he goes ballistic when it doesn't happen. We may never know what caused the incident this morning, but meltdowns are like that. One minute, the world is coming to an end, and the next, it's as if nothing happened." He paused and thought for a moment. "He could have been hungry or in pain. He might have been trying to tell them something and nobody got it. Or...maybe he was just plain ol' mad.

"I suspect sometimes he's late getting his meds but when they finally kick in, he's able to settle down. I worry about him, though.

"People tend to underestimate Sonti. He understands every single word you say and it's a huge mistake to assume that he doesn't have an opinion about something because he's unable to speak. He has opinions on lots of things."

The dismissal bell rang out in the yard. Mister Wilson glanced over his shoulder. "Oops! Gotta go. Here comes the stampede. See y'all tomorrow."

Just as Mister Wilson walked away, J.D. came rushing past Grady on the stairs. "Let's go. Huwwy. I'm weddy to go."

"We have to wait for the others, J.D. Have a seat. It won't be long."

Clara helped him with his backpack. "Where's your hoodie? And your hat and wand?"

"I...I...dwopped them."

Grady turned his direction. "If you want to go back and get them, J.D., we'll wait for you."

"Uh...no...I put them...in my...uh...lockuh. I will keep them theyuh. They will be safe." He slouched low in his seat. "Can we pwease go now? I'm weddy."

Clara studied J.D. for a minute. "Are you okay, J.D.? Is there something wrong?"

"No. Nothing is wong. I just want to go home is all."

"Would you like a blanket?"

Before he could answer, Prissy showed up at the lift brandishing something soft and black above her head. "Miss Johnson said to show you this, J.D. Is it yours?"

Clara smiled and walked toward the door to help Prissy onto the bus. "Looks like you got lucky today, J.D."

Finally inside, Prissy rolled up beside J.D. and handed him a hoodie. "They found it in a corner of the hallway by the girl's bathroom."

"Oh. Then it is pwobably mine." He turned it inside out. "Yes. It is definitely mine." He showed her the label. "See? That is my name. J.D. Pawkuh."

Clara began strapping Prissy into place. "By the girls' room? Whatever were you doing by the girls' room? I thought you said you put it in your locker."

He hurriedly draped the hoodie over his head. "I...I...um...I foegot."

Grady frowned. J.D. had a memory like a steel trap and was far too persnickety about his possessions to be that careless.

Clara waited a few seconds then said, "J.D., do you have something to say to Prissy?"

"Oh. Yeah. Thank you, Pwissy."

Prissy sent back a gracious, "You need to be more careful of your stuff, J.D."

"Be quiet, Pwissy. You not my mothuh."

Clara shook her head. "Be nice you two."

J.D. shifted in his seat. "Can we pweeese, pweeese go home now?"

The rest of the trip that day was spent in relative sanity, but Grady was completely drained when they finally arrived at the Transportation bus lot.

Clara packed up her things and prepared to leave but paused at the top of the stairs and turned toward him.

"I know it's been a hard couple of weeks for you, Mister Redwine. In this job, you see things you couldn't imagine in your wildest dreams. You witness heartbreak and injustice and hurt. But I promise you that if you persevere, you will experience the greatest personal and professional fulfillment any job can offer. Anywhere. Ever."

She went down a couple of steps then turned toward him again. "The greatest leap for most people new to Special Ed is learning how to understand what you're watching without judging it." She sent him a reassuring smile. "Just hang in a while longer. You'll get there."

Grady waited to shut things down until she reached her car. He knew she was trying to be kind and pump him back up, but he already knew what professional fulfillment was. He had it in spades as a coach. There was no possible way this job could give him feelings like that. Ever.

WEDNESDAY
January 23, 2019-Morning

Grady and Clara were parked outside Prissy's dorm and had the lift already down when she arrived at the bus that morning. She was a little more tentative than usual when she boarded.

"I'm sorry I was late this morning. I wasn't sure what to wear today. Miss Miller says it's supposed to rain, so Sonti's Mom is keeping him home. Oh! And Miss Miller said to tell you Bennie isn't coming today either. BennieBot's at NASA getting a tune-up..."—Grady exchanged surprised glances with Clara. — "... He will be back home tomorrow. Are we still going to clean up the park for Citizenship?"

"Nope! They've scheduled you for P.E. this afternoon. We'll do Citizenship tomorrow."

"Ooo P.E. I love P.E. They let me run laps on the walking track. I can start getting in shape for my next 4K."

The coach in Grady perked up. "Oh? When's that?"

"Father's Day. June Seventeenth. This will be my fourth one."

"Wow, Prissy, that's great!"

J.D. and an Aide were standing on the sidewalk outside his dorm when they drove up. The Aide was wearing a trench coat with a name plate identifying him as Paul. He was gripping J.D. by the arm with one hand and dangling his backpack with the other.

Grady opened the door and saw that J.D. had been crying. "What's going on, J.D.?"

J.D.'s voice shook with emotion. "Pleese Mistow Wedwine, don't make me go to school today."

"Why not?"

J.D.'s eyes seemed to search around in his brain for an answer. Grady grew nervous. J.D. always had an answer for everything.

"I...I don't feel good today. I don't feel like going to school."

Paul looked apologetic. "He doesn't have a fever, a cough, or a runny nose. He hasn't thrown up...."

"I twied to thwow up. I stuck my finguh down my thwoat but nothing hap-pened."

"...He's not bleeding anywhere, and nothing appears to be broken. He has to go to school."

"I...I did not eat a good bweakfast. Does that count?"

"That's true. You didn't."

J.D. looked inspired and hopeful. "Then I can stay home?"

"I'm sorry, J.D., those are the rules. You have to go."

J.D. hung his head and dragged his feet up the stairs. He turned at the top and made a final plea. "I think I will pwobably have a vewy bad cough by lunchtime."

Paul handed his things to Miss Clara. "Sorry, J.D."

Clara waited for J.D. to reach his seat. "Do you want your computer?"

J.D. stood in the aisle for a moment then sat down and covered his face with his hoodie like he always did. "No. You can just keep it up theyuh."

Grady and Clara exchanged shocked looks.

Grady released the brake and headed for the school as the rain began hitting the windshield.

A pitiful voice came from the back of the bus. "Miss Clawa, I'm hungwy. Do you have a banana I can have oh something?"

"You can't eat on the bus, J.D., honey. You know that."

"I know, but since I was cwying and couldn't thwow up, I thought you might be nice and make an ex-cep-shun."

"I don't have a banana, honey. But if you try hard to be happy until we get to the school, I can give you a cookie to eat when we get there."

J.D. grunted and tightened his hoodie. "Who could be happy when they hungwy...on Wednesday...in the wain...going to school when they don't want to go." He shifted in his seat. "And can't even get a banana."

In a minute or two, Prissy perked up. "We get to have P.E. today, J.D."

After several seconds of uncomfortable silence, she took on a more playful tone. "You get to play basss-ket-baaall. That should make you feel happy."

Grady glanced at J.D. in the mirror. "You and I can shoot some hoops, my man. It'll be fun!"

All he got back was an icy stare.

Guess not.

Afternoon

Grady wasn't expected to go to the gym with the kids, but since he would be responsible for their P.E. classes soon, he decided to drop in anyway and see what the athletic department was doing for them now.

He reached for his ID in the lanyard around his neck, intending to run it through the scanner, but his hand hovered above it a moment. This would be the first time he'd been in this building since…since…he took a deep breath.

Pull yourself together, Redwine. You're here on official business. You haven't done anything wrong, and these guys know that. There won't be any doubt in anyone's mind that you know what you're doing when it comes to this stuff.

He swiped through the scanner and pushed through the ground level doors, enjoying for a moment the tin-can acoustics and locker room smells that were such a big part of his life for so many years. Ahead, he spotted Charlie Carlson, an Assistant Coach and old friend of his, watching a couple of casual half-court games.

Charlie smiled when he saw Grady walking toward him. "Well, Grady Redwine. As I live and breathe!" Charlie offered a fist bump. Grady took it. "Looks like you could use an umbrella. How are ya man?"

Grady started shaking off some rain. "Doin' well, Charlie. Doin' well."

"It's good to see you, Coach…"

Grady's hand paused mid-motion. *Coach*. That meant a lot to him.

"You've been at the top of my call list since forever, but you know how it is. Time just flies by around here." He clapped Grady on his back. "We all really hated having to miss the funeral, but there was that away game and… everything…." Charlie's voice faded away.

Grady was about to tell them how much he appreciated their card and flowers when he was interrupted by a familiar voice from the running track above them. "Hey look, evwybody. It's Mistow Wedwine."

Grady looked up and saw dozens of little faces appear around the mezzanine railing rather like popcorn. "What? Who?" Where?"

Well, this is new.

Prissy peered over the rail sporting her feathered quiet ears and waved wildly. "Hey! Mister Redwine. Heyyyyy!" She turned around to others behind her. "That's Mister Redwine. He's our bus driver."

J.D. chimed in. "Yeah. He dwives owuh bus."

The little faces chimed in. "Oh!"; "Wow."; "Since when?"

J.D. and Prissy answered in unison, "Since two weeks ago."

The two of them sounded so proud, Grady had to chuckle, but the shine faded off the moment Charlie got a look of pity in his eyes.

"We heard about that, Coach, and we think it stinks. Just stinks."

Grady could only shrug. *Whaddaya gonna do.*

Charlie motioned him toward the hall. "Why don't we talk out there. It's a little louder in the gym these days."

As they walked, Charlie turned toward him. "So, what brings you to this part of the world today?"

"Well, I'm working with an experimental program for the *Special Needs* team. Looks like I'll be taking over responsibility for the P.E. classes for our kids, so I thought I'd check out what you've got them doing now."

Charlie shifted from foot-to-foot. "Oh! Uh. Well! I guess you haven't heard about the changes."

"Changes?"

"Yeah. The School Board decided that P.E. for *Special Needs* students would be taken online from now on."

Grady felt a heavy layer of sweat forming under his shirt. P. E.? Online? *How do you take P.E. online? How do you teach P.E. online?*

He fished around in his brain for what he thought might be a relevant technical term and said, "So what do they do? Log in somewhere and…"

"And they get a list of possibilities, find something they want to do and set a goal. Then after they do it, they fill out an activity report and get a grade…pass/fail."

"Let me guess. Nobody fails."

"Pretty much…unless they just do nothing."

Grady watched as the kids wandered around the track in joyful aimlessness. "So, is that their version of jogging or something?"

"Well, sort of. They only have to walk around the track nine times this semester to make a mile."

"Anyone counting laps?"

Charlie leaned in close and said under his breath, "Grady, those kids spend so much time up there, they could do a mile by accident. Nobody's going to miss their goal."

"So, everybody's goal for the semester is to walk a mile?"

"I guess so, yeah. For these kids, anyway."

An unexpected roar erupted on the basketball court. "Coach Carlson! Jason finally sank a free throw!"

"Great! That's great!" He turned toward Grady. "Outstanding football arm. Terrible on the court."

Grady heard Halim's voice up in the mezzanine stirring up the crowd. "*Whoop Whoop!…Whoop Whoop!…*"

Charlie rolled his eyes and raised his voice. "We have to listen to this stuff All. Day. Long."

"...*Slam-it-in-the-Hoop-Hoop!*"

Grady raised his voice too. "So do you happen to know the schedule?"

Charlie shuffled through some papers on his clip board until he found a chart. "Yeah, here it is. The teachers bring them down around eight fifteen and leave them for fifteen minutes of *exercise*...kind of like a recess. Then they bring them back after lunch..."

Grady made a slight wave with his hand. "That's when I get them...right after lunch. Except Mondays, I think, and Fridays."

"So, I guess that means they'll miss their usual *Leisure Choice* time from twelve to twelve-thirty, but their official *P.E.* time is one-twenty to two-fifteen."

Grady glanced at the clipboard. "Any way I could get a copy of that?"

"Sure." Charlie unclipped the page and handed it to him. "Take this one. I have more in the office."

"Thanks." Grady scanned through it quickly and frowned. "This says they have *P.E.* every day."

"Yep."

"So, that means I get them at Noon, and then..."

Charlie shrugged. "I guess you bring them back at one-twenty, load them onto the track for fifty-five minutes so they can walk, and then you get them back again...unless you want to bring them here for another *recess* at two-forty-five so they can work off some steam before you take them home at three."

Someone's voice from the balcony again. "Helllooooo." And the echo answered back, "Hellllooooooo, loooo, looo."

Charlie rolled his eyes.

A kid wearing a Packers, *Rodgers 12* jersey responded with a withering, "Goooood. Bye-yiiiiiiiie -yiiiiie." And under his breath, "You dummy."

"Excuse me a minute." Charlie headed back to the court and said over his shoulder, "I've gotta handle this."

He blew a tweet on his whistle and waved the kid over to him. "What have I told you about that, Jason?"

The kid replied with an off-handed, "Oh. Yeah. Sorry, Coach," then began skipping backward toward the foul line.

Charlie screwed up his face. "He thinks he's the next number one draft pick for the NFL. He's not." He glanced at the clock on the wall. "Well, the bell's about to ring. Anything else I can help you with?"

"Nope. Not right now. Thanks so much."

"Any-thing. Any-time, Coach. Just give me a call." He ran onto the floor and began herding kids toward the locker room. Over his shoulder Charlie shouted, "It was great to see you. Don't be a stranger, okay?"

Grady didn't answer. He knew Charlie wasn't listening. He just looked down at the chart in his hand and shook his head. *What a mess.*

Grady slumped behind the wheel of his truck and gazed at the schedule Charlie gave him. *What kind of lazy, needle-necked geek thought this up?*

He tallied up the track times in his head. The kids were spending three hours and forty minutes out of a seven-hour day down there. If he counted lunch, they spent more than half a day at school wasting time.

This was just wrong.

He couldn't do this. He *wouldn't* do this.

When it was time to pick up the kids after lunch, Clara was already waiting for him in the shade of the bus. Grady handed her the schedule. "Have you seen this?"

"What is it?"

"It's the kids' daily school schedule. I just got it from the guys in the gym."

"Why did you need a schedule?"

"Well, I figured since I'm expected to teach gym, it would be helpful to build on what they're doing with them already."

She raised her eyebrows. "Makes sense."

"So have you seen it?"

"The schedule?"—He nodded. — "Then that would be, no. I haven't seen it." She scanned down the page. "What goes on in school isn't considered a Bus Monitor's business."

He reached up and unlocked the door. "Well, prepare to be *appalled.* It's like six drunks got together in a bar one night, threw a bunch of stuff together, and called it a plan."

He slumped against the window and chewed on his thumbnail for a while, then gestured toward the schedule. "Do you know what that is? I'll tell you what that is. It's free daycare with two hours of," he flashed finger quotes, "school—and some lunch."

He reached across the aisle to retrieve the paper from her and continued without taking a breath. "I mean, really? Really!? And we're supposed to go along with this?"

He slumped back into his seat. "Well, I'm tellin' you right now, Miss Clara Foster," he slapped the back of his hand on the page as he spoke, "We. Are. Not. Doing. This."

He mumbled under his breath, "P.E. online with an accidental unguided mile on a track. My. Hairy. Butt."

Clara waited a minute then scrunched up her mouth and raised her eyebrows. "Finished?"

Grady smiled. "Let me check." He patted playfully around his chest. "Yeah. It's safe. Go ahead."

"You've just discovered why our program exists."

###

The schedule conversation instantly ground to a halt when the first bell rang, and J.D. piled onto the bus all lathered up. "Go, Mistow Wedwine. Huwwy. I'm weddy to go."

Grady and Clara exchanged nervous glances in the mirror. Grady kept monitoring while J.D. rushed for his seat and went through his usual routine. But when he pulled the hoodie out of his backpack and prepared to drape it over his face, Grady spoke up. "What's going on, J.D.?"

J.D. sent a wild-eyed glance out the window. "Nothing. Nothing is going on..."

Clara and Grady followed his glance up the yard but saw no particular reason for alarm. J.D. slouched down in his seat. "I just want to go home is all. I have stuff to do." He pulled the hood over his face. "Can we please go now, Miss Clawa? I'm weddy."

Clara looked at Grady and shrugged, obviously bewildered. "The second bell hasn't rung yet, J.D. We have to wait for everyone else, you know that."

"But..."

"But what, honey. What's going on?"

"I said **alll-wead-dy**, Miss Clah-wah. **Nuh-thing**. Is. **Go-ing. On**."

Grady watched J.D. silently rocking and fidgeting behind his hood for a while, then looked over at Clara. "Something's going on."

She mouthed back, "Definitely."

They didn't have time to pursue the discussion further because the second bell rang, and the rest of the crew came galumphing out of the gym entrance headed in their direction.

Prissy arrived at the lift all wound up. "Miss Clara! We saw Mister Redwine in the gym today! And Jason Weatherly finally sank a free throw." She made a wild fist pump over her head: "Whoop Whoop!"

Bennie was broadcasting his robotic version of "Whoop Whoop!" as he rolled in right behind Prissy, then J.D. threw in his bored two-cents from somewhere behind his backward hoodie: "Wooop-*peeee*."

THURSDAY
January 24, 2019-Morning

Clara was running a little late that morning, so they spent most of their pre-check time getting ready. But when they finally got off the lot and merged onto the highway, Clara took a sip of her coffee and said, "I wonder what's going on with J.D. He seems so uptight lately."

"I'm sure if it's important, he'll let us know when he's ready. You know, J.D. He tends to plan out everything."

Clara agreed, then followed up with, "Or Prissy will tell us."

He chuckled. "You know that's true."

###

As usual, Prissy was full of news when they picked her up that morning. "Miss Miller told me to tell you Sonti isn't coming today." She wheeled into her place. "And just wait until you see J.D. He looks like a movie star."

"Oh yeah?"

"Yeah! He's wearing the suit Mister Hamilton bought him for Christmas. Miss Miller spent an hour last night ironing it."

He and Clara exchanged surprised glances. Maybe things were looking up for J.D. *Wow.*

"Why is he wearing a suit?"

"He's going to ask Nikkie if she will go with him to the mixer."

Grady raised his eyebrows. "Sounds pretty serious."

"Oh, it is. J.D. is crazy about Nikkie. Everybody knows it." Prissy readjusted her wheel alignment. "She's in the computer class he takes with regular kids. They're doing a project together."

He sent an uneasy glance to Clara. She screwed up her mouth.

Uh Oh.

When Grady made a left turn at the corner instead of his usual right to pick up Sonti, Prissy rose up and gazed back down the street in the direction of his house.

"Sonti has missed school twice this week. He seems so sad lately. I hope he's okay."

Miss Clara patted Prissy's arm. "So do we, honey. So do we."

When Grady pulled up to the dorm, J.D. was already at the curb. Rather than his signature black hoodie, he wore an oversize trench coat with a nameplate identifying him as Paul.

This is new.

J.D. tripped on the stairs a little and got tangled up in the hem of the coat again when he walked back to his seat. The stuff in his arms went flying. "Good gwief! I keep getting stuck."

Miss Clara helped him pick everything up. "Take your time, honey. We'll figure it out."

After stowing his computer, J.D. unzipped the top of the coat, exposing a dark, nicely tailored suit jacket, a sparkling white dress shirt and a designer tie.

Wow.

By the time the zipper reached J.D.'s waist, however, the *Wolf of Wall Street* had turned into a bum from the neigh-buh-hood. For some unfathomable reason, J.D. had removed the trousers from his suit and replaced them with a pair of threadbare sweatpants tucked into white gym socks and high-top sneakers.

Prissy almost came out of her chair. "J.D.! What-have-you-done? Nothing matches!"

J.D. pointed at his shirt. "What coloh is this?"

"White."

He pointed to his sweatpants. "What coloh is this?"

Prissy screwed up her face. "I'm not sure."

"They both white, Pwissy. They match."

"But why aren't you wearing the pants Miss Miller ironed?"

"They ah too tight. They cwal up and give me a wash."

The last thing Grady wanted to discuss was J.D.'s crotch rash, so he decided to try to change the subject and head for Bennie's house. "Hey guys! I hear Bennie's back from NASA."

Prissy was having none of it. "So, what are you going to do about Nikkie, J.D.?"

"I have it all figuhd out. I am going to keep my coat on all day and sit down a lot. Nobody will even notice…"

Grady glanced at his thermometer. *Sixty-five degrees.* People would probably *notice*.

"…Wight befoe computuh class I'm going to get a headache and go to the clinic. Then I'm going to put my pants back on…and..."

Prissy interrupted. "Where are your pants?"

"In my backpack."

Oh Lord.

"J.D.! They'll be all wrinkly."

J.D. was getting indignant. "I am go-ing to smooth them out."

"What about your shoes?"

"I am going to ask the nuhse to help with my shoes."

Prissy opened her mouth to speak but J.D. cut her off. "This is not you business, Pwissy. Leave me alone."

Grady saw Clara send Prissy the tick-a-lock sign, but Prissy took one last shot anyway. "Miss Miller is going to kill you."

Clara tried again. "It sounds like you've given this a lot of thought, J.D."

J.D. settled into his seat. "Wight. I have. A lot."

With the exception of a few more indignant harrumphs from Prissy about stealing Paul's coat, they rode in silence until they rounded the corner to Bennie's house and parked.

J.D. ripped the hoodie off of his head. "Is Bennie back? I want to see him!"

When the garage door opened, Prissy went berserk. "O.M.G.! Look at BennieBot! He's walking! He's walking! Can you believe it?"

J.D. gave Bennie the once-over. "Coooooool."

Bennie's beaming face appeared on a helmet screen when he arrived at the curb with an Aide wearing NASA coveralls. "Look everybody! I'm really a BOT now! I have joints and hydraulics!" He shrugged, flexed his arms, bent his knees, wiggled his hips, every move emitting the smooth high-performance sound of hydraulics singing *wa whoop, wa whoop, wa whoop*.

"Look!" He lifted his right arm. The bot did too. "I can raise my arm to ask a question in class now!"

Grady saw Bennie lift his left leg, then watched the bot raise its left leg too. Bennie turned around and playfully shook his booty. The bot turned and mirrored the action exactly. *Grady's eyes* grew wide, and his mouth flew open in disbelief and pure amazement.

Behind him, he heard J.D. go all ga-ga. "Ooooo...niiiice.... woooowwwww!" Grady watched him examine everything more closely. "Wireless. Have you got a Gamepad?"

"Ohhhh-yes."

Bennie pointed to his belly. "They put scanners in where the fax machine was. And I have a neck! I grew two inches!" He rotated his head from shoulder to shoulder. "We're going to call him BennieToo."

Grady was spellbound. "Bennie, you're magnificent."

"Thank you!"

Clara started down the stairs to lower the lift for him, but BennieToo raised his new arms in protest. "I can do the stairs now. You don't have to go out in the rain anymore."

"I'd go out in the rain any time for you, Bennie, honey, but it's nice to hear I don't have to." She glanced around the bus a little disoriented. "Do I tie you down or do you use a seatbelt now?"

The man in coveralls handed up a wheelchair. "Just sit him in this and strap him down, ma'am. There are loops for the hooks in the middle of his back, under each arm, and at his hips. He's titanium and relatively light, but a little too big for a regular seat." He handed Clara a card. "This is my direct line. Give me a call if you need anything…anything at all."

Clara seemed a little awe struck. She held the card against her chest a moment before stowing it in her pocket and became rather breathless when she thanked him.

He saluted. "Happy to help, ma'am."

Clara's eyes followed the man as he walked sharply back toward the house. She sort of sparkled all over when she met Grady's eyes in the mirror and mouthed, *NASA! Can you believe it?*

Grady chuckled. "You're definitely connected now, Miss Clara. Don't forget the little people."

She sent him an *Oh shut up look* and turned back to figuring out how to get BennieToo safely seated.

J.D. twisted around in his seat. "Can you hold a egg without bweaking it and stuff, Bennie?"

"I haven't tried but I bet I can." Two rods appeared in the projection of Bennie's grinning face. "The mouse is gone. I've got joysticks now!"

Grady scrunched up his mouth and frowned. *Joy stick? What a term.*

"And even better! I have a Motion Capture suit."

"Nooo Waaaayyy. Like in the movies!?!"

"Uh huh! I put it on and BennieToo copies everything I do."

J.D. looked in awe. "I'm so jealous."

"And…I can work off a satellite signal if I have to, so I can go to Westlake with you guys now."

"Wow. Wow."

BennieToo was halfway to his seat when he stopped and shifted his attention to J.D.'s pants. "Please. Tell me you're not wearing those pants to ask Nikkie to the dance."

J.D. shot dagger eyes at Prissy. "Did you blab to ev-wy-body?"

Prissy shrugged "Don't blame **me**. Everybody I told already knew."

Grady prepared to pull away from the curb and Clara took over. "Settle down you two." She turned to BennieToo. "And as for you, Mister Troublemaker, let's get you buckled in so we can go. We're late."

Bennie reappeared. "Yes-ma'am. Buckling in now ma'am."

While Clara fussed with attaching the new anchor hooks, Prissy turned around to Bennie. "What was the first thing you did when your BOT woke up?"

"I hugged my Mom."

"Was hugging her now different than it used to be?"

"I could never hug my Mom before."

"On accounta germs?"

"Uh huh. The arm sleeves for my *Shelter* only faced in, and BennieBot's arms couldn't move, so...." His voice faded away.

"So, what did your Mom do when you hugged her?"

"She cried. Called them happy tears."

Prissy continued on. "I probably would have cried too."

"I did. I cried."

Clara smiled. "I'm so happy for you, Bennie."

For some unknown reason, Bennie fell quiet, and the silence grew awkward. Not even Prissy seemed to know what to say.

In his mirror, Grady saw tears flowing into the projection of Bennie's eyes. "Is everything okay, Bennie?"

Bennie's eyes searched about him uneasily and the tearful, awkward pause continued.

"Bennie?"

Bennie still didn't answer.

Clara stepped in. "It's okay to cry, Bennie...lots of people cry when they're happy."

Bennie finally responded in a hitching voice. "C...can I tell you something, Miss Clara?"

"Of course you can."

"Do you promise not to tell my Mom?"

Her voice grew soft. "If you ask me not to, I won't."

Bennie's tears began flowing harder. "When I saw people hugging in movies and stuff, they always looked so...so happy to me. And when I hugged my Mom, it was a happy time, but..." he took a halting breath, "...but all I really felt...I only felt... I felt..."

"What, darlin'...tell me."

"Lonely, Miss Clara. I just felt lone-ly."

An awkward hush fell over the bus.

Grady's eyes flew to the mirror. Every face was focused on him.

Me? ME?!

His eyes cut to Clara. *Say something.*

She turned away, swiping at tears.

When Grady glanced back at Bennie, still visibly upset, Mary's face flashed through his mind and he shared Bennie's feelings of loneliness, as if they were his own.

Finally, like answer to prayer, Prissy's voice drifted over them all. "I feel lonely too sometimes, Bennie when I watch the news. I worry my daddy won't come home from the war."

Oh-Lord, now we'll all be in tears.

Remarkably, though, Bennie seemed to perk up. "What do you do when that happens?"

"I try to flip to a good thing. Like—instead of thinking about how much it hurts, you could think about how you made your Mom happy and feel good about that."

Relieved that the crisis seemed to be over, Grady forced his anxiety down and concentrated on the road while Clara and the children chatted behind him. He'd digest it all later. Right now, his job was getting everyone safely to school.

###

When they arrived at the bus loop and parked, Prissy turned to Bennie's face on the screen and threw down a challenge. "Bet I can still beat ya to the door."

Bennie grinned from ear-to-ear. "In your dreams, maybe. Your days of winning are officially ooo-ver."

"We'll just see about that."

Miss Clara wheeled Prissy to the lift while Grady helped BennieToo maneuver the stairs. On ground level, they lined up along a crack in the cement.

Prissy rocked forward and back a few times to build momentum and then shouted, "Ready-Set…" She took off like a shot and ended the sentence over her shoulder with, "Goooo!"

Bennie was a yard behind but soon gained on her, shouting, "Hey! Not fair! No fair!"

Grady and Clara cheered them on, rooting for them both. Grady shook his head in wonder. "Can you imagine the skill it takes to operate that thing remotely?"

Prissy wheeled madly alongside BennieToo, but he surged ahead and entered the school as victor of the race for the very first time. "Wooo-hooo!"

J.D. trailed behind the others and turned back toward the bus, tripping on the hem of Paul's coat again. "Hey! How about me?"

"Good luck, J.D.! We're rooting for you too."

Grady slowly shook his head. "I have a really bad feeling about this Nikkie thing, Clara."

"So do I."

He trained his eyes on the closing door. "Can you think of anything we can do to help him?"

"It's hard, but sometimes we just have to let them live their lives and learn. Right now, all we can do is hope for the best and be here to pick up the pieces at the end of the day."

Afternoon

Grady watched Clara chew nervously on her lower lip as she stared at the exit doors of the school waiting for J.D. to emerge.

"Well, here we are at the end of the day ready to pick up the pieces...have you got tissues?"

"Yes." She pointed at a box beside her. "I bought a new box."

Grady's eyes began shifting between the bushes and the door right before the bell rang. Today, his money was on seeing J.D. in the bushes, but he was hoping for the door.

Shortly after the bell, Clara gasped and covered her mouth in astonishment. "Oh, my Lord, Grady. I think I see him coming out the door. The door!"

Sure enough, J.D. walked casually through the front entrance and paused a moment on the sidewalk, looking completely calm and cool.

Well, I'll be damned. He actually managed to pull it off. Right pants...zipped up. Right shoes...tied. A little rumpled, but overall, everything is in excellent order.

"Gosh, Grady. Just look at him. Doesn't he look fine?"

"He does. He really does."

The kids flowing from the building shot some surprised sideways glances at J.D and a few elbowed each other, but there was more admiration than mocking in the crowd.

Wow.

Clara clapped a little. "He could be standing outside the stock market in New York now and fit right in."

They prepared for a hero's welcome, but halfway on his way to the bus, J.D. began patting his pockets and searching around as if he had forgotten something.

Uh oh.

Eventually, when he seemed to remember what that something was, J.D. turned and raced back down the sidewalk into the school.

Uh-boy.

Clara leaned over his shoulder. "I think he might have forgotten Paul's coat."

"Well at least we know he's okay. I wonder what Nikkie said."

Clara re-stowed the tissue box. "How could a girl say no to that? He looks wonderful."

"He didn't seem upset about anything. Maybe she did say yes." Grady shrugged a shoulder as he closely monitored the building for him. "Or she was out sick today. "

Clara glanced up the walk. "Here come Prissy and Bennie. They'll know what happened."

Prissy wheeled to the bottom of the stairs and looked up at them. "J.D. didn't ask her."

What?!

Clara went out to work the lift. "What happened?"

Bennie answered, "Maybe he chickened out."

While everyone settled in, Grady resumed monitoring the building for J.D., eyes shifting from the door to the bushes and back to the clock on his dashboard.

This is taking far too long.

Sweat began to form in his arm pits. *Something's wrong.*

The crowd in the yard was still milling around but thinning out, either heading for a bus or beginning their walk home.

Come on, J.D. .... Come on... Come on ... Come out.

It wasn't long before Grady became aware of the sounds of a commotion at the rear of the side yard. He shaded his eyes from the glare of the afternoon sun and squinted. "What's going on up there?"

Prissy craned her neck to see. "Is it J.D.?"

Clara gasped. "It is!"

Everyone on the bus smashed against the windows to watch.

As heavy footsteps pounded their direction, Grady leaped to his feet and froze in place at what he saw. J.D. was literally running a gauntlet of laughing kids with at least five more hot on his heels. He was breathing hard…gripping his computer case against his chest for dear life and dragging his backpack behind him.

"What are they do-ing? They can't do that to my kid!" Grady rushed to the door.

Clara blocked him. "We have kids on board."

"We have a kid out THERE and they're trying to hurt him."

The bus erupted.

"J.D.?"; "Someone's going to hurt him?"; "Where is he?"; "What's happening?"; "I've got my wand. Do you want my wand?"; "Run, J.D., run!"

Clara grabbed the mike. "I'm calling for an S.R.O."

Grady stepped around her. "I'm going to *find* one."

Heart pounding, Grady sprinted down the stairs; leaned out the door. "Officer! S.R.O.! Officer!"

The gang closed in.

Grady called to the crowd milling around in the yard. "Someone! Get an Officer!"

The gang was right on J.D.'s heels when a football flew through the air and ricocheted off the back of his head.

He heard Clara gasp behind him. "Oh my God!"

Grady lost it. "Hey! HEY! Are You CRAAAAZEEE?"

J.D. whirled around to look for the source of the ball.

Grady's hands flew in the air with disbelief. "No! Don't look back, J.D.! Run! Just run!" He took off his hat and waved it while he searched the bus loop. "S-R-O-! We need an S.R.O. now!"

Clara and Prissy and Bennie joined in. "Run! Run J.D. run!"

Apparently, the gang in the yard heard Grady calling for a cop and grew nervous. They began to slow down and slide to a stop. A voice from somewhere shouted, "Aw, let him go," and they swiftly blended into the crowd.

J.D. finally came to his senses and hot-footed it toward them, all pigeon-toed and knock-kneed. He angled across the grass and reached the bottom stair completely out of breath. Grady hauled the sweat-drenched boy aboard.

Clara scanned him from top to bottom as he struggled up the stairs. "He doesn't have both shoes! J.D.! What happened to your shoe?"

"I-do-not-know."

Grady turned him around. "Let me check your head."

J.D. winced as Grady searched. "Is there blood?"

"No blood." Grady gently patted the hair back in place. "What happened, J.D. What's going on?"

J.D. didn't answer him, just ducked his head and charged toward his seat, swiping at his eyes. "I don't want to talk about it."

Clara reached out a hand. "J.D...."

J.D. pulled his hoodie out of his backpack and put it on his head, switching it around to hide his face. "Miss Clawa, I do **not** want to talk about it."

Everyone stared transfixed as J.D.'s hands traveled from his lap to his eyes, wiping them dry on his hoodie.

Grady looked up the sidewalk and saw the crowd all staring down at their phones and laughing.

I hope that's not what I think it is.

He started down the stairs. "Call the *Food Bank*, Miss Clara. Tell them we're not coming today."

Prissy let out a shriek. "Mister Redwine! J.D. is on social media."

J.D. groaned. "Oh nooo. Oh nooo. Evywone will see. Evywone will know."

Grady backed up and flew down the aisle. Prissy handed him her phone.

Grady pulled out his reading glasses and focused on the unsteady video while Clara looked over his shoulder.

> *J.D. was cornered in a crowded hallway with a girl standing in front of him, laughing and clutching her books against her chest as if she needed protection. A crowd gathered around them, spurred on by a boy in a number twelve football jersey, sniggering, pointing their phones to record the scene.*

Grady gritted his teeth. "Jason."

Clara came unglued. "Those children! What a horrible crowd! Where's their teacher?!"

The video continued as J.D., looking completely overwhelmed, inched his way around a corner and began to run toward the exit. Jason blocked him and reached down to pull at J.D.'s shoelaces. J.D made a pitiful attempt to kick and resist but lost a shoe as he dropped his coat and continued to sidle toward the doors. Finally clear, he made a run for it.

#

Grady gave Prissy her phone back and searched the crowded clusters of gawking students, slowly beginning to disperse.

"Where the **Hell** is that S.R.O.?"

J.D. shouted from beneath the hoodie. "Please! Don't do anything, Mistoe Wedwine. You will only make it wuss! I am used to it. Weally! It happens all the time!" He burst into tears again. "If you do something It will only get wuss."

Grady's eyes seared into Clara's, daring her to try and stop him as he headed for the stairwell. "I'm going to go get J.D.'s shoe."

To his surprise, she stepped aside, clenched her jaw and whispered, "You go get that little bully, Grady. Get him good."

He had just reached the stairwell when he felt a hasty jerk on the back of his shirt and heard Clara whisper again, "Be careful. Don't touch him. There are cameras with microphones everywhere."

###

Fighting against the rage welling up in him, Grady approached a crowded throng of kids in the schoolyard that parted like the Red Sea when they saw him, then closed in again behind him when he passed. He retrieved the football and wove his way through the throng further until he found Jason. He was motioning an intended receiver backward while pumping J.D.'s shoe over his shoulder, preparing to throw it like a football.

Grady stepped between Jason and his target to give him a friendly wave. His eyes shot lightning, but his voice remained friendly. "Well, hey there, Jason…"

The kid grew pale; tucked the wingtip in his armpit.

Grady casually spun the football in his hands. "Remember me?"

Jason's eyes were riveted on the ball. "Uh…."

Grady helped. "In the gym? The other day?"

"Uh, sure. I remember. You were with Coach Carlson."

"That's right! Coach Carlson and I go way back."

"Oh?"

"Uh huh." Grady held out the football "This yours?"

He could see the kid weighing his answer. "Uh, no. No it isn't."

"Know whose it is?"

"N...No I don't."

"Actually, I'm looking for a shoe. You haven't seen one lying around by any chance, have you?"

The kid removed the wingtip from his armpit and handed it over like it was on fire. "I, uh, I found it. I was taking it to the lost and found."

Grady added it to the hand holding the football. "We're also missing a coat. You wouldn't by any chance know where that is, would you?"

Jason pointed toward the door. "I think it might be back there. Turn left at the corner."

Grady turned his head toward the doors to look, but his feet remained in place. "Why don't you show me, Jason. I'm new here. I might get lost."

"I can't. I have to suit up for practice. I'll be late."

Grady dug in his feet and centered his weight. His face showed a smile, but his eyes didn't. "If you think it would help, I'd be happy to go with you and explain to Coach Carlson what happened."

Jason switched direction on a dime and headed back to the school. "You're making me late. I'll have to run laps."

"Hate it when that happens."—Grady opened the door and ushered Jason in— "Guess we better hurry."

Inside and alone, Grady scanned for surveillance. *No people. One camera over the exit.*

Jason turned toward him. "Do you know who my father is?"

Grady turned his back to the door. "Don't know. Don't care." He reached into his pocket and pulled out his phone. "Do you know what this is?"

"It's a phone. So what?"

"So, this happens to be a special phone. This phone can speed dial any Coach in any high school, any institution of higher learning, and the owner of every pro team in any sport in the United States. Those people answer when this number shows up on their Caller ID and every one of them calls the owner of the phone by his first name...which just happens to be *mine*."

Jason pulled out his own phone and turned it on. "Maybe I should call my dad."

"Great idea. Sounds like fun. Let's do this: while you talk to your dad, I'll call the Coach and Principal Gordon…maybe even the parents of the other kids standing around and laughing today, then we'll get some popcorn…maybe a few soft drinks…and we'll all watch the videos your buddies shot at the crime scene."

Jason searched around like a badger in a trap. "Crime scene?"

Grady reached down to retrieve Paul's coat. "Yeah, afraid so. Aggravated assault is definitely a crime."

"Wait a minute. Nobody touched J.D."

"He got hit in the head by this football, Jason. Someone had to throw it. We'll know who when we get the fingerprints."

Jason swallowed hard.

Grady sucked some air through his teeth and let it go with a shrug. "*Assault*. Definitely *assault*. It could have broken his neck."

He pointed at Jason's phone. "Just for fun, sometime. Why don't you look up the penalty for *assault*. And after you do, I suggest you tell everyone who starred in or downloaded the video today, that if J.D. gets mad enough, they could end up in court soon too…just sayin'…" He paused for effect and watched Jason squirm. "Actually, J.D. just wants to forgive and forget the whole thing. I have to confess that I'm not quite there yet, but I might reconsider if you start being nice to him and cut out the trash-talk. I think the three of us could become close friends. You're here every day; J.D.'s here every day…*I'll* be here every day. You're in class together. It could work, right?"

"Uh…"

"Right?"

"R…right."

"Great!" Grady talked as he ushered Jason back through the door. "I'll look forward to seeing you again tomorrow, then…" He tossed the football playfully in the air as he spoke. "And every. Single. Day. After. That."

He sent a friendly wave to Jason's intended receiver, then turned and sauntered toward the bus as if absolutely nothing important had happened.

Still at the curb of the drop-off, Clara was hovering in the doorway of the bus when Grady returned. "What did you do?"

He prominently displayed the football on the dash against the windshield. "Just a little blackmail. And a big buncha lies."

She motioned to the deserted school yard. "Well, it obviously worked. Look at this place."

"How's J.D.?"

She shook her head; mouthed, *not good.*

He walked to J.D.'s seat. Under the hoodie, J.D. rocked forward-back-forward-back-forward-back-forward-back, while his hands took turns wiping tears away.

Grady instinctively laid a comforting hand on J.D.'s shoulder. J.D. went stiff.

Clara shook her head and flapped her hands *no, no, no.*

Grady quickly moved his hand away then spoke softly. "What happened, J.D.?"

J.D. spoke from behind his hoodie. "At fuhst I did not ask Nikkie. I would look at huh, Mistow Wedwine, and the woods just would not come out of my mouth.

"Then I went outside and said to myself, 'J.D. Pawkuh, you get back inside and ask that gull to go with you. You can-not gwow up a spineless cowud,' so I went back into the school. Nikkie was out in the hall."

J.D. took a shuddering breath. "I...I asked huh to go to the dance with me. She went back into the computuh woom and told Jason about it and he stahted yelling at me in the hall."

"What did he say?"

"He said, 'Who do you think you ah, asking Nikkie to go with you. You a gimp. You wide Bus 86...a gimp bus. Do you know what 86 means? It means it is no good foe nothing. 'Nobody wants a date with someone who wides a gimp bus! You can't even talk wight. You pwobably can't even dance.'"

J.D. pulled down his hoodie, exposing teary, bloodshot eyes. "Mistow Wedwine, I pwacticed and pwacticed. I wote it all down. I told huh she looked nice today. I chose woods without 'ahs' in them so I could say it wight. 'Would you please go to the dance with me next week, Nikkie?' I didn't say mixuh oh Fwiday. I said dance and next week."

Everyone on board was frozen in their seats as they watched J.D. take a hitching breath and bare his soul. "I thought she was my fwiend. I helped huh with huh homewuhk. I woe my suit so she would know I could look nice foe huh and she would not be embawassed."

J.D.'s eyes filled with pain. "She laughed at me, Mistoe Wedwine. They took videos. And evywone will know. Evywone can watch. How can I evuh go back to school?"

Clara handed him some tissues. "Don't worry, honey. We're going to fix this. Mister Redwine will fix this."

J.D. was inconsolable. "Jason called me we-tah-ded and said, 'You nothing but a dead man walking, widing on the Last Mile Bus.'

"Then anuthuh boy called me *Dead Man Mike*."

Prissy popped up. "Your name isn't Mike. Maybe he was talking to someone else!"

Clara flashed Prissy the "tick-a-lock" sign.

Prissy pressed on anyway. "Isn't that a TV show, J.D.? I think it is…or something like that…something about dead people. It's the biggest show on TV right now. If you were that guy, you'd be practically famous."

J.D. became calmer.

Grady was mystified by Prissy's logic but decided to roll with it anyway. "Do you know what The *Legend of the Last Mile* is about, J.D.?"

J.D. answered in a quivering voice. "N-No."

"It's a story about a special person just like all of us on this bus. He couldn't talk really well or walk really well, but he had a special gift. He could heal people."

Prissy looked amazed. "Wow."

"All of us have a special gift. We just have to find it. I'm just guessing, J.D., but I bet you're better at computers than Jason."

BennieToo joined in from the back of the bus. "He sure is! And everybody knows it."

"So, you have a special gift too."

"Do you think so?"

"Absolutely. And you know what? I think Jason might be jealous because Nikkie likes you for helping her with her homework."

"Maybe."

Grady looked toward Prissy. "What's your special gift?"

"I can run 4Ks."

"That's right! And we know Sonti can run fast and sink baskets. And Bennie, what do you think your special gift is?"

"I can do the computer too. And I'm great at research."

Grady threw his arms wide. "So that's us. We're all *Last Mile kids*…And that makes us all practically famous."

Grady looked toward Clara. "And to celebrate, Miss Clara is going to call *Indy's Chicken*. She's going to tell them we want a private room, and six ice creams!" He turned to BennieToo. "And, Bennie, I bet your Mom would bring you a yogurt too."

Bennie said, "Mom keeps them in the refrigerator. I'll get banana."

Prissy spoke up. "But Mister Redwine. What about the *Food Bank*? We won't earn any money today."

"The ice cream is my treat. And I'm buying everybody's lunch on Friday, so don't worry about your money."

"Then I want sprinkles. Are we having the ice cream with sprinkles?"

"You betcha."

J.D. joined in. "Oh! With hot fudge?"

"Yep! And sprinkles too, if you want them." Grady pulled away from the sidewalk and looked in his rear-view mirror. An Officer was running along the sidewalk trying to wave him down.

"*Now* you show up." He lifted his microphone. "Eighty-six to base."

"This is base."

"We've been calling for an S.R.O. to help us at State High School."

"He was directing traffic. Someone was sick."

"Copy that. Everything is under control here. Tell him thanks for the help."

"Ten-four."

Grady finished his thoughts with the kids. "And tomorrow, when we have our lunch at *Indy's Chicken*, we're going to have a meeting and make some plans."

After School

After the kids had been delivered home, Grady and Clara rode in silence back to the bus yard, each one lost in thought.

Finally, Clara turned toward him. "Poor J.D."

Grady parked the bus while he searched around for something appropriate to say, but could only come up with, "Yes."

Clara continued on: "He seems better now."

"Hot fudge and ice cream. Works every time."

They sat there enveloped in silence again, except for the sound of the ignition key click-click-clicking against the starter.

"I feel so guilty, Grady. All the signs were there...not wanting to go to school...hiding...losing his hoodie." She dabbed at her eyes. "How could we miss them?"

"I don't know."

More silence.

"You did a good job with that little thug today, Grady. I was proud of you."

"Thanks.

"I bet he doesn't do anything like that again."

"Better not."

Evening

Grady reached home still ticked off at that jock wannabe and what he did to J.D. He also felt somewhat guilt-ridden.

He'd spent most of his life in locker rooms with the best-of-the-best where trash-talk was considered good-natured ribbing—motivational even. Everyone gave just as good as they got, then went out on the court to make the other guy eat his words.

Trash-talking was part of the game. You gave it. You had to be able to take it. Hell, they handed out *awards* for it.

There *were* a few unwritten rules lying around: you didn't trash a guy in front of his mom or grandma; you didn't insult his sister; and you didn't write anything on walls. That was about it. There was never much mention about picking on little guys like J.D. because there weren't many little guys hanging around in the locker room.

The writing on walls rule was mostly meant more to protect property than to save someone's dignity.

He gazed over at his phone and reflected on the video posted online of J.D.. Witnessing first-hand the degree of emotional damage done by that incident was brutal for Grady. He hoped he hadn't turned out any Jasons. He hoped he'd coached his boys into good men.

FRIDAY-SUNDAY
January 25 - 27, 2019

Friday Morning

Grady was all bleary-eyed that morning after spending a restless night still distressed over J.D.'s situation. He wandered around the house for a while until it was time to leave, then climbed into his truck and headed out to get coffee.

When he drove up to the window at the truck stop café and Minnie's smile popped up in the window, rather than thinking she looked like bread in a toaster today, Grady found himself mentally calculating how many dozens of times that poor woman had to step up and down on a stool every day in order to feed her family.

He knew he was still the same person he had been before, but yesterday somehow seemed to have changed him. It felt almost as if his view of the world had been as a 6, and he just noticed it was an upside-down 9. That knowledge didn't change a single fact in his life. — Everything was exactly the same, but he was looking through different eyes.

###

Grady was deep in his own thoughts and Clara was deep into hers, when they started the route that morning. Clara eventually broke the silence. "Do you think J.D. will be riding today?"

"I doubt it. Poor kid. But. I didn't get a text telling me he wasn't."

"Sure do hope he's okay. I know he'll be upset if he has to miss the meeting. Do you think we should delay it?"

"Let's wait and see how things turn out this morning before we make a decision. I'm sure Prissy will catch us both up on things." —He pulled up to the curb outside Prissy's dorm. — "Here she comes now."

Prissy handed Grady a note when she got on board. "Miss Miller wants you to call her."

Grady pulled out his phone and turned off the bus so he could go down to the sidewalk and talk in private while Clara got Prissy settled in. He put on his glasses and dialed. Miss Miller answered on the first ring. "Thank you so much for calling, Mister Redwine."

"No problem at all. How is J.D.?"

"He had a rough night—nightmares. He woke up with a headache so I'm letting him sleep in this morning. I'll get him to school in time to ride with you this afternoon. He was upset when I told him he had to stay home -- made me promise to let you know he would be at the meeting today...so...I am."

"Tell him we're looking forward to seeing him—we wouldn't have the meeting without him."

"Thank you, Mister Redwine. Thank you for all you do."

"He's a great young man. I'm just glad I can help." He looked at the time. "Gotta rush. Don't want to be late."

Back on the bus, Clara waited for the news. "J.D. is staying home this morning, but Miss Miller said she'd have him at school in time to go to the meeting with us this afternoon."

"Oh good. So, he's okay."

"I hope so. He had a rough night."

Prissy added her two-cents. "Miss Miller sat up with him all night. His neck really hurt." She took on a serious tone. "Today's a special day, isn't it, Mister Redwine?"

"Yep. We're having a meeting and making some plans."

"Is Sonti going to be able to come?"

"I hope so. I didn't get a text not to pick him up, anyway."

"I feel like I haven't seen him in forever."

"Where has he been?"

"Mostly with his Mom."

"So, you didn't see him at dinner last night?"

"No. He was in the quiet room."

Again?

He pulled around the corner to the other side of the building. "Looks like Sonti *is* coming. They're walking this way."

Sonti was calm when he and his Aide arrived at the stairs, but he looked like he'd just been mugged in an alley. There were ugly red scratches all over his cheeks, swollen cuts on both of his lips, a big bruise on his forehead and evidence of an emerging black eye. When he reached out for the railing to get up the stairs, his sleeve slipped above his wrist, exposing a thick band of scar tissue and at least a baker's dozen of inflamed donut-shaped bite-marks.

Oh, My Lord.

His eyes shot to Sonti's Aide. "Who would do such a thing?"

The Aide turned his way with a sorrowful look and silently mouthed, "He would."

Grady sent back a silent, "He did that?! Sonti did that to himself?!"

The Aide raised his eyebrows and gave a slight nod. "It happens."

For a moment Grady found it hard to breathe.

The Aide spoke up. "Nobody's certain what set him off. It's happened before." He walked Sonti back to his seat and added, "We were hoping to give him more time to heal, but we had no choice. He's missed too much school. If he stayed home today, the school would have to report it to *Protective Services*."

Sonti dutifully sat down in his seat. The Aide held him there. "Don't slide over, Sonti. We have to sit on the aisle side today."

Clara got a pleading tone in her voice. "Do you *have* to put him there? He loves looking out the window when riding."

"He's been banging his head. It wouldn't be safe to let him sit near the glass." The Aide fastened the clips and tested them. "He's really tired. He might just go to sleep."

Clara walked with the Aide back to the stairs. "We'll call the school—tell them what to expect. Do we still take him to his mother's tonight?"

"Mister Wilson will tell you when he brings him out. It depends on how the rest of the day goes."

Prissy adjusted her quiet ears and looked across the aisle at her friend. "It's Chicken Nugget Day, Sonti. Your favorite. It's going to be fun."

Sonti ignored her. He was busy trying to force his way to the window.

Grady whispered to Clara. "Can't we just park down the block and move him over?"

She whispered back, "Better not."

Clara placed the purple blanket on Sonti's lap. "Here, honey. Try to rest."

He wadded it up; side-armed it back and began moaning.

Ohhh-man.

Grady broke out in a serious sweat while switching between the road and the mirror, trying to monitor events and drive safely.

By the time Bennie came aboard, Sonti had worked himself into a first-class frenzy. Clara helped the boys dodge some serious kicks and get safely settled down in their seats, then she returned to the front and leaned in close. "I sent Mister Wilson a text. He says to meet him at the back door. We'll let Sonti off first so the rest of the kids can get off more easily."

Grady wiped his sweaty palms on his pants. "Will do."

###

Mister Wilson was waiting for them with a wheelchair when Grady pulled into the back drive. Sonti had reached full combat mode by then—thrashing wildly around and shrieking.

Grady turned off the bus and opened the door, braced for battle, ears ringing. "How can I help?"

Mister Wilson answered from the side of his mouth, "Just don't let him get off without me."

With the exception of Sonti, the bus was dead silent when Mister Wilson walked toward him slowly. He paused beside his seat and spoke softly, "Sounds like you're having a hard time today, son."

Sonti upped the ante—pitched his screams an octave higher.

"Let's go inside. We can discuss it in there."

Sonti banged his body forward and back in the seat.

"Whadda ya say we get off the bus. I saved you some chocolate from yesterday."

Sonti perked up; dialed everything down a bit.

Mister Wilson began to reach out but paused. "If you lean forward, I can unhook you." He gently guided Sonti's upper body forward. "I'm going to unhook you now, okay?"

He unhooked the waist clips then guided Sonti's back against the seat. "I'm going to unhook your shoulder clips now. But you have to stay in your seat until we're ready to go inside, okay? Nod your head if it's okay."

Sonti hesitated.

"I can't let you out unless you nod, son. Will you stay in your seat if I unhook you?"

Sonti finally nodded.

Mister Wilson sent Grady a get ready wink. "Good boy."

Grady shifted sideways; prepared to block...or tackle.

Mister Wilson unsnapped the last two clips. "There ya go! Let's get you out of here and go eat some chocolate." He held out a hand. "Here. Let me help you."

Sonti took Mister Wilson's hand and quietly followed him down the aisle.

Grady set his feet firmly and prepared to aim low in case Sonti bolted as the pair made their way down the stairs.

On the ground, Mister Wilson pointed to the wheelchair. "You get to ride to class today." Sonti stiffly settled in and let Mister Wilson fasten the belt.

Clara handed Sonti's backpack down. "Goodbye, honey. See you at Noon."

Grady breathed a sigh of relief and cranked the bus. After a tight U-turn into the alley, he made a beeline for the front door to try and beat the last bell.

Clara rushed Prissy onto the lift and hustled everyone else off the bus. "I'll call the office. Just run straight to class!"

Grady shouted at their retreating backs, "Good job, everyone! *Indy's* today!" He watched as the kids disappeared through the doors. "They'll never make it."

Clara picked up her phone. "I'll call."

Grady turned to Clara when they passed the alley on their way back to the main road. "I wonder what set Sonti off."

"We'll probably never know. Sonti may not even know."

Grady drove all the way to the bus barn fighting intense frustration and feeling guilty—like he'd somehow let Sonti down. "We should have let him move to the window."

"We have to let the medical staff have final say. There'd be Hell to pay if something bad happened because we didn't."

"It's my bus. I should have some say."

"Uh, it's the School District's bus and you're an employee. You have no choice but follow orders."

They were silent a while, then Clara said, "You can't beat yourself up over things like this, Grady. Sonti's pot boiled over long before he got on the bus. It could be he just didn't want to go to school."

But his face, Clara! His face looked like raw hamburger! He needs a doctor…not a ride to the school.

I'm certain a doctor saw him at the Shelter. He's safer at school than at home today, Grady. Mister Wilson's a good man. Sonti has missed too many days of school this year. If he stayed home today, the school would have to report it to *Protective Services.*

"All we can do is try to give him a couple of hours a day where he can get a smile, know he's safe and riding with people who care about him." — She leaned back In her seat. — "We got him and the other kids safely to school. That's our job. That's what we do."

Friday Afternoon

Grady's ears were still ringing from Sonti's screaming when he headed home to change into a dry shirt and rest awhile before he had to pick up the kids again. Sonti didn't look in any kind of shape to stay in school all day. *Hope he's going to be okay at the meeting.*

Grady had seen enough scratches and scrapes as a coach to be able to evaluate the seriousness of a kid's lacerations. He wouldn't be surprised to learn that some of the injuries he'd seen on Sonti's arm had occurred the previous Tuesday morning when he was locked inside the shed. But the sheer volume and variety of them were evidence that all had not been well with him for quite a long time. But those were worries for another time. Right now, he had four other children to care for.

###

Grady casually twirled the football he had retrieved from the lawn the previous afternoon while he positioned himself at the foot of the sidewalk and waited for the dismissal bell to ring. He wanted to be sure to be able to send a friendly head nod to his newest buddy, Jason Weatherly, before J.D. arrived with Miss Miller.

He spotted the familiar Packers jersey making its way down the hall long before he actually saw the kid's face, so he was able to maneuver around and make sure he would be in full view. Jason burst through the door with his gang of buddies all full of himself, but the minute Grady caught his eye and smiled, Jason ducked his head and quietly hurried on his way.

Yeah, that's right. Run you little weasel.

###

Everyone cheered when both J.D. and Sonti arrived on the bus. J.D. looked a little embarrassed, but smiled as he moved to his seat and buckled in. Sonti actually looked A-Okay.

Prissy twisted around in her chair. "We're having a meeting and making plans, today, J.D."

"I know."

###

Grady dropped everyone off at the door of *Indy's* and drove around to the back to park the bus. When he walked through the front entrance himself, he could see Clara with Prissy, Sonti, J.D. and Bennie already gathered around the table in the private room.

The children's excitement had obviously transferred to nerves and, for this group, nerves turned into motion—forward-back, forward-back, forward-back. Even Bennie, in his bubble, was rocking.

Grady wiped his palms along the front of his thighs as he approached the room. *You've been building teams for twenty-five years, Redwine. How hard can this be?*

He peeked through the door, caught Clara's eye, and mouthed, "No Grundel?"

She shrugged a single-shouldered, *Guess Not.*

They shared a delighted smile.

Grady entered the room rubbing his palms together with excitement. "Okay, kids, let's huddle up here and have some fun."

The room erupted in full-volume, simultaneous confusion: "Hud-dle up?"; "Ah we playing football today?": "We can't play football in here!"; "J.D. got hit in the head with a football yesterday."; "We don't have a football. How can we play?"

The cherry on top came when J.D. leaned toward him and whispered, "Mistow Wedwine, I don't think Sonti is supposed to play football. He wuns away."

Grady shook his head, bewildered. *Five minutes you've been here and look at it.*

Prissy took command. "This isn't football, you dummies. All he's saying is that we're going to have a team meeting...which we already knew."

The room erupted again: "Don't call names, Pwissy. It isn't nice."; "Team? What team?"; "We're not a team."; "I'm hungry."; "I thought we were having lunch."; "Can we eat fuhst?"; "When are we going to start having fun."

To Grady's relief, Clara took over and turned toward him. "Let's try this: I'll place orders for everyone today and you can have your meeting while I go get the food. How does that sound?"

The kids didn't give him a chance to answer. "Do you know how to order?"; "What if you get it wong?"

Clara chuckled. "Let me guess. Everyone wants six Chicken Nuggets, French fries, and a chocolate shake, right?"

Sonti nodded and smiled; Prissy responded, "Right."; Bennie added, "Four-dollars-eighty-cents."; then J.D. closed with, "And stwahs. Don't fohget the stwahs."

Clara chuckled again. "Got it. While I'm gone, Mister Redwine is going to talk about some things, and we're going to listen carefully, aren't we...not all talk at the same time."

All heads nodded.

She smiled in his direction. "Go ahead, Mister Redwine. Hold your meeting."

Grady took a seat at the head of the table. "Thank you, Miss Clara." He wanted to make eye contact with each member of the group, but, with the exception of Prissy, and in his bubble, Bennie, he met lowered heads. "Raise your hand if you've ever been a member of a team."

No one did.

"How about a club. Does anyone belong to a club?"

The question launched serious rocking in every chair...forward-back, forward-back, forward-back. Finally, J.D. raised his hand. "Miss Milluh sometimes takes us shopping at a food *Club*."

Grady saw an opportunity and jumped on it. "Thank you, J.D.! And what good conversation skills you used—raising your hand." He scanned around the table. "And all the rest of you, taking turns to talk—great work! Does anyone else have an example?"

Prissy raised her hand and said, "We have *Good News Club* at school. I belong to that."

"That's great! Good for you!" Grady waited a minute. "Anyone else?"

No one.

"Well, I think we should fix that. Let's just make one of our own."

J.D. hopped right on that. "Ah we making a team oh a club?"

Prissy looked bewildered. "What's the difference?"

Grady scrambled up an answer. "Well...uh...members of teams have fun doing things like...uh...sports or...uh...work, annnd people who belong to a club have fun...uh...just-doing-things-they-like-to-do."

Another simultaneous reaction ensued. Bennie spoke first. "I'd rather belong than just be a member"; "Me too"; "I pick club"; "We alweady wook evwy Wednesday, I want club too."

Grady mentally rolled his eyes. *So much for talking one-at-a-time.* He responded. "Then it's unanimous. Club it is."

J.D. raised his hand again. "What kind of club ah we making?"

"Well, since we have fun doing things together, like coming here for lunch and going to the park, I think we should have a club for people who ride the bus. Whaddaya think?"

He was met with complete silence, but the rocking slowed.

Pedal faster, Redwine. "Who remembers the story of The *Last Mile*?"

Prissy raised her hand and spoke up. "It's about a special person just like all of us. He couldn't talk really well or walk really well, but he had a special gift."

"And who has a special gift? Do you remember, J.D.?"

J.D. looked startled—sort of cornered. He hesitated for a moment. Grady held his breath, but J.D. recovered. "All of us have a special gift. We just have to find it."

"Good job! And that makes us what, Prissy?"

"Practically famous."

"Right! Yay! So, the next thing we have to do is come up with names for things. Let's start with the bus."

"The bus alweady has a name, Mistow Wedwine. It is called **The Bus**. It is Numbuh *eighty-six*."

"Yes, you're right, but this will be a secret club name that only we know."

The group perked up.

"Raise your hand if you think it would be fun to make our secret bus name, *The Last Mile Bus.*"

Everybody's hand went up. Even Sonti made a try.

"Great! And since our club is going to call Bus Eighty-Six, *The Last Mile Bus*, I think we should call our club the Milers."

Bennie's screen lit up. "Mile-ers? What are mile-ers?"

"Milers are people who run a whole last mile of a race without stopping…no matter what. If they fall down, they pick themselves up and run some more, even if they're tired. They never stop until they reach their goal."

He looked around the table. "So how does Milers sound?"

J.D. raised his hand. "Do we have to wun a mile?"

"No. Only if we want to. It's just a name—it's not what we do."

J.D. continued. "Do we get to have a t-shut?"

Grady resisted smacking himself on the forehead. "Yes. Yes. Of course you do. It wouldn't be a real club without a t-shirt."

J.D. smiled. "Sounds okay to me, then. Since we get a shut."

Miss Clara showed up with the food. "Time to eat, everybody. We can finish our meeting when we're done."

"Good."; "Yeah. Good."; "Can I have my shake?"; "I want my fwies please."; "Did you remembuh the stwahs?"

Grady rolled his eyes. "One at a time, everybody. Please! One at a time!"

After a fun-filled lunch, the meeting reconvened and the rocking began again.

Grady smiled and asked, "Who can tell me what a goal is?"

Forward-Back- Forward-Back- Forward-Back-

Prissy perked up. "I go over a goal line when I run a 4K."

J.D. added, "Isn't it called a goal when someone makes a basket?"

Grady gave a little shout of approval. "That's right, you two! Very good!"

Bennie took a stab at an answer. "Is it like my I.E.P.?"

Clara stepped in. "That's an excellent answer, Bennie. It is like your *Individual Education Plan*, only for *this* goal, you are the *only* one who decides what the goal is."

Grady looked around the table. "A goal is all of the things we talked about, but it can also be a wish— or a dream— or a promise you make to yourself."

Prissy added, "Cinderella says a dream is a wish your heart makes."

"Good! That's good, Prissy."

"So, what do you want us to do Mistow Wedwine?"

"I want you all to spend the weekend thinking hard about something you really, really want to do."

Forward-Back. Forward-Back.

"It could be something you want to do with your special gift, or what you think you might want to be when you grow up..."

Forward-Back. Forward-Back.

"Or it could be somewhere you would like to visit, or something you've always wanted to do..."

Forward-Back. Forward-Back.

"Even if it's very hard... or even if it feels scary."

Grady paused. "And when you have decided what it is..." He ripped some pages out of his notebook. I want you to wriii..." Clara gave a quick little headshake. "Uh...I want you to tell me what it is, and I'll write it down on these papers." Clara smiled. "Then we will get together on Monday again and set some goals. How does that sound?"

The rocking around the table got harder. Everyone's eyes grew larger.

Oh-Lord.

J.D. looked puzzled. "Ah the goals going to be fo-evuh?"

"Great question. They can *be* forever, but they don't *have* to be. You know why?"

Heads shook no.

"Because they are *your* goals. They belong to you, so you can change them whenever you want to." He looked around the table. "Any other questions?"

There were a few seconds of silence, then the kids responded: "Are we going to get Chicken Nuggets Monday?"

"Can we have ice cream today?"

"When do we get our T-shuts?"

There wasn't much chatter on the way home that night. Everyone conked out in their seats.

"Carbs," Clara said.

Grady drove for a while then whispered. "Looks like we've got some work to do this weekend to get ready for Monday."

"Looks liiiike."

"You think, and I'll think, and we'll put what we accomplish together Monday morning, okay?"

"Deal."

Friday Evening

On the way home, Grady started planning his weekend. He had two days to pull together an agenda, prepare his back up materials, design a logo and get t-shirts made for the Milers. He was going to be a busy man.

Just to get a head start on the project, he decided to stop at the big-box store on the Square because they were the most likely to have everything he would need for the meeting. He roamed the aisles, hoping to get inspiration; bought coloring books; tablets; tape; and some pens.

In the magazine isle, he picked up a TV viewing guide to sneak a look at the weekend schedule.

On Saturday, the NBA games didn't start until 3:30, so he would have tomorrow morning and early afternoon free. He knew most of the stores on the Square downtown all opened around eleven. There was a t-shirt shop there known for good custom work. He'd go there.

Sunday, the morning would be free as well. The Pro Bowl itself began at three, but he didn't want to miss pre-game programming.

On the way to the checkout line, he remembered he'd need some paper to wrap something, and the display just happened to be beside the beer cooler.

He stared at the cooler for a while. *Then there's that.* He began to push his cart forward and leave the cooler behind but went back. *Maybe a few Ponies would get him by.*

Grady stared at the six-pack of Ponies he'd placed in the child's seat of the cart all the way to his truck parked in the last row of the lot.

> *"You're trying to do something good this weekend, Redwine. You know if you drink that, you'll ruin it. You never stopped at six Ponies in your life."*

He passed four trash cans before he could make a decision, but at the last one, he picked up the six-pack and dumped it.

WEEK FOUR

MONDAY
January 28, 2019-Morning

After a chaotic weekend at home preparing for today's planning meeting with Clara, Grady arrived at the bus early and waited anxiously to see what she came up with on her end. He leaned back in his seat and sipped at his coffee. *Hope she came up with something good.*

As he thought back over the events leading up to today, Grady felt an excited rush of urgency in his body that hadn't hit him since he was at the peak of his coaching career. The sensation never seemed to be triggered by anything obvious. It just slipped into him out of nowhere in the form of an unshakeable belief that something big was about to happen.

He didn't have any time to reflect on it further because Clara climbed onboard all wound up too. "Look what I've got for our meeting today." She pulled a pack of balloons from her purse along with a few dollar bills.

"Ohhhkaaaayyy."

"I'm going to call these *Goal Balloons*. I thought we'd write everyone's goal on a piece of paper and stuff it into a balloon with a dollar bill and a bunch of confetti and glitter. Thennnn..." She pulled a small container of canned air out of her bag and held it up. "We blow them up with this and tack them on the rail above their seat. That way, when they see the balloon every day, it will remind them to work on their goal. And when they achieve it, we have a big celebration where they pop the balloon and get to keep the dollar."

"That's just genius, Clara. I love it."

She made a small head bow. "Thank you. I love it too."

She pulled out a black marker. "We can write their name on the balloon with these."

"Perfect!"

He reached over to the dashboard and passed a plastic bag in her direction. "I put some stuff together this weekend too."

Clara reached into the bag. "Ohhh, Grady, t-shirts. J.D. will be so happy." She held one up. "They're beautiful! What a great color green."

"I call it *Last Mile* green."

"Well, it's perfect. Oh! I love the logo and the slogan! *'Go for your Goal.'* It's simple and understandable. I'm impressed."

"Look at the back." He watched her turn it around and read: *"We Reach for the Stars and Get There."*

"Too much?"

"Not at all."

"There's one for you and one for me, too. We can wear them on Fridays."

Clara pulled out one that looked about the size of a blimp. "I know you had to guess my size, but..."

He laughed. "I got one for BennieToo."

"Well, that's a relief. I was worried there for a minute."

"It took all day Saturday, but the guys at the t-shirt shop really came through for me when I explained what the Milers Club is and that we were setting our goals this afternoon."

"Is Sonti coming today?"

"I think so. I didn't get a text saying he wasn't. I figure if they had to send him to school last Friday for *Protective Services*, whether he's ready or not, they'd be forced to send him today too."

"Have you thought about what you're going to do with him in the meeting?"

Grady handed her a file folder. "I remembered Mister Wilson telling me that they communicated with Sonti through pictures, so I decided to give it a try."— He passed it across the aisle to her. — "This isn't pretty, but I think it'll work."

She opened the file and pulled out a sheet of paper. "Oh! I seeeeee."

"My plan is to show him that page of pictures and ask him to choose what he wants to work on."

"So, you've got basketball, dancing, football, track, a beachball and a roller-coaster."

"Yeah, I thought he might like to go to the beach or an amusement park or something."

"You never know."—She returned the paper to the folder and handed it back to him— "My money's on basketball."

"Mine too. But I think it's important to let him choose for himself."

"I like how you think."

Grady took a glance at the sky. "Looks like it's going to be a sunshiny day."—He shifted his gaze to the clock. —

"Whoa. We've gotta go get the kids."

Afternoon

The air was filled with excitement in the main meeting room at Indy's that afternoon. After the gang had gulped down their Nuggets and shakes, Grady went to the head of the table to set the agenda.

"Welcome to the first official meeting of the Milers Club, everyone."

Pleased looks spread around the table.

He watched Sonti rock in his chair— peaceful and surprisingly connected to what was going on. *So far so good.*

"So, let's begin. Everybody, repeat after me: "We are Milers.""

'We ah Miluhs—"; "We are Milers—"; "What? What are we supposed to do?"

J.D. took charge. "We ah supposed to pay a-ten-shun, Bennie."

Grady continued. "We set goals and…" He left the end of the sentence open. "What do we do? Who can remember."

Bennie said, "I remember...but I forgot." He paused. "Oh yeah, now I remember. We achieve them."

Prissy smiled. "We achieve them."

"Perfect. And if we fall, what do we do?"

Prissy answered with great conviction, "We pick ourselves up and keep going until we get there."

Grady got goosebumps. "Great job."

He moved on. "Does everyone have their goal ready?"

"Uh huh."

"I do."

"Yeeeessss,"

"Uh, sort of."

"That's great! So, this is how this meeting is going to work. One-by-one we are going into the other room, and I am going to write your goal in my notebook to make it official."

"Who wants to be first?"

Prissy's hand shot up. "Me! Pick me!"

"Okay. Prissy is first." Everyone else looked a little relieved.

Grady escorted Prissy through an archway at the side of the room where the gang hung out and opened a door that led to a smaller meeting room, set up for a more intimate meeting with only a table for four.

Grady set his materials on the table and sat down. Prissy parked across from him, obviously all wound up. "I have my goal! But I need to talk to you about it first."

"Okay. Shoot."

She leaned his way. "Well, you know I like to run 4Ks."

"Yes."

"So, I thought for my goal I could maybe run a little farther."

"Oh! A stretch goal! Very good!"

"I don't feel ready to do a 5K yet, so I thought instead of just a 4K, I could step it up to a 401K this time. What do you think?"

Grady hid a smile—cleared his throat. "I haven't heard about any 401K races scheduled around here, but there are lots of ways to do a race better. One way is what you are thinking about already— running a little farther. Another way is to do what you're already doing, only run it faster. Maybe that would be a good goal."

"Oh yeah. I never thought about that."

"How fast are you running now?"

"Thirty-five minutes."

"Maybe you could try for thirty-four minutes next time."

"Okay. That's good—or even thirty-three."

"Yeah! Maybe! Let's put together a program to make you stronger, see how you do, and decide on the final goal then. Whaddaya think?"

"Good. I think that's good. Let's do that."

He recorded the goal in his notebook. "Okay, you're official, Prissy."

She glowed with pride.

He handed her a small slip of paper. "And this is your official receipt."

She pressed the paper against her chest and glowed even brighter. "So, what do I do now?"

Take your receipt to Miss Clara. She'll tell you what to do next."

Grady watched with a warm heart as Prissy wheeled through the archway to the larger room. She stopped and turned back toward him. "Oooo I'm just so excited!"

"So am I, honey. So am I."

J.D. came in next and before Grady could ask him if he had his goal ready, J.D. flat-out announced, "I want to luhn how to dwibble."

The coach in Grady perked right up. "Oh yeah?! That's very interesting, J.D. What made you decide to do that?"

"Coach Cahlson said if I could dwibble, they might let me go down to the gym flooh with the wegulah kids."

"Would you like a few tips? I might be able to help you."

J.D. weighed the suggestion for a minute. "Okay."

"I have to warn you. There are lots of things to learn and it takes a lot of practice."

"How many things do I have to luhn?"

Grady knew J.D. well enough to realize he'd better be accurate. "Probably fifty if you want to be really good."

J.D. gave the number some consideration. "Fifty is okay. I guess. I can luhn fifty."

"It could take a few more. It just depends on how much you practice. Are you willing to practice?"

"Yes. I will pwactice. Weally, weally hahd. Evwy chance I get."

Grady wrote the goal in his notebook and handed J.D. his receipt. "You're official, J.D., Thank you for being so prepared. Take this out to Miss Clara and when we're all finished in here, we'll tell you what to do next."

Grady chuckled as he watched J.D. do a pretty darn good fake dribble on the outside of one knee as he went back through the archway. *The boy is serious.*

BennieToo walked in and stood across the table from Grady.

"Hi Bennie! It's good to see you here today."

The look on Bennie's face in the monitor showed how much he wanted to please, but he couldn't seem able to bring himself to speak.

Maybe something's wrong with the Wi-Fi. "Bennie? Are you there?"

"Yes, Mister Redwine, I'm here."

"Do you have your goal ready?"

There was a long, awkward pause. "Bennie?"

"I don't think I can be a Miler, Mister Redwine."

"Why not?"

"Because everything I want to do is impossible."

Grady dug desperately through memories of his old half-time talks to find something appropriate to say and finally emerged with: "I had a coach in college who talked about achieving impossible goals, and he told us, 'Things that once seemed impossible become reality every day because someone decided to try to do it anyway.'"

He leaned closer to the camera. "Miracles happen, Bennie—all the time. Let's see how close we can come to making one."

There was a pause, then Bennie said, "Okay."

"So, let's set a goal. What would you like your goal to be?"

"I want to feel like a regular kid, Mister Redwine. I want to fit in—like a regular kid—just for a day."

Whoa. Grady had to swallow hard before he was able to reply but managed to force himself to steady his voice and soldier on. "Okay, then. Let's see what we can do. Let's start right now. Close your eyes."

Bennie did.

"Can you imagine what you might be doing when you feel that way?"

There was a period of silence. Eventually, Bennie opened his eyes again. "I'm sorry, Mister Redwine. I can't."

"That's okay. You don't have to know what it is right now. Let's start by making it your goal to come up with some possibilities."

"Okay."

Grady's hand trembled when he reached for his pen. He wiped it on his thigh and tried again.

Finally successful, he began to write. "This is a very good start, Bennie. I'm putting it in my book now."

He put the pen down, smiled into Bennie's camera and held the entry up for him to see. "You're official, Bennie. I'm putting your receipt on your tray to take back and give to Miss Clara."

As Bennie left the room, Grady took a big gulp of coffee, wishing the cup held something stronger. *You probably stepped deep in it this time, Redwine—making promises that could mess with the mind of Victor Hamilton's son.*

###

Clara wheeled Sonti into the room and parked him in a place at the table. "Have fun you two. I'll just leave you alone to talk."

Grady looked across the table. "Hello, Sonti. I'm glad to see you again."

Sonti's eyes wandered around the room, ignoring him.

"We're forming a club, Sonti, and we want you to be a member. Would you like that?"

Sonti's eyes continued to stray.

"We're choosing some things we'd all like to do in the club." Grady pulled the conversation sheet out of the file and slid it across the table toward him. "I made this so you could choose yours."

Sonti glanced at the paper and seemed to recognize what he was expected to do.

"Is there something on this list you like best, Sonti? Something you'd like to do?" Grady pointed out each item as he named it. "Would you like to play more basketball? Learn a new dance? Run in a race? Go to the beach? Or ride a roller-coaster?"

Sonti seemed to be following along.

"Can you point for me? Tell me what you would like to do?"

Sonti stared at the paper for a minute, pointed at the runner, then moved to the basketball and finished up with some serious eye contact.

Grady made a couple of mental fist pumps. *Yesss! Yessss!*

By the time he finished his personal celebration, Sonti's eyes were wandering again. Grady moved on. "So, you'd like to think about two things, Sonti? Track and basketball?"

Sonti's eyes returned to his. "That's great! We'll take a look at them both—see what we can come up with."

Grady picked up his pen. "I'm writing your choices in the book for you now." When finished, he looked up and smiled, "Looks like you're official, Sonti. Good job."

Sonti smiled back.

Grady took hold of the handles on Sonti's chair and headed for the archway. "Let's go back in with the others and give them your good news."

Even though he felt they deserved the equivalent of a NASCAR burnout, or at least a couple of victory laps, Grady resisted. It would probably be a mistake to get Sonti all wound up like that. But—

What a high.

###

Back in the main room, the other kids were still gathered around the long lunch table holding their inflated balloons and flapping them around by the stem.

"We have *Goal Balloons*, Mister Redwine. They have dollars in them."

"I can see that."

Clara took Sonti's receipt from Grady's hand. "As soon as we put Sonti's together, we can put them over your seats."

Grady returned to the head of the table. "Close your eyes, everyone. We have another surprise."

Chaos returned to the room: "Ooooo I looooove surprises."; "What is it?"; "It's a sup-wise, Pwissy. You don't ask what a sup-pwise is."

Clara pulled a plastic bag out of her tote bag and handed it to Grady. "Now don't open your eyes until we tell you to."

Grady removed the shirts from the bag and placed one on the table in front of each child. "Ok, you can open your eyes now."

Oohs and ahhhs spread through the room. J.D. shouted to Bennie, "It's ah shuts, Bennie. We got ah shuts!"

Grady placed himself in front of Bennie's camera and held up a t-shirt. "We have one for BennieToo—and we'll also send yours home with him today. Your Mom may have to adjust it—maybe cut a few holes, so it doesn't get in the way of transmission or anything."

"Wow! Thank you, Mister Redwine."

"You're more than welcome, Bennie."

Grady stood at the head of the table and stretched his arms wide as if embracing them all. "I now pronounce you official members of the Milers Club."

Prissy took the shirt and held it against her chest for a minute. "Can I put it on?"

"Yes. It's yours. You earned it."

She pulled it over her head and smoothed it down. "I looove it. I looove green." The others shimmied into theirs as well while Clara first helped Sonti into his, then put Bennie's on a tray for BennieToo to carry into the house with him.

Bennie beamed with joy on the screen. "Thank you so much!"

J.D. admired his reflection in the window. "Wow. "We ah a club."

Sonti managed a small, silent smile.

Prissy smoothed hers down again. "Mister Redwine, can we wear them to school tomorrow?"

"No. These will only be for special occasions. Keep them in your closet in your room. Miss Clara and I will tell you when to wear them."

Back on the bus, Clara stuck a thumb tack through the neck of the balloons and pinned them to the cork strip above the window of each person's seat.

"Now that you have your *Goal Balloon*, you can look at it every morning and decide what you are going to do that day to make your goal come true. And when you reach your goal, who can tell me what happens?"

Prissy raised her hand and said, "You get to pop it and keep the dollar."

"Right! And then what. Can anybody guess?"

The group was silent for the first time that day.

Grady spoke up. "When you achieve this goal, you make a new one and work on getting another dollar."

J.D. obviously loved that thought. "We ah going to be witch!"

TUESDAY
January 29, 2019-Morning

Grady and Clara hurried through their preparation for the route that morning still feeling high about the meeting the day before.

Clara looked up at the balloons above every child's seat. "I think we were a success yesterday, what do you think?"

"Exceeded my expectations, I'll tell you that."— He started the bus and began driving for the exit. — "Now comes the hard part—following through. "— He surveyed the sky. "Looks like another sunny day."

Clara replied. "Unusual this late in January."

Grady knew when Prissy came aboard the bus with her wand, that it was *Wizard Day* in *American Lit* again.

He chuckled.

"We're reading the first book today." She leaned toward him and lifted her shoulders in a small shrug, obviously about to confess a secret, and whispered, "I cheated and read ahead. I have a favorite line. Do you want to hear it?"

"Of course."

She settled back in and gathered her thoughts. "Okay. Okay-um—The Wizard of Wizards says, 'Joy can be found anywhere if one is willing to look for it.'"

Clara smiled. "That's a beautiful line."

"It sounds like something my mother would say. Only, she would want me to change it to, 'if *you* are willing to look for it' because it would make me feel more responsible."

Grady thought maybe he should change his mind about that *Wizard* stuff. There might be something to learn in it after all.

Grady and Clara loaded the rest of the Wizards and wands onto the bus, reminding each one to look at their *Goal Balloon* and decide what they were going to do that day to make their dream come true.

Afternoon

When the Wizards flew back onto the bus that afternoon, they were still full of Wizard lore. Grady heard Clara in the back asking what each of them liked best about the book. Prissy hopped right on it by repeating her quote from that morning about joy and trying.

J.D. countered with, "I liked the one that says…" He opened his book and shuffled through the pages. When he couldn't find it, he said, "*It goes something like, 'Bad stuff sometimes happens to good people.'*" He paused and looked up. "But *t*his is my favowite paht, Mistoe Wedwine: *'We just have to wemind ahselves that we ah good people.'*"

Grady thought maybe he should change his thinking about *Wizards* altogether.

Thirteen Weeks On The Last Mile Bus

WEDNESDAY
January 30, 2019-Morning

Grady and Clara agreed to meet at the bus a little earlier this morning so she could brief him about the work activity that afternoon, since it was quite different from the usual sorting of cans at the *Food Bank*. He had to admit he was a little nervous about the concept of those three kids shredding paper at City Hall.

He took a sip of his coffee as she settled in. "So how does this whole thing work?"

"We set up a relay much like we do at the *Food Bank*. The materials we shred are already stacked in a hallway outside the shredding room and we station Prissy there because of the noise."

Grady tensed up. "Ear plugs again?"

"No, she can use her quiet ears for this one." He gave a big sigh of relief. "She opens the binders, removes the paper and searches through for any paper clips so they don't jam the shredder."

"Are staples okay?"

"Yes."

"BennieToo does most of the heavy work. He lifts and carries the binders to Prissy and moves filled containers into the alley. J.D. feeds the shredder."

Grady kind of shivered. "Sharp things?"

Clara chuckled. "Don't worry. A three-year-old could use this shredder safely. "The blades are a long way away from the feeder."

Grady smiled. "That's a good thing."

Afternoon

Grady and Clara agreed that it would be great if the afternoon went as smoothly as the morning route did. It had been relatively uneventful and peaceful…which was a good thing, considering the activity they were doing that day.

The kids seemed excited about the upcoming events when they boarded the bus at the school.

Prissy came on board all excited. "We get to shred paper today," Mister Redwine!

J.D. closely followed with, "And we get to play Volcano!"

Grady looked at Clara and mouthed, *"Volcano?"*

She looked at him sideways.

"Never mind. I know. Laaater." He drove the bus up to City Hall and parked in the *Handicapped Zone*. Miss Clara stood up and said, "Don't forget to take your quiet ears everyone. You know how noisy it is in there."

As they headed down to the bowels of the building, Grady saw Clara glancing up the hall. "Oh! Here comes our contact."

A tiny middle-aged woman with a toothy grin gathered them into a circle. "Hello everyone! My name is Miss Thornburg. Welcome back to City Hall." She pointed to several tall stacks of binders along the wall. "As you can see, we have lots of work to do this afternoon, so we really appreciate your help."

"Just a few reminders." She held up a bundle of papers held together by a clamp. "Is it okay to put this in the shredder the way it is?"

The consensus of the group was "No."

"Very good. What should I remove?"

J.D. hopped all over that. "You have to wemove the clamp."

"That's right! You remembered!" She held up the bunch with the paper clip. "How about this one?"

Prissy answered, "No. You have to take off the paper clip."

"Excellent. So, is the staple ok?"

The answer was a fairly unanimous: "Yes."

She held up a huge fistful of papers. "How about this? Is it okay to put this in the feeder?"

Prissy answered, "No. It's too fat. No more than thirty-five pages."

"Very good! You remembered too!" She turned and grabbed a stack of papers on the long side then held it sideways. "And I put the papers in the feeder like this, right?"

Bennie answered. "Wrong. You hold the paper at the top of the short side."

"One more question. What else am I careful not to put in the feeder?"

The gang answered in chorus. "Fiiiinnnnggggeeerrrsss!"

"Wow. That's right! We always use the pushing tool. You guys are really experts."

The gang looked around, self-satisfied.

"And what do we do when we're finished?"

A chorus arose. "We go to the bagging room to eat I-I-I-I-Ice cream and play vol-ca-a-a-a-no."

Miss Thornburg began to wrap it up. "Any questions?"

Grady raised his hand. "What if it jams? What do we do then?"

"It seldom happens, but if it does, just pull the plug from the wall and call me." She gave Grady a not-so-subtle once-over. "Or, if you need some help with *anything else*, my number is right over the light switch."

Clara watched Miss Thornburg swish away. "Whoah, Mister Redwine. Want me to write her number in my notebook..."

It was his turn to look sideways.

"...Just in case you *need* something *else*, and you aren't near the *light switch*?"

He looked sideways harder.

She shrugged a shoulder and smiled. "Just asking."

After the gang had worked their way through the stack of binders and convinced J.D. he didn't have to count every bundle up to exactly thirty-five pages or check just once more for paper clips, they headed for the back of the building. Clara stopped at a door with a brass plate that said *Volcano Playroom* and they all piled in.

Not far inside the door, the group came upon a mountain of ticker tape at least five feet high. Off to the side of the mountain was a stack of large paper bags and a table set with sippy-cups, ice cream bars, and a five-dollar bill for each student.

Clara looked toward Grady. "Do I still have to explain volcano?"

"Uh. No. But you'd think equipment like this would be self-bagging."

"Oh, it is. They do this for the kids. People have birthday parties here. It's like one big snowball fight. The kids love it."

Prissy wheeled in. "Miss Miller hates it when we come here. She has to use the vacuum to clean us up before dinner. Last time, she was still picking strips out of our undies at bedtime—said she didn't want anyone to get a paper cut on their patootie."

J.D. passed by. "Miss Miller didn't exactly call it a patootie, though."

Prissy finished. "She said you haven't lived until you've cleaned up poo in a pull-up with paper strips in it."

THURSDAY
January 31, 2019-Morning

It looked like a Japanese shadow play outside the high-security building at the top of the hill when Grady pulled into the drive at *The Hamilton Home* that morning. It was obvious Sonti had escaped again. His silhouette was quite easy to pick out of the crowd as he ran around in what appeared to be his tidy-whities—dodging—ducking— creating chaos.

When Sonti spotted the bus, he bolted down the drive, made an enormous leap across their bow and sprinted into the woods, followed closely by an angry mob of medical staff carrying flashlights and constraints.

Grady counted back in his mind. This was the sixth meltdown he'd witnessed during the three-and-a-half weeks he'd been driving this route. Heaven only knew how many more of them took place that he hadn't seen. No reasonable person could doubt that Sonti led an overwhelming and frustrating existence, but his meltdown this morning seemed different.

Grady reflected on the look he saw on Sonti's face as he sailed past the windshield. There was no fear in the boy's eyes—no trace of the black, fathomless look Grady had witnessed during previous meltdowns. He saw fun there.

Grady suspected Sonti had added a game of *Chase* to his other two standbys: *Teacher Push the Wheelchair* and *Toss the Shoes*. He was obviously having a ball this morning, getting chased.

Late Morning

After all the kids had been left off at school, Grady shared some of his thoughts about Sonti with Clara.

"I've been thinking a little about our Milers meeting with Sonti."

"Ohh?"

"I started out thinking I should start working with him on basketball because that's something I know how to do—I'm really not that much of a track guy. But after what we saw at Sonti's dorm this morning, I'm starting to think that track is a better choice because it would be faster to implement. Basketball is a team sport. Track and field are mostly individual performances—except for relays."

Clara seemed to mull it all over a while, then said, "Sonti can run, that's for sure. He obviously enjoys it. And I think it would be great if he had a constructive way to work off all that stored up energy. So, what are you thinking?"

"I think Sonti belongs in *Special Olympics...*"

Clara smiled. "What a great idea!"

"...and I think I'm going to discuss the idea with Coach Riley this afternoon."

"I'll cross my fingers. Let me know if there's anything I can do."

Afternoon

Grady searched the parking lot at the gym for fifteen minutes before he finally had to give up his plan to use the shortcut to the Coach's Office. He drove up the hill to the old VIP lot and lucked out with a spot not far from what was formerly the main entrance to the lobby. Technically, he wasn't supposed to park there anymore, but his window to talk with Jack was too small to hunt any longer. He decided just to take his chances and plead ignorance if he got caught.

It felt like home to Grady when he walked through the door. Over the years when he was a coach, it had become a ritual for him to assemble his team in the hall at the start of the season. He'd gather the boys around the picture of Vince Lombardi and ask someone to read the words that hung on the wall of every locker room: *Winning isn't everything, it's the only thing.*

After the boys had digested it, he'd say, "Those are truly great words and you see them everywhere, but I'll let you in on a little secret. Lombardi often told his friends that what he really said was, *'Winning isn't everything. The **will** to win is the only thing.'*

Grady smiled as he strolled over to the trophy case to reminisce a little longer. The slightly tarnished trophies from his three consecutive State championships still held places of honor, flanked by the customary team photos. He scanned the rows of skinny, big-eared boys, stopping on the ones he'd helped get to the majors.

He loved them all but lingered longest on his favorites: superstars Malik Perry and Brandon Baldwin, two of the five who had grown into wonderful athletes and now played in the NBA.

Grady felt a few goosebumps rise on his arms as he remembered those simpler times...back when he was a king.

Wow.

Grady felt even more nostalgic as he walked down the hallway leading to the office of Jack Riley, the new Head Coach of the *War Eagles*. He loved that office when it was his. It was deep in the bowels of an old section where peeling walls and yellowing posters made you feel frozen in time.

Out of habit, he took the shortcut through the boy's locker room and found himself falling into a ritual that began as a bet with Charlie Carlson the night before the finals of their first championship.

They were going into the game as massive underdogs the night Charlie bet him twenty bucks he couldn't name all the NBA stars in the order their posters hung in the hall without looking. Not only did Grady manage to pull it off and collect the money, but he also called a brilliant long shot play in the final seconds of the game, and the team went home with the trophy.

Grady was just superstitious enough to worry about accidentally jinxing something if he didn't call out the posters every time he walked the hall, and that concern carried over to this day.

As always, he started to walk, eyes straight ahead, ticking off names: Rafer Alston, Royal Ivey, Kevin Love, Lamar Odom—picked up some speed at Bill Russell, Wilt the Stilt and Karl Malone—moved into a trot at Kareem, Shaquille—then warped into high past Magic and Michael then slid to a stop at the top of the stairs with Kobe.

He paused to catch his breath for a while, then descended the stairs and headed for the athletic department.

Jack was busy scotch-taping a poster to the window in the office door and didn't notice him as he approached. Grady recognized the poster as the one advertising the annual *Half-Court Shot Contest* sponsored by the local pro team, the *Comets*.

He sort of sneaked up on Jack and said, "Anything new this year?"

Jack looked a little startled when he turned in Grady's direction but smiled widely when he recognized who it was.

"Well, look who's here!" He applied the final strip of tape. "I've always wanted to go to one of these things but have never been able to. They always seem to schedule it on my anniversary, and for some reason, my wife doesn't consider going to a basketball game a romantic evening out."

Grady chuckled.

Jack motioned him into the office toward the guest chair across from the desk. "Come on in! Have a seat." He tilted his chair back and casually crossed a foot over his knee. "How the heck are ya, Grady?"

Grady sat down and, in the mirror over Jack's head, he noticed that his picture had been moved from the center of the coaching staff to a place behind the door. He cleared his throat. "I'm doing well, Jack, thanks."

"To what do we owe this honor?"

"I have a great prospect for track in the *Special Olympics* and need your help getting him ready."

"Well, as far as I'm concerned, you have best eye for raw talent there is, Grady, and I'm anxious to hear about him." Jack squirmed in his seat a little. "But *Special Olympics* is kind of a new area for you, isn't it?"

Grady shrugged a shoulder. "It's a long story."

Jack lowered the front of his chair to the floor and leaned forward across the desk. "I think you got a bad deal, Grady. A really bad deal."

After an awkward silence, Jack leaned back in the chair again. "What's the kid's name?"

"Sontiago Smith."

"Sonti! I know him well."

"Oh yeah?"

"We worked with him two years ago. Failed. Fabulous runner. He could have been a star if it weren't for…well, you know."

"What happened?"

"Well, I'm sure I don't have to tell you, Grady, that there's a big difference between talent and ability. Sonti was extremely talented…just didn't have the ability to be a track star."

Grady scrunched up his mouth. "What was missing?"

"Well," —Jack leaned forward, laid a loose upside-down fist on the desk and began to recite his *What's Missing* list by raising a finger with each point he was making:

- "When you're doing cross country, you need to realize you aren't running away from home.
- You need to understand that when the starting gun sounds, it's not a signal for you to *decide* if you're going to run.
- When you're running relays, you need to understand that the baton isn't a gift for you to keep forever.
- When you're jumping hurdles, you need to jump the ones in your own lane, not the ones in a lane you like more. And…"

He ended the list with his thumb.

- "You have to understand the concept of taking turns. Every race isn't yours to run."

Grady digested those points for a moment then began to brainstorm. "How about teaming him up with someone like they do on ski slopes?"

Jack settled back in his chair. "I never thought these words would come out of my mouth, but in addition to everything else, he's just too competitive."

Sonti was like *Sea biscuit* out there, Grady. He'd look another runner in the eye and have to win. Teamwork just isn't on his radar."

Grady digested it all but said nothing.

Jack got a dismissive look in his eyes. "We tried, but he was a total disruption all the time and it was impeding the progress of the team, so we had to turn him down."

Grady made a small smacking sound with his mouth and stood up. "Well, I hoped I was on to something, but I guess not." He stuck out his hand. The two of them shook hands and Grady headed out the door. Behind him, Jack said, "Come back any time, Grady. It's been nice to see you."

Grady waved a wide, sideways goodbye as he walked away. "Will do. Thanks for your time, Jack." He didn't look back.

FRIDAY
February 1, 2019-Morning

In spite of his discouraging meeting with Jack Riley the afternoon before, Grady woke up fairly happy and felt light-hearted after driving a completely uneventful route that morning.

It was the first day of February—his second favorite month of the year because it was short...it started on Friday this year...he got three weekends, two teacher workdays and an entire week off for *Winter Break*...annnnd...he could start building his brackets for *March Madness.*

It just didn't get much better than that.

Afternoon

Miss Grundel wasn't there when Grady, Clara and the gang arrived in the lobby of Indy's and still hadn't shown up after everyone waited fifteen minutes.

Grady stretched his neck to survey their surroundings. "You'd think she would tell us if she was late or just wasn't coming."

Clara got a disgusted look on her face. "Ya think?"

Grady made an executive decision. "Well—the cat's away. Let's play a little." He gathered the Milers around him. "We are going to have an adventure and order for ourselves today."

He was surrounded by silence and faces with saucer eyes—including Clara's.

Finally, Prissy managed to say, "But..."

"No buts about it. You know how to order already. What do you say to the lady?"

J.D. responded. "Six-Chicken-Nuggets-Fwench fwies-chocolate-shake-Fo-dollahs-eighty-cents."

"Cor-rect! Very good, J.D. But today, we're going to take turns and let the lady say, 'four dollars, eighty cents.'"

There was an immediate explosion. "What if the lady can't wemembuh?"; "What if she gets it wrong?"; "Do we still get our two monies back?"

Clara mumbled, "Are you out of your mind?!"

Grady pressed on. "Don't worry, you guys, everything will be fine. Miss Clara will go first. Just watch her and do what she does. We'll help you if you need it."

He glanced down at Prissy. "Are you with me, honey?"

Prissy began fidgeting nervously in her chair "Yes."

"Bennie?"

His screen lit up. "I guess I can. I'll try."

"J.D., don't forget to say thank you."

"I won't fohget."

Grady was about to start an order for Sonti when Clara said out of the side of her mouth, "Time to duck, Grady. We've got Incoming."

His eyes shot to the window just in time to catch Miss Grundle pulling into the lot and parking carelessly, taking two spaces. He felt a pained look fly to his face. *Just stay calm, Redwine. Just stay calm.*

Clara softly said in his ear, "Fasten your seat belt. Three seconds to launch."

Grady watched Miss Grundle clip her keys to her lanyard, then notice that she was in the meeting room alone. But when she did, she obviously panicked. And when she finally spotted them in the lobby standing in line, she rushed toward them waggling a finger.

"No no no no no no. *What* are you *do*-ing?"

Prissy piped up from her place in line. "We're ordering for ourselves today, Miss Grundle. Isn't it exciting?"

She glowered at Grady. "What-have-you-done? This-isn't-how-we-do-this."

"I thought it would be fun to have a different kind of experience today."

People behind them started shifting around or moving to other lines. The young girl at the register appeared very confused. A Manager headed their direction.

Miss Grundel looked awkwardly around the room. "I'm sorry. I apologize." She pulled the children from the line and stepped out of the way of the next customer. "Please. Order. I sincerely apologize."

She began to herd the kids toward their private room, sort of backing out of the lobby, bowing like someone leaving the Pope.

Prissy looked bewildered "But…"

"Do what you're told, Prissy. You know how Fridays work."

She got a universal reaction from the others: "I'm hungwy, Miss Gwundle, ah we still going to eat?"

"I thought we were going to order our own lunch today."

"What hap-pened?"

Clara: "God help us."

Prissy persisted. "But Mister Redwine said…"

"Mister Redwine is new," Clara said. "It was a mistake. He didn't understand." She pointed to the room. "Be quiet and go. Go **now**."

Grundle glared at Clara. "I'll have a word with *you* later."

After the children were arranged around the table, Miss Grundel instructed them to hold out their money.

She snatched Sonti's bill from his hand. "We all know you want Chicken Nuggets today."

Grady clenched his teeth and thought, *"Don't you dare take this out on the children."*

She moved on. "What would you like for lunch, Prissy?"

Prissy produced her five-dollar bill and recited, "Six-Chicken-Nuggets-French fries-chocolate-shake-Four-dollars-eighty-cents."

Miss Grundel took her money without comment; moved on to take J.D.'s five dollars. "And You?"

"Six-Chicken-Nuggets-Fwench-fwies-chocolate-shake-¬Fo-dollahs-eighty-cents."

She turned to BennieBot. "Did you get your order, Bennie?"

At home, Bennie focused the camera on his tray. "Yes. Six chicken strips, Sweet Potato fries and a banana yogurt."

Miss Grundel's voice suddenly turned into honey. — "That's great, sweetheart."

Grady's stomach churned with disgust as he watched her stomp to the register.

Everyone ate in deathly silence and when finished, Miss Grundel stood up and announced, "I'm riding with you home on the bus."

Grady glanced at Clara who looked like a deer in the headlights.

The bus had never been so silent for so long on the ride home. Other than a few horn honks and the grind of the brakes, the only sound anyone heard were the keys bouncing around on Grundel's bosom.

When the route was complete and they returned to Indy's to take Grundel back to her car, she pointed to a place on the lot.

"Pull over there. We need to talk."

When parked, she glared in Clara's direction. "You knew better than to do what you did. What could you possibly have been thinking?"

Grady answered her. "Miss Grundel, we were told our mandate is to give these children life skills that will help them function well on their own someday. I felt the group had the, uh, elementary skills down and it was time to expand the experience."

Miss Grundel spun around to face him. "You are a bus driver, Mister Redwine. You drive a bus. That's what you do. That's what you're here for— to drive a bus. Not make decisions about what is taught to these children."

Grady figured now was probably not a good time to mention they put him in charge of P.E..

Clara opened her mouth to speak but Miss Grundel charged on. "During one single lunch, you have violated every agreement I had to make with the Manager of this establishment so these lunches on Friday could be possible. I assured him that we wouldn't interfere with their regular customers. And look what you've done. I'll be shocked if they let us come back."

Grady suspected any hesitation on the part of the staff at Indy's might rest more on their fear of her running into the place with her hair on fire than on the kids asking the cashier for six-chicken-Nuggets-french fries-chocolate-shake¬four-dollars-eighty-cents.

She harrumphed and adjusted her clothing. "Do you know how long it took me to get these kids to the point where their parents can take them out for a meal without spills or a meltdown? They know they're supposed to sit down and tell their parents what they want to eat. They know how much it costs. They know they're supposed to get something back. They also know not to go to someone else's table and take their food."

Grady tried to manage the look on his face as he waited for her to take a breath, but Miss Grundel wasn't finished.

"These children need structure, consistency, and routine in their lives to feel secure. Change is hard for them. They find it very unsettling and frightening. God only knows how much damage your,"— she flashed finger quotes, — "expansion experiment has done to these kids."

He stared across the bus at Clara who was giving him a slow, serious shake of the head. *Don't do it.*

Nope. Sorry. She crossed the line.

He leaned toward Miss Grundle, forcing apology into his voice. "I feel badly that I messed up your lesson plan, Miss Grundle, and sincerely hope that I haven't done any serious harm to the children by this." He adjusted his sitting position. "I do have a couple of thoughts, however, and a little feedback."

She snapped out, "What?"

"In the future, it might help if you briefed us on your lesson plan and stopped leaving us in limbo about whether you were going to bother to show up that day. OR even better, maybe you could just start showing up every Friday and arrive on time like you're supposed to." He shrugged. "Just sayin'."

She drew herself up to her full sitting height, neck veins bulging. "You're awfully high and mighty there, aren't you Mister Bus Driver. You've been in the program…what…thirty minutes? And you're already giving me 'feedback.' Remarkable.

"You wanna judge me? Get a black gown and buy a gavel." She gathered up her things. "Give me a call in five years. Let me know how you're doing."

She turned toward Clara. "I've had serious doubts about this program from the beginning, and you've just proven me right." She stormed down the stairs. "Trust me. You haven't heard the end of this."

Grady looked over at Clara. She was leaning against the window watching him. "Okay. Go ahead and say it."

"Be afraid," she said. "Very afraid."

Late Afternoon

Grady was halfway home when he heard the faint sound of bell tones floating up from his backpack and in the corner of his eye, caught a glimpse of something glowing through the fabric of the side pocket. It took a moment before it dawned on him: Mary's phone! It was ringing!

I get emails! I get texts on that thing! I don't get phone calls! Who could be calling?

He kept his eyes strictly on traffic while he stretched over to try and unzip the pocket by feel.

Come on, come on.

It wouldn't budge, so he jerked the backpack onto the console beside him to check out why the zipper wasn't working. His eyes darted between the road and the console as he fought with the zipper. The truck drifted slightly, and it was a struggle, but he finally managed to fish out the phone.

I hate this thing.

He quickly held it at arm's length in front of the windshield and squinted so he could read what it said with his driving glasses. The screen showed a header that said, "Transportation."

Beads of sweat burst out on his forehead.

He glanced down at the bottom of the screen and saw a graphic indicating he should "Slide to Answer."

He frantically felt around for a lever. There was no lever. He swiped at the button. Nothing happened. He tried again, with a little more pressure and it seemed to work, so he held the phone up to his ear and said a tentative, "Hullo?"

He heard a faint, slightly muffled voice drifting into his ear. "Is that you, Mister Redwine? I can hardly hear you."

"You sound far away to me too," he replied.

"Do you suppose you might accidentally have the phone upside-down?"

Grady flipped it. "How's this?"

"Oh, that's perfect." —There was a pause. —"This is Nora from the office. Would it be possible for you to come to Transportation before you go home this evening?"

He felt a sharp jolt of alarm in his gut. Nora always asked in the form of a question, but Grady knew a command when he heard one. He managed to get a casual air in his voice. "I'd be glad to. What's up?"

"I'm not sure, Mister Redwine. Everybody's in an uproar about *something* around here. All I know is they wanted me to give you a call and make sure you came in tonight."

Oh Lord.

"I'm on my way. Be there in about ten minutes."

"Okay. I'll let them know."

Grady felt a cold sweat rise on his body. *Them?* There's a *them* waiting for me?

His heart began to thump wildly in his chest. *Miss Grundel's as good as her word, alright. Didn't waste much time getting even.*

He glanced at the clock on his dash—thirty minutes. *She must have flown down on her broom.*

Grady parked and walked to Transportation like a man on Death Row. *Why didn't you listen to Clara, Redwine? You should have listened to Clara.*

It was 23 degrees outside and windy, but he still had to mop away sweat on his forehead before he took a deep breath and entered the lobby. Behind the window, Nora was in the middle of a conversation but held up her index finger to ask him to wait. A few minutes later, she disappeared into another room, still talking.

He soon heard footsteps in the hallway and sounds of an opening door, then fragments of an angry conversation drifted his direction. A voice he recognized as Margaret Sorenson's was reading the riot act over her speakerphone: "Totally unacceptable...has been told...not happen again."

Looks like that mouth of yours has done it again, Redwine. Kiss those benefits goodbye.

He loitered around alone awhile, anticipating the worst, growing more anxious as Margaret's conversation continued: "Constant turmoil...absolutely ridiculous...who does he think he is?"

Resigned to his fate, Grady fished the bus keys out of his pocket; removed the weathered old lanyard from around his neck and mentally prepared to turn them both in. He slouched in a chair and stared at the picture of him on his ID, reminded once again why he always wore it backwards.

He didn't waste any time making up an excuse. He was on probation—he'd been warned—and—he was guilty. What could he say that would make any difference?

After what seemed like an hour passed by, Grady heard footsteps heading his way and steeled himself for what was about to come.

He expected to see Nora emerge from the hall and lead him to the back office for the bloodletting, but Margaret herself came out. The woman who mere minutes ago was dragging someone over hot coals, greeted him warmly, with a broad, toothy smile.

Grady was shocked, nearly speechless.

"It's nice to see you, Grady. I'm sorry we had to make you wait. You're here because P.R. is planning to take publicity pictures first thing on Monday morning, and as usual, they waited until the very last minute to let us know. They want the pictures of the drivers to match, and Nora reminded us we hadn't presented you with your official shirt yet, so we had to call you back." She plunked a lime green golf shirt with the *County* logo on it in his hands. "Congratulations. Welcome to the *Special Needs* family. Here's your shirt. Wear it on Monday. Extra-large. Will that work?"

He managed to nod.

"There won't be any official posing or anything, but don't be surprised if someone comes by at the worst pos-si-ble mo-ment Monday morning and expects to snap a few photos."

He choked out, "Thank you."

"Well, I'm up to my ears back there but wanted to say hello. You doing okay?"

"Uh huh. Yes. Doing fine. Just fine."

"Good! Gotta go." She headed back down the hallway and shouted over her shoulder. "Let's get together and catch up soon. Enjoy the rest of your day!"

###

Grady walked back to his truck all rubber-legged and slumped behind the wheel awhile, feeling shell-shocked and raw. He returned the keys to his keychain and slid his ID back into its lanyard.

You got lucky today, Redwine, but you know it's just a matter of time. People like Grundel don't let things like this go.

He cranked up his truck and headed for home. After running on nothing but coffee all day he knew he should have something to eat, but his stomach was so tied up in knots, the thought of his usual cheeseburger made him feel queasy.

He figured he should just stick with liquids for a while and decided to stock up on Tall Boys when he checked out the Lottery.

###

Grady had planned for a fast in and out at *Qwick Pick*, but soon learned his luck hadn't changed. He'd already grabbed a case of beer, hauled ten pounds of ice out of the freezer, and was on his way to the register, when a woman all in an uproar rushed through the door and stepped between him and the counter. Always the gentleman, Grady said nothing and let her go first.

"I'm-late-for-a-meeting-back-at-the-office," she said over her shoulder. "My-workgroup-set-a-new-record-this-month-and-we-want-to-celebrate."
She continued to rattle on and on as she removed a huge carry-all from her shoulder and began to rummage around in it. "I'm-going-to-be-late. I-just-know-it. Oh-where-did-it-go? I-know-I-put-it-in-here." She started piling the contents of her bag on the counter—keys, scarves, papers, candy wrappers, mints, utility bills.

The clerk at the register glanced along the growing line behind Grady with the look of a man taken hostage.

"Oh! Here it is." Her hand emerged from the bag with a big wad of ones, secured by a thick rubber band. She smiled at the clerk, then held up the wad.

"Everyone pitched in two dollars. Fifty Power Balls, please. We all want our own number."

An audible groan surged through the line, but the woman was obviously oblivious.

For some unknown reason, she twisted toward Grady. "We thought it would be more fun this way—and if someone wins, there won't be a fight over money."

While Grady tried to pretend that he cared and fought off a strong urge to kill her, she whirled back to the counter, returned to the wad, unwrapped it and set about counting—ssslooowlyyy—to one hundred.

Grady was weak-kneed and getting the shakes, so he grabbed two cans of an energy drink and a big bag of beef jerky to make sure he'd have something healthy to eat. He juggled around the ice and the beer to make room for his new acquisitions and searched for signs or the sounds of another cashier.

Crickets.

In time, he felt so drained, he had to place the ice and beer on the floor while he waited. Just to pass the time, he pulled out yesterday's Lottery ticket and checked his numbers against the sign.

It was no big surprise to learn he had a loser. As a matter of fact, the ticket was such a big loser, he didn't get a single number—not even a number close to a number.

When the clerk finally finished counting out the lady's fifty tickets, the line breathed a communal sigh of relief and prepared to move forward. Then, without warning, the woman struck again. She pulled a five-dollar bill from her purse. "I'm feeling lucky. Give me five one- dollar Scratchies."

Grady ran his hand down his face. All he wanted in the world right then was to go home. *He Needed. To. Go. Home.*

When his turn at the register finally came, the clerk quickly tallied his order then looked at him with lifted brows, obviously scared to say the word *Lottery*. Grady cracked up. "Thanks, but I'm certain I've already used up any luck that was allocated to me for this day."

Grady would have knelt down and kissed the ground when he got home, but he knew if he did, he might never get back up again.

He hauled his purchases through the front door, picked up the Styrofoam cooler and dumped everything unceremoniously beside Mary's clock.

He slumped against the wall and slid to the floor next to his case of *Tall Boys*, then rested his head on the side panel of the clock and closed his eyes, unwinding. "You'll have to forgive me tonight, baby. I've had a *Really. Bad. Day.*"

In time, he emptied the ice into the cooler; loaded in the energy drinks and beer; popped open a tall boy and chugged it down.

He popped the tab on another; shifted so he could press his back on the clock and listened to the tick, tick, tick of the pendulum while he tuned in to Mary's soft, soothing heartbeat.

He sipped at the beer and relaxed a little, grateful for the first full breath he'd been able to draw since being called back to the office.

Eventually, his thoughts returned to his fight with the Grundel. Could he have been more diplomatic? He shrugged a shoulder. Probably.

Was he sorry he said what he said? He had to think about that one awhile.

I probably should be, and maybe someday I will be, but I don't care what anyone says, it's just wrong to turn those kids into robots. They're people—with dreams—not just a litter of puppies you paper train and consider yourself finished when they no longer poop on the floor.

He crushed the can; chucked it aside and reached into the cooler again. His hand paused for a moment or two at the energy drink but picked up a beer can instead.

He sipped. Debated. *Okay-okay-okay. Let's be fair. You-gotta-be-fair. Paper training is important. Everybody knows you can't give an untrained puppy the run of the house. But even puppies are given a chance to build a bigger life.* He began making a list in his head—*theyyyy become police dogs and... fire dogs and... help hunt down the enemy in wars.*

He sipped some more. *What else.*

Theyyyy get work finding truffles; they help hunt for game. They detect diseases and explosives and drugs. Theyyyy rescue people and help out veterans and even sometimes lead the blind. They're actors and models and mascots. They're sled dogs and watch dogs and help herd sheep.

Hell, some of them don't use the damn paper at all and end up just fine—like hunters and rescue dogs—they're mostly outside—they don't need it, so why bother to learn?

And what about the rest of them—the ones that just sit on your lap and make you feel better. That could be the most valuable job of them all.

He chuckled. "Me-me-remmer Kreeng—uh—Kr-Kringle, honey? You know, that Elk Hound the neighbors got one year for Christmas? Escaped from the yard about eight times a week; marked every bush for miles and still couldn't find his way home.

"John—I think that was the father's name. Or was it, Don. Yeah. That was it—Don. Don wanted a dog to take hunting and kept trying to teach Kreen-nel to track. Took him out in the woods all the time and they would both get lost." He took a sip. "Embarrassing."

"Musta called the rescue team for them six times b'fore a vet found out the poor dog had a damaged nerve in his nose and couldn't smell.

"Sweetest dog in the world, though. Good old Kreen-nel. Poor old dog Kreen-nel...couldn't smell."

He pondered Kringle's dilemma and sipped awhile.

"Ol' big-hearted Don wanted to put Kreen-nel down when they found out about his nose. His kids were all in an uproar—me-rem-er that day? His wife was gonna leave him...should have.

"Had a happy ending though. Was all o-ver the papers. Kreen-nel heard a baby crying in a dumpster one day and helped save her. Found out completely by accident his hearing was as good as his smelling was bad.

"Turned him into a rescue dog—saved lots of lives."

Grady crushed the empty can, chucked it back into the cooler and reached for another beer. "Sure says somethin' important 'bout giving second chances...you ask me."

He took a couple slugs and spent time studying the can. *Beer good ol' beer.*

A slight spinning started in Grady's head and his eyes floated toward the bathroom door. Hmmmm. Could it wait? He'd prefer to wait.

Out of the question.

The world spun wildly as he staggered to his feet— braced himself on the furniture as he made his way to the bathroom. And that was the last thing he remembered.

SATURDAY
February 2, 2019-Morning

Grady woke up with a blinding headache, sprawled face down on a stack of laundry scattered around on the guest room bed. Next to him were half a dozen crumpled beef jerky wraps which helped explain the strange, greasy garlic taste in his mouth and the stomach cramps causing his urgent need to head for the bathroom.

He felt a slight tremble in his legs and a stiffness spreading up the back of his neck when he bent over the sink to splash water on his face and gargle away some bitter stomach acid aftertaste. *What were you think-king?*

He tried hard to steady himself against the vanity but grew dizzy again and slumped to the floor—ice cold—heart pounding— blood rushing in his ears. And in a few seconds, the world went blurry then faded abruptly away.

###

For a moment, Grady wasn't quite sure where he was when he opened his eyes and saw what turned out to be the underside of a toilet bowl against his cheek. How he got there in the first place was a foggy blur, but he ended up grateful to have something sturdy to pull against when he hoisted himself to his feet.

He looked around in wonderment at the state of the room. *What happened here?* The door of the medicine chest was open, and all the contents were either in the sink or on the floor. The vanity drawer was open and empty as well, and all the towels were wet and wadded-up in a pile.

When did I do this?

He decided he'd just have to deal with it later because right now, he was half blind from the pain in his eyes. He spotted an open bottle of pain killers on the floor near the sink and grabbed it. *Thank you, Lord.*

The bottle felt rather light, but it rattled, so he figured there was at least one tablet in there. But even though he'd anticipated getting a pill in his palm when he tipped the container over, what came out was only a weird little plastic tube that they used to keep the pills dry.

Swell.

After taking a moment to steady himself and give one last look around, Grady decided there was nothing left there to help him, so he stumbled away from the mess in the bathroom, past a mess he'd made beside Mary's clock, and miraculously managed to flop into his recliner.

He put his face in his hands, placed his elbows on his knees and rested in that position for a minute or two, feeling a dull, pulsing pain in his temples and a horrible throbbing inside his eyes.

Grady, Grady, Grady. What-have-you-done.

He glanced down at the cooler and got inspired. A compress might help. Maybe he could make one for his eyes using the ice in the cooler.

He fished a few napkins out of the trash on the floor and was bending over filling a few with ice, when a sudden tingling sensation on the back of his neck sent shivers down his spine. *Woah!* He dropped the napkins and froze there. *What was that?!*

In an instant, everything seemed to be slightly off in the room, and he started to feel strangely unsafe inside—as if someone or something was there in the dark, watching him.

He glanced quickly behind him and held his breath, listening for any strange sounds in the house. But even though he heard nothing out of the ordinary, there was something about the silence itself that he still found seriously disturbing.

Grady stood up slowly, heart beating hard—listening—eyes straining left—straining right. But after he listened a few seconds longer and heard only the usual house sounds, he had to admit to himself that no matter how real the present danger may seem, last night he consumed almost a six-pack of Tall Boys, and those menacing creaks and cracks could merely be figments of his imagination.

Maybe. They might be. But they still gave him the chills.

Just in case, Grady made another sweep of the room before bending over again. But halfway down to the cooler, he was certain he caught sight of something shifting around in the shadows at the foot of the sofa.

Oh My Lord.

Grady glanced at the door, heart pounding. Should he run? Try to hide? *What if it's a guy with a knife? Or a gun!?*

He hesitated, then got stubborn and set his jaw hard.

It is what it is. I'm standing my ground.

He frantically searched for a weapon—found a plastic fork on the floor and grabbed it, then whipped around to a fighting stance, fully prepared to confront whoever it was man-to-man.

"I see you there. Come out." There was no response. He inched his hand over to the floor lamp: "Who are you? What do you want? Why are you here?"

Only silence.

Sweating bullets, Grady switched on the lamp to better see his attacker, only to stand there slack jawed and astonished to learn he was completely alone in the room. And worse, to discover that the shadow he saw moving down by the sofa was his reflection in his grandmother's mirror.

Really?! Really!! You have got to be kidding.

Grady remained motionless for a minute trying to recover his breath but felt slightly weak in the knees and sank down on the sofa.

Gee-zus!

Normally, he would attempt to brush off something as stupid as this; make a joke about fighting a gun with a fork—then get on with making his ice pack. But right now, he just couldn't tear his attention away from that gaunt, gray face in the mirror staring back at him. He'd had his share of looking wasted in college, but this? This was a whole new level of awful.

He spent a long time studying the dark sunken eyes. They looked so much like his grandmother's; he had to blink a few times just to make sure they were his. Perhaps it was caused by the pain so apparent in them—the same pain that appeared in old black and whites taken of her unveiling his uncle's badge on the *Wall of the Fallen in The National Fallen Firefighters Memorial,* and in others at Arlington, placing a flag on his grandfather's grave.

He stretched out on the cushions a while, eyes closed, recalling the first time he saw that tormented look first-hand. He was sitting with his grandmother on that very same sofa—gripping her hand and choking back tears while the two of them listened to two cops tell them how his Mom and dad had been killed by a drunk backing up on the highway.

He was nine at the time, trying his best to be brave like a man—a true Redwine. But when the officers finally packed up their reports and were gone, she lifted his chin with that haunted look in her eyes and gave him permission to cry.

"You just go on and cry, Grady honey," she said. "Cry until you run out of tears. And I'm going to cry along with you until I feel empty. But the day we lay your mommy and daddy to rest, you and I have to try hard to send any leftover tears with them and find enough strength to move on. There's one thing I'm sure of, honey, life is short, but *Eternity* is forever. So, we're going to concentrate on living lives to be proud of, so when our time comes to be judged, God finds us worthy enough to be with our loved ones again—in *Eternity*—forever."

He glanced back into the eyes in the mirror. They reflected his fear and had the look of death embedded in them. Then he heard his grandmother's voice. *Life is about forks in the road and you're standing at one of them, Grady. If you keep on drinking like this, you're going to die, and you'll never see your loved ones again.*

He studied that gaunt, gray face some more.

"Who are you? What do you want, Grady? Why are you here?"

He turned to face his picture of Mary. Was he living a life to be proud of? Would he be judged worthy enough to be with her again in *Eternity*?

He turned his head away, feeling sick with shame.

Afternoon

Grady slept awhile after his fight with the mirror and woke up ready to make amends. Even though he knew what had to be done to put this incident behind him, he placed mucking out the living room, bathroom, and hall at the top of his to-do list and took a shower because—well—he just had a need to feel clean.

Ultimately, he ended up outside Mary's office door, gathering the nerve to go in. He reached for the doorknob and drew his hand back several times before he finally forced himself to step inside. Once in there, however, all he could manage to do was stare at the box with its golden cross on the cover, placed carefully in the corner of the desk.

What should I do? What should I say?

Eventually, he made his way to the desk and rested a trembling hand on the cross. To his amazement, words just poured from his heart, and he felt a strange calm settle in.

"You probably think I've got a lot of nerve coming here, Lord, especially since I've brought this up to you before, but I'm not here to ask you for anything. I just need a few minutes of your time to help me make a promise to my wife, because—he choked up a bit; gathered himself—because I love her and making a promise by doing it this way is important to her, so it's important to me.

"I seem to be failing at everything, these days, Lord—I'm bad at my job—I've messed up my life. And I'm worried that if I don't start turning things around now, I may never find my way back.

"I haven't figured out what to do or how to do it yet. I just feel this is the best way to start."

He took a deep breath and in a broken voice said, "All I'm asking you to do is forgive me for all my failures, Lord, and let me have a chance to be with my Mary again. I promise I will do my best to deserve it.

"And maybe—maybe if you see a good opportunity—a small something you might do—you could help me." He swallowed hard. "Amen."

SUNDAY
February 3, 2019-Morning

Grady had mostly been sleeping in his chair since Mary died, and he slept there again the previous night because it was habit. But for the first time in months, he slept through the night, dreamless and in total peace.

He yawned; stretched; and noticed a new little bounce in his step as he headed for the shower, stripped, and turned on the hottest water his body could stand.

He stood with his head under the pelting hot stream and soaped down his body, then perched on the small bench in the stall while the room filled with steam. After half an hour of sweating, he soaped up again, scrubbed down and rinsed, then toweled off and pitched the towel in the corner on top of his dirty clothes.

Halfway to the sink, he stopped and pivoted back to pick up the pile. He placed it all in the dirty clothes bin—pleased for a sign he was already doing better.

He even attempted five push-ups on the bathmat, did a few lame deep squats, and considered trying some lunges but knew better.

Amazed to be able to look himself in the mirror and smile while he brushed his teeth, he carefully stored away everything cluttered around the sink and ran his fingers through his hair.

"You need a haircut, son." He scruffed up his beard. "You could use a trim there too." He considered the situation: shave everything off or continue to grow a beard and wear a hat to hide his hair like he'd been doing.

The voice said, *"You're making a new start, Grady. Do you really think taking a shower and putting dirty clothes in the bin is an adequate effort? Get dressed and go see your barber."*

###

When Grady pulled into the parking lot of the shopping center where the Open-Every-Day barber shop was, he thought all the cars were there for the grocery store. So, it was a shock to him to find the place packed to the rafters.

"It's Sun-day morn-ing in In-di-an-a. There's church. There's basketball. There's sleeping in. Why is everyone *here*?!"

Grady had been going to that barber shop for years and the owner was a big basketball fan. It was a natural thing for him to leave his customer and come out to greet him. "Coach! Great to see you! I haven't seen you very much since the—since Mrs. Redwine passed. She was a wonderful lady."

Grady smiled a thank you. "She was."

"Where've you been lately?"

"Busy, Joe. Just really busy."

Joe glanced at Grady's hair and laughed. "Well, one thing's for sure. You haven't quit me and gone somewhere else."

"How could I leave you, Joe? You're the only one who knows how to hide my bald spot without making it look like a comb-over."

Joe laughed. "I'm sorry you have to wait today. Did you know you can make a reservation using our app now?"

Grady cringed. *App. What in the world is an app?*

"Make yourself at home. I'll be with you in a few."

Grady hated waiting rooms—mostly because he was really bad at waiting—but also because they had horrible magazines. Everything was outdated, dog-eared, creased, and probably contagious. At least this shop had a decent selection with something interesting in them to read, even when the magazine was old. He fanned through one to the trivia page that turned out to contain questions about mascots. *What is the most popular live mascot in college sports? Easy. Bulldog—English Bulldog.*

He passed over the rest of the questions and began to cruise around, checking out the walls covered with old photos and paraphernalia. He was particularly attracted to a huge, framed article from the New York Times that he'd never noticed before. It was centered around a photo of Wilt Chamberlain standing out in his yard with three Great Danes.

Wow.

He shouted back to where the chairs were. "Hey Joe! I never noticed this picture before. Where did it come from?"

Joe's voice drifted back to him. "Isn't that a nice one? Actually, I've had it forever, back in the storeroom. We had to rearrange some things in there and it kept getting in the way. My wife scraped her leg on it and finally put her foot down—told me to move it or lose it, so I hung it up there in the corner. Just did it this morning."

Grady began to read the article with interest. He knew a lot about Wilt and his records, but he'd never heard about his dogs. According to the article, Great Danes were a hard breed to train but, apparently, Wilt found out he was good at it. He told the reporter that he thought he was successful because he didn't take a traditional approach. He only taught the pups basic obedience skills: heel, sit, down, and come. Then, once they got those mastered, he watched them awhile to see what they were good at and built skills from there.

Wilt didn't believe in docking their ears—left them floppy like they naturally grew. To him, it was cruel, and he didn't think they had to look like every other Great Dane, anyway. They should just be themselves.

Grady chuckled. He figured Wilt had fallen back on his personal experience. He was a great player, but he was also famous for his challenges with free throws. Rumor had it, he wasn't so good at some of the basic obedience skills either.

When he finally got called to the chair, Grady spent his usual thirty minutes listening to Joe chit-chat about basketball while he cut. "The team really stinks since you left, Coach. Everybody wants them to put you back in there."

"Well, I appreciate the thought, Joe, I'd love to be back there. But I don't think anyone should bet their ranch on it happening."

###

Back home and ready to relax, Grady pulled on some sweatpants and picked up the phone to place his usual Sunday food order: one extra-large Deep-Dish Pizza Supreme, extra mushrooms, double meat, double cheese—only this time he added four liters of diet soda.

While he waited for his food, he moved his cooler back to the living room and dumped in the ice. Then he rewashed the clothes he'd messed up on the guest room bed two nights before, cleared the hall of the clutter and hauled the trash from around the couch to the barrel outside.

Finally finished, he sat in his chair and looked around for a while, feeling different—lighter—hopeful.

When the pizza arrived, he chomped on a slice and resisted turning on the television so he could consider all the possibilities for what he could do to make amends. He decided to up the ante from *something hard* to *something especially hard* to make up for failing the last time.

He looked at the cooler full of ice and shifted his eyes toward the kitchen. Maybe his *hard thing* should be to start using the kitchen again. He immediately jumped to *No. Definitely not. He wasn't ready. No way.*

Was he being ridiculous? Maybe. But he took refuge in the fact that way back when this whole Making Amends thing started, Mary made it clear that the rules weren't there to punish you. They were there to make your sacrifice worthwhile and help you become a better person.

He mulled everything over in his mind for a while and concluded that making the kitchen his *hard thing* would be inappropriate anyway. It was easier to park in the garage than the driveway, and it was definitely less of a hassle to enter the house through the door into the kitchen. It just made sense that if his *hard thing* actually made his life easier, it would be more selfish than sacrifice—so that made using the kitchen out of the question.

Grady knew he was spinning the issue, but he didn't care. The kitchen was too hard. It still felt like a knife plunged into his heart every time he went in there.

He wasn't ready. He couldn't do it. He knew he *wouldn't* do it. What's more, he knew he'd probably end up doing something really stupid like sleeping in the truck just to avoid it.

There weren't any deadlines in Mary's process, so he decided to watch TV for a while and return to the issue later.

He clicked through the Sunday lineup. *Celtics* at *Ravens*. *Lakers* at *the Heat*. Perfect way to finish the weekend.

Late Night

Grady sat straight up in bed at two in the morning with a sense of clarity he hadn't experienced in months. Wilt Chamberlain! Wilt Chamberlain was a *sign*—he had to be.

He grabbed his phone off the nightstand and dialed. He just *had* to share his thoughts with Ryan.

A rattling sound followed by a befuddled voice answered at the other end. "Mon...Monsignor uh Goodman."

"Ryan!"

"This better be good, Grady."

"Listen! I've got it! I'm so excited, I'm floating, Ryan. Soaring."

"Let me guess. Three beers."

"No! I've had nothing! Nada! I've never been more sober in my life. It's just that I...well, I sorta feel almost like I discovered Penicillin or something."

"I'm fairly certain someone already did that."

"Funny."

Grady leaned into the phone. "Ryan, it really is like Penicillin. Everyone's been looking at the Petri dish, but nobody got the message until I woke up and got it just now. I got it. I just woke up and got it."

"Got what?"

"The answer."

"Which is…"

"Wilt Chamberlain! Wilt effin' Chamberlain!"

"What's the question?"

"How can you help kids with Autism."

"You've cured Autism with Wilt Chamberlain."

"No, not cured it, but…"

"Enough, Grady. Enough. Where do I go. How much is the bail."

"I'm serious, Ryan. I'm clean. Completely clean. It's just that I think I've figured out a way to help my kids and I need to share it with you while it's still clear."

"Call back. Share it after one o'clock."

"No! No listen! You're the only one who'll understand!"

"I'll understand better at one."

"No! Really! It's gotta be now. If we don't talk now, it might slip away by then."

"What, Grady. What can't wait."

"Answer me this. Who was the most awesome offensive force basketball has ever seen?"

"Michael Jordan."

"Damnit, Ryan, work with me here."

"Well, he was."

"Okay wise ass. Who was the most horrible free throw shooter in the NBA to be MVP four times?"

"Wilt Chamberlain. What's your point."

"What made that possible?"

"Tell me."

"For seven years, the Sixer's coaching staff spent hours and hours trying to improve Wilt's free throw technique because he was killing them on the foul line. He'd become such a liability, everybody was wanting to let him go, but Alex Hannum, who probably woke up at two in the morning like I just did, decided to try one last thing. Remember what it was?"

"Yeah, he let him shoot fouls granny-style and turned him into a rebounder."

Grady leaned into the receiver. "Correctamundo. One night at two in the morning he finally got the message in the Petri dish. The dish said, 'Quit wasting your time on Wilt's free throws, Alex. He's never going to get better. Concentrate on what he's good at…his offensive capabilities under the basket.'

"Voilà! Wilt Chamberlain was the very first person to score a hundred points in a single game and it will never, ever happen again. Sixers?! Sixty-Eight-to-Thirteen, the best record in league history at the time, and Chamberlain?! Most. Valuable. Player. Four. Times.

"So, what do you think? Am I making sense?"

Ryan's voice sounded amazed. "This is scary, Grady, but I think you are."

There was a pause while they both digested the magnitude of it all.

Finally, Ryan spoke. "So, what are you going to do with this revelation?"

"I don't know. I'll call you and let you know. All I'm sure of is that I've finally found my *hard thing*."

There was sort of a stunned pause on the line, then Ryan said, "I'm not even going to *try* to figure out what you mean by that, Redwine. Call me back when you can make some sense—

"I'm going to. I will."

"But make it after one o'clock. Please."

Grady was so excited, he leaped out of bed and rushed to Mary's office. Without hesitation, he stood beside her desk, placed his hand on her Bible, and with a voice resolute and unwavering, began:

"I solemnly swear that no matter how complicated, no matter how crazy making, no matter the sacrifice or consequences..." He dug his feet deeper into the carpet and centered his stance. "I'm going to do my best to help these kids...and..." Grady wanted to continue but the emotion of the moment seemed to catch in his throat. He tried hard to swallow it down, but was so overcome, he could only manage to whisper, "Amen."

WEEK FIVE

MONDAY
February 4, 2019-Morning

When Grady woke up that morning, it dawned on him that he was supposed to get his picture taken that day. Thank heavens he got a haircut yesterday…he could hide the top of his head with a hat, but his neck would have looked a disgrace.

He cringed when he pulled on that horrible green shirt Margaret gave him on Friday. At least it was a decent golf shirt and seemed to fit okay. He checked it out in the mirror. "Well, I guess I won't have to worry about going hunting and get mistaken for a moose."

He left home a little early and stopped by to get his coffee on the way to the bus lot and when Minnie appeared at the window, she looked a little startled before she greeted him.

He grinned. "Like my new shirt?"

"Uh, well, uh…"

"School picture day today."

She laughed, "Need some espresso?"

"No, I don't think so. I already glow in the dark."

###

Grady parked in the bus lot and opened up the bus, then sipped at his coffee and waited for Clara. When she climbed on board, she took one look at him and chuckled. "Nice shirt."

He pointed to his pocket. "Logo, even."

"Wow! Nice haircut too. I'm impressed! So, what's the occasion?"

"Publicity department. Taking pictures today. All us drivers gotta match." He started up the bus. "We're going to look like a bunch of grasshoppers driving around town all day."

"Or a swarm of locusts."

"Yeah, if they take a group shot—except I think locusts are more brownish."

"Does it glow in the dark?"

"Can't say for sure, but when I got up at midnight to use the facilities, I noticed I didn't need a light."

She settled into her seat. "So, who's riding today?"

"Everyone this morning but Sonti. I think he'll be with us this afternoon, though."

"He probably heard about your shirt and didn't want to miss it."

They pulled into the Hamilton property, laughing, and saw Prissy waiting on the sidewalk for them.

Clara squinted forward. "Wow. Our little girl is eager today."

After Clara hustled down and brought her onto the bus, Prissy slid into place behind Grady filled with excitement.

"I am totally amped, Mister Redwine."

"Oh? Tell me about it."

"I got the paperwork all filled out for my next 4K and I can hardly wait."

"Wow. That's great! What got you interested in racing, Prissy?"

"I don't really remember how it began. All I know is I love it. I get out there at the starting line in the middle of the crowd, and everybody's so glad to see each other again. And we talk about the race and our strategy; not about how come I'm in a chair. They only see me, Mister Redwine, me... a real competitor. And then, when they shoot the starting gun, I'm suddenly floating. I'm racing down the road feeling free," she said, raising her arms wide above her head. "Just free."— She shifted in her chair. —But my other favorite part is that you don't have to finish first to win. Everyone competes against the course and themselves. Just finishing is winning. And next year you can win better if you beat your time."

Prissy rearranged her blankets. "I have three certificates all saved up to surprise my daddy when he gets back from protecting America. This new one will make four. I do a race every Father's Day. That's my present."

"I'm sure he's very proud of you."

"I hope so. I know I'm proud of him. He's an American hero, you know."

"When was the last time you saw him?"

"I don't remember. My Mama told me I was just a baby."

"Oh."

"Before my Mama went to live with Jesus and they gave me up to the State, she told me she wrote him a letter telling him to be careful because we needed him. She said right now, we have to sacrifice, but someday soon the war will be over, and he will come and get me. He's going to take me to California to live with him."

"That's so great. I hope it's really soon."

"Sometimes I worry though. I wonder, will I remember him? Will he remember me?"

"I bet he will."

"My Mama said she told him I would carry a red balloon when I went to meet him so he would know for sure it was me. Mama gave me one to keep in my drawer."

"That's a great idea."

Her voice grew wistful. "Sometimes when I go to bed, I dream about seeing him, and it's so real, I expect him to be standing right beside me when I wake up. But he never is. Has anything like that ever happened to you, Mister Redwine?"

Mary's face flashed through Grady's mind. "Oh yes. Yes, it has."

"It hurts, doesn't it."

"It's the worst."

"I have lots of questions for my daddy. My Mama said to save them up and one day I'll get a chance to ask him. So, I have a notebook, and I write them down...like if he still loves Mommy and if he knows how I caught the Scoliosis."

Grady fought against the lump in his throat. "That's a good idea too."

"Do you think maybe you could go to the race and take my picture at the finish line so I can keep it for him?"

"Absolutely. We'll be there, won't we, Miss Clara?"

Clara swiped at her eyes. "Of course we will. Just tell us when and where."

The bus fell silent until they pulled up to the dorm to get J.D. He climbed onto the stairs but stopped short halfway up. "Gween. You have a gween shut on today."

Grady smiled. "Yes, I do. It's my new bus driver shirt."

"But you always weah blue."

"That's true. I do." Grady kind of posed a little. "Whaddaya think?"

"I think it is a weally ugly shut. You look like a cahtoon."

Grady and Clara cracked up. Clara shrugged and said, "Ask J.D. a question—get an honest answer."

Grady smiled. *A really honest answer.*

J.D. wasn't finished. "Do you have to weah it?"

"Afraid so."

"Oh bwuthuh."

Bennie paused when he saw Grady and scanned him up and down but was polite and didn't say anything.

Grady turned in his seat and watched Bennie roll into place. "Go ahead, Bennie. Let me have it. Everybody else has."

"I'm not ready yet. I have to give it some thought."

The rest of the trip was filled with shirt jokes and spotting other grasshoppers driving past. At school, Bennie finally came alive. "Okay...okay. I've got it. The perfect thing to say."

Grady opened the door. "Let us have it."

"No shoes, that shirt, no service."

Afternoon

All the kids were wearing their Willy Wizard gear when they emerged from the building that afternoon. They frolicked joyfully around on the grass for a while, waving wands and pretending to fly while they worked their way toward the bus.

Clara watched them and smiled. "That would make a good picture for P.R."

Rising above the joyous chaos came a succession of startling screams from inside the building that grew increasingly louder until their source was finally revealed.

Sonti.

Mister Wilson looked like he'd been through a war when he appeared in the doorway pushing a wheelchair containing the firmly anchored, outraged child swaddled in his purple blanket.

Sonti's head was thrown back, eyes squeezed shut against the sun, shrieking like an endless fingernail scratch on a blackboard as he struggled to break free.

Shivers shot through Grady's body.

Hair rose high on the back of his neck.

He gritted his teeth and turned toward Clara, forcing his voice to sound calm. "Looks like it's going to be one of those days."

"Loooks liiike."

Mister Wilson parked the chair beside the lift; leaned over and locked the wheels. "Okay big boy. Settle down. You're on your way home now."

Grady went out to meet them. "Need help?"

At the sound of Grady's voice, Sonti's eyes flew open and, as if someone suddenly jerked out his power cord, he fell silent and sat there, gawking at Grady's shirt.

Prissy's voice drifted its way from the lawn. "Looks like Sonti hates your shirt too, Mister Redwine."

Howls of laughter swirled around them.

Grady held out his arms. "Evvv-ry-body's got an opinion."

Mister Wilson smiled, then shifted his focus back to Sonti. "He's been upset ever since he got back from the doctor today. I had to keep him sitting on my lap half the afternoon—he was hurting himself."

Sonti began to struggle again. Mister Wilson steadied the chair. "His Mom knows we're coming. I think we should just leave him in the chair to ride and take him up the lift. He's calmed down enough for me to unwrap, so—"

His sentence remained unfinished because a young man with a Nikon camera appeared from behind the bus. He got the look on his face of someone walking in on a kidnapping.

Grady waved him over. "Everything's okay here, son. Come on over."

"Uh. I'm Roary? I'm the photographer?"

Clara took charge and gathered the other kids. "Why don't ya'll go up there on the lawn and let this nice man take your picture."

Roary hesitated. "Can the robot go on the grass? I was told to get the robot."

J.D. became indignant. "That is *not* a wobot. That is Bennie. He is a *boy*."

Roary grew a little wide-eyed and took a small step backward. "Uh, the picture is supposed to be beside the bus?"

Grady left Sonti with Mister Wilson and Clara to handle, then took charge. "This isn't a good time, son. Let's all gather up by the door. Bennie, you stay on the sidewalk and the rest of you uh, just-stand-around-him."

"But they're supposed to be able to read the..."

Grady pulled the magnetic number off the side of the bus and handed it to Prissy. "Variety is a good thing, Roary. She'll be in the picture holding the number. We're going to the door."

"I'll get in trouble. All the pictures are supposed to be same."

"I'll make a phone call. They'll understand."

Roary looked nervously in Sonti's direction. "Is—is he on this bus?"

"Yes, he is."

"Should he be in the picture?"

Wouldn't Margaret love that?

He started steering Roary toward the door. "I don't think it would be a good idea to include him today. P.R. will understand."

Roary finally gave in and started directing like a real photographer: "Okay then, let's put the girl in front? You boys stand behind her and smile? Okay, now all of you spread out then point your wands at each other? Okay, now point your wands at the camera? Okay—"

Grady ran out of patience. "Please. Last picture, Roary. This isn't an art book we're talking about here. We've got to get these kids home."

Roary looked his direction. "Do you want to be in the picture?"

"That would be no."

"Just one? Please? They want to show the shirts…soooo..."

"Will you leave after that?"

"Yes. Absolutely."

Grady moved in behind the group and pasted on a plastic smile.

Roary aimed the camera. "Okay, on three? Wuhhhhnnnn—toooo—thrrrrrr..."

Grady's patience hit the wall. "Okay. We're done."

Halfway down the sidewalk, he took pity on the kid and turned back. "Thank you, Roary. You did a great job." He turned back to the kids. "Say thank you to Roary, everyone."

"Thaaank youuu."

"You did a good job."

"We had fuuun."

Roary waved. "Don't forget to make the calls?"

"I won't. Don't worry. Everything's going to be okay."

Mister Wilson was gone, and Sonti was asleep in the chair when they returned to the bus.

Clara met them at the top of the stairs. "Shhhhhh—tippy-toes, everyone."

She didn't have to tell anyone twice.

TUESDAY
February 5, 2019-School Closed

Grady had been awakened by thunder and the heavy pounding of rain long before he heard the ding and saw the light flash on in his phone. He groped around for his reading glasses and squinted at the screen.

School Closure Notification
Dates: *Tuesday, February 5, and Wednesday, February 6*
Dear East High School Community,
Due to a lightning strike that has caused significant damage to the school's heating system, classes at East High School will be canceled for the following periods:
Tuesday, February 5: *All classes are canceled.*
Wednesday, February 6: *Morning classes are canceled. Weather permitting, classes will resume at* **1:00 PM** *on* **February 6.**
Please Note:
No lunch will be served on Wednesday, February 6.
Parents and guardians are encouraged to plan accordingly for these schedule changes.
We will provide updates and additional details as they become available. Thank you for your understanding and cooperation as we address this unexpected situation.

Wow! Bonus! He hated running his route in a downpour before sunrise... kids racing for the bus in the dark... so dangerous.

Grady placed his glasses and phone on the bed beside him and punched at his pillow, intending to go back to sleep. An hour later, he was staring at the ceiling still wide awake.

He finally gave up and headed for the living room hoping he could sleep in his chair. Halfway down the hall, his plan screeched to a halt when a low rumbling shook the house, and he was plunged into darkness.

Swell.

He managed to feel his way to the recliner and locate the emergency lantern he kept nearby, but he hadn't been seated for five seconds before his stomach started demanding some coffee. He knew the drive-thru was open all night, but they were on the same power grid he was, so they probably wouldn't be serving.

Who'd want to go out in this mess, anyhow.

His eyes drifted toward the kitchen. There was coffee in there—instant coffee— probably older than he was— but it might still be good. Maybe a couple of teaspoons in some really hot tap water...

Uh, no. He wanted coffee, but he wasn't crazy.

Grady resigned himself to drinking a warm diet cola he found stuck in a corner of the cooler, then out of boredom, adjusted the lantern and began casually flipping through the notebook where the goals from the Milers meeting were recorded. Today would probably be a good time to start doing some planning.

He scratched his beard awhile, mulling everything over. Grady realized that he didn't know anything about *Special Needs*, but he believed he'd created enough winning strategies for championship games to be able to fumble around and come up with one for this project too.

He found a pen and began by writing the name of each child at the top of an empty page and spent an hour putting together a specific goal statement for each one.

You can't get there if you don't know where you're going.

Grady always looked for quick wins first when he started a project, so he decided to start with J.D. He had a definite deadline, enough determination to succeed, and could work well on his own. He put Prissy second. Her goal was straight-forward and she was fairly independent too.

He pictured Bennie sort of floating around in the atmosphere, always there, ready to pounce when he found something right for him. And that left Sonti for last...but not least.

What Bennie and Sonti had to accomplish was more long-term and complicated and Grady had to get up to speed himself before he could help them in any meaningful way.

He put his pen down and stretched, feeling satisfied. *Done and done.*

He laid back in his chair and settled in. He could sleep now.

WEDNESDAY
February 6, 2019-Afternoon

Grady was awakened early that morning by a text from the Administration. Even though the storm had been forecasted for two days, it passed early, so school was officially declared back in session for the afternoon.

He decided to go to work a little early in case something had to be done to get the bus ready. The sun had been up for most of the morning so everything on the lot was dry. He decided to give the windows a once-over and was finishing up when Clara arrived. He waited for her to climb onboard and settle in then decided to catch up on their agenda.

"I'm assuming we're still on for Citizenship today. What are we doing?"

"We're taking the kids to Westlake High to work on a task for Kiwanis. Someone from the Club goes there early and litters up the tennis courts, then they pay us five dollars each to collect the trash and bag it. It's a really good program—it's safe—and it's in a perfect location. The courts have big, tall mesh fences and a gate that locks, so the kids can just roam around as much as they want to. It's especially great for Sonti because he can just be Sonti, and we don't have to worry about him climbing over the fence or bolting away."

"What do we do with BennieToo?"

"We have to leave him behind for this one. The Wi-Fi signal is too weak."

"We'll miss him, but it sounds like fun."

"This task is everyone's favorite. The court has a basketball hoop at each end, so we take a couple of balls along with us and the kids play when they're done working. I think you'll be a little amazed today."

"By what?"

"Not telling. It's a surprise."

"I hate surprises."

"I think you'll like this one." She was silent for a couple of minutes, then continued on. "The only downside of going to Westlake is the marching band. They practice in the adjoining field and the kids have to transport their instruments from the school to the field themselves. They're supposed to take the long way around, but you know kids. There's a lot of lazy ones who take a shortcut past the tennis court. Annnnd, when they see a short bus, they feel obligated to be as obnoxious and loud as possible—there's a big bunch of them— drums—cymbals—trumpets. It's bedlam and it drives our kids crazy."

"Have you complained?"

"We've asked about it, but they're quick to point out that it's their school not ours, and that particular period is called *band practice*. They made it pretty clear that if we wanted to go somewhere else, it would be okay with them.

"I have to admit they have a point. Even if the kids tiptoe by us, it will be noisy ten minutes later when they begin marching anyway."

"Well, maybe they'll cancel practice today. After the storm, they'll be sloshing through mud."

"Unlikely, but we can hope."

###

After Clara and Grady picked up the gang at school, they headed for Westlake.

"We get to do trash today, Mistow Wedwine."

Prissy chimed in. "And play basketball."

"Sounds like a good time to me!"

Westlake was only a mile or two down the road from where the kids went to school. It was an upscale private school in a park setting with a pool, a track field, a football stadium and a tennis facility.

Grady pulled into the main drive and parked beside a large oak tree in the green space next to the tennis courts and opened the doors.

J.D. galumphed down the stairs to wait at the lift for Prissy and Sonti, who Mr. Wilson had strapped into a wheelchair again as a precautionary measure.

Grady unloaded the trash collection equipment and two basketballs, then followed along behind everyone.

"Fortunately, the sun dried the rain off the pavement, so we'll be able to collect trash today." Clara obviously had everything in hand, so he ended up lounging against the wall in a shady spot to watch.

J.D. wheeled Sonti to a spot on the court and opened a trash bag. Miss Clara handed out simple grabbers to help them lift the trash safely and take it to a tub in front of Sonti, whose job it was to place it in the plastic bag.

Sonti's eyes remained riveted on the basketball hoop as if he was searching for something while he waited for paper deliveries. He only reluctantly turned away when asked a question or was handed some paper to put in the trash by one of the other children.

After he finished filling his bag and turned it over to Clara, J.D. retrieved a ball from the bin and placed it in Sonti's lap. The two of them dodged carefully around the tennis nets and avoided cracks in the cement, wheeling joyfully toward one of the hoops. J.D. parked the wheelchair and took back the ball so Sonti could stand up and make his way to the free throw line.

Clara joined Grady at the fence. "Watch this."

On the foul line, Sonti adjusted the purple blanket on his head and accepted the ball back from J.D. He dribbled it twice and spun it awhile then looked at the ground and began circling around like a puppy chasing his tail.

Clara scrunched up her nose and forehead. "We have never been able to figure out why he does that."

Grady chuckled. "He might be looking for the nail."

"The nail?"

"There's usually a nail at the middle of the free throw line...sometimes just a painted dot. Players use it to line up their shooting foot."

Sonti stopped spinning. Grady smiled. *He got it.*

Sonti's tongue twisted through his lips and moved from side-to-side as he carefully pointed his feet in the direction of the basket.

He fiddled with the blanket and tugged at the shoulder seams of his shirt. He dribbled twice in front then once to the side and wiped his forehead with his elbow.

The kid has more ticks than a clock.

At long last, Sonti glanced toward the basket, ducked his head and unceremoniously side-armed the ball through the hoop.

Grady's head snapped back. "How-did-he-do-that?"

Prissy cheered. Clara chuckled. "Told ya you'd be surprised. It's a mystery to everyone."

"Does he have relatives...cousins?"

"Nope."

"Neighbors? "

"Don't think so. Why?"

"I saw a hoop in..." Sudden shivers shot down his spine. *The tie-out cable.* He finished his sentence, "...their driveway."

Clara skipped a beat or two before she answered. "Mmmm. He spends most of his time at the Shelter these days and I don't think they teach basketball in his unit there, either."

J.D. chased down the ball and moved Sonti to the side court.

Grady watched Sonti spin the ball, readjusting. *He's searching for its center.*

Clara grabbed Grady's elbow. "Uh oh. Here comes bedlam."

A loud clattering approached from the direction of the main building. It grew in volume as a parade of instruments rumbled by, base drums pounding, trumpets blaring, symbols clashing.

Prissy squealed and covered her headset. "Make it stop, Miss Clara. Make it stop!"

Clara rushed over to console her. "Deep breaths. Deep breaths."

Grady immediately returned his attention to Sonti and prepared to chase him down in case he made a bolt for the gate, but Sonti hadn't even flinched. He was as calm as if he were alone in a bubble without any sense of space or time. He remained focused…completely absorbed in what he was doing.

Grady had never seen Sonti so peaceful and relaxed as he shifted his eyes between the ball and the hoop, obviously measuring the arc of the ball.

Eventually, Sonti turned away from the hoop and began fidgeting through his routine. Finally ready, he casually side-armed the ball right into the center of the net.

Swish.

J.D. moved Sonti again. Another side-arm hit.

How can this happen? He throws like a damn catapult. He never stands still and has no follow-through at all.

Grady walked over to J.D. and said softly, "Try taking him out to mid-court."

Once again, Sonti fidgeted and dribbled the ball, but this time he side-armed a throw that hit the rim and bounced away. J.D. chased it down and Sonti tried again. This time, the ball fell short.

J.D. chased the ball and shouted, "He must be tired." He bounced the ball a couple of times then playfully threw it to Grady. "Try it Coach."

Propelled by a little blast from his past, Grady popped his neck left and right, drove to the basket and executed a perfect underarm lay-up.

God that felt good.

Wild applause broke out from the kids.

Grady smiled…took a bow.

As Grady walked with the kids back to the bus, J.D. sidled up beside him. "Why did you do that Mistow Wedwine?"

"Do what?"

"Cwack you neck."

"I don't know. It just seems to make me feel… ready."

"Oh."

The kids piled onto the bus and prepared to head home. Grady noticed a peace around Sonti when he settled into his seat. His usual fidgety, jerky demeanor was gone, and for someone who never quite seemed at rest, slept soundly.

###

The kids all slept during the route home after Westlake. Grady dropped them off at the usual destinations then returned to Transportation and parked. He switched off the bus and turned toward Clara. "Sonti's family doesn't *have* a dog. Do they."

She swallowed hard. "No. I don't believe they do."

"Miss Clara, how did Sonti end up at the Shelter?"

She sank down in the seat across from him. "Please don't judge his mother, Grady. She's an enterprising, extremely hard-working woman who loves him deeply."

"Yes. Yes, it shows all over her. There is no doubt about that."

"Sonti's files are sealed and confidential. And we aren't supposed to discuss our children or their issues with others…" —She rose from her seat and continued to talk as she began packing up her belongings. — "…but I promise you, anything that may have happened and everything she may have done to care for him and keep him safe was motivated either by love or utter desperation."

She paused at the top of the steps. "Hope you believe me."

He replied with a sincere, "I do," but continued to feel haunted by the tie-out cable in Sonti's driveway as he drove home. Shooting free throws was a skill that had to be developed—and practiced—it wasn't as simple as learning to sit down in a chair. There were talented athletes who couldn't do what Sonti just did.

###

Grady sat in his recliner reflecting on what happened with Sonti at Westlake. If he were a more religious man, he would have sworn that he had witnessed a miracle of Biblical proportions that day.

He reflected back on what Coach Riley told him about Sonti and track. He had the talent of a champion to run, but not an ounce of ability to work as a team. Now that Grady knew Sonti was also a basket-making machine, he'd start working with that.

A story Shaquille O'Neal told about Kobe Bryant in an interview one time when they both played for the Lakers drifted into Grady's mind: "I told

Kobe, 'There's no 'I' in team,' and Kobe told me, 'No, but there is an 'M' and an 'E.'"

Sonti wasn't a team player either, but he had chosen basketball as his Miler's goal. If basketball worked like baseball where you could use him as a pinch hitter, it would be easy to find a team that would let him play for a night or two. But basketball was a team sport through and through. Individual efforts like passing, rebounding, and scoring— while valued— have to be combined with actions from other people to make a difference.

Then, out of the blue, it hit him: ***scoring***! Free throws! The *Half-Court Shot Contest!*.

Who'd ever dream you could find an individual effort in a team sport? He looked toward the ceiling and threw up his arms.

*My mother thanks you. My father thanks you. And **I** thank you.*

There were a hundred things that needed to be done to get Sonti ready. First, though, he had to get his hands on a copy of that Flyer.

THURSDAY
February 7, 2019-Afternoon

There were no feelings of nostalgia when Grady rushed down the hallway of the high school toward the Head Coach's office—only dead determination.

Unfortunate parking logistics forced him to enter the building too far away from the boy's locker room to go through his usual ritual in the hallway.

He rushed past the poster-filled wall and homed in on the table outside the Coach's door where he knew he'd find a few flyers and a stack of brochures containing information on the upcoming Comets' Half-Court contest. He grabbed a couple of each off the stack and headed for home to study them.

Grady was careful not to change anything else in his usual routine. He was superstitious enough to feel nervous already about starting on his Sonti mission without going through the hall ritual.

For the majority of his adulthood, Grady lived the predictable, well-structured existence of a Basketball Coach. From six in the morning until nine at night, his calendar was packed with routine activities and lots of people. Except for the highs and lows of competition, his life had a steady rhythm to it, and he liked it that way.

When everything went to Hell after Mary's diagnosis and he was walking around in a fog for nine months, his routine—his systems—were what kept him alive. His coach's mind preferred to call it "Conscious Goal-Directed Behavior," but if anyone stopped to think seriously about it, sticking to a routine was just a way to make it through another day without going off the deep end.

Over the years, he learned that living a predictable life was surprisingly efficient. It didn't take long for Minnie to realize that it was fruitless for her to correct him every time he ordered his *Large, Double Expresso with lots of cream*, so the two of them finally agreed that she'd just brew up a large strong one with extra cream when he requested "the usual."

The guys at the pizza parlor recognized his voice on the phone and recited his order for him before he had to place one; waiters at upscale restaurants knew he wanted a ribeye — rare; and when he went through the drive-thru to pick up his dinner tonight, he knew they would have two bacon cheeseburgers, a large order of fries and a chocolate shake packed up and waiting for him at the window.

He picked up his dinner and stole a couple of fries from the bag to chomp on as he scanned through one of the *Half-Court* flyers at stop signs, composing a mental to-do list as he worked his way through the rules.

*Age Limit: You must be at least 18 years
to be eligible for the contest.*

Whoah. How old is Sonti? He had no idea. It was tough with these kids. You couldn't judge their age by what grade they were in.

Sonti had a little fuzz on his chin and along his jaw line. He had to be at least fifteen. But nineteen? He didn't know. This could be a deal-breaker, but he'd worry about that when he had to.

He pulled into the driveway then made one of those quick motions people make without thinking to open the garage door. He pulled inside, still adding things to his mental list.

Grady had three ways to carry things: right hand, left hand, and lips. Mary teased him constantly about looking look like a dog carrying a sock around all the time. But with the load he had today, he had no choice. The flyers ended up in his mouth.

He managed to balance everything without spilling when he pushed the button to close the garage door and walk up the two steps to the kitchen. He plunked everything on the counter and kept reading while making his coffee:

*Note: You must not be a current or former
professional, semiprofessional, college
and/or Olympic basketball player or Coach.*

No problem there.

*Note: You are not eligible if you have been a
current or former high school basketball player
or Coach within the past 5 years.*

I hope that doesn't apply to sponsors too. He made a mental note to ask.

When finished brewing, he grabbed the cheeseburger bag, the brochures, and the coffee then headed for his recliner. He placed his dinner on the coffee table and sat down. Then froze.

He was in the Livingroom.

He looked at his drink on the table. *I didn't stop at the drive-thru.*

He looked at the floor inside the front door where he kept his stuff. *Empty.*
How did I get here? What have I done?
Grady tried to recall how this happened and couldn't remember a thing.
He ran his hand across his beard and brought himself back to reality. *You came in through the garage, Grady. You made coffee in the kitchen.*
Wow.
He leaned back in his chair. *Wow.*

FRIDAY-SUNDAY
February 8-10, 2019-Friday Morning

Clara was jubilant when she met Grady at the bus that morning. "Boy, do I have news for you. Miss Grundel is finally retiring from teaching. She's getting a staff job of some sort."

"Wow. How long has she been in the job?"

"Fifteen years or so."

"I'd say it's time."

"I'll say." She tried to hand him a sheet of paper. "Here's the announcement."

He waved her off. "Gotta do my pre-trip."

"Ok. I'll read. You work."

She settled onto the edge of her seat and read. "After ten years of dedicated service as *Department Chair* of the *Special Education Program*, Helen Grundel has set her eyes on a new career in *Administration*.

"She has been a devoted coach and mentor to *Special Needs* students her entire career, as well as a trusted and valuable member of the *Cabinet* representing *District Four*.

"Miss Grundel is a graduate of *Vanderbilt University* yada yada *Teacher-of- the Year* yada yada. A farewell luncheon is planned... "

She stopped and looked at Grady. "Wanna go?"

"Really do, but I've got plans for the flu that day. When is it?"

She returned to the announcement. "Her last day will be March 18."

"Got it. I'll write it down—feel feverish already."

Friday Afternoon

Grundel was nowhere to be seen when they arrived at *Indy's* that day. Grady leaned toward Clara. "She's probably just gonna ride her teaching job out at her desk."

Clara obviously agreed but offered a cautious approach to the day. "We should wait awhile to order, anyway—show a little respect. But in the meantime, I've been reading about a contest they're going to have at the school, and I thought it would be fun for the Milers to participate. She reached into the bag she carried and pulled out Twisty Puzzles for everyone. "*I thought we deserved a head start.*"

The kids went bonkers: "Ooo I love these!"; "Twisty Puzzles!"; "This is so coool, Miss Clara."

Even Sonti seemed intrigued.

She looked at the screen of her computer. Bennie was streaming that day. "Did your Mom give you yours, Bennie?"

"Yes, she did. Thaaaank yoooouuu."

"You are most welcome."

Soon the room was filled with the loud, ratchety Tchk- Tchk- Tchking sounds of kids manipulating the layers of their cubes, as they attempted to solve the puzzle.

J.D.'s fingers flew around his cube, and he frowned constantly as he concentrated. "Our computah teachuh told us about this contest today. The contest will last two days: The fuhst day is Monday when they give evwybody in school a Twisty and ten dollahs to students who can solve one. The second day is Tuesday when they give five moh dollahs to the puhson who can finish it fastest. I am going to pwactice all weekend and be the fuhst one to finish and the fastest!"

Prissy leaned Grady's way. "Jason Weatherly bet J.D. five dollars that he could beat him."

J.D. worked away even faster. "I am going to beat that Jason Weathuhly. I will have his five dollahs in my pocket if it is the last thing I do."

Grady got enthusiastic also. "I bet they would teach you how to solve it on the U-Tube, don'tcha think?"

Clara elbowed him in the side. "We're teaching cheating now, are we?"

"No! We're teaching self-motivation and initiative."

"Sure, we are."

"Miss Clara. You know J.D. would have thought of going to the U-Tube all on his own, anyway."

"Uhhh Huhhh."

As Grady predicted, Miss Grundel was a no-show, so they just ordered, ate and headed home.

Back at the bus barn, Grady had to admit that he'd had it up to here with Twisty Puzzles. "Sounds like an invasion of locusts."

Clara chuckled. "Miss Miller is probably going to kill me."

"I suspect you're right."

She packed up her things. "What are you going to do this weekend?"

"I found a bunch of last year's *March Madness* specials the other night, and I'm going to binge-watch them the whole weekend. How about you?"

C.A. Caldwell

She rolled her eyes. "In-laws. All weekend."
He chuckled. "You need say no more."

WEEK SIX

MONDAY
February 11, 2019-Morning

When Grady arrived at Prissy's wing of the dorm that morning, he pulled into the curb, waved Clara up to the front of the bus and motioned toward the front door. "Look up there."

Clara stretched over his shoulder, removed her reading glasses, and squinted in that direction. "Is that Miss Miller wearing Prissy's headphones?"

Grady chuckled. "Yep. Pink feathers and all."

"Well, that's a picture to draw to."—Clara watched awhile longer. — "She looks a little frazzled."

"I'll say."

Eventually, Miss Miller reached into a grocery bag, withdrew a small square object, took off the headphones, and placed both of them in Prissy's backpack as she passed through the doorway.

"Ohhh, Grady. I think she confiscated the Twisty toys."

They watched Prissy zoom toward them down the driveway. "Guess we'll find out soon enough."

One thing was for sure: Prissy wasn't her usual cheerful self when she arrived at the bus; and she didn't have much to say to Clara, either, while on the lift. She just pulled her sound suppressors out of her backpack and fiddled with them while Clara anchored her in.

Grady attempted to be cheerful. "What's up, Prissy?"

"Miss Miller borrowed these to wear all weekend cuza the Twisty Puzzle noise...said it was either that or shoot herself. I didn't mind except she got my feathers all steamed up when she did the dishes..."

Grady didn't have to look at Clara to see the guilt on her face.

Prissy continued preening the feathers while she completed her news. "She said she was going to buy a couplea drums and have them delivered to your boys, Miss Clara, so they could start onea those garage rock bands."

Clara smiled. "Too late—already happened. They practice every Saturday."

Grady laughed and looked at her in the mirror. She appeared little proud when she said, "They're actually getting quite good…in a headbanger, loud rock kinda way. I go to the gym."

Grady released the brake and headed around the building for Sonti. "How did you do with your cube, Prissy?"

"I had fun, but I gave it to J.D. so he could beat that Jason Weatherly."

"Why did J.D. need two cubes?"

"Not sure. He said it was for the sake-uh insurance."

There was an Aide waiting for them at the bottom of the driveway in front of Sonti's wing of the dorm when they pulled around the corner. He smiled and waved them on.

Grady looked at Clara. "No Sonti today. Wonder why."

"I know he was with his Mom over the weekend. Maybe she wanted to keep him another day."

"She's been really good about texting me." He glanced at his phone. "Didn't get one this time."

"Maybe it was a last-minute thing."

"Maybe."

When they pulled around the corner to pick up J.D., he climbed aboard brandishing a completed cube. "Look Mistow Wedwine! I got it! I solved the puzzle."

"Wow, J.D. Congratulations."

Prissy watched as he passed by and headed down the aisle. "Is that your cube or mine?"

"This one's mine. I put yohs in my backpack foe inshuance."

Miss Clara followed him to his seat. "Why do you need insurance, J.D.?"

"So I can pwove I solved it in case I foeget how to do it in class."

Grady spoke over his shoulder. "How long did it take you to do it?"

"Six owuhs to get the stickuhs pwied off and eight owuhs to get them glued back on wight."

What?!

Grady's eyes shot to the mirror. "Whatever made you think to do that?"

"YouTube."

Grady could feel Clara's "told you so" drilling into him. He tried a quick Hail Mary. "That's not how you solve the puzzle, J.D."

"Well, it's not the twa-di-shun-al way, but it wuhks."

"But isn't that cheating?"

"No. It's not cheating. I wouldn't cheat, Mistow Wedwine. The wules say you get ten dolluhs if you get the design all lined up wight on evwy side. They don't say you have to tuhn the watchets to do it."

"So, what are you going to do if they ask you to solve it again in class?"

"Oh, I figuhd out how to do it that way too. This is just fo inshuance so I get twenty-five dollahs—five fo being fuhst, ten fo getting the design all lined up wight, and the vewy best of all, five fo beating that Jason Weathuhly."

"How fast can you do it the other—uh, traditional—way?"

"About five minutes."

"That's a great time, J.D."

"Not weally. A kid in Ahstwalia did it in awound five seconds. Next to him, I am a snail. That makes Jason Weathuhly pwobably a slug."

They laughed all the way to Bennie's house and when BennieToo came aboard, Grady asked how he did with his Twisty toy.

"Oh, I gave up after an hour or two. I got bored."

J.D. perked up. "That's a good sign. Maybe some of the othuh kids will give up too. It will be less competition."

Grady drove for a few minutes then glanced at J.D. in the mirror. "Maybe it would be a good idea to wait until everybody else gets their Twisties and have a chance to try before you turn in yours."

J.D. seemed to ponder the thought for a moment, then asked, "Why?"

"Because the one you got Friday might not count. They would say you had a head start so that one wouldn't count."

"Ohhhh. I see what you mean."

"Besides, I bet you can finish another one in class faster than everyone else anyway, because you've had so much practice…you can already solve it in five minutes."

"Pwobably. I will think about it."

Grady glanced at J.D. in the mirror. "One thing I can tell you for sure, J.D., is that it feels a lot better to know that you lost doing your best than to spend your whole life knowing you had to cheat to win."

They rode in silence a while then J.D. said, "If I lose, that Jason Weathuhly won't evuh let me fohget it."

"Then don't lose!"

After they let the kids off in the bus loop, Clara watched as they entered the building. "I'd say, J.D.'s on a mission."

"Sure is. Hope he wins…he has a win coming."

"Yes, but he's considering cheating."

"J.D. has his issues, but he's basically a good kid. Let's see how it all plays out and worry about what to do then."

Afternoon

J.D. wasn't lingering in the bushes that afternoon when Grady and Clara arrived at the school. He rushed right for the bus and flashed a ten-dollar bill in the air with a sly look on his face. "How do you think the Twisty Puzzle contest tuhned out Mistow Wedwine?"

Grady surveyed J.D.'s money display. "I think everything went well."

"Co-wect."

Clara helped buckle him in. "Did you need to use your insurance?"

"No. They gave us new messed up cubes and made us actually do it in class."

Prissy piped up. "J.D. was first to finish. He beat everybody—In—To—The—Grrrouuuund today. Tomorrow is the speed contest."

J.D. interrupted. "And I am going to be the fastest tomohwow too. I am going to pwactice all night."

Grady and Clara exchanged guilty glances.

Grady waited for J.D. to get settled into his seat before he walked down the aisle and stood beside him.

"I'm buckling, Mistoe Wedwine. I'm buckling."

Grady smiled. "I'm not here to check on buckling, J.D. I want to ask you a question."

"Okay."

"Do you think you could show me how to do the *research*?"

"The what?"

"You know, the *searching*. On my cell phone."

J.D. shook his head with obvious disappointment. "Mistow Wedwine, Mistow Wedwine, Mistow Wedwine. You have a Smaht Phone not a Cell Phone. Cell Phones don't such. You supposed to say, 'J.D., I need to such foe something. Would you show me how to such on my Smaht *Phone*?' And then I say, 'Yes I will.'"

"Ohhhkaaay. Do you want me to say that now?"

J.D. held out his hand. "Foe you I will make an exception today."

Grady put his phone in J.D.'s palm.

J.D. tilted the screen of the phone so they both could see it. "Fuhst, you-tap-this-then-tap-heuh-input-what-you-ah suching foe..." He looked at Grady. "What *ah* you sutching foe?"

"Brackets."

"Bwackets foe basketball oh bwackets foe hanging a shelf?"

"For basketball."

"Okay-put-bwackets-heah." His fingers flew on the screen. "Tap-such-up-heah. Then, when-you-want-to-go-back-push-this-button-at-the-bottom. Simple." He handed back the phone.

Grady stood there wide-eyed and bewildered, but the NCAA Brackets *did* appear on the screen, so he faked it and nodded.

A minute or two later, Grady reached into his shirt pocket and pulled out a pen, intending to ask J.D. to write it all down for him—just in case he forgot how.

Standing behind J.D., Clara gave Grady a warning finger wave...no...then mouthed, "He can't write."

J.D. put on his hoodie. "Don't hang up until you done suching, Mistow Wedwine. You too new to staht ovuh."

After Grady had settled back into his seat, Clara reached out for his phone. "Um, maybe I can help a little too." She swiped right several times and showed him the *Home Screen*.

"Just go to this screen and think CATS. See this compass-looking thing? Think 'C' for compass. Tap there. Now, think 'A.' That stands for AOL. Tap there. 'T' is for type..."

J.D.'s voice drifted from under his hoodie. "Input, Miss Clawa. Not type."

Clara mouthed, "type," then continued to say aloud, "up here in this box, *in-put* what you're looking for—in this case, that would be *brackets*—then over here, tap 'S' for *search*. To repeat, it's CATS: Compass, AOL." She mouthed *Type*, but said, "Input—then, search. That's all you need to know."

Grady gave her a wink. "Got it. C.A.T.S. with 'T' for 'Input.' Thank you both very much."

He released the brake and made plans just to forget about searching. He'd make his own brackets...photocopy the format from his completed ones from last year.

TUESDAY
February 12, 2019-Morning

Grady worked feverishly on his *March Madness* brackets until just after midnight the night before, so it wasn't easy to get up when the alarm went off at four. He wasn't finished completing them, of course—filling them out was a process—but he believed his left-over adrenaline with a boost from two lattes could get him fueled up for the day.

He cupped his hands; splashed his face with cold water; ran his nails through the scruff on his cheeks; swished some mouthwash around in his mouth and tilted his head back to gargle, then spit it out in the sink. After hiding his hair under his favorite cap, he rushed out the door to meet up with Clara and deliver his kids to school.

Grady heard Prissy and Clara discussing last night when they loaded her onboard that morning. Apparently Miss Miller had a Twisty victory dinner for J.D. the previous evening.

Prissy rolled in and parked behind him, then let out a loud yawn and continued her story. "...and now everyone in the house wants him to teach them. Miss Miller said J.D. probably should rest his wrist for a while, so she had everyone put their Twistie in a basket and let us stay up late last night to watch a movie.

She said this weekend; he could teach everyone outside in the yard if the weather is good and she would make us a picnic."

He and Clara exchanged smiles, then she put a blanket on Prissy's lap and tucked it around her.

Grady pulled the bus away from the curb and headed for J.D.'s wing as Clara continued the conversation. "So did everyone enjoy the movie?"

"Everybody did but J.D.. He wanted to practice his speed for the contest today."

J.D. was already waiting at the curb and leaped aboard quickly. "Mowning evwybody."

Clara greeted him at the top of the stairs. "Good morning, J.D. I hear you had a victory dinner last night..."—He went to his seat and opened his backpack then turned back toward her and answered, "Yes!"—Clara continued. "What did Miss Miller cook for you?"— "My favowite: poke chops and applesauce. And then we all watched a movie."—Clara finished the agenda. "...and you're going to have a picnic this weekend., I hear."

J.D. pulled out his computer and settled into his seat. "Well, we wuh. But not any moh. It just now got canceled."

"Oh? Why?"

Prissy whirled around in her chair. "Did Miss Miller find out you had two Twisties?"

"Yes. She discovuhed youhs in my pocket when she handed my coat to me."

"Oh brother. Thanks a lot, J.D. Now we're both in for it."

Clara glanced around. "I'm confused."

Prissy twisted back around in her chair. "Miss Miller said we could stay up late and watch a movie last night if we didn't play with our Twisties. She told everyone to leave theirs in a bowl on the hall table."

J.D. took over. "And we did."

Prissy gasped. "Nuh Uhhhhh. You didn't leave yours."

"I did too. I left *mine* like she told me to…I just didn't leave *yohs*."

Clara went to her seat and sat down. "So, what happened?"

The bus was suddenly silent. Clara prodded again. "JaayyyDeee. What happened?"

"On the way into the den to watch the movie, Miss Milluh asked evwyone if they had left *they* Twisty toy outside in the basket and evwybody told the truth and said, yes. Then we all watched the movie the way we wuh supposed to and went to bed."

"Annnnnndddd?"

"And I had to get weady foh the contest today…sooo, I hid unduh the covuhs and pwacticed…"—He hurried on. —"…but vewy slowwwly."

Prissy picked up the story. "Miss Miller always leaves the intercom on at night in case we have a emergency. It would be all quiet in the house, then suddenly, you'd hear a click-click-click sound in your room, sorta like water dripping, and everyone would burst out laughing because they knew it was J.D. practicing."

J.D. spoke again. "Miss Milluh would stick huh head into my woom evwy once in a while and listen, but I would pwetend to be asleep."

"She woked me up one time and asked if I had my Twisty. I told the truth and said no it was in the basket."

Clara spoke up. "JayyDeee. Shame on you. How could *no* be the truth?"

"Because I wasn't playing with my Twisty. I was *pwacticing* with *Pwissie's*.

"When she found it in my coat pocket this mohning while she was calling the plumbuh to find the leak and fix it, she canceled the picnic."

Lunch Break

February weather in Indiana was not conducive to teaching a gym class outside, so during his lunch break, Grady picked up the phone and dialed Charlie Carlson to see what he could do to fix the ridiculous practice of letting the kids wander around on the track for an hour each day.

"I need to ask a favor, Charlie. I have something important coming up for my kids and I need some gym time."

"How much gym time?"

"Every day. At least for an hour."

Charlie cleared his throat. "I'm looking at the schedule, Grady. We're completely booked."

"But the official school schedule you gave me calls for an hour of P.E. for my kids every day."

"That's on the upper track, Grady. Not downstairs."

"Just a corner and one hoop. That's all I need."

"I'm sorry, Grady, but it's impossible."

"Okay, half the floor one day a week."

"No can do. Coach Riley won't mix the groups."

"What you mean is, *my kids are distracting and not welcome*, is that it?"

There was complete silence at the other end.

Grady moved on. "How about full use of the track upstairs for an hour and a basket set up at regulation height on one end."

"Do you know how much those things cost?"

"Okay, full use of the track for an hour and you let me buy a driveway hoop and install it up there myself."

"What am I supposed to do with the rest of the kids?"

"They can—watch."

"Good luck with that one."

"So, it's a no?"

"Yes. It's a no."

"Non-negotiable—even for a good cause?"

"Sorry, Grady. I would do it if I could."

It was a lie, but he said, "I know," anyway.

"Have you called the Y? They might have some time. And the Salvation Army has a court. You might try there."

Grady hung up politely then stared at the phone and said, "Bastards."

Tuesday Afternoon

For the second day in a row, J.D. wasn't lingering in the bushes when Grady and Clara arrived at the school. He rushed right out the school door waving two five-dollar bills in the air, grinning from ear-to-ear. "How do you think the Twisty Puzzle contest tuhned out to-*day* Mistow Wedwine?"

Grady admired J.D.'s money display. "I think everything went well until you tried to collect from Jason Weatherly."

"Co-wect. He was so shoe he was going to win, he didn't bwing his money. He says he will bwing it tomowwow, but like Miss Milluh always says, 'I am not holding my bweath.'"

Grady heard Prissy bragging about J.D.'s performance when she rolled onto the lift. "He wiped the floor with that Jason Weatherly and leffft him innn the *dussst* today."

All J.D. had to say was, "I hope we get left-ovuhs tonight. I don't think Miss Milluh will cook fwesh poke chops foh me today 'cuz I'm pwobably gwounded again."

WEDNESDAY
February 13, 2019-Morning

After Grady delivered the kids that morning, he sat down at home with the intention of finding some gym time. He searched through the phone book, located the YMCA and dialed.

The call was answered: "It's a wonderful day at the YMCA. This is Millie. How can I help you?

"Well Millie! I'm hoping you can. My name is Grady Redwine and I'm working with a group of *Special Needs* children who need some gym time and I'm wondering how I can get on your calendar to see if we can line up some time."

"Well, let me pull up my calendar here and see what we have available. What time were you hoping for?"

Their school P.E. class is scheduled for one-twenty to two-fifteen. But we could probably work with any time after twelve-thirty."

"And what days of the week were you looking at?"

"Every school day, if possible, but we'll take about any day you have open."

"You're all members, I presume."

"I'm assuming we'll all have to join. There will be two adults and five children."

He heard keys clicking on a computer keyboard. Ok, for two adults and any number of dependents, it will cost ninety-five dollars to join and ninety-five dollars a month."

He'd foot the bill. It would be worth it. "That's fine."

"Okay, Good. So let me check the schedule and see what we can do. Ohhhhhh."

"What?"

"I forgot. We're starting *Adult Aerobics* and our *Mommie and Me* classes this week. The gymnasiums are completely booked until June."

Grady's heart sank. "Do you have any available time at all?"

"We have a half hour at nine A.M. twice a week."

"No can do. They're in class then. Well, thank you for trying, Millie. You've been very helpful. Have a wonderful day."

Time to go to Plan B. He hung up, reached for his old Rolodex and flipped around to the card containing the name and number of his buddy Mike Patterson...a Commander in the local Salvation Army.

Mike answered the phone himself. "Salvation Army. How can I help you today?"

"Hi Mike. This is Grady Redwine."

"As I live and breathe! How are you?"

"Doin' fine. Doin' fine."

"I was so sorry to hear about Mary, Grady. She was a wonderful woman."

"Thank you, Mike. I appreciate the thought."

"So, to what do I owe this honor?"

"I'm working with a group of *Special Needs* children..."

"Oh yes, I heard. You got a darn rotten deal, you ask me, Grady."

"Well thank you, Mike. I appreciate it. Anyhow, I've got to find a way to get these kids some gym time and I'm wondering if you might have some time available over there."

"I'd be happy to help you if I could, my friend, but we had a leak in our roof last month and it completely ruined the floor—warped the Hell out of it—leaked into the basement—warped that floor too. We've had to shut down and replace the whole thing. We're wrangling with insurance right now and have started a fund drive so we can pay the deductible. Wanna throw in a few bucks?"

Grady rolled his head left and right, thinking. "Sure, Put me down for a C note."

"Great! Cash or credit?"

Grady opened his wallet, pulled out his credit card and gave Mike the number.

"Thank you, Grady. Thanks so much. That's very generous of you. Thank heavens for the Redwines. You always come through. I'll call you and keep you updated on the gym. Maybe we can work something out over the summer."

"We may have to put it off to the fall. I don't think they have classes this summer but keep in touch anyway."

"Will do." Grady finished the call and hung up. *Well, that was expensive. What am I gonna do now?*

Afternoon

Grady and Clara met at the bus after lunch. She settled into her seat then said, "The kids were still flying high over the contest this morning. Hope they've calmed down a little this afternoon."

He smiled at her in the mirror. "Good luck with that one."

When they reached the school and pulled into the bus loop, Grady could tell the kids were still pumped the minute they burst through the doors of the building blowing kazoos. They wore pointed hats with streamers and carried goodie bags overflowing with what he assumed was birthday party booty.

He patted his pocket to make sure he had his aspirin then opened the doors to greet them.

Prissy held up her goodie bag. "You'll never believe what happened today, Mister Redwine."

Grady looked at the hat she was wearing with Happy Birthday printed on it. "Well, let me guess. Hmmmmm. Did someone have a birthday?"

The whole gang shouted, "Yessssss!"

J.D. followed closely in Prissy's wake. "Guess what we got!"

"Uh...kazoos?"

J.D. blew into his. "You wight!"

Prissy played *Row Row Row Your Boat* all the way up the lift and wheeled into place on...*merrily, merrily, merrily, merrily, life is but a dream*. She took the kazoo out of her mouth and shouted, "Okay, Now! Evvvvrrryyyyyboooddddy."

The whole bus joined in, sounding like a pond full of wounded ducks.

Grady reached into his pocket, shook two aspirins into his mouth and swallowed them without a drink.

Clara leaned his way and mumbled, "At least there aren't any horns."

She spoke too soon.

J.D. reached into his goodie bag and pulled out a plastic tube attached to a paper coil that unrolled and fluttered when he blew. "It's called a tooty-tooter."

Oh God.

Prissy pulled out a whistle and suddenly it was New Year's Eve.

He looked at Clara in the mirror and mouthed, "DO SOMETHING."

She smiled, stood up and said, "Did you get anything else?"

Prissy reached into her bag and pulled out a paddle ball. "We got these." She unhooked the ball and swung at it.

Grady's head started throbbing.

Boinga boinga boinga bam!

Boinga boinga boinga ouch!

Boinga boinga boinga darn!

Clara walked to the front and said quietly, "Don't worry. Everything will be broken soon."

He didn't find that helpful.

A mile down the road while at a stoplight, Grady saw Sonti pull out his paddle too.

Oh God, not more. Not now.

He returned his attention to the light and soon the bus filled with a new sound.

Bam…Bam…Bam…

He glanced in the mirror to locate its source and discovered it was Sonti with his paddle.

Bam…Bam…Bam…overhanded…Bam…Bam…Bam…under--handed…Bam…Side-armed…Bam…Bam…Bam.

Grady completely forgot his headache. It was as if he had Bjorn Borg on board. Sonti never missed.

In spite of the revelation of Sonti's fabulous hand-eye coordination, Grady was approaching the limits of his sanity by the time he pulled up to the tennis courts at Westlake.

He and Clara switched Bennie Too to satellite feed, watched the kids gather up the paper trash, then handed out the basketball equipment when they were finished.

BennieToo grabbed Sonti's wheelchair, and they headed for the hoops, but J.D. went to a corner alone.

This is new.

Grady watched J.D. toss the ball up, let it bounce, catch it against his chest with two hands, then take a step forward and do it all again.

After J.D. made a couple of trips across the court, Grady approached him. "What are you doing, J.D.?"

"I'm pwacticing my dwibble foe my *Goal Balloon.*"

"That's really great! Would you like a few tips?"

J.D. thought about it for a minute. "Okay."

Grady picked up the ball. "Then let's get started. Hold out your hand. Let's see if you can bounce with one hand." He placed the ball in J.D.'s palm.

J.D. tossed it upward like the start of a bad volleyball serve and chased it all over the place when it bounced.

"That's a good start, but rule number one is: 'There is no way-up-high-in-dribble. Only down. And low.'"

"Oh."

Grady held his arm out at his side with the ball in the palm of his hand. "Let's see if you can do this." He turned his palm over. The ball bounced straight down and returned lower but straight up.

"Now you try." He helped J.D. hold his arm out straight to the side and placed the ball in his palm.

J.D. concentrated hard and struggled to hold the ball steady.

"Don't look at the ball, J.D. Just feel it in your hand."

The ball still wobbled around.

"Try closing your eyes."

When he did, the ball stayed still.

"Okay. Great! Now just slowly turn your hand over. The ball will bounce and come back up."

"And then I push and wun. Wight?"

"No. No pushing. No running yet."

J.D.'s eyes popped open, and the ball fell to the ground. "You supposed to wun with the ball, Mistow Wedwine, not stand still. I think you need to study up on dwibble."

Grady laughed. "Yes. Running is important, but you want to *tell* the ball which way to go, not chase after it. So here we are at rule number two already. What's rule number one? Do you remember?"

"They is no way-up-high-in-dwibble. Only down."

"Annnd..."

"And low."

"Good job. Rule number two is: You are the boss of the ball. The ball is not the boss of you."

"Got it."

Grady retrieved the ball and placed it in J.D.'s hand. "Show me what you got."

J.D. lowered his face to the ball. "I am the boss of you. You ah not the boss of me."

He stretched his arm out sideways with the ball in his palm, closed his eyes and turned his hand over. The ball bounced down and back perfectly.

J.D. became ecstatic. "I felt it, Mistow Wedwine! I felt it come back."

"If you do it *that* way, it will always come back. You just have to learn to trust it. It's called physics."

"So, if I let it go and twust it, physics will bwing it back?"

"Every time."

J.D. grew silent for a moment, obviously mulling something important over.

"J.D.?"

"I am just wonduhing, Mistow Wedwine. If I twust it, would physics bwing my mothuh back?"

THURSDAY
February 14, 2019-Morning

Prissy was already talking when she rolled into her spot behind Grady on the bus. "Boy, do I have news for you. J.D. got in big trouble last night."

"A-GAIN? What did he do?"

"He was bouncing the basketball in his room at three o'clock in the morning."

Grady cringed. *Oh-boy.*

"He woked ev-ery-body up. Miss Miller's bedroom is right under his and she stomped up those stairs so loud, you would think a elephant was coming."

Prissy talked as she organized her stuff. "Miss Miller asked J.D. if he was out of his ever-lovin' mind and J.D. said he promised Mister Redwine he was going to practice every chance he got, and this was a chance, so he was practicing..."

Grady rolled his eyes and started shaking his head.

"...So, Miss Miller told J.D. that if he knew what was good for him, he'd stop bouncing that damn ball right now because if he got Sonti all in a frenzy, she was going to kill him."

"So did he stop?"

"Yes. He had to because Sonti started his frenzy." She lowered her voice a little. "Miss Miller blamed J.D. for it, but I think she was the one who woked Sonti up when she said, 'damn ball' and called his name."

Prissy leaned back in her chair. "So anyway, when Sonti started screaming his lungs out and pounding on his door, Miss Miller exploded all over the house. I heard her say, 'Give me that damn ball this second, J.D. Parker, or you won't see another dessert as long as you live!'"

Clara scrunched up her mouth.

Prissy forged on. "J.D. told her 'No!' He said a promise is a promise and he had to practice his dribble..."

Grady let out a groan.

"There were some struggle sounds, and Miss Miller shouted, 'You are groun-ded, J.D. Groun-ded for a week.'" Prissy adjusted her position. "She was holding the ball when she stomped past my door, so I know she took it away from him." Prissy lowered her voice again. "I never saw her face so red, Miss Clara, I thought she might have a stroke or something."

"So, what happened then?"

"Well, things got worse! While Miss Miller was at the other end of the hall trying to get Sonti back in bed, for some reason, J.D. started shouting for a Psychic to make Miss Miller bring his ball back..."

Clara turned his way. "Psy-chic?"

Grady gave a helpless shrug. "Physics. He meant, physics."

"So, when it was all over, she grounded J.D. for a-nother week and told him if he ever talked back to her again, she was going to kick his ass around the block, and he wouldn't see the light of day for a month."

Clara gasped. "Oh my-gosh!"

"So now J.D. is grounded over all of Winter Break! He has to do chores every day and he's not going to have any fun at all." She arranged her blanket on her lap. "They're going to let Sonti sleep off his frenzy, then they're sending him home to spend the holiday with his Mom."

At that moment, J.D. climbed aboard and went directly to his seat without saying a word. He jerked his hoodie over his face, then shouted from under it. "You told me a L-I-E, Mistow Wedwine. You told me Psychics, would always bwing my ball back."

He crossed his arms across his chest. "I laid awake all night, Mistow Wedwine, waiting foe my ball to come back. But it did not. You said I could twust Psychics. And I did. But Psychics. Did. Not. Do. His. Job."

Grady was driving and had to just let the subject drop. But the atmosphere in the bus was so heavy, everyone he picked up seemed to sense immediately that something was wrong. They all just kind of tiptoed to their seats and rocked silently.

When they offloaded at the school, Grady turned to Clara. "Did you notice?"

"Notice what?"

"J.D. didn't say a word about getting grounded....and it's over ten days of Winter Break too! He only wanted his ball back. What a commitment. What a guy!"

Clara crossed her arms over her chest. "I hope you are planning to call Miss Miller and get him off the hook over this. You're partially to blame, you know."

"I know. I will. J.D. needs to practice."

Afternoon

When Grady and Clara pulled into the bus stop that afternoon, the kids came bubbling out of the doors carrying decorated shoe boxes.

Clara smiled. "Valentine's Day cards. They must have had a party."

Prissy zoomed aboard. "I got thirty valentines, Mister Redwine! The only person who got more than me was Jason Weatherly."

Figures.

"He's got eight girlfriends—one of them he even likes."

My kinda man.

Prissy moved on. "The other kids got one from every person in the class—it was the rule. The teacher said she didn't want any hurt feelings this year. But you could still tell who didn't really want to give you one because their card just said Happy Valentine's Day and didn't have a sugar heart glued on. I got thirty-seven sugar hearts—Jason got thirty-eight. But the teacher gave everyone a whole box full just in case somebody didn't get any."

Nobody asked J.D. how many sugar hearts he got and BennieToo didn't bring up the subject either, but Grady knew all of them had already opened the box from the teacher because he saw them chewing something when they got on the bus.

They're going to be riding sugar highs all the way home. This should be fun.

###

Ten miles down the street, a series of flashing signs appeared: *Road Work Ahead Expect Delays.*

Not again! Not a-gain!

He stretched up and saw traffic beginning to back up and turned on his blinker to make a left turn. He'd find a back way home.

J.D. yanked the hoodie off his face. "Mistow Wedwine! Mistow Wedwine! We don't tuhn heah, Mistow Wedwine!"

Oh-Lord.

He answered J.D. in the mirror. "There's road work ahead, J.D. We're going to go a different way today."

He saw J.D. grip the back of the seat in front of him, obviously a little frightened. "Will we be lost? I don't want to be lost."

"Don't worry. I know the way."

Grady drove a couple of blocks then swung a right onto a back road running past *Saint Agnes* Parochial School.

J.D.'s voice got an octave higher and two decibels louder. "This isn't ah school, Mistow Wedwine. We going home now—it's affff-tuh school—not tooo school. I think you lost all-weady."

Grady rolled his eyes—took a deep breath—let it out slowly.

He watched Clara head J.D.'s direction and mouthed a *Thank You* to her in the mirror.

She smiled back and sat down in the seat beside J.D.

"Ah we going to be late? I don't want to be late, Miss Clawa. It's Thuhsday—*Treasure Troop* day."

Prissy turned his way. "You can't watch *Treasure Troop* today anyway, J.D. You're grounded."

"Oh. Yeah." He looked over at Bennie. "Bennie?"

Bennie's face appeared on the screen. "Yeesssss."

"Can we stweam *Treasure Troop* today?"

Grady glanced in the mirror at J.D., *Stream?*

Bennie responded to J.D., "Let me check."

They could hear Bennie tapping on a keyboard for a while, then he looked up and reported, "Yep! You can watch it online."

"Miss Milluh has the intuhnet at the house. If she won't let me watch on the big TV, I'll stweam it on my computuh and watch it in the closet…"

In the closet?!?

Prissy offered her usual two-cents. "If she doesn't take your phone away too."

J.D. finally got a chance to finish, "I'll call you and we can talk about it tomahwow."

Grady returned his attention to the road then let out a groan when he spotted a flagman at the end of the bus loop signaling for him to stop.

Why now? Why to-day?

He slid his window open as the man approached. "Sorry, sir. This road is closed tonight. We're bringing in some heavy equipment. If you cut down the alley at the back of the building, merge onto Brady and turn left, you should be able to get around most of it."

"Oh! Good! That'll work. There's absolutely **nothing worse** than sitting with a bus full of kids waiting for traffic to move…" It was his intention to thank the man and leave, but when J.D. screamed, "I have to go to the bathroom," Grady's chin slumped down to his chest.

He stared at the chuckling flagman over the top of his glasses and spoke: "Except for this. This is definitely worse."

In the mirror, he saw Prissy turn around in her chair. "Didn't you go at school? You're supposed to go before you get on the bus."

"I did Number One! This is Number Two!"

Grady leaned toward the flagman. "Don't suppose there's a facility we can use around here."

"School's all locked up. Been pretty much shut down for a month or two 'cuza renovations, but they let us use the boys' locker room. I'm not supposed to do this, but it's an emergency. I don't think they'd mind if I made an exception and walked you back there."

"I'm not really supposed to do this either, but..." He unhooked his seat belt. "Come on, J.D., we're going inside."

He could see Clara looking doubtful about his decision but after she glanced at the look on J.D.'s face, she waved him on anyway.

Grady heard horrible noises rumbling around in J.D.'s belly as he quick-stepped into the building. "Ahh. Ahh. Ahh. Ahh. Have-to-hurry. Ahh. Ahh. Ahh. Ahh. Please-don't-go. Please-don't-go. Ahh. Ahh. Ahh. Ahh. Almost theyuh. Aaahh. Aaahh. Aaahh. Aaahh."

The flagman switched on the lights and J.D. tore into a stall.

Grady shouted over the door. "Do you need help in there?"

"No. I'm okay."

"I'll be right outside the door; J.D. Wash your hands when you're done."

As Grady emerged from the boys' locker room to wait, he stepped through a ray of light from a stained-glass window and stopped dead in his tracks at the end of the hall, for the first time fully aware of his surroundings. It suddenly sank in that he was in a gym—an empty, unused, functional gym—and he lost his mind.

Oh-my Lord. This is it! This is the answer! Oh-my Lord! I can't believe it! Oh-my Lord!

His eyes swept around the mahogany walls, stopping to admire a magnificent old-world cross with an intertwined heart carved into one of the panels.

"What a beautiful place! What a crazy co-in..." He hesitated a minute—glanced at the cross again. *Was this a coincidence? Could it be that it wasn't?* Grady wasn't sure, but he had no doubt in his mind what Mary would say.

A moment later, he felt a tug on his shirt tail and heard J.D. say, "I'm duuun."

Grady turned his way and said, "Then let's go home, whaddaya say?"

"I say yes. We late. Let's go home."

Grady was still totally pumped about the Saint Agnes gym when he returned to the bus, but he didn't mention it to Clara. He was superstitious about discussing something not set in concrete because he might jinx it.

He cut down the alley at the back of the building, merged onto Brady and turned left like the flagman suggested. Fortunately, the flagman was right. They avoided a lot of congestion and got the kids home in time for most of *Treasure Troop*.

He and Clara wished them all a happy Winter Break, told them they'd see them in ten days and drove on.

Finally, back at the bus barn, Clara packed up. "Well, we made it. Winter break. Fourteen free days of what at our house, we callll." Her arms shot up into two high overhead victory signs. "Feb-ru-air-ee Freak-out! What are you going to do?"

"Sports. Work on my brackets. Maybe noodle around with some balloon-goal stuff."

She headed for the stairs. "Have a great time! Give me a call if..." She turned back toward him. "I take that back. Please. Don't call me."

He knew she was referring to his infamous drunk-dial debacle and got her point. But he didn't want to make a promise he might not be able to keep, so he just said, "I'll lock up my phone."

Grady went out on the back porch when he got home, watched the sunset for a while, sipped at his coffee and mulled over the remarkable events of the day.

How weird was it that he'd lived in that town for sixty-three years and had never been in that building. He coached basketball twenty-five of those years and his team never played Saint Agnes either—their school was too small for his classification.

Grady was no mathematician, but even *he* knew the odds had to be staggeringly high against him being on that road, meeting a flagman willing to break the rules and let J.D. inside a parochial school to use the bathroom in the locker room of an unused gym inside a building that in sixty-three years he'd never gone into and had no conceivable reason to go into anyway, just when he had failed to find a gym for his kids on his own.

He began to form an unsettling belief that the events of this day couldn't have been accidental. Without a doubt, he knew what Mary would say, but right now, for him...well...the jury was still out.

He rose from his chair with a slight case of jitters and tried hard to dismiss it as too much caffeine, but Grady drank enough *Venti lattes* each day to know deep in his heart that caffeine could not be the culprit.

Well...okay, Mary honey. Let's just test it and see. I'll call Ryan first thing in the morning.

FRIDAY
February 15, 2019-Morning

First Day of Winter Break

Grady woke up too early to call Ryan about using the gym, so he killed some time by making a swing by the drive-thru to grab a coffee. He was so excited he practically had to sit on his hands to keep from lifting the phone and dialing but reminded himself he was about to ask a big favor, and Ryan was usually more willing to be helpful when he'd had enough sleep.

At ten sharp, he dialed Ryan's number. It rang twice, then he heard, "Okay. What do you want."

"Is that any way to answer the phone? What makes you think I want something?"

"It's not two o'clock in the morning. Whatever it is, you must want it bad."

"Actually, I do. I'm calling to find out if *Saint Agnes School* is going to close."

"Yes, it is. We're still having a few classes there, but it will close for renovations this summer. Why are you asking?"

"Does the gym still have heat—and Wi-Fi?"

"Yes, for both, but the girls' locker room is a mess...the flood wiped it out. What are you up to? Tell me."

"Well, you know this new program I'm assigned to? They won't let my kids use the regular gym. They just dump them on the upper level every day, let them wander around for an hour and call it going to gym class. The kids aren't learning anything. They aren't getting any cardio. They're just wandering around in circles making a lot of noise."

"Doesn't sound real fair to me."

"It isn't. So, I want to use your gym and see what I can do with them. I have a little girl in a wheelchair who wants to run a 4K this year. She's run some 4Ks in the past and I want to help her up her fitness. I also have some boys who want to play basketball, and I want to teach them something about the game."

"Wow. Sounds like you've done a one-eighty about the job. That's great!"

"I'm trying really hard to make the most of it."

"I'm proud of you for that, Grady. I really am. I'm pretty sure I can let you have an hour or two on Tuesdays and Thursdays. How does that sound?"

"Anything—anything right after lunch."

"One o'clock?"

"Perfect. Thanks."

"I'll double check and call you if I can't. If you don't hear from me, just show up. You'll have to share the boys' locker room with the young lady in the wheelchair and the construction workers."

"No problem."

"I'll arrange for you to get some keys at the front desk. Ask for Sister Mary Mercy. You'll have to bring your own equipment."

"Will do—and thanks so much. You've helped make five little kids really happy."

"Glad I could do it. Gotta go. Keep in touch."

Grady said his goodbyes then hung up the phone, smiling. He walked down the hall, opened the door to Mary's office, stuck his head into the room and whispered toward the Bible, "Thank you."

SATURDAY
February 16, 2019-Bob Day

The third Saturday in February had been one of Grady's favorite days of the year ever since one brawly night in a bar back in college, when he and his friends threw down their gauntlets after a spirited basketball discussion and issued an official call to combat they called: *The Annual Red-wine-Gen-u-ine-March Madness-Knock-Down-Drag-Out-Winner-Take-All-Battle-of-the-Brackets.* After they sobered up some, they whittled it down to *The Battle of the Brackets.* Then it was *B.O.B. Day* for a while, but out of sheer laziness, they finally landed on plain ol' *Bob Day.*

His buddies were all gone now—moved on or passed away—but for the past 39 years, Grady continued to set aside *Bob Day* to begin researching team trends, injury reports and player stats in his never-ending quest to produce a perfect March Madness bracket.

After he got organized, Grady glanced over at Mary's empty chair. In days gone by, she'd be sitting there making reservations for the week-long "Get Outa Town Girls' Trip" the wives demanded when they found out they were going to be widowed and knee-deep in crazy for an additional month every year because of the *Bob Day c*hallenge.

Grady felt grateful to have lived a life lucky in love. Mary was a died-in-the-wool Hoosier like he was, so when they became a couple and she learned about his passion for basketball and his goal to become a coach someday, it didn't seem outrageously odd to her that he was such a big fan. Unlike some of the other wives, she never complained about his descent into madness each March, but she never missed a *Get Outa Town* trip with the girls, either.

Today, Grady loved having a chance to crawl back into his old skin for a while. He was at peace with the world, living the life he always loved...doing things he knew how to do well, all weekend.

SUNDAY
February 17, 2019

Grady slept in this morning because he was up past midnight watching some luke-warm basketball. The Bucks beat the socks off the Heat 116 to 87. Then the Celtics knocked out the Knicks 113 to 99. And the Suns shot down the Clippers 130 to 122. But, as Grady was often heard saying, *a bad night of basketball is better than a wonderful day at work any time*, so he woke up happy.

Before *Bob Day* came about, he spent most of Winter Break parked in his recliner next to a full cooler of beer, binge-watching ESPN. It was high on his agenda again this year, but he decided it was time to throw caution to the wind and see if he could get Sonti into the Half-Court Shot Contest first.

He knew the best way to accomplish that was to go right to the top, so he pulled out Bennie's paperwork and turned to his emergency contact information. Right where it was supposed to be, was the private office number of Bennie's father, Victor Hamilton, owner of the Comets and founder of The Hamilton Children's Shelter.

Bet that's worth a dollar or two on the black market.

He carefully recorded the number on a paper pad next to his phone and stared at it for a while. It was Sunday…he wouldn't bother the man on a Sunday. But, tomorrow, he would make the call.

WEEK SEVEN

MONDAY
February 18, 2019-Morning

Winter Break

Grady woke up in his recliner again this morning. Sleeping there seemed to be becoming a habit. Somewhere around ten, he picked up the slip of paper with Victor Hamilton's contact number and stared at it while he sipped on some coffee.

Okay, now what?

He stared at it a little longer—had a conversation with himself.

Call the man, Redwine. What's the worst thing that can happen?

Well, for one thing, there's termination for abusive use of a student's personal information.

Yes, there's that.

And unsanctioned solicitation of a parent for a commercial cause.

And that.

And don't forget a little matter called violating the terms of your probation.

Hmmmmmm.

He rested on his elbows and chewed absent-mindedly on his thumbnail.

Who needs insurance and a pension anyway?

Uh, you do?

Is it worth the risk?

He didn't hesitate for a second. *Yes. For Sonti, yes it is.*

Then damn son, call the man.

Grady ran his hands through his hair and forced a deep breath, trying to shake the tension from his body as he dialed Bennie's father.

A rich baritone voice anyone could pick out of a crowd answered, "Victor Hamilton."

Oh-my-God! Oh-my-God! It was really his personal number! He'd expected a secretary.

"Um, this is Grady Redwine, Mister Hamilton. I'm, uh, I'm Bennie's bus driver."

"Mister Redwine! This is an unexpected surprise. What can I do for you today?"

"I'm really sorry for bothering you, sir."

"Any time, Mister Redwine. Any time. Bennie speaks very highly of you."

"Thank you. He's a wonderful little boy. I really enjoy having him on the bus."

"So how can I help you?"

"Has Bennie told you about the Milers Club and our goal setting project?"

"Yes he has. He's a little nervous, but excited about it,"

"Well, sir, I have a couple of ideas I'd like to discuss with you that will help two of my kids achieve their goals, and I'm wondering if you might have some time open on your schedule when we could get together and I could run them past you."

"How much time will you need?"

"Thirty minutes?"

"Fortunately, you've called at a propitious time."—Grady hoped that meant good. —"We're taking a *Winter Break* too and I'm not traveling. Let me check my schedule."

Grady heard papers rattle then Hamilton's voice returned. "Could you come today? I have an open half hour at 2:30."

Grady was so shocked he could barely breathe. "Uh...two thirty? Uh...let me check my calendar too." — He sat down and attempted to regain his composure before he returned to the conversation. "Um two thirty...two thirty...yes...I have some time then. Where should I go to meet you?"

"I'm working out of my home office this week. When you come onto the property—You have the gate code, I guess." — "Yes, I do."—"Good. Just drive around to the right of the three-car garage where you pick up BennieToo in the morning, then follow the road around the right side of the house. You'll find a small parking area near a side entrance under a blue canopy. Just push the button on the speaker beside the doors. Someone will answer and show you in."

"Will do. Thank you, sir. I'll see you then."

"Looking forward to it."

"Me too." Grady heard dial tone and collapsed in his chair.

"Ho-lee-*shit*! What do I do now?"

He looked at his watch. *Ten O'Clock.* He had two and a half hours…make that two. It would take thirty minutes to get there.

###

Grady set a world record for showering but shaved carefully so he wouldn't cut himself. He usually just wet down his hair and hid it under a hat, but today, he took the time to blow-dry it.

What in the world should I wear?

A suit? He hadn't had on his suit since Mary's funeral, and it was still lying in a heap on a chair.

He decided it was best to stop guessing and start looking through what was actually clean. Jeans? No. Khakis? Yes…that's it… Khakis. Did he have any that still fit? It took two tries, but he found a pair.

He flipped through a series of hangers holding golf shirts, work shirts, a couple of dress shirts, some jackets and sweaters, until his eyes landed on the Milers high-end t-shirt that the designers gave him as a thank you for all the business.

That's it!

He was going to be meeting with Hamilton on official Milers' business, so it made sense. He'd wear that with a pair of Khakis under a light jacket and tennis shoes. Perfect.

###

When Grady pressed the backlit call button beside the carved wooden doors under the blue awning, a woman's voice came through the speaker. "How can I help you?"

He leaned down toward the speaker. "I have an appointment with Mister Hamilton."

"Your name?"

"Uh, Grady Redwine."

"One moment please."

Grady rocked on his heels and whistled while he waited, trying to remain calm, but stopped short and caught his breath when the doors opened. He was expecting a housemaid or a secretary. But standing framed by the doorway was a man wearing dark slacks, a starched white shirt open at the collar with the sleeves rolled up, and a friendly smile: Victor Hamilton.

He stood aside and ushered Grady inside, offering a warm handshake when he arrived in the foyer. "Welcome! It's high time we met, Mister Redwine." He gave a subtle nod toward a short hallway. "We're down this way."

Grady walked with him past a few small offices then they entered double doors at the end of the hall. Hamilton's paneled office was elegant and masculine but furnished with surprisingly simple and understated overstuffed black leather furniture. A Fireplace with flaming gas logs under a pale gray marble mantel dominated the far wall. Hung above it was a dramatic rendering of what he recognized as the *Comets* logo: a blaze of light streaking across the night sky, trailed by a tail of dazzling ice blue and silver embers.

The fireplace was flanked by an easy chair and a glass case fitted with LED lighting displaying several trophies and four gleaming championship rings on finger-shaped black velvet ring stands.

Hamilton gestured toward a chair across from the desk— "Have a seat."— Grady sank into the soft leather. After settling into his own high-backed chair, Bennie's father shifted aside the project he must have been working on before Grady arrived, then gave him his full attention.

"So why are we here?"

"I'm hoping to discuss some ideas I have for Milers' goal setting and the Half-Court Shot Contest."

Hamilton held up his hands. "You need saaay no more. I've still got a few courtside seats open, and I'd be glad to have you, and your kids, come and watch as our guests."

"That's very generous of you, Mister Hamilton, thank you. We'll definitely take you up on that aspect of our attendance at the game. But I also have what I think is a great idea to make the event even more exciting."

"Ohhh? What's that?"

"I would like one of my kids to be a contestant."

Hamilton's eyes grew wide. "Well…that's certainly an interesting idea, Mister Redwine, but I'm afraid you're a little late. We follow a strict protocol for contestant selection to ensure that the process is fair. Everyone has to meet some basic requirements to qualify for the contest, then fill out and submit an entry form and attend a public gathering where we draw names at random. We've already held the drawing and selected our candidate for this event. If I were to insert a contestant outside that process at the last minute, the tabloids would have a field day and we'd be up to our eyeballs in lawsuits."

Grady felt sweat begin to form on the back of his neck as he pushed onward. "I've been hearing about the charity events you've incorporated into the flow of the game on the nightly news."

Hamilton smiled. "Yes, we're having the Salvation Army bring their kids and *Athletes for Hope* are sponsoring some activities."

"Well, in a way, this exception could also be considered an act of charity, Mr. Hamilton. I was hoping people would feel inspired and support it."

"I think it would be wonderful if everyone climbed on board, but, we've only had one person able to make the shot from half-court this season, so the prize pool has reached half a million dollars. It's unfortunate, but ambition and greed are powerful forces in this world, and they tend to overshadow compassion and caring. There is a shameful amount of fraud in the world of charities today, and your suggestion involves entering a contestant who is the beneficiary of a charity *that I sponsor*, so it is imperative that we remain beyond reproach in everything we do.

"It's unfortunate that we've missed the window for *this particular* season, but if you come back again next year, only earlier in the process, we'll open it up for discussion again. How does that sound?"

"If we were discussing *most* children, it would seem to be perfectly fair. But I'm afraid *this child* might not have another year."

Hamilton seemed genuinely moved by that statement. "Who is it?"

"He's one of your kids at the *Shelter*, sir: Sonti Solari."

There was a brief moment of silence, then Grady watched regret flow into Hamilton's eyes. "I know your intentions are good, Mister Redwine, and Bennie has mentioned how good Sonti is at making baskets, but I vowed a long time ago that I would never exploit my children for personal gain. I have no choice but to give you a definitive no now."— Grady felt a sinking feeling in his stomach as Hamilton continued. — "Sonti already has enough pain in his life to contend with, and I would never allow him to be exposed to that much potential humiliation."

Grady slid to the edge of his seat. "I swear, neither would I, Mister Hamilton. But I am completely convinced that Sonti is capable of making that shot."

"So, you're telling me you haven't actually seen him do it."

"No, I haven't...not yet. He's still short and off to the left, but I feel certain by the night of the contest, he'll have as good a chance as anyone else of doing it."

Hamilton shifted in his seat. "I am aware of your remarkable coaching career, Mr. Redwine, and have no reason to doubt your professional judgment...but It's hard to imagine that a young man with Sonti's limitations would have a chance of success or be able to cope with the conditions he would face in this situation."

Just then, the intercom came alive, and a woman's voice entered the room. "Mister Hamiton, Your three o'clock appointment is here."

"Thank you, Marie. Have them take a seat and I'll be right down."

Hamilton stood and spread his arms with a display of obvious regret, then walked Grady back down the hall to the door. "I would appreciate it if you didn't say anything about our conversation to Bennie. I don't want to get him upset."

"I promise I won't. Not a word."

They shook hands, then Hamilton closed the conversation with, "I look forward to seeing you and your kids at the game, Mr. Redwine. I'll make sure you get the tickets."

"Thank you. It was very nice meeting you, sir. Thank you for taking my call."

"Call me any time."

Grady flashed him a smile then turned away and the door closed gently behind him.

###

Grady drove home in a funk, slumped into his chair in the den, popped open a can of beer and took a slug. *Well, you tried.* He picked up the remote and surfed through the channels for a while, staring blankly at the screen.

Grady, you're better than this. If you were down by one with two seconds on the clock, would you give up? Hell no. You'd kick butts all over the court if someone just stood there and didn't try to make a shot. The man said you could call back any time. Try again! Play until the game is over, son. Shoot the effin' ball.

Afternoon

Before he dialed Victor Hamilton back, Grady glanced over at a framed poster propped on the back of the couch across the room. It was the only thing he had saved from his coaching office when he left:

"I can accept failure, but I can't accept not trying."
–Michael Jordan

Well, Michael, here we go.

He double-checked the number, dialed, counted three rings and heard a beep.

"You have reached the office of Victor Hamilton. We are out of the office at the moment. Please leave a message and we will return your call as soon as possible."

"Uh, This is Grady Redwine, Mr. Hamilton. "I've been thinking about the situation we discussed, and I have another idea to run by you.

"How about this. We aren't on the program. However, if the person already chosen doesn't make the shot…and only if he doesn't make the shot… we put it up for a vote with the fans at the game. Let *them* decide if Sonti gets a chance. That way, nobody should feel cheated. If the person *sinks* his shot, we just chalk it up to bad luck for us.

"Every dime will go to Sonti. Nobody else will get paid anything. Not a cent. You said you only picked one contestant this year, but I know you've usually had two, so you should have enough time to work Sonti into the program. Please, just give it a little more thought. Two of my former students are playing for the Ravens in the game that night: Malik Perry and Brandon Baldwin. I'm sure they would be willing to sponsor him. I think the fans would love that fact too. Um, Uh, Thank you. Uh, Goodbye."

TUESDAY
February 19, 2019-Morning

Winter Break

Grady slept fitfully all night and was wide awake long before sunrise. He never thought he'd regret not having to work, but today, it would be nice to have something to do.

What are you going to do if Victor Hamilton doesn't buy your idea?
He didn't know.

Mary's voice flew into his mind: *"Geez, Redwine! Who said you could only have one idea? If he says no to this, go find another way."*

He stared at his phone lying on the seat, silent, and willed it to ring. For twenty-four agonizing hours, it didn't.

WEDNESDAY
February 20, 2019-Morning

Grady had to sit down when his phone rang that morning and Victor Hamilton's name appeared in his Caller ID.

This is it! This is really it!

He struggled with his fingers a bit as he entered his security code and answered. "Hello?"

"Hello Mister Redwine. This is Victor Hamilton."

"Mister Hamilton. Thank you for calling me back so soon."

"Well, I knew this was important to you, so I didn't want to keep you hanging any longer than necessary."

"Thank you. I really appreciate that."

Grady heard him take a deep breath and exhale. *Not a good sign.*

"I want to assure you, Mister Redwine, that I took your idea to my attorneys and public relations people, and they all insisted that what you're asking us to do will reflect negatively on the integrity of the promotion and lead to nothing but trouble."

Grady's heart sank. "Oh." He tried to remain professional. "Well, thank you so much for…"

"Now wait, hold on just a minute, there's a little more to the story. They all told me no, and I have to admit I was resigned to sticking with no as well, but eventually we were all outvoted."

"Oh? Oh! Who? How?"

"Well, it just so happened that Mrs. Hamilton was the one who picked up the message you left on the telephone Monday afternoon, and she thought it was an interesting idea. So, she went up and discussed it with Bennie and he said he thought Sonti could make the shot too.

I shared with her what our attorneys and P.R. people said, and we discussed it a while." —There were a few moments of silence, then he continued. — "I don't know if you're a married man, Mister Redwine, but around here, that means I lose."

Grady laughed.

"Mrs. Hamilton made it clear that for something like this, we should be willing to handle a little trouble. And, as only she can, gently reminded me that's why we have attorneys on retainer…" He paused. Grady held his breath. "…so, I guess you've got a yes."

Grady leaped to his feet. "Oh wow! Oh wow! Thank you so very much. So very, *very* much. I'm going to do my best to make sure you're proud of this, Mister Hamilton."

"It's yes with a few conditions, though."

"Anything, sir. Just name it."

"One. You can't tell anyone about this agreement prior to the event."

"Not-a-word."

"Two. Absolutely no money goes to Bennie or back to the foundation."

"Not-a-dime."

"Three. You have to do this with full permission of Sonti's mother."

Grady's stomach clenched. *Steady. Steady.* "I have a signed release for special events, so I suppose it will apply."

"Well make sure it does."

Grady swallowed hard. "I will."

"Four. As you proposed, if our candidate makes the shot before it's your turn, you are out of luck. You can only participate if he fails, and the crowd votes you in."

"Absolutely. That's only fair."

"Five. You can do absolutely nothing that even remotely looks like favoritism played a role in this."

"Agreed. If there's any question about anything, I'll run it by you first."

"And last but not least, the league has a mandatory fifteen-minute half-time limit, and the rules of the contest are still the rules. He gets three shots in two minutes, and the ball has to have completely left his hand before the buzzer sounds."

"Understood."

"He will have to walk out to half-court. We can't have wheelchair marks on the floor. Remember, we will be working with an extremely strict time limit, so he can't dawdle. If there are fewer than two minutes left when he shoots his first ball, it's on you..."

Grady cringed. "Understood."

"And, last but not least, he's allowed only one other person on the court with him."

"That works for us."

"Then it looks like we have a deal, Mister Redwine. Congratulations. Oh, by the way, Mrs. Hamilton loved the idea of having Malik and Brandon sponsor him. You can arrange that if you trust them not to let the cat out of the bag. As we have discussed, there will be serious ramifications if this leaks."

Grady pumped a fist. *Yesssss!*

"I'm so excited, Mister Hamilton. I wanted this so much for Sonti and it's actually going to happen. I can hardly believe it."

"Bennie showed me Sonti's stats. I agree with you. He just might sink that ball. We'll be rooting for you."

"Thank you, sir. And thank Mrs. Hamilton too. Please tell her she can trust Malik and Brandon. They're both stand-up guys. Mum's the word. And…hug Bennie for me."

There was a slight pause. "I'll be sure to tell them. You can pick up the tickets at *VIP Will Call* just off the lobby any time after tomorrow. Five tickets, right?"

"Yes. Three kids. Two chaperones."

"One wheelchair, right?"

"Yes."

"Will do. See you at the game."

Grady hung up and hurled himself back into his chair, arms high above his head, tingles surging through his body.

*What was that? What was **that**?*

A win. He'd had an effin' *win!*

Oh-my-God! Oh-my-God! I can't be-lieve it!

He grabbed Mary's photo and looked her in the eyes. "I did it, darlin'! I did it!" He gave her a big smack on the lips and clutched her hard against his chest trying to feel her presence. "I had two minutes and I…I…I did it."

A large, painful lump began to form in Grady's throat. He fought against it, but today there was no stopping months of pent-up tears. They burst through the dam a drop at a time then grew into a bottomless flood of heavy sobs. "I'm so happy. So happy."

Afternoon

Grady checked his calendar. He had six weeks to get Sonti and the rest of the kids in shape for the contest.

I need a plan.

He mentally walked his way through his conversation with Victor Hamilton and created a quick to-do list.

1. Visit auditorium- verify distances.
2. New permission slip from Sonti's mother. (Check to see if the current signed release for special events applies.)
3. Figure out how to ditch that blanket on court.

4. Memorize contest rules.
5. Work on shot speed and timing between shots. Three shots in two minutes.
6. Increase stamina. Has to walk to half-court. No wheelchair.
   That one's going to be a stickler. Sonti can run like Jesse Owns when he wants to…but he meanders like a gray-haired granny when he walks.
7. One person on court.
   I'll station J.D. somewhere where I can see him.
8. Practice. Practice. Practice every chance we get.
9. Call Ryan. Get gym days increased.

THURSDAY
February 21, 2019- Morning

Grady started working on his to-do list, last item first. He had agreed not to tell anyone about this, but since he would be unable to pull off the event without having a gym to use, he picked up the phone and called Ryan. He knew he could trust him not to tell anyone if he asked him not to…he was a priest.

He picked up his phone and dialed.

Ryan answered, but Grady didn't give him a chance to talk…just blurted out, "How would you like to die knowing you were part of a miracle?"

"Is this another Wilt Chamberlain thing?"

"No. I think it's God. Actually, God."

"Okay, I'm game. Tell me what it is and what you want."

"I have a young man in my group of kids named Sonti."

"Isn't he the one you were in here complaining about a few weeks ago who screams his way to school every day?"

"Actually, yes, but I'm smarter now. I understand what's going on and I've discovered he has an incredible natural talent to make baskets."

"So, what do you want us to do…sell them in our stores?"

"Not *woven* baskets. *Basketball* baskets."

"Oh. And…"

"And I've convinced Victor Hamilton, owner of the *Comets* to give him a chance to make a try for the big prize at the Half-Court Shot Contest."

"That's wonderful. So, what do you need from me?"

"Well, for one thing, I'm only calling *you*. I'm not supposed to tell anyone about this, so you have to treat it like a confession, ok?"

"Of course."

"I need to be able to use the gym every day instead of just Tuesdays and Thursdays so he can train for this."

"I'm assuming his mother is on board."

Grady hesitated for a moment. He didn't want to lie.

Ryan pressed on. "I take it by your silence, that his mother isn't quite sold on this yet."

"I have a signed release from his Mom for field trips. Does that count?

"No."

"What do you need?"

"I need a signed, notarized, release for this specific event. Do not call me back until you have one."

Grady stared at his phone when he got dial tone again. *Well, this is a fine mess you've managed to get yourself into.* He flopped back in his chair. *Maybe I shouldn't have told him.*

Grady thought for a long time, then picked up his phone and dialed Ryan's number again in spite of his warning. As he anticipated, it went straight to voicemail.

> *You have reached the office of His Eminence, Monsignor Ryan Goodman. We are not in the office right now, but please leave a message and tell us how we can help you. Someone will get back to you just as soon as possible. Feel free to leave details. You have two minutes.*

When he heard the beep Grady said, "Ryan, it's me. I-know-I-know. Please. Please listen. It's really important.

"Could you please, Ryan, please rethink your requirements for the use of the gym? This is the chance of a lifetime for this boy, and I need every minute I can get with him to help him be successful. Getting permission from his Mom to do it is going to take a while and I don't want to lessen his chances more by delaying his fitness and training.

"I promise I won't go through with the plan without her permission. But I truly believe that there's something bigger than all of us at work in this.

"There's an infinite list of gifts God could have given Sonti. I don't know why He chose shooting baskets from that list and I don't know why I ended up driving Sonti's bus. It could just be a strange coincidence. But when you add Victor Hamilton into the equation...the fact that his son is riding on the very same bus with us...the fact that he owns the *Comets* and the *Comets* just happen to be holding a Half-Court contest next month that Sonti has a real chance to win, it's mind-boggling. All that cannot be just coincidence, Ryan.

"But what if winning isn't the point at all? What if what God wants is for someone to care about this boy...someone to see his talent and help him do something wonderful.

"Please. Help us. Let me use the gym. Don't hurt this boy's chances because I'm...well, because of me."

Grady had to wait an hour before his phone dinged and Ryan's name appeared on his screen.

Keep the keys. Use the gym every day if you want.

He put the phone down and nearly cried. *"Whoah. What a relief.*
He texted back. *Thank you buddy.*
He could relax now and enjoy the next three days off.

SUNDAY
February 24, 2019

 Grady was sitting on the back porch recovering from his three-day television binge, sipping at his *latte* and studying the Sunday sports section. There was an article about a recent basketball game lost by his old high school team, the War Eagles, lamenting the fact that Coach Riley seemed to be fumbling his way through the season.
 He took no pleasure in reading the article and felt sorry for Jack who was actually a very good Coach. It couldn't be great to read something like that about yourself in the newspaper…and the *Boosters*? As the gang would have said…*Fuhgeddaboudit.*
 Grady knew the team was out there battling their way through every game—doing their best. But he also knew from experience that there were times the ball just didn't bounce your way, and when it happens, you lose.
 He missed coaching. He missed the kids—the travel—the excitement—and, yeah, the glory of being a winner.
 Would he go back now if they asked him?
 After reading that article, he wasn't sure.

###

 Grady spent some time scanning his completed brackets and smiled, remembering better days when he and his buddies spent endless hours agonizing and arguing about the lineup. For weeks, they analyzed team statistics, player performance, injuries, and trending. They'd overlay some old-fashioned gut feelings and a few rumors and protect their final version from each other until their unveiling party on the first day of the First Round.
 Then, Mary and her friends who hadn't watched a game all season, would return from their girls' trip, issue a challenge to the men, spend an hour in the kitchen filling out their brackets based on selections made from some random criteria like favorite school colors or cutest mascot, and routinely massacre them in the end.
 He glanced over at Mary's picture. *Not this time, darlin'. You haven't got a chance. I've aced it this year. You wait and see.*

WEEK EIGHT

MONDAY
February 25, 2019-Morning

Grady woke up early this morning to the high-pitched whine of the TV station sign-off signal. He'd fallen asleep in his chair in the den again, with his brackets scattered across his lap.

That signal always triggered a headache in him and he hated it, but he was grateful to be able to get an early start this morning because he knew he'd need time to crank up his pickup and warm up the bus. Both vehicles had been pretty much sitting out in the cold for ten days and he wanted to make sure there weren't any issues.

He rushed through his usual morning fresh-up routine, swallowed a couple of extra strength aspirin, then pulled on his parka and rushed out to his pickup hoping it wouldn't give him any trouble. She was slow but started up fine and he headed out to buy his coffee.

At the truck stop, Minnie popped into the window and smiled. "Back to the ol' grind, today, Mr. Redwine?"

"Yep, 'fraid so."

"Hope you had a good vacation."

"I did. And you?"

"Worked, but the tips were good."

"Glad to hear it. Give me two of the usual today, Minnie…with jet fuel."

"Two espresso lattes, coming right up!"

At the bus lot, he did his pre-check and started up the big yellow *Titan* with a different attitude that day. It coughed and rumbled to life then sort of hummed along as if it understood they were facing more than the start of a new day. It was as if both of them knew something significant had changed for them during Winter Break.

When Clara arrived, he handed over the latte he'd bought her on the way there. "Welcome back sunshine!"—She smiled and did a little curtsy. "Why thank you, sir!"— He finished his greeting. "Did you have a good two weeks off?"

"I had an excellent Winter Break, thank you."

"So did I." He climbed into his seat and took a sip of his dark roast as he fastened his seat belt. "Oh! Before I forget, put the night of April sixth on your calendar. We're going on a field trip."

"Oooohhh Kaaaay." She pulled out her phone and opened her calendar. "Grady, that's a Saturday."

"Yep! We're going to a basketball game...the Half-Court contest for the *Comets*."

His announcement was met with a groan.

"What's that all about? This is great news. Do you know how many kids would kill to go to that game?"

"But it's a Saturday...at night."

"And?"

"It's a fieldtrip. On a weekend. We have to get approval. There's red tape all over the place."

"We'll figure it out." He signaled left. "Let's do some planning this afternoon. The kids have assembly."

"Works for me." Clara looked ahead at the road. "I take it we're going to Sonti's first this morning."

"Yep. Guess he spent the break with his Mom."

"Wow. Nine days at home. He's bad enough after a weekend." She shifted in her seat. "Poor kid is probably thinking school's finally over forever, and suddenly...." She wiggled her fingers above her head. "Weee'rrrre baaaaa-ack."

Grady was easing into a right turn at the center of Sonti's intersection when his eyes froze on a junky old car covered with patches and primer speeding toward the corner across from them.

I don't think that guy's gonna stop.

He waited a couple more seconds, calculating.

Nope. He's not.

"Hold on, Clara!"

He gripped the wheel, braced himself; braked hard.

Tires squealing, the Junker swiped left and literally flew past their front bumper.

Clara was thrown to the floor, coffee flying. "Whooah!"

"You okay?"

Her head appeared above the seat bottom. "Yeah."

She scrambled up using the safety bar and wiped coffee off her arms while she watched the car tear down the street. "W-T-F, Grady! Is he craa-zy?!"

"Guess the guy didn't want to follow a school bus this morning."

"Yeah, but that was just completely uncalled for. Thank God there weren't any kids on board."

"People do stupid things when they're late."

"Tell me about it."

Grateful for having a good cup holder, he finished off his coffee and managed a chuckle. "Everyone hates following a school bus. Even school buses hate following school buses."

Clara squinted down the street. "Grady, do you think there's a chance that might have been…"

"The car that parks at Sonti's house sometimes?"

"Uh huh."

"Not sure. Maybe."

When they finally arrived at Sonti's house, the street was deserted except for a couple of cars disappearing over the hill. Grady could tell from the high-tech taillight design that one of them was an expensive import and the other had to be an old Junker because it had one of its lights dangling on a wire swinging around in the back. When he pulled up in front of Sonti's house, however, the conclusion turned into a toss-up. *Their* old Junker was parked in its usual place against the curb, but he knew it had been driven because for the very first time, it was facing inward.

I'd bet the ranch that if I touched it, that hood would be hot.

Grady's thoughts changed course in an instant when the lights in the house switched on like dominos and shadows with wildly waving arms flashed across the shades.

Looks like it's going to be one of those days.

He felt like a kid crunched down in the seat of a movie theater watching scary sci-fi…stomach all crawly and tense…wondering who or what would leap from the darkness.

Clara leaned over his shoulder. "Everyone's obviously awake up there. Sonti should be—ohh myyy Gohhhhd."

His eyes shot to the side yard just in time to see Sonti burst out the door with a flurry of screaming people flying after him.

A new, unsettling sound drifted toward them as he headed in their direction, sending a chill down Grady's spine.

"Do you hear that? What *is* that?"

She shrugged. "Don't know."

He studied the hill again. "I think this is more than a meltdown. There's something really wrong up there."

"Why?"

"Sonti's running toward us. He never runs *toward* the bus...especially the first day after a long holiday."

She drew closer to the window. "Wow."

Grady squinted up the hill. "And that sound. What is that sound?"

He placed his hand on the lever, preparing to open the door.

She lifted her hand to stop him. "He isn't wearing his safety vest. We can't let him in 'til his Mom gets here."

He whipped around, incredulous. "Clara. What if he takes off down the street? He could get hit by a car."

"We have to leave it closed, Grady. We have to. We can't control him without his vest. If he got hurt on the bus there'd be Hell to pay for everyone, including him."

Sonti was only a few steps away when the source of the sound hit Grady.

"Clara, I don't think he's screaming. I think Sonti is speaking."

Clara leaned toward the door. "Oh-my-gosh! He is!"

Through the glass, they heard a high-pitched, monotonal voice shrieking, "MaaaMaaa!"

Grady felt shell-shocked. He'd never heard Sonti say anything.

"MaaaMaaa! MaaaMaaa!"

Grady decided to Hell with it. He was going to open the door when Sonti reached them. "Is your Mama okay, Sonti? Is she okay?"

He was answered by what sounded like a frightened baby lamb. "MaaaMaaa! MaaaMaaa!"

Grady turned toward Clara. "Should we call the police?"

Before she could answer, two shadows emerged high tailing it out of the dark: Sonti's sister, followed closely by a man he'd never seen before.

She gestured in the man's direction. "This is our...uh...Tío...our uncle. He is...visiting." She reached for Sonti's hand. He slapped it away. "Sonti cannot go to school today. We will take him back inside."

Clara bent toward the door. "Where is your mother?"

The girl motioned toward the house as Sonti paced back and forth in front of the door. "Up there."

Above them, a curtain in the front window lifted and Sonti's mother appeared, wrapped in a ragged old robe. It was an eerie sight to see her bathed in light, motioning feebly for them to continue on. When they acknowledged they'd seen her, she slowly turned and let the curtain fall behind her.

The man managed to jump Sonti from behind. He clamped the boy's arms to his sides and lifted him off his feet like he was about to move a roll of carpet. Sonti struggled desperately as he was hauled up to the house.

"MaaaMaaa! MaaaMaaa!"

Grady remained at the curb for a while just to make sure Sonti wasn't hurt on the hill, then pulled away.

Clara dabbed at her eyes. "I'm feeling a little devastated, Grady."

"It's a tough situation."

"Do you think he was trying to tell us something?"

"Don't know. We saw his mother. She seemed okay."

"Yes, but she was so far away!"

The two of them rode silently toward *The Hamilton Home* to get Prissy and J.D. About halfway there, he looked in his mirror and saw Clara studying him.

"What are you thinking, Grady Redwine. I see you thinking."

"Just going over what happened, is all."

"It's their family business. We're not allowed to get involved."

"I know."

"I'm serious, Grady. You cannot get involved."

"Trust me, Clara. I'm not going to get involved in their business."

All I'm going to do is have Transportation pull the video from our route this morning. They'll watch it and turn it over to the police—or not. It will be up to them.

###

They rode in silence to *The Hamilton Home*, each of them talking themselves off the ledge after the events of the morning so far.

Prissy was all excited when she boarded the bus. "Look, Mister Redwine. Look what I've got."

She held out a fluffy little bunny...all pink with a white muzzle and front paws. "Miss Miller made it for me. It used to be a slipper, but she stuffed it and sewed it shut for me so now it looks real." She hopped it across her lap sending the long ears flapping. "It has a sole on the bottom, but I don't care. It will keep her from getting dirty."

Clara watched with a smile. "I love those button eyes."

"I found it in the lost and found at Church on Sunday. Miss Miller said there was only one of them so no one would care if I took it."

Grady grinned. "Does it have a name?"

"I call her Rosie."

Clara fastened the last clip on Prissy's chair. "Perfect. It's a perfect name."

Prissy unzipped the rear section of her backpack and pushed Rosie in up to her paws. "I'm going to let her ride back here."

"That's perfect too."

Prissy perked up. "Oh, by the way, Miss Miller said to tell you Sonti's mother called. He isn't going to school today."

As they approached the school, Grady saw Mister Wilson waiting at the back door. Grady pulled up to the curb and opened the door. "No Sonti today. He's not feeling well."

Clara bent into the stairwell. "We didn't find out he wasn't coming to school until we got to his house, and I thought you should know; we heard Sonti speak this morning."

"He did?! My goodness! What did he say?"

"He said MaMa."

"That's—that's so *great*! Wow!"

Grady waved at him from behind the wheel. "You never know, you might see him sometime around Noon."

Mr. Wilson waved back. "That's true! It's happened before. We'll just have to wait and see."

The radio crackled to life and the dispatcher's monotonal voice filled the bus. "Base to Bus Eighty-Six." Grady picked up the mic. "Eighty-six."

"The school has scheduled a safety drill and assembly this afternoon. All Special Needs children will remain at the school to attend. You are to pick students up after second bell this afternoon."

"Roger that. Eighty-Six out."

After they had delivered the kids, Grady and Clara sat at the front of the bus. Grady turned to Clara. "I'm worried about Sonti."

She gave him a gentle smile. "I'm sure everything will turn out okay. We've been through this with Sonti before. He'll probably be fine at the end of the day. I'd rather go home for a while, but I think we'd better talk about going to the game."

"I don't get what the big deal is. We take them on a field trip every day."

"But it's a Saturday…at night."

"And?"

"We have to get approval to go. There's a ton of paperwork involved."
"Have you done one before?"
"No."
"How much paperwork can there be? We've already got releases for field trips in their files."
"Not for weekends, we don't."
"Well, Miss Miller signs for three of the kids. This is a Hamilton event, so she's not going to object. Who signs for Sonti?"
"I think it's his Mom."
"So, he's not a ward of the home?"
"No. I'm pretty sure she still has to sign."
"Well, his mother has to know how much he loves basketball, so she shouldn't have an issue with it either. We can take care of that in no time."
"That part, maybe, but we also have to get sign-off from the school."
"Okay. So, we'll find out everything we have to do and walk it through."
She shot him an apologetic look. "It's all done online."
"Do we HAVE to do it that way?"
"It's a process. No one's allowed to go outside the process."
"Swell. Just swell!"

Afternoon

After lunch, Clara climbed on board with enthusiasm. "I am happy to report that during lunch I managed to print out the official School Sponsored Field Trip Checklist."
"Wow. Sounds impressive."
"Doesn't it though." She handed him a copy. "I've brought one for you so we can discuss it, but I think we should talk about something else first."
"Ok."
"We need to decide when we're going to tell the kids about this. There's a lot of paperwork involved. There's a chance we could be told no, and they'd be disappointed…or word might get out somehow and they would get teased at school."
"We definitely don't want anything like that to happen, but Bennie *already* knows…he's a big part of how this all happened."
"We could ask him not to tell anyone."
"I know he would try to keep it secret, but you know kids…they get excited. Slip-ups happen."
"So, what should we do?"

"I think our only choice is to have a Milers meeting, swear everyone to secrecy. then remind them about it every day."

"Okay. Makes sense. I agree."— She handed him a copy then settled into her seat. — "I thought maybe we should fill out the form old-school first and hand-write it. Then I'll go home and put it in the computer, and we can go on from there. How does that sound?"

"Sounds like a plan."

She arranged the papers on her lap. "I've never filled one out before, but I've seen a few."

"Okay. Good. Where do we start?"

"I think we should confirm the deadlines first."

"I agree."

She scanned the document with her eyes. "Okay... here it is. It says, "The completed form has to be faxed to *Transportation*, the *Middle School Liaisons*, and the *Cabinet Secretary* two workdays prior to the date of the *Cabinet Meeting*."

"When's the meeting, again?"

She pulled out her phone, logged on to the school web site and swiped around the screen for a minute. "They're on the calendar for March 18th. That means we have to have everything completely signed off on by March 14th to get on the agenda."

"I thought the deadline was two days prior. The 14th is four days."

"It says two *workdays*. The meeting is on a Monday, so we have to have it in by Thursday because of the weekend."

"Oh."

She studied the calendar some more. "Today is the 25th. That means we have exactly"—she counted—"ten workdays to get this through the process."

"Okay, so, I'll work some weekends."

"I will too, but they won't!"

"Okay. Ten days. Now we know. Where do we start?"

"I also managed to wade through some of the form while I printed, and according to the checklist, this trip is a *Class Four* field trip. That's because we have what they consider," she read, "'unique requirements of distance, time, transportation or other costs.'"

"Okay. Class Four it is. What else?"

"We need Parental Permission Slips for the event."

"We figured that. What else?"

"We have to have permission to use the bus. Transportation has to verify that we will: use a *certified* driver and not interfere with the regular transportation system."

"I can handle that one. I'm *certified*. And the rest of it's a no-brainer on a Saturday night."

"We have to have one adult chaperone for every two students."

"Piece a cake. Next?"

"We need what is termed, 'evident…sound…and educational goals.'"

He scrunched up his mouth. "Well…we'll figure it out. What else?"

"We need the approval of seven people."

"Sev-ven!?"

"Yep, we need sign-off from the Program Administrator, the Department Director, the Assistant Superintendent…"

"We know them. No problem. Who else?"

"All members of the Cabinet."

"Who's on the Cabinet?"

"Apparently, there's one representative from each of the four County Districts."

"Do you know who they are?"

"No, but we can look them up really quick. "She picked up her phone and switched screens. "Okay, here we go. *District One* is Leonard Jones."

"Don't know him."

"Me either. *District Two* is Roy Gillum."

"Don't know him either. Do you?"

"Nope. *District Three* is Scott Davis. I do know him. He's a nice man. He should be an easy yes."

"Great. Who's *District Four*?"

Clara turned pale. "Oh-my-God." She looked at him like his dog just died. "*District Four* is Miss Grundel."

Grady's heart stopped. He leaned back in his seat and tried to deal with his feelings. He'd worked so hard…tried so hard to do something good. And now his project was practically dead-on arrival. He looked at Clara. "We're screwed, aren't we?"

She nodded sadly. "Probably."

TUESDAY
February 26, 2019-Morning

Grady showed up at the bus lot early this morning, hoping to have time for a more in-depth conversation with Clara about the situation with Sonti and see if he could find some way to convince her to stick with their plan. Fortunately, she arrived early too, and the minute she climbed on board they both blurted out the same thing. "I've been thinking about this."

They had a good laugh, then she continued on. "I think we should at least try." He nodded. "So do I."

Clara pulled the checklist out of her bag. "I sat up late last night filling in what I could. Actually, all that's left is agreeing on our, evident, sound, educational goals part. So, I went online and pulled up checklists for some trips that have been approved in the past to try and see what they consider a good answer." She handed him the paper. "Here's what I found."

He read the list then put the paper down and stared at her. "You know this is all a bunch of crap, don't you?"

She shrugged. "Welcome to academia."

He scanned down the page again "What is there—some magic list of active verbs and adjectives that have to be used to make it a real application?"

"Well, sort of, yeah." She pulled out a list and handed it to him.

He read. "Unique. Enhance. Visualize. Discuss. Encourage. Dream. College." He handed it back to her. "What happened to *Just Plain Fun*?"

She got an impatient expression on her face. "Look. Do you want to complain? Or do you want to go to the game."

"I'm sorry, Clara. You're doing a great job. Let's go with what we've got and do what we have to do...as long as we can just go to the effin' basketball game and have some fun in spite of them."

Afternoon

When they picked up the kids at school that afternoon, Clara handed out blindfolds. "Put these on, everyone. We're in for a big surprise. Noooo peeking."

The kids chitter-chatted all the way to their destination, trying to guess where they were going. Finally, when they reached Saint Agnes and took off their blindfolds, J.D. looked out the window, obviously disappointed and said, "I don't have to go to the bathroom, Mistow. Redwine."

"I know, but we're still going inside."

Prissy looked around, obviously bewildered. "We're all going to go to the bathroom? I just went."

J.D. watched Clara unbuckle BennieToo. "Why is Bennie coming? He doesn't go to the bathwoom."

Bennie added his two-cents. "Do you have to go to the bathroom, Mr. Redwine?"

Grady and Clara herded them into the gymnasium and turned on the lights. "TaaaDaaaa!"

The kids looked around and gave a unanimous reaction. "Wow!"

Prissy looked around the room. "Why are we here, Mister Redwine?"

"We're going to start getting you ready for your Goal Balloon and, we've got some good news. It looks like Sonti has a chance to get his balloon too and we're going to help him."

Prissy joyfully clasped her hands in front of her. "Really?!"

Clara gave her a big smile. "Really."

Grady continued his introduction "Thanks to Bennie and his family, and if Sonti's mother will let him, he's going to be in the Half-Court Shot Contest at a basketball game and we get to go there and watch him."

The room was filled with a universal "Whoahhhhh" and a lot of, "Thank yous" aimed at Bennie.

J.D. followed up with: "Weally?"

Grady nodded. "Really. But right now, it's a secret and we have some rules. Miss Clara? What is the first thing Milers do when they get on the bus?"

"They look at their balloon and think about what they're going to do to help make it happen that day."

"Right. So now, *I'm* going to tell you what Milers are going to start doing every night when they get *off* the bus: They're going to look at Sonti's balloon and do this..." He pretended to turn a key in a lock over his lips: "And they say, 'Tick-a-Lock' so they remember to keep the secret."

He looked around at the group. "Let's start now, okay? Do it with me." He turned the key in the lock over his lips and said, "Tick-a-Lock. Now, you do it, Miss Clara—"

Clara turned her key and said, "Tick-a-Lock."

Grady swiveled right. "And Prissy?"

Prissy took her turn. "Tick-a-lock."

Grady swiveled right again. "J.D.?"

J.D. turned his key. "Tick-a-lock."

Grady swiveled one last time. "And Bennie?"

Bennie turned a key. "Tick-a-Lock."

"Okay. We're set. Good work, everyone. Are there any more questions?"

Prissy piped up. "Are we coming here every day?"

"There may be some days it's not possible, but we're going to try to always come here first, then go on with our usual activities after."

He formed them all into a huddle in the middle of the room, squatted down and took out a schedule. Then he looked up at BennieToo.

"Bennie?"

The screen lit up. Bennie's smile appeared. "Yes."

"We're going to try and improve Prissy's fitness and runtime, so I'm sending her workout schedule over to you. Your job is to roll the laps with her and keep track of her time. Keep her on schedule. okay?"

"Yes."

Grady fed the schedule into BennieToo's scanner. "Here it comes."

At the other end, Bennie's eyes lit up. "Got it!"

Grady squatted beside Prissy's chair. "Okay. Let's go over it."

"We have eight weeks until the race, so I've built your program with the goal of making sure you peak on your race day, April ninth."

"Yay!"

"We've got to try to do it at least three times a week—more if possible. So, here's what you do—Bennie are you listening?"

BennieToo lit up. "I am."

"Prissy is to warm up rolling laps very slowly for five minutes then cool down for at least five minutes more when she's done. After that, you count off one set of eight repetitions for each of the motions I have on the list, beginning with the two-pound weights."

"Bennie, you roll the laps with her, track the time and count the reps, okay?"

He waited for Bennie's reply of "Okay," then continued his explanation. "Remember the rules with the weights. Slowly up, pause. Slowly down, pause." He looked toward Prissy. "And what?"

She quickly responded, "Resist gravity. No bouncing."

"Perfect! Great answer." Grady switched topics. "Each week we'll increase your time by five minutes and your distance by a quarter of a mile until you reach three miles. Saturday and Sunday, you rest."

He turned toward BennieToo. "Have you got all that Bennie?"

BennieToo lit up. "Got it."

Grady smiled. "Very good."

Grady continued with Prissy. "Today, since we spent this time planning, just roll laps at your normal speed for thirty minutes then rest."

"Okay." Prissy searched around the room. "Where's the track—oh I see. It goes around the outside of the floor."

"While you two are doing that, J.D. and I will be working on getting ready for Sonti when he gets back."

Grady looked at J.D. "Do you have your phone with you?"

"Yes."

"See if you can find an app that measures distance and download it."

J.D. grinned. "Hey evwybody! Mistow Wedwine knows about apps!" Various ooo's and ahhhh's arose from the others, then J.D. turned back to Grady. "I alweady have a app called *May-zuh*. What do you want me to do?"

"This basketball court is designed for a high school. NBA game courts are ninety-four feet long and the mid-court line is forty-seven feet from each baseline. We have to make sure Sonti is practicing the right distance—forty-five feet from the shot line to the center of the hoop."

Grady pulled some masking tape out of his pocket. "We'll mark the new lines on the floor with this."

"Bennie, you help Prissy today and then next time when Sonti is here, you'll be the placer, the ball chaser, and official warmer upper."

He refocused on his project with J.D. and when finished, the two of them stood back to admire their work. "Looks like we've got Sonti set up for success."

"He's gonna need all the help he can get, Mistow Wedwine. I did some we-such. The odds of making a shot from heah ah fifty-to-one."

"So, are you saying you think it looks pretty hopeless?"

"No! I am saying we just have to make shoe he's not the fifty, he's the ONE."

WEDNESDAY
February 27, 2019-Evening

Grady was stretched out in his recliner drinking a beer while he reviewed the events of the day. It had turned out to be fairly routine, all things considered. The stop at the gym in the afternoon came off as planned and there weren't any emergencies. So far, so good.

He and Mary were never big fans of TV viewing on Wednesdays until they decided to turn it into O*ld Movie Night*. They'd put on their pajamas, make a nice fire, open a bottle of their favorite wine, fix a big bowl of butter-soaked popcorn, and settle down to watch a black and white movie or a season of classic TV. They found it rather refreshing, actually, to return to their childhoods awhile and re-living life in a simpler time.

Being the creature of habit that he was, Grady saw no reason to completely change Wednesday's routine even though Mary was gone—especially since the TV lineup had failed to improve. He switched from pajamas to skivvies, forgot the fire, the wine and buttered popcorn, but other than that, left the viewing concept the same.

He ordered an old basketball movie in honor of the season and spent the night watching the hero turn a struggling high school team into winners. Grady mouthed his favorite words with the coach when he said them: "Give it your all—focus, work hard, and push yourself to be the best version of you."

THURSDAY
February 28, 2019-Late Afternoon

Just like they always did, J.D. grabbed Sonti's wheelchair and headed for the hoops when they reached Westlake. After a while, Clara and Sonti settled down in the shade for a snack and J.D. approached Grady carrying a basketball. "Can we wuhk on my dwibble some moe Mistow Wedwine?"

"Sure! Where do you think we should start?"

"I will wecite the wules."

"Great idea."

Grady got things started on the way to the court next door. "Okay, J.D., recite away."

"Wule numbuh one. They is no way-up-high in dwibble."

"Great. And rule number two is…"

"I am the boss of the ball. It is not the boss of me."

"Excellent." He placed the ball in J.D.'s hand. "Show me what you do to start."

J.D. stretched out his arm with the ball in his palm, closed his eyes and turned his hand over. The ball bounced down and back perfectly.

"Wow, J.D. That was great."

"I have been pwacticing."

Grady cleared his throat. "I heard."

J.D. snatched up the ball. "Now watch this. Watch me wun." He went smoothly through his start ritual, but this time when the ball bounced back, he slapped it down with his palm, sending it flying wildly away at an angle. J.D. took off in mad pursuit, managing only to get his hand on the ball every once in a while.

Grady leaned against a post and watched while J.D. whacked away. He wasn't a graceful runner like Sonti. He was all pointy elbows and knock-knees, but Grady had to admire the kid's stubborn pursuit of his goal. In spite of being punished for practicing his dribble, and even though he failed more often than he succeeded, J.D. pushed on.

Surprisingly enough, it wasn't a new experience for Grady to see something like this. None of the kids he'd sent to the pros were natural athletes. But they put in the work, focused on their goals, and it made them millions.

Grady realized that J.D.'s future probably lay in the world of technology, but if it weren't for the unfortunate circumstances surrounding his Autism, the fact that he was pigeon-toed would have made him a prime prospect for several coaches he knew. It was fairly common knowledge among old-school recruiters that running toe-in tends to make an athlete explosive and faster.

The benefit of that physical advantage, however, wouldn't be at all evident to anyone watching J.D. clomp around the court at the current moment.

Grady switched his focus when J.D. turned the far corner and charged in his direction all breathless. "Did you see? Did you see me wun?"

"Yes I did. You ran a lot. But I have a question for you."

"What."

"Who was the boss when you ran, J.D...you or the ball?"

J.D. shifted from foot-to-foot. "I twied to be boss, but the ball kept wunning away."

"You were spanking the ball, J.D. If someone was spanking you, would you want to run away?"

J.D. heaved an exasperated sigh. "Pwobably, but I want to wun with the ball, Mistow Wedwine. If you don't dwibble you can't dwive the lane."

Grady was trying to figure out how to explain that you had to know how to dribble before you could drive when Miss Clara's voice drifted their direction. "Okay everyone. Time to pack up and go home."

Grady looked down at J.D. "Keep up the good work, J.D. We're going to figure this out."

FRIDAY
March 1, 2019-Afternoon

It turned out to be a glorious sunny day, so Grady thought they should take the kids back to Westlake and turn them loose for some more exercise and fun. But since it was their Indy's day, he went through the drive-through, picked up their usual lunch and took them all for a picnic.

Grady watched the boys scamper around for a while and critiqued Prissy's wheeling technique as she did some laps around the courts. Eventually, he glanced over at the basketball in the corner, knowing it wouldn't be long before J.D. would ask him for help again.

How am I going to keep that boy from beating the Hell out of the ball all the time?

He noticed Rosie's floppy-eared head and front feet hanging out of Prissy's backpack and got inspired. He shouted up to Prissy. "Is it OK if Rosie plays with J.D. and me for a while?"

Prissy looked conflicted and took a long stare at her bunny. "What are you going to do?"

"Nothing bad. I promise."

"Ooooookaaay but be careful. If you hurt her or get her dirty, Miss Miller and I will both kick your butts."

Grady retrieved the bunny and held it out to J.D. "Let's play *Pretend*."

"Pwetend what?"

"Just for a minute, we are going to pretend Rosie is a ball."

J.D. shifted his weight from foot-to-foot. "Bunnies don't bounce, Mistow Wedwine. They hop. You need to wead up on you wabbits."

Grady rolled his eyes. "Work with me here."

J.D. rolled his eyes too. "We ah wuhking. We wuhking on my dwibble. I thought."

"I want you to hold out your arm and pretend Rosie's a ball."

J.D.'s eyes shifted nervously toward the other kids. "Do I have to?"

"What's the problem."

"They going to laugh at me."

"If they laugh, J.D., they'll be laughing at me."

He started to place the bunny in J.D.'s palm, but J.D. pulled in his arms and clutched his waist. "Woesie is going to get duhty. Pwissie will be mad at me."

"No she won't." He held the bunny upside-down. "See, she's got a sole like a slipper. She won't get dirty. I promise."

J.D. sighed and let him put Rosie in his hand.

"Now, turn your hand over and let Rosie bounce." J.D. did as he was told and sent Rosie falling toward the ground.

Grady caught her mid-flight. "Excellent. Now watch."

He lowered the bunny to the ground and lifted her to a height just short of J.D.'s hand. "See where Rosie is?"

"Yes."

"What do you want her to do now?"

"Is she still a ball?"

"Yes."

J.D. shifted foot-to-foot. "Do I want huh to bounce again?"

"Yes. Only it would work better if she bounced a little higher, don't you think?"

"Yes."

"So how do you think you could get her to do that?"

J.D. thought for a moment. "I would do this," he said as he hauled off and slapped her hard on the back. Rosie went hurtling headlong toward the ground.

Grady managed to rescue her in time and hugged her against his chest. "Pooor Ro-sie, J.D. You spanked her hard, and she didn't do anything wrong. Do you think she might want to run away from you and hide?"

"Maybe."

"If that happened to you, would you still want to play?"

"No."

"What do you think might make her want to play?"

"I don't know."

"Well, if it was me, I would pet her… like this…." Grady stroked his fingers along Rosie's back, "And I'd say, 'good job, Rosie. Bounce for me again.'"

He held her out toward J.D. "Now you try it."

J.D. ran the flat of his hand down her back. "Good job, Wosie. Bounce foe me again."

"That's a good start but only use your fingers." Grady demonstrated again. He spread his fingers and gently ran them down Rosie's back. "Like this."

J.D. did it right that time.

Ok. Let's review. What is rule number one?

"They is no way-up-high-in-dwibble. Only down. And low."
"Excellent. And rule number two?"
"You ah the boss of the ball. The ball is not the boss of you."
"Good job. So now we're going to add rule number three."
"What is it?"
"Repeat after me. There is no spanking in basketball."
"They is no spanking in basketball."
"Great job. Let's try again." Grady lowered Rosie and brought her back to his hand. J.D. petted her.
"What do you say?"
"Good Wosie. Bounce again."
Grady lowered her once more, brought her back up to the right height.
"Good Wosie."
Grady took a step forward, lowered and lifted her.
J.D. took a step too. "Good Wosie."
Another step.
"Good Wosie."
Then another.

Grady ended it all with a creaky, old-man version of a duck walk across the width of the court, pretending to bounce Rosie so J.D. could learn to pet her correctly, get a feel for the rhythm, and run.

Completely winded when they were done, Grady sank to the ground by the fence, barely able to slap J.D. a high-five. "I'm proud of you, son. You were perfect."

J.D. did a little victory dance, laughing with joy while Grady caught his breath. He set Rosie aside and got to his feet by climbing hand-over-hand up the chain-link in the fence.

Grady took a deep breath when he got to his feet, exhaled hard and inhaled again. "O.K., now pretend the ball is Rosie, J.D." He picked up the ball. "Ready?"

"I guess so."

"Okay, here we go. Hold out your hand." J.D. did. Grady placed it in his palm. We're at rule number two. What do you say?"

J.D. lowered his head and whispered, "You are not the boss of me. I am the boss of you." He turned his hand over and the ball bounced back to his hand as expected, but J.D. obviously lost concentration and slapped it down hard to the pavement. They both stood and watched it fly wildly away, then Grady sent J.D. off to retrieve it.

When J.D. finally returned with the ball, Grady screwed up his mouth. "What happened?"

J.D. hung his head. "I foegot wule thwee. I spanked huh and she wunned away."

"Right. So, let's try again. Pet the ball, J.D., exactly like you did Rosie."

J.D. did. The ball bounced correctly. "Pet her!"

J.D. did.

"Pet her!"

J.D. did.

"Pet her again!" ... "Again!" ... "Again!"

Prissy's voice carried to them from across the court, "Look everybody! Look at J.D.! He can do it! He can dribble! Look at him go!"

J.D. tucked the ball under one arm and took a victory lap, waving the other one, holding his hand high. "I am the boss! I am the boss! I am fin-al-ly the boss of the ball!"

Late Evening

Grady was stretched out in his chair drinking a beer...already a little high over his success with J.D. What a great day! Not only did he have that fun time at Westlake, but it was payday and the first day of March—his all-time favorite month of the year—and that meant March Madness was only three weeks away.

His mind drifted back to watching J.D., knock-kneed and awkward, taking whacks at the ball all afternoon yesterday, and contrasting it with him dressed up in his suit, sprinting back into the school to get his jacket six weeks before. You'd never know the runner coming back out the door that day wearing only one shoe was the same one who first ran inside wearing two. Nor would you confuse that boy in the suit with the boy who was chasing after Rosie on the tennis court this afternoon.

Why?

He ran the memories through his mind like clips from three old movies. Play. Rewind. Play. Rewind. Slow motion. Roll it back again. Bingo!

Shoes! The difference had to be shoes! J.D. ran brilliantly when wearing his wingtips, less well when he'd lost one, and it was just a mess when he clomped around in his worn-out old sneakers.

I don't care what anyone says. That boy has a problem with his feet. Not his legs.

When J.D. had the support of good shoes, his legs would stay straight, and he could run really fast. Without that support, his knees went all bandy, making him awkward and slow.

Grady had true admiration for people who tried, even if they ultimately failed. Back when he was recruiting, he'd take determination over talent any day. J.D. was obviously starved for success and Grady had seen him make sacrifices for it already. So, now that he had figured out a way to help him, Grady was determined to make it happen.

Inspired, he looked at his watch. Eight O'clock. Still early enough. He picked up the phone and dialed an old buddy of his, Marshall Woodward, the orthopedic surgeon who worked with the *War Eagles* and the athletic department.

"Hey Marsh! It's Grady Redwine."

"Well, hello there Coach!..."

Grady smiled. *Coach.*

"We haven't talked in ages."

"I know. Far too long."

Marsh's voice saddened. "We were awfully sorry to hear about Mary, Grady. What a loss."

"Thank you, pal."

"So how the Hell are ya? What's going on?"

"Are you still working with *Athletes for Hope*?"

"Sure am. We've been missing you, by the way."

"I've been missing all of you too and I've come up with an opportunity for us to get together again."

"Any-time. Any-where, Coach. After all you've done for us."

"Well, I have a young man who's got some issues with his feet and really needs some new shoes. Do you think you and the *Hope* team might be able to help us out?"

"Absolutely. Call the office in the morning...we're open on Saturdays...and tell them I want to work you in. We'll do some catching up then."

"Will do. I knew I could count on you. See you soon."

He hung up and rubbed his hands together with enthusiasm. "Allll-Right. We're cookin' with gas, folks."

Grady reached for his *phone* and squinted at the screen. He was used to getting a text first and just answering, so when there was nothing to read on the Messages Screen with an empty box that said *search*, he was a man alone in a foreign land.

He squinted at the long list of numbers on the screen. *Hell.* He put on his glasses and squinted. Fortunately, he found an old message from H. Miller but no empty box to type in. It took a while before he thought to tap the backward arrow and brought up an option to reply.

Good grief!

He entered his message in the text message box, fervently hoping it was going to her.

Miss Millrr sprry to bother you do myte but IM womdring if you hsve any plas fr JD tomorrow.

He stared at the screen. *Well, that's a fine mess.* He intended to erase and start over but heard a sudden swish and realized too late he'd hit *send*.

Oh-Lord.

He heard an immediate ding, and a message appeared.

Mister Redwine, is that you?

He managed to reply, *yes.*

Why don't I just call you back so we can talk.

He searched around for a thumbs-up thingy but the phone rang before he could send it.

Miss Miller's voice came through. "Hello, Mister Redwine. I thought this might be easier."

"How did you know it was me?"

"Texts are sent with your phone number, and I recognized it from our messages before."

"I apologize for the confusion. God used cigars for my fingers."

"What counts is that you tried." She paused. "To tell you the truth, I'd rather talk on the phone, anyway. So, what can I do for you?"

"I was wondering if you have any plans for J.D. tomorrow."

"No. Not really. Just the usual chores. Why?"

"I would like to borrow him for a couple of hours. I want to buy him new shoes."

"How wonderful! He's been saving his chore money for some for a while. He'll be thrilled."

"I'll get back to you with the time when I have everything ironed out."

"Okay. See you then."
Grady smiled to himself. *Well, Redwine. You can finally text.*

SATURDAY
March 2, 2019-Early Morning

Grady had never been what you'd call a physical specimen but staying fit had been a big part of his job as a coach. Unfortunately, the more sedentary lifestyle of driving a bus and—okay, let's face it—frequent consumption of fast-food and beer, had taken its toll on his current conditioning. He realized the moment he opened his eyes and attempted to get out of bed, that he probably should have considered that fact before duckwalking around on cement for an hour using Rosie to teach J.D. how to dribble.

He threw off the covers. *Ahhhh! My back! Oh Lord, my legs! Not my legs! And my arms! My elbows are creaking!*

A voice from somewhere inside him said, *"It's your own fault, Redwine. You had it coming."*

Okay, so it was probably stupid to forget he wasn't twenty-four anymore, but when he remembered the smile on J.D.'s face and that joy on his victory lap, Grady was convinced it was worth it.

You're getting J.D. a new pair of shoes today, Redwine—You've gotta get yourself up and mobile.

Late Morning

The only time in his life Grady wished he had an automatic transmission was this morning. Every push on the clutch felt like agony.

J.D. came running out of the dorm hauling what looked like a very heavy load in his backpack. He opened the door to Grady's truck and tossed the backpack onto the seat. It landed with a noticeable clank.

"Whatcha got in there, pal?"

"Miss Milluh said we buying shoes so I bwought my bank. I want wed ones. Black toe Mid-tops with a swoosh."

"Oh yeah? How much have you got in your bank?"

"Two pounds."

"Two pounds? You weigh your money?"

"Mis-tow Wed-wine…" J.D. fastened his seatbelt. "Why would anyone want to count eighty quahtuhs and fifty dimes when all they had to do was stack them on a scale until it gets to two?"

Grady felt a little flabbergasted. "You've got a point there."

J.D. continued. "I have a pound and a half of quahtuhs and a half a pound of dimes. That makes twenty-five dollahs. I left my nickels at home. It was too heavy."

Who even won-ders about something like that?

J.D. was on a roll. "Did you know ten doluhs in quahtuhs weighs the same as ten doluhs in dimes?"

Actually, no. He didn't. But he decided to play with J.D. a little. "How much is a pound of dollar bills?"

"Foe hundwed fifty foe dollluhs. But I don't have any money that folds wight now."

"This is all very interesting, J.D. How did you figure it out?"

"In-tuh-net."

"Do you know how much those Mid-tops cost?"

"They have used ones on eBay foe Fifty Dolluhs. I thought we could go halfsies."

About that time, they pulled into the *Ankle and Foot Clinic.*

"Why don't we lock your bank in the car for now. We don't have to pay until they fit and everything's right."

"Okay."

They were met in the waiting room by a tall red-headed man in a white medical coat. He gave Grady a big handshake and glanced over toward J.D.

"So, this is your young man. Nice to meet you, J.D. I'm Doctor Woodward."

"I want ...wed ones. Black toe Mid-tops with a swoosh."

The doctor got a little wide-eyed.

Grady could only shrug.

"Those are really good shoes, but they mostly help you jump. Mister Redwine tells me you need to run better, so for now, let's see if we can find some magic shoes that will help you with that."

The doctor began to guide them toward a cubicle in the back when J.D. pulled Grady aside. "Mistow Wedwine. I don't want Magic shoes. I woot foh the Bulls."

Grady did his best to hide a smile. "I promise, J.D. We won't buy magic shoes."

Dr. Woodward took some x-rays and examined the alignment of J.D.'s knees with his feet. Then he measured his foot and selected a sample pair from a shelf running along one wall of the cubicle.

He spoke mostly to Grady. "We need to give him shoes that correct the alignment of his feet and knees to balance the forces on the ligaments. He'll need a wider width shoe with more cushion, but we'll design them to leave the rotation in his foot the same. This will correct his knees but maintain the efficiency of his push off."

"That sounds perfect. We're aiming for fast from the get-go."

The doctor slid the samples onto J.D.'s feet. "It won't be long, young man, before you will run like the wind." He paused. "Do you want to tie them, or do you want me to?"

J.D. hung his head. There was a little shame in his voice. "I can't tie, Doctow Woodwud."

The doctor perked up. "Well, we can fix that, right now J.D." He picked another pair off the wall. "Watch this." The shoe he chose appeared to be one with the usual type ties but when he pulled sideways on the saddle of the shoe, it burst open like a faulty zipper.

Both Grady and J.D. said, "Wow!"

"Now watch this." He slid the open shoe onto J.D.'s foot and gave the ties a flip. As if alive, they zipped themselves together again and looked like any old tennis shoe on any old foot.

The doctor looked toward Grady. "They're super magnets…self-attracting and self-centering. Sewn in. Extra strength. Can't tell the difference between these laces and the real thing."

J.D. was fascinated. "Oh my-gosh!" He pulled them open. Then closed. Then open and closed again. "Oh, can I keep these, Doctuh? I want these."

"Climb down and walk around a little. Let's make sure they fit."

J.D. hopped off the examining table and began to walk. He was graceful. Confident. Straight.

"Let's see you take a couple of laps down the hallway, son."

J.D. took off out the door; reached the front door like lightning, then spun around, absolutely jubilant. "I can wun, Mistowe Wedwine. I can wun!"

"Yes! I see!"

Grady turned toward the doctor. "Are they safe enough to run distances? I mean, they're not going to just pop open on their own, are they?"

"No. They have a really good safety record. I wouldn't recommend them if he was going to run in the Olympics, but for J.D., they should work just fine."

J.D. looked shyly at the doctor. "How much do they cost, Doctuh Woodwuhd?"

Grady winked at the doctor and held up ten fingers twice. "J.D. brought his bank today. Tell the doctor how much you've saved."

J.D. sounded proud to say, "Twenty-five dollahs." He was quick to add, "But if it's not enough, I have some nickels left back at the dohm we could use if we need them."

Dr. Woodward smiled at Grady. "That's perfect. They're twenty dollars for the shoes and four dollars and fifty cents for the laces."

"How much tax?"

"Oh, yes, I almost forgot. Fifty cents tax."

Grady leaned back in his chair. "So, since we're going halvsies, J.D. that's twelve dollars and twenty-five cents for you and the same for me."

The doctor smiled. "That means you have twelve dollars, and twenty-five cents left in your bank, J.D.—plus your nickels. That's a really good start on something else."

J.D.'s face could barely hold his smile.

The doctor began to slip the shoes off J.D.'s feet. "These shoes are for display, J.D. But you're lucky because we have a lab right here in this building and we can have your real ones built by Tuesday."

J.D. looked very disappointed. "Can I pleeze keep these until then?"

The doctor hesitated for a moment. "We don't usually let our demos out…but for you, sure."

"Can my weal ones be wed?"

"Red it is."

"But no swoosh, though, wight?"

"No. No swoosh."

J.D. thought for a minute. "I weally waan-ted a swoosh." He thought for a minute more. "But-I-want-these-laces-moh-than-a-swoosh—so that's okay—I'll take these."

J.D. was already out the door and halfway to the truck when Grady turned toward the doctor and shook his hand. "I can't thank you enough, Mitch."

"I was happy to help. He's a fine boy."

"How much do they cost really?"

"Don't ask."

SUNDAY
March 3, 2019

Grady woke up that morning to cartoons blaring on the TV. How he got to that station was a mystery.

He fished around him in his chair for the remote, but it was nowhere to be found, and he wasn't ready to get up yet, so he just sat there and watched a kid dancing with some animated robots awhile, then checked his guide for the sports lineup. Golf all day. Not his cup of tea. He resigned himself to doing some more work on his brackets, and generally just chill.

And then he heard a reference to *Joystick* and actually recognized the term.

Joystick — I think that's what Bennie uses to control BennieToo.

I bet BennieToo could do that. I'm pretty sure Bennie can dance...or could learn. It would be perfect! Just PERFECT for the Talent Show.

And then it hit him. *Oh-my Lord!* His eyes shot down the hall to Mary's office. *Oh. My. Lord! I can't believe it! This might be a way for Bennie to get his balloon!*

He'd have to first ask his Mom and dad, of course, and clear it with the drama teacher.

WEEK NINE

MONDAY
March 4, 2019-Morning

When Clara arrived at the bus barn and climbed onboard that morning, she stopped at the top of the stairs. "Well, you look happy today."

"I am happy. I'm a Very. Happy. Man. I think I found a way for Bennie to get his balloon."

Clara's face lit up with excitement. "How wonderful. Tell me!"

Grady loved that it was finally his turn to say, "Tell ya later."

Prissy was bubbling over when she boarded the bus. "J.D.'s got a big surprise for you, Mister Redwine."

"Oh yeah? What is it?"

She smiled and switched to a sing-songy voice. "I-I-I'm no-ot tell-ling…"

That's new.

"Besides, J.D. said he'd kill me if I did."

"Well, we can't have that, can we? Guess we better get over there and find out what it is."

"You're gonna love it."

"I'm sure I am."

She looked out the windshield. "Is Sonti riding today?"

"Nope, no Sonti today."

"Well, he can see it tomorrow, I guess."

When they pulled up in front of the dorm, Grady knew it had to be a special occasion because Miss Miller was standing on the porch. She gave them a wave then turned and shouted behind her, obviously signaling the start of something.

J.D. came out the door wearing his loaners and twirling a basketball. He sort of skipped down the stairs, grinned toward the bus and began dribbling like he'd been doing it for twenty years. He dribbled halfway down the sidewalk with his right-hand then smoothly switched to his left and dribbled the rest of the way.

Grady went wild with excitement. "J.D.! My Man! Look at you! How did you do that?"

J.D.'s smile looked wider than his face. "YouTube."

Grady mentally scratched his head. He'd heard of a U-joint puller and a U-bolt clamp, but he'd never heard of a U-tube.

"I studied up on Fwed 'Cuhly' Neal the gweatest dwibbluh the wuhld has evuh seen."

Prissy piped up. "He played the videos over and over and over and over and over. If you ever want to know anything about Fred 'Curly' Neal, you can just ask me."

Miss Miller shouted from the porch. "He drove evvvvverrrrrrybody craaaazy all weekend, practicing so he could surprise you today."

Wow.

J.D. stopped outside the door. "Watch this, Mistow Wedwine." He bounced the ball a couple of times and attempted to pass it from right to left behind his back but missed.

"You're definitely on the right track, J.D. Just a little more practice and you'll have it nailed."

J.D. chased down the ball and piled on board, then dribbled his way to his seat. "I am going to luhn how to do the Low Dwibble, Speed Dwibble. Change-Of-Pace Dwibble...."

Oh-Lord.

"Cwossovuh Dwibble. Hockey Dwibble. Revuhs Dwibble. Half-Revuhs Dwibble. Hesitation Cwossovuh, Behind-the-Back Dwibble. Slip Scissuhs and the El Tohnado Flick."

Grady went on alert. *The Flick is soccer.* He opened his mouth then shut it fast. *Let it go, Redwine. Just let it go.*

Never one to slow down when he was on a roll, J.D. continued talking while he arranged his things. "Did you know Cuhly Neal was bald Mistow Wedwine?"

"Actually, yes, I did."

"They called him that because of Cuhly in the *Thwee Stooges*..."

"I didn't know that."

"He was bald too." J.D. fastened his seat belt. "Cuhly was numbuh twenty-two. And he was the most famous Globetwahttuh of all."

"That I did know."

"If I get a numbuh someday, I want it to be twenty-two, too."

"Great idea."

"I'm going to luhn evewything about him."

"Sounds like fun."

There was a welcome pause, but J.D. wasn't finished. "I wunduh if he was welated to Shaquille Oh-Neal."

"Maybe."
"I'm going to look that up."
"Great idea."
J.D. leaned toward the stairwell as his friend came aboard. "Hey Bennie! Have you huhd of Fwed 'Cuhly' Neal?"

###

Normally, Grady tried to tune it out when one of the kids started spewing reams of information, but J.D. was so over-the-top excited that morning, he got a kick out of listening to him repeat it all for Bennie.

"I played the video, then pwacticed. Then played it, then pwacticed..."

Grady smiled. *Patient man, that Fred "Curley" Neal.*

"...And then, one day I got it! I woked up and pwacticed and suddenly I could dwibble with my left hand! It was like a miwacle."

Bennie sounded excited. "I can hardly wait to see you."

At the school, Grady watched J.D. dribble into the building. "It won't be long before he won't go anywhere without dribbling."

Clara laughed. "I think we're there already."

After School

The dribbling miracle J.D. pulled off over the weekend nagged at Grady all day. While they waited in the bus loop for the kids to come out, he turned to Clara. "I can't stop thinking about what J.D. has done with his dribble. What the heck is a U-Tube, anyway?"

Clara thought for a moment. "It's...it's..." She pulled out her *phone*. "I can't explain it. Let's ask Siri."

Who the Hell is Siri?

She spoke into the phone. "Hey Siri, what is *YouTube*?"

A woman's voice came from the phone's speaker.

> *YouTube is a website designed for sharing videos. Millions of users around the world have created videos on a wide variety of topics and have uploaded them to the site which allows them to be viewed by anyone any time on any day.*

Grady sat in silence.

Clara laughed. "You didn't understand a word of it, did you?"

"Oh, I understood every word. I just haven't got a clue what the words *meant*. You didn't dial the phone number, but she answered you anyway. How could some woman just sit on the phone all day and wait for you to ask her something."

"Well, first of all, Siri isn't a *she*. She's more of an *it*. She's...well she's...I guess you could call her sort of a female...uh...robot...uh...kind of a... librarian. They call her an app—short for application."

"That's just creepy...someone listening all the time."

"Siri only pays attention to what you say after she hears her name. She doesn't listen to ev-ery-thing."

Grady scrunched up his face. "How can she hear her name if she's not listening all the time?"

"She's not a person, Grady. She's just a feature on your phone—like speed dial. She's always there, but she only does stuff when you ask her to. You'll be able to understand it better after you've tried it. Do you want it or don't you."

"I'm not sure."

She reached out her hand. "Here. Give me your phone. I'll ask J.D. to turn it on and if you decide you don't like it, I'll have him turn it off again. How's that?"

He handed it over. "Okay, I guess. If you're sure I can turn it off again if I want to."

"I'm sure. But I kind of suspect that after she's been around for a while, you might start thinking of her as your best friend."

Just then, the bell rang, and they saw J.D. dribbling in their direction. He stopped long enough to walk up the stairs but dribbled down the aisle to his seat. "Pwissy won't be widing this aftuhnoon. She got sent home. She's not feeling well."

Grady and Clara exchanged worried looks. "Do you know what's wrong with her?"

"No. She's just not feeling well, I guess."

Clara helped him stow his backpack. "I want to keep the ball on the seat with me."

Grady turned toward him. "No dribbling while I'm driving, J.D. It's too dangerous. Okay?"

J.D. got a disappointed look on his face. "Couldn't I just be cahful? I have to pwactice."

"You just never know what might happen with the bus moving. You can keep it on the seat, but we'll have to take it away if you bounce it. Okay?"

"Okay. Can I just woll it awound in my hands? I won't bounce it."

"No, because you might accidentally drop it."

"What if I pwomise I won't dwop it."

Grady sent him a "*no*" look.

J.D. crossed his arms roughly across his chest and sank down in his seat all in a pout. "I bet you would let Fwed 'Cuhley' Neal pwactice on the bus."

Grady escalated his answer in the mirror to the evil eye.

"Okay. Okay. I will leave it on the seat."

Clara changed the subject. "J.D., Mister Redwine and I were just talking about Siri. Do you think you could help us launch her on his *phone*?"

"If you give me his phone, I can tuhn it on, but I can't teach him how to use it."

"Why's that?"

"Sihwi can't unduhstand me, Miss Clawa. I can't woll my ahs."

Grady's eyes flashed to the mirror. It was tough to see the embarrassed look on Clara's face and watch her grope for the right thing to say.

Fortunately for everyone, J.D. just continued on in his usual matter-of-fact way. "I can text Sihwi questions, but it's fastuh foe me just to do evwything old-school."

Clara handed Grady's phone to him and in less than a minute, J.D. had the process completed. He began to hand it back to Clara but hesitated. "I bettow show him how myself. I will do it when I get off the bus, okay?"

"Good plan."

When they reached J.D.'s dorm, he paused beside Grady on his way out the door and held up his phone. "Just pwess this bottom button on the wight side—you can wemembuh it because wight also means cowwect—pwess the button and say, 'Hey Sihwi' and when you see a swuh-ly thing, she is weady foe you to tell huh what to do." He handed the phone to him. "I asked foe an Amewican voice. If you want something else, I can change it. Some people find Austwalian fun."

Grady took the phone and tucked it away. "Thank you, J.D. You have helped me a lot."

J.D. responded, "I know." He started down the stairs but turned back. "It's almost Motch Madness, Mistow Wedwine."

Grady knew...boy did he know.

"I am going to do my bwackets tonight."

"Ohh? You do brackets?"

"Yes. Evwy yeah."

"How do you do them?"

"Bawock Obama publishes his evwy yeah. I wait until his is done then I download them and cowwect them."

Grady blinked a couple of times. "You correct them?"

"Yes. He has only been wight once—back in two thousand nine—and even then, UNC wasn't weally his fust choice. It was just a accident that he wote them in. He usually makes it okay until the fohth wownd, so I let him do all the hahd wook to put it togethuh and then I download it and cowwect the west."

"So how often are you right?"

"I am wight sixty-nine puhcent of the time...he's somewheah awound twenty-five."

Grady chuckled.

"I am going to watch as much as I can, ah you?"

"Oh-yeah."

"Maybe someday we could watch a game togethuh."

"I'd like that, J.D. I really would. You have a great weekend, okay?"

"Okay. I am going to pwactice my dwibble this weekend."

"I'm sure Miss Miller will be glad to know that."

J.D. turned to leave. Grady loudly cleared his throat and J.D. turned back to him. "Oh. Yeah. Tick-a-Lock Mistow Wedwine."

"Tick-a-Lock, J.D."

Night at Home

When Grady reached home that night, he sat in his chair and smiled at the memory of J.D. dribbling up the sidewalk from the bus to the door of his dorm. What a difference those shoes made. What a difference good ol' patient Fred "Curley" Neal made. And, with a little help, J.D. pretty much did it on his own. Heaven knows he was motivated—he wouldn't quit talking about it.

Maybe there was something to that online learning stuff after all—the right kid—the right project—a little help on the side. Who knew? It might just work.

After dinner, he figured it was time to start working on his *phone* skills.

With new confidence based on his discussion with Clara and J.D. that morning about the new—what was it? —oh yeah— app as in app-lication— he picked up his phone, searched out the bottom button on the left side, waited for the swirly thing and said, "Hi Swirly." He heard nothing but silence.

I thought she was listening! She's supposed to be listening!

He tried again. "Hi Slurry." "Hello Surry...Circe...Sheri." Silence still. *Some best friend.*

Wait! Maybe it's Hey. I think Clara might have said, "Hey". "Hey Sheri." Nothing. *Come on—come on. I haven't got time for this.* "Please. Surry. Talk to me. Help me."

Grady was disgusted but not defeated. He was on a mission and would not be deterred. He stared at the screen for a moment then went to *Plan B*.

Clara said to think CATS when I'm searching. He remembered to tap on the compass-looking thing, but after he did, five squares appeared: APPLE, Bing, Google, Yahoo, AOL.

Grady slumped back in his chair and let out an exasperated sigh. There were *two* As—APPLE and AOL.

Of course there are. What the Hell do I do now?

He tentatively tapped the square with AOL in it and all kinds of news articles appeared. Not what he wanted.

Great guess, Redwine.

He began pushing random places on the screen, growing more frustrated with each additional failure. *How the Hell do I get back where I want to be?*

It was quite by accident that he managed to hit the spy glass at the bottom. *Ahhh, finally, the search.* He looked at the ceiling. *Thank God.*

He picked AOL, typed in *Gted cugley neesl*, got completely disgusted, hit *cancel,* then tried again a few times until he finally managed to enter *Fred Curley Neal* and tap *search*.

Almost instantly, he had a screen full of squares filled with pictures and a logo indicating he had reached *YouTube*.

Oh! YouTube! Not UTube! So, that's a You Tube!

Grady spent two hours spellbound on the site watching all the tribute videos, game re-runs and dribbling tips. *So that's how J.D. learned to dribble. Wow.*

In time, he located the *search* box and thought for a moment, then just for the heck of it, entered, *Satchmo*. In seconds, at least a dozen items popped onto his screen about *Satchmo Armstrong*.

Whoa!

He watched a few videos, listened to recordings, interviews, tributes and a few speeches. *Who **did** this? Who would even **think** of doing this?*

TUESDAY
March 5, 2019-Morning

J.D. was bubbling over with excitement when he bounded out of the dorm and climbed on board. "Pwissy has a doctow's appointment. She will be widing this aftuhnoon though." He hustled back to his seat and settled in then stuck his legs out in the aisle and waggled his feet. "I tuhn in my loanuhs and get my new shoes today, don't I Mistow Wedwine?"

"Yes, you do."

"Miss Milluh said I couldn't bwing my bank to school, though. We will have to go back home fuhst to get my money."

"We'll go right after school."

Grady glanced at J.D. in the mirror. For the first time in memory, he didn't have his hoodie over his face. Instead, he sat perched on the edge of his seat and greeted everyone as they on-boarded.

"I get my new shoes today, Bennie."

Bennie smiled. "Good for you! Can't wait to see them."

"I get my new shoes today, Sonti."

Sonti said nothing.

J.D. remained undeterred. "I'll tell Pwissy about them this aftuhnoon."

Afternoon

As soon as J.D. saw Prissy sitting on the bus, he started speaking at the bottom of the stairs. "I get my new shoes today, Pwissy."

"I know. I'm excited for you, J.D."

BennieToo came aboard next, and J.D. pounced on him, too. "Did you know I get my new shoes today, Bennie?"

Everyone else looked a little bored with the subject. "We knooooowwwww, J.D. You tolllld us this morning and at lunch."

Clara shot them the evil eye. "We're all very excited for you, J.D. ***Aren't. We.***"

She was hit with a bunch of mumbled uh-huhs and yes-we-are's.

J.D. forged on. "Mistow Wedwine and I ah going to get them wight aftuh we get home tonight. You can see them in the mohning, isn't that wight, Mistow Wedwine?"

Grady looked at J.D. in the mirror. "Uh huh."

Bennie smiled. "That's nice."

Prissy added her two-cents. "Can't wait to see them."

J.D. wrapped it all up with, "I got wed ones. But we couldn't get a swoosh."

After School

J.D. rode with Grady and Clara the entire route, sitting on the edge of his seat, overflowing with excitement.

When they left Clara at the Bus Barn, they climbed into Grady's truck and headed for J.D.'s dorm to pick up his savings.

He raced inside and emerged hauling the same heavy load in his backpack that he brought with him the first time they went to the clinic.

"I weighed evwything again this mohning—twelve dollahs and fifty cents."

"Good job."

"Did you check you twelve dollahs and fifty cents too?"

"I brought my credit card. Have it right here in my pocket."

"That's good. This is vewwy, vewwy impohtant to me, Misow Wedwine."

"To me, too, J.D. I can hardly wait to see them."

###

Doctor Woodward met them at the door holding a box.

J.D.'s eyes lit up. "Ah those my shoes?"

"Yes. Red ones. Just like you ordered."

"Can I cawwy them?"

Doctor Woodward handed the box to him. "Of course you can."

J.D. practically raced down the hall. "I can't wait. I can't wait."

He sat down and dropped his bank on the floor with a clunk. The doctor looked a little bewildered.

Grady smiled. "J.D. brought his savings."

"Oh?"

"Tell the doctor how you got your money, J.D."

"House Duties. I get ten cents a day to mop the kitchen."

Grady watched as Doctor Woodward calculated and saw him mist up a little. "You mopped the kitchen floor two hundred times to buy your shoes?"

"Actually, two hundwed and fifty-six. Sometimes I buy Tootsie Wolls at the school stow instead of saving. But now that Mistow Wedwine and I ah going halvsies, it was weally only about one hundwed and twenty-thwee times."

The doctor swallowed hard before he spoke again. "Well, let's get these on your feet, shall we?"

J.D. waggled his feet in front of him. "Yes. I'm weady to wun like the wind."

The doctor slid them onto J.D.'s feet and smiled. "Want to tie them yourself?"

"Oh yes. I loooove to tie my shoes." J.D. gave them a flip and the magnets flew into place. He gave the doctor an enormous grin. "I smile evwy time I tie now, doctuh. I can't help it."

"They are fun, aren't they." The doctor straightened up. "Looks like they're perfect. Walk around for me and tell me how they feel."

An obvious wave of excitement ran through J.D.'s body as he stood in the shoes the first time. "They feel gweat, doctuh. Gweat!"

The doctor studied J.D. as he walked. "Good walk. Now run for me."

J.D. took off like a shot. "I can wun Mistow Wedwine. Wun like the wind."

"They have arch supports in them, J.D., and your feet might get a little sore after you wear them for an hour or two. I'm going to let you take the loaners home with you. Wear your new ones for an hour today then change back to the loaners. After that, add an hour every day for a week then you can wear them full time."

The doctor patted J.D. on the shoulder. "Bring him back in a week and we'll check everything out again."

J.D. paused and admired his shoes in the mirrored wall, tipping them every which way—smiling—obviously pleased.

J.D. eventually made his way to the checkout window and set his bag on the ledge with the usual clank. Grady smiled and winked at the bewildered nurse.

"I have thwee fohths of a pound of quahtuhs and a fohth of a pound of dimes. That makes twelve dollahs and fifty cents."

Grady wrote her a quick note and passed it over the counter. "Just put it all on my credit card. I'll come back for the bags of change."

She flashed him a kind smile and mouthed back, "Thank you."

Back in the truck, J.D. turned to Grady. "I saw a postuh in the caf-uh-tewia this week about the Dwibble-Off competition. Can you help me get in, Mistow Wedwine? I have my new shoes now, and I think I would like to twy."

Grady's eyebrows shot toward his hairline. He certainly didn't see *this* coming. "I think that's a great idea, J.D. It could sort of be the *last mile* for your balloon."

WEDNESDAY
March 6, 2019-Morning

Clara was carrying two large steaming coffee cups when she met Grady in the Bus Lot that morning. "I splurged and got double shots."

"Perfect. We're gonna need 'em."

She settled into her seat. "So, what's the run-down."

"First, no Prissy this morning. Got a message from Miss Miller that she wasn't feeling well."

Clara sipped at her coffee. "She seemed fine yesterday afternoon. Wonder what happened."

"Don't know. She didn't say."

"So, what else."

"No Sonti—his Mom is driving him this morning. We'll have a full load this afternoon, though." He reached over and turned on the air conditioning. "Gonna be a scorcher today. Seventy-five."

"In March, no less." She sipped at her coffee again. "So, what else is going on?"

"Got the shocker of all shockers when we picked up J.D.'s new shoes last night."

"Oh yeah? What happened?"

"He told me he wants to enter the *Dribble-Off*."

Clara's coffee froze mid-air for a moment, and her eyebrows shot to her hairline. "Noooooooo. Really?"

"Really."

"***Well. Good. For. Him.***"

Grady shot her a big grin. "I can hardly wait to tell Coach Riley."

THURSDAY
March 7, 2019-Mid-Morning

Grady felt it was only fair to give Jack Riley some warning about his plans for the afternoon, so he dialed him up right after his morning run because he knew the Coach's calendar was held open around then. He also knew his name showed up on the phone in the office when it rang. When he was sent to voicemail, he considered just calling back but went ahead with a message anyway.

"Hi Jack! It's Grady. Just wanted to let you know I'm going to enter J.D. Parker in the *Dribble-Off* competition this afternoon. I think it's going to be a lot of fun!"

Grady couldn't have counted to five before Jack called back. "Grady. My man! You have got to be kidding."

"Actually, no. No, I'm not."

"Really? Really!"

"Jack, you know J.D. has the right to compete just like everyone else."

"The contest is for representatives from school districts and club teams, Grady. You know that."

"He'll be representing the Milers Club."

"Grady. Please. This is important to the school and the War Eagles I'm asking you, please don't do it."

"Actually, I feel fairly good about it, Jack. I've been working with him a little and I'm pretty pleased with his progress. You might be surprised at how far he's come."

"I have to put my foot down on this, Grady. It will just be like the *Special Olympics* and Sonti again. I can't be party to letting that poor boy get into a situation where he might be shamed and bullied."

"And you think *I* would?"

"Honestly?!? It's starting to look like yes. Yes, you would."

"Why thank you, Jack. It's nice to know you hold me in such high regard."

There was an awkward silence. Jack's voice came back sounding nervous. "He's not going to ask to go out for the team, is he?"

Grady began to feel a little guilty about how much enjoyment he was getting from Jack's discomfort. "I don't think so, but you never really know what J.D.'s going to do. He might. But I think what he wants the most is to be allowed to go down to the main floor with the other kids."

"I can't let him down there, Grady. He's a constant distraction. It causes mass confusion. You know how mean kids can be."

"I say give him a chance to earn the right to be there, Jack. It's only fair."

"I'm warning you, Grady. You mess me over on this, and…"

"I know. I know. I'll never work in this town again."

Grady hung up and headed straight for the t-shirt souvenir store to buy a size small Milers Jersey with Globetrotters number twenty-two on the back.

Afternoon

J.D. and Grady walked along the hallway following the signs directing everyone to the *Dribble-Off.*

"It is two fifty-five, Mistow Wedwine. It stahts at thwee. Ah we going to be late?"

"No, J.D. We should be just on time."

"They will not let me do it if we ah late."

"Don't worry, J.D. We'll be fine."

J.D. picked up the pace. "It is two fifty-six and we ah not theyuh."

Grady synched his watch with a school clock on the wall. Everything was fine.

"Two fifty-seven!"

"Really, J.D., it's just around the corner down there."

The pitch of J.D.'s voice went up an octave. "Eight! Two fifty-eight!"

The alarm on J.D.'s cell phone went off just as they rounded the corner to the event, catching everyone's attention as they took their place in line behind the other contestants.

Grady was relieved that the first face he saw was a friendly one.

Charlie Carlson stood at the door smiling. "Hello, J.D. Welcome to the *Intermural Dribble-Off.*"

"I set my alahm."

"I can tell."

"We wight on time. Thwee o'clock."

"Yes, you are."

Charlie smiled and handed J.D. a piece of paper. He winked at Grady…code for *I'm not supposed to be happy about this, but I'm glad to see you anyway.*

"Please write your name on this piece of paper and who you are representing, J.D. We'll call your name when it's your turn."

Grady filled out the form for J.D. and handed it to Charlie. "We're representing *the* Milers Club today." Charlie accepted his submission gracefully, but Grady noticed that he folded the forms of the two boys ahead of them in half before they were put in the bowl, but J.D.'s was folded into quarters. They were obviously cheating on the draw. He figured J.D. would either be first so they could get him out of there, or maybe last in case there were issues.

J.D. peered through the doors at the bleachers lined up courtside next to the team bench, filled with families and friends waving banners and holding handmade signs.

J.D.'s eyes darted around as if searching for a place to hide. "I didn't know all those people would be heah. Who ah they?"

Grady fished around in his mind for terms other than *parents* and *friends* and landed on, "**Fans**. All sporting events have fans; you know that J.D."

A hush fell over the room as Grady and J.D. entered the gym. Everyone looked a little stunned for a moment, but the silence soon filled with coughing sounds as kids tried to cover sarcastic remarks.

J.D. made an immediate U-turn out the door. "I changed my mind."

Grady guided him into an alcove out in the hall. "What's going on, J.D.?"

"I am shaking all ovuh inside, Mistow Wedwine. I can't do this…all those people."

"Shaking is a ***good*** thing, J.D.! It's just your body telling you it's pumping adrenaline to give you the energy to do your best. Just take a deep breath and let it out slowly."—J.D. did. —"It will go away soon, you'll see."

Grady squatted down to J.D.'s level. "Actually, I'm glad you brought us out here because…"— He stretched up and glanced around like a spy on the run. — "…I have three secrets to share with you."

J.D. seemed to enjoy the intrigue and glanced around too.

Grady whispered. "Did you spot anything?"

J.D. took one last look left and right, then whispered back at him. "All good."

"Are you ready for the secrets?"

"Weady."

Grady leaned closer. "The first secret is that everyone thinks the *Dribble-Off* is a ***contest***, but it really ***isn't***."

"What is it?"

"It's a ***race***. And *that's a* big difference."

"Why?"

"In a contest, there's *only one winner, and* everyone who doesn't win is called a *loser*."

He watched J.D.'s eyes grow wide.

"But races are different! Can you remember what Prissy says she *loves* about *racing*?"

"She says, evwyone competes against they self to see how fast they can do it."

"That's right. And everyone who doesn't drop out of the race is…what?"

"A winnuh."

"Right. And you are a Miler, J.D. What do Milers do?"

"They finish the wase no mattuh what."

"Even if they are tired or scared?"

"Even then. They nevuh stop until they weach they goal."

"So, the *second* big secret is that you are a winner already, J.D., because you're a Miler and you're going to finish."

"Wow."

"And now for the *biggest* secret."

"What is it?"

"Put your hand on your heart." —J.D. did. — "Can you feel it beating?"

"Yes."

"And can you hear it too?"

J.D. seemed to search around in his head and soon answered, "Yes."

"What does it say?"

"Thump-thump, thump-thump, thump-thump."

"That's what it says *most* of the time, but during a *Dribble-Off*, it's different. During a *Dribble-Off*, it changes to—" Grady patted his chest as he spoke, — "buh-bounce, buh-bounce, buh-bounce. And if the *only thing* you listen to after the whistle blows is your *heart*, and you bounce the ball to its beat, it will help you get through the course much faster."

J.D.'s eyes grew large. "Weally?"

"Really."

"Wow! What a gweat sequwet! Oh Wow!"

Just then, Charlie Carlson stuck his head around the corner and said, "They're getting ready to start down there. Better hurry!"

Grady stood up and looked at J.D. "Are you ready?"

"I am *wead-dy*."

When Grady and J.D. leaned against the wall with the other competitors, first one, then another, and soon everyone around them began to sidle away.

Fortunately, the awkwardness was broken when Coach Riley took center stage.

"On behalf of the *War Eagles*, I would like to welcome everyone to the fourteenth annual *Dribble-Off* competition. I'm Coach Riley and I'm here to describe for you how today is going to work.

"As you can see, there are two lanes marked off the length of the gym. One lane goes away from the start line and the other lane comes back around to the finish.

"Everybody's name has been placed in this bowl. When your name is drawn, it will be your turn to come to the starting line. I will count down from five, and your time will begin when I count down from five and say, 'Go!'"

"You will dribble right-handed, zigzagging around the cones to the end of the left lane, change your pace around the end cones, then dribble left-handed around the cones in the right lane to the finish. Jason Weatherly, the representative from our home team, *The War Eagles* of *District 1* will demonstrate."

Jason rolled the ball in his hands as he strutted to the starting line. He took a swipe across his nose with the back of his wrist, bent to a start position, then nodded toward the coach. *Ready.*

The coach counted down to 'Go!' and Jason took off. He dribbled in and around the cones like a pro, slightly lost balance when he struck a shoe, but recovered well. Energy in the room climbed to a peak and cheers erupted as he approached the finish line. "You're on *fire*, Jason, keep it up.!"; "Way to go!"

Coach Riley smashed the stopwatch with a flourish. "Eleven and a half seconds. Great job, Jason!"

Jason made a fancy bounce between his legs, took a bow toward the stands, and winked at a blond in the bleachers who was gushing, "You crushed it!"

Coach Riley continued his address to the contenders. "Jason has just set the bar." He gestured around the group with fanfare. "*Your* job is to *beat* him.

"The person with the fastest time wins. If there is a tie, there will be a *Dribble-Off*. Are there any questions?" J.D. started to raise his hand.

Oh-Lord.

Grady stopped J.D.'s hand and leaned over to him. "Let's go out in the hallway again. I'll answer any question you have."

Fortunately, J.D. complied without complaint, and when there, he said. "Why do I have to dwibble with my wight hand in the left lane and my left hand in the wight lane?"

"Because those are the rules."

"The wules do not make sense, Mistow Wedwine. When I tuhn awound on the end, I will still be dwibbling on the left side when I come back to the finish line. The first left lane will be the new wight lane. The coach should study up on wules."

"J.D., do you want to dribble on the bottom floor?"

"Yes."

"Then just do what Jason does, follow the coach's instructions, and don't ask any more questions, okay?"

"Okay, but just one mow question. Since I will still be in the left lane aftuh I tuhn awound on the end, I should use my wight hand…since it's the left lane, wight?"

"No. You need to use your left hand."

"Okay. If you say so, Mistow Wedwine, but it still does not make sense. Those ah bad wules. Vewy confusing, bad wules."

Back in the room, Grady was grateful for their forced privacy along the wall while the coach made his closing comments:

"The names have been drawn, and the remaining contestants will compete in the following order: Jeremy Diamond from The Christian Academy *Saints*, Bobby Roman from the District 3 *Mustangs*, Clark Freeman from the District 2 *Warriors,* Nick Haley from the *YMCA*, and J.D. Parker representing the *Milers Club*."

J.D. looked up at Grady. "I'm last."

Grady smiled at him. "That makes you lucky, J.D."—He squatted down so they'd be head level, and whispered, —"You get to watch everyone else and learn."

Jeremy Diamond entered Lane One, bent to a start position and nodded toward the coach. *Ready.*

The coach counted down; the whistle blew; and Jeremy took off. He dribbled in and around the cones without error while the crowd cheered him on and he finished with a flourish, shouting, "Go! *Saints*! Go!"

Coach Riley smashed the button on the stopwatch. "Thirteen seconds! Good work, Jeremy."

A man in the stands who was obviously Jeremy's father shouted, "You'll get it next time, son."

Grady leaned toward J.D. and said under his breath, "What would Curly tell Jeremy, J. D.?"

J.D. leaned his direction and whispered, "Quit watching the ball. Watch wheah you going." Then he smiled and continued, "But **you** would tell him, twust Psychics."

Grady chuckled and whispered back, "Good man."

Bobby Roman was called next to Lane One. He took the position, nodded for the countdown, and the whistle blew. Bobby dribbled in and around the cones quite well. Energy in the room climbed to a peak and cheers from the crowd erupted as he approached the finish line. "Buck 'em *Mustangs*!"; "You got this!"

Coach Riley hit the stopwatch. "Twelve Seconds. Great job, Bobby!"

Grady leaned toward J.D. "What cost him that half-second?"

"He dwibbled moh with his palm than his finguh tips."

"Correct."

Clark Freeman was called to the lane. He took the position, nodded, and the coach counted down. Clark took off like he was shot from a cannon. He maneuvered in and out of the cones like a pro, with whistles and shouts from the crowd echoing around him. "That's how it's done!"; "Incredible!"; "Unbelievable!"

He finished his run to an explosion of applause and cheers, clocking in at an impressive eleven point seventy-five seconds. "Way to Go! Way to Go *Warriors*!"

Grady whispered to J.D. "What cost him the contest, J.D.?"

Obviously mystified, J.D. answered, "I don't know."

Grady leaned toward him. "He took the turn on the outside of his foot. If you take the turn on the ball of your foot, I think you can win."

J.D.'s eyes lit up. "I will do that!"

When Coach Riley called Nick Haley to the lane, he announced that Nick had injured an ankle the previous week during a game, but he worked hard to be able to compete today, so he wanted to participate anyway. The crowd shouted encouragement when he took the starting position. "Hang in there, you can do it!"; "Shake it off!" But Nick was only able to limp stiffly around the cones and shuffle off at the sound of the whistle.

Coach Riley ended it with, "Thanks for being brave and showing up, Nick! See ya again next year." Then he called J.D.'s name.

Grady stood up and gave J.D. a reassuring grin. "You're up!" He bent down and whispered, "You worked hard for this, J.D. You are the **boss** of the ball. Go out there and show 'em what you can do."

"I'm going to twy hahd Mistow Wedwine."

"We're not here to *try*, J.D. We're here to *do it*."

J.D. made somewhat of a sorry figure as he awkwardly walked onto the court, and a soft murmur rippled through the crowd when he entered the lane. But when it became time to take the starting position, he straightened with confidence, stood tall with enormous dignity, glanced toward Grady and placed his hand on his heart.

Grady placed his hand on his own heart as well and sent an encouraging nod. Coach Riley looked in J.D.'s direction. "Are you ready?"

J.D. mimicked Jason's signature back-wrist-swipe at his nose, bent to a starting position and stared at the line. "Weady."

Grady closed his eyes, knowing he could monitor J.D.'s progress through the course most effectively by tuning into the rhythmic bounce of the ball and the squeak of his shoes on the floor.

He sent up a silent prayer and whispered, "Come on, son, come on! You can do this."

The coach counted down. The whistle blew. Grady heard J.D. explode off the line and settle into the steady *buh-bump, buh-bump, buh-bump* of the ball down the straightaway; then crank up to a methodical route through the cones: *buhbump–buhbump– buhbump– buhbump – buhbump– buhbump. A*s he approached and made what had to be a flawless turn at the top of the course, *buhbump – buhbump–buhbump,* he sprinted hard for the finish line: *BumpBumpBumpBumpBump-buhBump.*

Jack smashed his thumb down on the stopwatch and studied it with startled eyes. "Eleven seconds flat!" He turned toward Grady and held out the stopwatch, obviously bewildered. "Eleven!!"

The gym was completely silent for a few stunned seconds then filled with audible whispers and gasps.

Grady shrugged *whaddaya expect* and jogged J.D.'s direction grinning from ear-to-ear.

Jason spoke up. "I want a *Dribble-Off*, Coach."

Jack responded immediately. "This wasn't a *tie*, Jason. Not even **close**."

J.D. pulled on Grady's shirt tail and whispered, "Maybe we **should** do it ovuh, Mistow Wedwine. I foegot to make the show-off bounce between my legs at the end."

Grady chuckled. "Don't worry, J.D. They won't count *that* against you. You made Curly *proud.*"

Coach Riley picked up the trophy and presented it to J.D. "You won, son. Fair and square." Then he turned and addressed the crowd. "Let's hear it for J.D. Parker!" There was a ripple of restrained applause.

J.D. clutched the trophy to his chest and remained speechless. Grady nudged him. "Thank the coach, J.D."

"Thank you, Coach Wiley. Can I dwibble on the bottom flooh of the gym with evwyone else now?"

"Any time you want to, J.D.. You have earned the right."

J.D. turned to Grady. "We can go home now, Mistow Wedwine." They walked past the bleachers filled with astonished looks and muffled muttering.

When they reached the hallway J.D. said, "Who is we-tah-ded now, Jason Black-buhn."

Evening

Grady hadn't been home for ten minutes before his phone rang, and Jack Riley's name appeared.

"Hello Jack."

"What did you feed that boy, Grady?"

"Pretty remarkable, isn't he?"

"I've been thinking about it all afternoon. Didn't expect such good ball handling around that course from J.D.."

"He worked very hard."

"I've been thinking. Basketball teams can always use good ball handlers. Do you think he might like to try out for JV? We can take a close look if he does—see if there might be something there."

Grady stretched out in his recliner and grinned. "Wellll, I can tell you that if J.D. was on the team, you could go through your game plan once and he would remember every move. He's got a great work ethic. He's goal oriented. With a little help, he could pass the ball about as well as anybody. And...you saw him dribble."

He left out what a nightmare J.D. would be playing defense. He could calculate like a genius but had limited ability to anticipate. Jack would go through Hell trying to convince him to change something between plays, but J.D. genuinely earned some time in the sun, and he was going to let him have it.

"I'd be happy to ask him if you want me to, Jack...or *you* can invite him."

"I think it would be better if *you* did, Grady. After all, you're the one who got him to the contest. If he says yes and you agree, then you and I can take it from there, how's that?"

"Let's play it by ear. I'll ask and get back to you. How does that sound?"

"Sounds good." There was a moment of hesitation, then Jack said, "Please. Try to be convincing."

FRIDAY
March 8, 2019-Morning

Last School Day Before Spring Break

Grady and Clara were sitting outside Prissy's dorm that morning waiting for her to arrive. They were expecting to receive one of her usual updates of the previous night's events and hear about the big celebration of J.D.'s victory at the dorm, but it was obvious that wasn't going to happen the minute she rolled onto the driveway. Her energy was low. Her usual smile was missing. She took her time getting to the bus and said nothing but, "Morning Miss Clara" when she reached the lift.

Grady watched her ease into place behind him, lethargically go through the routine of getting herself clipped into place, then slump back in her chair.

"You okay Miss Priss?"

"I just found out that I can't do my fast 4K, Mister Redwine."

He released the brake and began to drive. "What happened?"

"I have to have my foot cut off instead."

The bus swerved a little.

"They can't get the circulation right in it, so it's going to turn blue and die."

He saw Clara's eyes go misty. "Tell Mister Redwine how many surgeries you've had, Prissy."

"Thirty-Two."

Grady's voice came out an octave high. "Thirty-Two!?"

"I was hoping Thirty-Three would be my lucky surgery—the one where they straighten my back, but I guess I'll have to wait 'till Thirty-Four."

"I'm so sorry about your foot, Prissy."

"Oh, thank you, but I don't use the old thing much anyway. What I'm worried about is my daddy. How am I going to get a certificate to give him for *Father's Day* if I don't run the 4K?"

"He'll understand, honey. Don't worry about that one minute."

"Not having that foot is going to throw my balance off. I might not be able to win one again."

"Don't you worry about that either, honey. We'll figure it out and work through it together."

Grady was glad that J.D.'s pick-up spot was just around the corner from Prissy's. He was finding himself at a loss for words.

J.D. climbed on board in a sober mood and paused beside Prissy. "I hood about you foot, Pwissy. Does that mean you will miss the 4K?"

She nodded. "And I won't get to pop my balloon."

"I'm weally, weally sohwy to know that."

"Thank you, J.D. So am I."

The bus remained fairly silent the rest of the route. Grady intercepted J.D. as he left the bus. "Could I talk to you a minute, J.D.?"

"Will I be late for the bell?"

"No. I just have a message for you from Coach Riley."

"It is eight twenty-eight. Is it a showt message?"

"Sort of. He wants to know if you would like to try out for the *War Eagles* Junior Varsity basketball team."

"It is eight twenty-nine."

"Well, give it some thought. You can tell me later if you want."

"I have a minute left. I can tell you now. I don't want to be a basketball playuh, Mistow Wedwine. Pweese tell Coach Wiley all I want is to dwibble on the bottom flooh with evwyone else like he pwomised."

"Okay. I will. I'll tell him."

J.D. adjusted his backpack and took off for the door. "I shoe hope Coach Wiley has not made me late."

Late Morning

As soon as they had dropped off the kids and made their way back to the bus barn, Grady pulled out the folio containing their emergency data and ripped open the strip of Velcro.

Clara looked puzzled. "What's up?"

"I'm going to write the Commanding Officer of Major Milcamp's military unit and request that he be given humanitarian leave so he can come here when Prissy has her surgery."

He thumbed through Prissy's paperwork. "Hmmmm. It just has *Stateside* emergency contacts and only lists the folks at the *Shelter*."

Clara took a seat across from him. "It's my understanding that Prissy is a legal ward of the State."

"But she still has a father. Surely, they'll let him come here for something like this. She shouldn't go through an amputation alone." He kept shuffling through the documents. "I take it from how she talks, he's either in the Army, the Marines or Special Forces. He doesn't seem like a Navy or Air Force kinda guy.

"Grady?"

"We have to give them enough notice and make sure we've submitted the right paperwork." He kept searching for a blank sheet of paper to write on. "Yeah?"

"Grady. Look at me."

He turned toward her. "Okay...what's up?"

"Grady, Prissy's father can't come here."

"Why? Is he on some sort of secret mission or something? They've got to know where he is."

Clara lowered her voice. "Prissy's father is in prison, Grady. He's on Death Row for murder."

Grady felt like he'd been gut punched. "Please. Don't tell me it was her mother."

"Nobody knows. They don't ever give us details about confidential things like that."

"Well, you'd think it would have been all over the papers."

"Maybe so. But they're still keeping it on the downlow."

"How long has she been in the *Shelter*?"

"Seven years."

"So that makes her around four when everything happened."

"It could be they're keeping it from her because she's so young and has gone through so much with her health and all. Maybe they think believing he's out there free and alive gives her some hope to live on."

"Well, I'm glad I'm not the one making that call. There isn't a good answer. Both options are cruel.

"Her father is practically all she talks about—living with him in California when he comes home from the war."

"She's going to get a big shock someday...doesn't seem fair."

Afternoon

At the school, Grady couldn't take his eyes off the bushes outside the side entrance. J.D. wasn't hiding in his usual spot there today.

Uh oh. I sure hope he's okay.

After a tense fifteen minutes, the second bell rang, and J.D. appeared at the main entrance. In the past, Grady had seen kids let go of the door and allow it to swing back on J.D. to hit him, but today they held it open and waited. Grady noticed a slight strut in his step as he strolled down the sidewalk, straight and tall in his shoes. Heads were turning. Kids were pointing but not making fun.

A little girl's voice drifted into the bus from the yard. "Who is that?"

In his head, Grady answered, "That, little missy, is *the* J.D. Parker—star of the basketball *Dribble-Off*—the most talked-about prospect and runaway favorite to be hand-picked for a spot in the *War Eagles* Junior Varsity Team."

When all the Milers were settled into their seats, Grady drove out of the bus loop, parked in a nearby delivery lot and turned on his four-way flashers. Soon after, Miss Miller pulled in driving the Hamilton School van packed with J.D.'s housemates and parked.

J.D. looked somewhat gob-smacked: "What's going on?"

Grady opened the door to the bus, leaned out and shouted to Miss Miller. "Thanks so much! We'll have them back home by dinner."

She shouted back. "No later than six please! We're having a big celebration!"

Everyone left the Hamilton van, piled onto the bus and settled into seats, holding up signs that said, ***Congratulations!*** and ***We're Proud of You, J.D.!***

Grady watched Clara ceremoniously pull the magnetic clip holding J.D.'s balloon off the rail over his seat and anchor it on the pole at the top of the stairs.

When Clara was finished, Grady saw her hand her smartphone to Prissy and say, "Your job is getting Bennie on the phone and holding the camera so he can see everything that's going on."

Grady helped Clara hand out noisemakers and bottles of bubbles, then retreated to the driver's seat as chaos ensued.

Above the roar, Clara continued. "It's time for you to pop your balloon, J.D. Come up here and COL-LECT YOUR DOL-LAR!!"

The kids wildly clapped and hooted as J.D. rose from his seat and walked to the front of the bus.

Grady settled everyone down a bit and said, "This is an incredible accomplishment, J.D. You're the first one ever to get a ***Miler*** balloon and we're all so proud of you for your hard work and determination."

J.D. smiled and accepted the official stickpin from Clara, then everyone sang: ***"Congratulations to you, Congratulations to you, Congratu-laaaaaa-tions, Jay Dee-ee, Congratulations to you."***

When they were finished, Grady watched J. D. grab the balloon and pop it, sending a spectacular display of colored glitter into the air that settled all over him; covered the hair of the jubilant kids on the bus; and made a horrible, marvelous mess.

J.D. chased after the dollar as it floated around, and the kids gathered up handfuls of glitter amid squeals of delight. When he managed to catch his dollar, the kids began tossing the glitter back into the air and all over each other. Clara started some music and turned on the intercom.

J.D. threw up his arms, fists raised high in victory and did a darn good dance around the top of the stairs, eyes sparkling with pride and sheer joy. In time all the other kids joined in, and everyone rocked out in the aisles.

Late Afternoon

After they got everyone safely delivered home that evening, and were on their way back to park the bus, Clara let out a sudden howl of laughter.

"What's that all about?"

"I was just imagining bath time at the dorm tonight. Miss Miller thought pulling paper shreds out of poo in pull-ups after community service was hard. I can imagine what she's going through tonight with all that glitter."

Grady howled. "This is sort of different, though, don't you think? I believe she's proud of J.D."

Clara smiled. "So do I. But maybe we should lay low for a while just in case."

He drove for a while then glanced at Clara. "By the way, where did you get the music?"

"It's a recording of my sons' band practice from last week."

"It's really good! What do they call themselves?"

"They've tossed several names around, but I think they've finally settled on, *The Real Deal*."

"Well, I think it fits!"

"Thanks. I do too." He saw her look around, assessing the mess. "I'll bring the band down tomorrow to help clean this place up after they practice," she said.

"I'll help!"

"Thanks, but I think I should do it as penance for making Miss Miller's life miserable. The glitter was my idea in the first place."

Grady dropped Clara off at her car then headed down his favorite short cut -- the loading dock alley running behind the high school. He noticed delivery trucks unloading flats of scenery and taking them through the back door by the auditorium which set off an alarm in his mind. He pulled out his *phone* and looked at the date: March 8.

"Oh, my Lord! Bennie! I forgot about Bennie! Today's the sign-up deadline for the Talent Show."

Grady swung into a parking spot and raced through the back door of the building. He asked the first person he ran across standing in the hall giving instructions if he knew the theater teacher and watched the startled look in the man's eyes as they surveyed the glitter all over his clothes. Grady brushed a few flecks off his sleeve and said, "Uh, we had a party."

The man chuckled. "Looks like it was a good one. Wish I'd been there."

Grady repeated his question. "Do you know where I could find the theater teacher?"

The man smiled. "That would be me—I'm George Walsh."

"I'm terribly sorry to bother you this late, Mister Walsh, but I just remembered that today is the deadline for the Talent Show. I know it's late and I apologize for that, but I need to sign up one of my students."

The theater teacher glanced out the door. "Is that your bus?"

"Yes, it is."

"It's a *Special Needs* Bus."

"Yes, it is."

"Perhaps we should discuss some parameters. I won't be party to putting a child in an embarrassing situation."

"Nor would I."

"What would your student be doing?"

"I want to enter a boy and his dancing robot."

"Let me guess. Bennie Hamilton."

"Yep!"

Grady could read, *Nobody says no to the Hamiltons* in the man's eyes, but even so, Mister Walsh was still hesitant.

"Bennie's at home, as you know. How would this work?"

"Just like it works every day in school. Bennie himself will be at home and BennieToo will be here. Bennie's talent will be making BennieToo dance."

Mr. Walsh lit up all over. "I love the idea—simply LOVE it."

He paused to think for a minute. "We'll have to make do with the equipment I already have here. There won't be time to get anything else through budgeting and the rental process in time. I'll give you the paperwork tomorrow—parental permission, insurance releases, etcetera. We'll definitely need a *License to Use* for the music."

Grady felt his body break out in a sweat. "Uh, *License to Use?*"

"It's illegal to use published music without permission—even for educational purposes—which this isn't."

Grady glanced at the clock. It was four o'clock on a FRIDAY. "Hope you don't need it tomorrow."

"No just by the fifteenth—the day before the show." He flipped through some papers on his clipboard. "We're having individual logistics meetings with contestants all day tomorrow. Can you come in at ten?"

He didn't have a clue, but still answered, "Sure!"

"We can work out the props and logistics one-on-one. You can work on your routine however you want—at home, or I can check for openings in the schedule. The Talent Show is the night of the sixteenth. Can you be ready?"

Grady didn't have the foggiest idea but still answered, "Yes! We can!"

Grady didn't go home. He couldn't waste time, so he returned to the bus, turned it on, and called out to BennieToo still in the back seat. "Bennie, are you there?"

The screen lit up and Bennie appeared. "Hi Mister Redwine! You're working late."

"Do you have time for a brief conversation?"

"I do."

"I've been thinking Bennie, about your balloon."

"So have I. But I haven't come up with a goal yet. I'm sorry."

"No pressure, Bennie. Not to worry. But I have a question. Can you dance?"

"I **LOVE** to dance."

"What kind of music do you like to dance to?"

"Rock…hip-hop…just about anything."

"Great! I have an idea, but I need to talk to both you and your mother. Is she at home?"

"Yes she is."

"Could you call her and ask when we might have a short conversation, if at all possible, soon, and call me back?"

"Okay."

"Do you have my number?"

"Yes I do. We'll probably use *FaceTime*."

"Use what?"

"Um...I can't really explain it. Just answer your phone the way you always do, and you'll see what I mean."

"Oh—okay. Should I be nervous?"

Bennie laughed. "No. Not at all."

Grady stewed around for about half an hour, then Bennie called him back again. He tapped to answer and both Bennie and his mother appeared on the screen.

Grady was completely taken aback. *Whoah hohohohoho!*

Bennie's voice came over the line. "Hello Mister Redwine. We're using *FaceTime*. How do you like it?"

Grady studied the screen closer. "Uh, I—I think *FaceTime* is — wonderful."

Mrs. Hamilton smiled at him and said, "Bennie tells me you have an idea for his balloon."

"I do."

"That's wonderful!! Please tell us about it! We're anxious to hear what you have in mind."

"It's just an idea, and maybe a little bit crazy, but I thought I'd run it by you, Mrs. Hamilton."

"Shoot."

"I was watching a documentary this weekend about how *Motion Capture* is being used in movies, and it dawned on me that Bennie has a *Motion Capture* suit that he uses with BennieToo."

"That's correct. He does."

"Well, I've seen how proficient Bennie is at using BennieToo to help J.D. retrieve basketballs and it occurred to me that if Bennie can dance, we could use those skills in the upcoming Talent Contest for his balloon."

There was a pause then she said, "That's very interesting. How would he use them?"

"Bennie tells me he likes to dance."

"He does! He and BennieToo dance all the time,"

Grady continued. "Well, I was thinking we could find some appropriate music, light up the stage like a disco, and BennieToo could perform. I think it would be grand."

"What a fab-u-lous idea!" She turned to Bennie. "What do you think, honey? Do you think you and BennieToo can do it?"

"I *know* we can."

Grady grinned. "Then let's try it, okay? You can get your balloon!"

Bennie raised up and let out a jubilant "Yay!"

Grady hesitated for a second or two. "We have to use music that doesn't require a *License to Use* but I have an idea where we can get some. Do you remember the music from J.D.'s balloon celebration, Bennie?"

"Yes! It was great!"

"Do you think you could dance to one of the songs from that?"

"Oh yes! I would love to."

"I was hoping you'd say that. I'll check with Miss Clara tomorrow and see if we can get permission to use it, I can't imagine it will be a problem. When we get everything settled, I'll get a tape over to you so you can practice."

"If you could fill out the paperwork and help Bennie with the music and practice, Mrs. Hamilton, I'll handle the lighting and logistics."

She answered enthusiastically, "It's a deal."

Grady continued. "I'll fax over the paperwork from the School District as soon as I get it tomorrow morning. During our rehearsal time, I can check out the sound and lighting. I'm going to call J.D. and see if he can help me. I'll check everything out and get back to you…and if you have any questions, just give me another face call and we'll discuss it."

Bennie and his Mom lit up like Christmas.

Evening

Grady called Miss Miller rather than texting this time. It was too complicated. "I was wondering if I could borrow J.D. for a while tomorrow. I need him to help me with a project. Is he available?"

"Sure."

"Is he there? Can I talk to him?"

He heard her put her hand over the mouthpiece and the muffled sound of her voice shouting upstairs. "J.D. It's Mister Redwine on the phone. Hurry downstairs, please. He wants to talk to you on the housephone."

He heard J.D.'s footsteps on the stairs and his voice coming nearer and nearer to the phone. "Why did he call *you* if he wanted to talk to *me*? I was in the showuh."

"J.D.! Why didn't you put on your robe? You're wet! It's cold down here."

J.D. sounded bewildered. "I huw-wied."

He heard the transfer rattle of the phone and J.D.'s voice arrived on his phone. "Mistow Wedwine, I was in the showuh. Why did you call me on *this* phone?"

Sounds of people rushing around to get J.D. dry and decent echoed around in the background. "I called Miss Miller to ask if you could help me with a project tomorrow and she called you down."

"Oh. What pwoject do you need me foh?"

"How would you like to help Bennie get his balloon?"

"Bennie doesn't have a balloon yet."

"He has one now. Do you want to help?"

"I'm a Mile-uh. That's what we do."

"Great! That's what I like to hear. We only have a short time to pull it together."

"What do you need?"

"Bennie Too is going to do a dance on the stage at the Talent Show."

"Oh wow! That's gweat! What do you need fwum me?"

"I need you to help figure out the technology. I'm getting the music, but we need to tell Mr. Walsh what we need for sound and lighting. Could you give it some thought and figure out what we will need to do it?"

"Yes. I can do that."

"Tonight?"

"Yes."

"Mr. Walsh needs a list. Can you put one together on your computer and bring a printed copy tomorrow morning?"

"Okay. Yes. I can do that."

"I'll pick you up at nine o'clock. If you have any questions, just text me or call me at home tonight, OK?"

"OK."

"See you in the morning. Nine o'clock."

"At least I will have my showuh ovuh by then."

SATURDAY
March 09, 2019

First Day of Spring Break

When Grady and J.D. presented their list to Mr. Walsh that morning, he hesitated. "This is quite a list, J.D. I must say, you're very organized."

"Yes."

"I'm impressed."

J.D. skipped right over the compliment and began to read the list from his phone...all business. "I need twelve things."

"I hope we have them all. I'll do my best, but we'll have to make do with the equipment I have here already. There won't be time to get anything else through budgeting and the rental process in time."

J.D. continued his train of thought. "All we have to do foe sound is amplify the PA system. I can do that with a micwophone and a speakuh.

"I alweady have the music. I can play it eithuh fwom my smahtphone on my computah, but I need *Bluetooth* to do it..."

"Oh Yeah?"

"The amplifieuh weceives the signal from the micwophone, amplifies it with level contwol, and then the sound is output from the speakuh. So, weally all I need is a mixuh with a built-in speakuh; at least one loudspeakuh...two would be bettuh; a micwophone...wie-uh-less is best; level con-twoe-luh; and extwa bat-tuh-wies."

Mr. Walsh's eyes were about the size of chicken eggs. "Oookay then."

J.D. continued. "The lighting is a little moe complicated. Do you have a patch panel?"

"No."

"That's okay. I can get along without one. I definitely need a *follow* spotlight, though. Have you got one?"

"No, but I have several FRESNELs, will that work?"

"I could pwobably jewwy-wig one if you don't mine us taking it down and holding it. We definitely have to twack him."

Grady jumped in. "If we have to, we'll hunt one down and rent it ourselves."

Mr. Walsh replied. "Good. If we end up having to do that, I can hook it all up in no time."

J.D. finished. "I will also need a on/off switch and a dim-muh."

Grady watched a mystified look spread over Mr. Walsh's face. "How did he learn all this stuff?"

"Probably YouTube."

SUNDAY
March 10, 2019

Spring Break & Daylight Savings

Grady hated Daylight Savings time. *What **idiot** decided to change the time on a **SUN**-day! Nobody even gets a day off to adjust!*

*I get up at 4AM **now**! If it wasn't Spring Break tomorrow, I'd have to get up at 3!*

People rave about the long sunny evenings, but most of them never had to pick up a bunch of kids in pitch black and unload them again in the dark. It's dangerous and it makes nearly everyone grumpy for at least a week when the sun doesn't show up until 8:25.

The whole concept just sucks; you ask me.

After he got all that off his chest, Grady pondered the situation for a while and decided he should start getting used to the time change early. The best way to do that would be to start sleeping in the bedroom and set the alarm, because he knew that if he slept in the den, he'd end up just rolling over at three.

He locked the doors and turned off the lights in the front of the house and headed down the hall toward the master bedroom, stopping to place his hand on Mary's clock for a minute or two for moral support.

He heard Mary's voice in the back of his mind telling him gently, *"You've been in my office and gone through my things. You've conquered the kitchen, my love, and survived. Take advantage of this time away from your job and do your best to try and move on."*

After a minute or two, he walked down the hall and paused in the doorway of the room where he and Mary spent forty-five years laughing and loving. The king-sized bed was still neatly made, but it looked awfully lonely and empty from where he was standing.

Grady set the alarm. Then he curled up in the middle of the bed fully dressed; clutched Mary's pillow against his chest; and buried his face deep in its softness. The familiar scent of Lavender Oil Mary put on it at night to help her sleep remained in the fabric, so he inhaled deeply, hoping it would somehow help him rest too.

WEEK TEN

MONDAY
March 11, 2019-*Spring* Break

Grady got a text from Clara first thing that morning:

I'm almost ready to submit our application for the field trip but we still need the permission slip from Sonti's Mom to do it.

He picked up the phone and called her. She answered with, "Sorry to bother you with this, but I didn't know what to do."

"You can call me anytime, from anywhere, Clara. No problem."—He shifted in his seat. — "So, about Sonti's Mom. Let me ask a few questions."

"Shoot."

"Do we have to send copies of the permission slips?"

"No."

"Is there a checklist that we have to submit verifying we have everything?"

"No. It just says it's a requirement to have it."

"Does it say we have to have it before we submit the form?"

"Let me check." —He heard papers shuffling. — "No. It doesn't say we do."

"Well, I'm not going to lie to anyone and I'm not going to ask you to lie either…"

Clara jumped in. "Good. Because I wouldn't."

"…but I don't think there's anything wrong with submitting what we have so far, just to make sure we get it in on time…and as-suuum-ming we'll have it before the night of the event."

Clara hesitated a moment then said, "Let's agree up front, though, that if we don't have it by the night of the contest, Sonti can't go. It's hard, Grady, I know. But that's what we have to do."

"I agree one hundred percent. Victor Hamilton made having permission from Sonti's mother a requirement to let him participate and I gave him my word on that. But even if I hadn't, I wouldn't put him or the contest on the spot with this situation. It's too important."

"Good. Then it's a go. I'm pushing the *submit* button now."

TUESDAY & WEDNESDAY
March 12-13, 2019-Spring Break

Grady bounded out of bed that morning. The official NCAA Selection Committee was going to announce the full brackets for the tournament, and he was beside himself with excitement. There was a long string of events scheduled over the next two days: live broadcasts and updates; *March Madness* analysis; extensive game highlights; expert commentary; bracket predictions and updates on contests.

The schedule did not disappoint.

Gonzaga made Number 1 overall seed again—like he called it. Duke and Villanova nabbed Number 2, ahead of Tennessee and Texas Tech—bingo on those calls too.

On the bubble, were Indiana, Rutgers, Notre Dame and Wyoming—He got those—But how Michigan managed to get in, he'd never know. He missed that one. ***Hell.***

THURSDAY
March 14, 2019-Spring Break

Deadline Day

Clara's voice sounded strained when she called him that morning. "Grady, I've checked our request for the field trip. We've got signoffs from everyone but Miss Grundle. Today's the deadline. I suppose I could request an extension, but I don't think it would make much difference since she's the one standing in the way."

"So, without approval from her by today it's an automatic no?"

"I'm pretty sure it is."

The phone was silent a few seconds, then she said, "The kids are going to be so disappointed."

"Oh no they're not. We're go-ing to the game."

"But...."

"I'll go talk to her."

"Nobody can talk to that woman."

"I can be pretty convincing when I have to be."

"Oh yeah?"

"Watch me."

"It's *Spring Break,* Grady. Everyone's on vacation."

"She's gotta be *some* place. I'll track her down. Helen Grundel might win this battle, but I'm not losing the war. We're go-ing to go to that game."

Afternoon

Grady thought through the situation for a while and sent Marie Sleidell a text.

Are you working today?

He got a thumbs-up with a note. *They don't give Administrators Spring Break off.*

Got a minute?

Can you come to my office?

He sent a smiley face. *Room number?*

Admin Second Floor first office on left.

###

Marie greeted him with a smile. "What's up?"

"I have something very important to one of my kids coming up that requires a weekend field trip. I'm really new when it comes to the process of getting approval for something like this and I just found out about the requirements and deadlines.

"I figure you've gotta be an expert on this stuff by now and I'm wondering if you could give me a few tips on getting the paperwork expedited. I'm way over my head and a little behind."

Marie glanced nervously at the open window in the wall separating her office from the one next to hers. Her voice became a little formal and stilted. "I'd really like to help you get approval faster, Mister Redwine, but I can't. I can give you a couple of general *guidelines*, though."

He felt himself frown…confused. This didn't sound like her at all.

She sent a nod toward the open window and said, "First of all, it would be a big mistake to **take the paperwork for your field trip to Miss Grundel in person**." —He began to realize from the look on her face that he should be reading between the lines because there were people listening. — "The process to submit everything to the Committee through their website is strictly enforced and they just don't make any exceptions. If they weren't so strict, she'd be buried in people all the time wanting her *to expedite* their request because it's common knowledge that *she has the power to do it if she wants to*…"

Ohhhh, I get it.

"…She's a very busy woman and her schedule is so packed…" Mary made serious eye contact. "…*she has to bring her lunch every day because that's the only way she can get a break.* You can understand, can't you?"

He sent her a wink and replied in a rather formal voice, "I do. Thank you."

She reached into a drawer, pulled out a piece of paper, and began to write while she talked. "Make sure you answer every question and check every box." —She handed him the note. — "Use *this* email *address* and get your application in as soon as possible. I believe the deadline is coming up soon."

Grady took the paper and read. **This floor. Down the hall to the Executive Wing. Next to the Supply Room.**

Marie walked him to the door and said a little too loudly, "I'm so sorry I can't help you with this, Mister Redwine. Just make sure everything is filled out properly and get it in email on time."

He wanted to hug her but didn't. "Thanks, anyway. I'll get to work on it right away."

He headed down the hallway. Behind him, he heard a sincere, "Good luck!"

Grady always compared visiting the *Executive Wing* of the *Admin Building* to going on vacation in Australia: they try to convince you you're in paradise, but underneath, everything there is really trying to kill you. So, when he learned from Marie *that wing* was the location of Miss Grundel's office, only one thought came to his mind:

Of course it is.

But Grady was on a mission. He set his personal feelings aside and wandered down the hall until he found a door marked *Supply Room* just past the *Special Needs* bulletin board. He'd always worked in buildings where bulletin boards had amateur shots of teachers glued to colored construction paper randomly thumb-tacked to an oversized cork board. This display, however, was an obvious marketing tool designed to impress parents coming to evaluate the programs offered by the *District*. All staff photos were professional graduation shots from a university yearbook, mounted behind an expensive acrylic frame.

Smack in the middle of the group and slightly higher than the others, was Helen Grundel. Ph.D., LPC, NCC, BC-TMH. Unlike the rest of the staff, she had two frames: a citation from when she was *Teacher-of-the-Year* and her *Vanderbilt* graduation photo with the caption quote: "I want to make a difference in the world."

Just beyond the board was an open office door with light leaking into the hall.

Good. She's there.

When he knocked on the door frame, Miss Grundel glanced up, saw who it was and returned to what she was doing. "If you want to talk to me, get an appointment."

"I only need five minutes."

Head down, she waggled her fingers, shooing him away. "Get...an...appoint-ment, Mister Redwine. And close the door behind you."

He closed the door but didn't leave.

After a short, cold standoff, she rolled her eyes and tossed her papers down in a huff. "I'm very busy. What do you want?"

"I want to know why you turned down the application for our field trip."

"Easy. Uncrossed t's. Undotted i's."

"What t's aren't crossed? Which i's aren't dotted?"

"Well, for one thing, you indicated that you'd be driving the bus for the event."

He shifted on his feet. "I'm a bus driver. That's what I do."

"It says very clearly on the checklist, Mister Redwine, that *Class Four* field trips require a certified driver. You are not a certified driver."

"Miss Grundel, I drive these kids on field trips nearly every day. How could I not be certified?"

She replied in the slow, patient tone often used in kindergarten. "You drive during the week, Mister Redwine. This trip is on a weekend. It's a totally dif-fer-ent an-i-mal."

The four-year-old in Grady wanted to kick her in the shin, but he managed to remain a grown-up and resist the temptation to point out the hundreds of week-ends he spent over the years, driving bas-ket-ball teams to games.

"Wow. Looks like I better find out how to get certified."

"Yes. I guess you should." She shifted the papers around on her desk. "There will be a class sometime this summer."

"Oookayyy. Guess I better get busy and find someone certified to drive us."

"Well, that's a start, Mister Redwine, but we still have to address problems with your *Section Ten*.

"Oh?"

"Yes. *Section Ten* asks for *Additional Thoughts, Concerns, or Challenges*. You answered, None."

"That's because I didn't have any."

"Well, I have a few."

"Oh? What did I miss?"

"First of all, these children are sensitive to sound, Mister Redwine. The decibel levels in an arena that size are likely to be painful and it could do serious damage to their hearing."

"We were worried about that too, so we made plans to bring medically approved sound suppressors for everyone."

"Does it say that on your application?"

"No. It doesn't."

"Why not?"

"Because the form asks for **Additional** *Thoughts, Concerns, or Challenges*. We identified noise as an issue early on and solved it, so it was no longer a concern.

She returned to kindergarten. "Mis-ter Red-wine. How could we possibly know what issues you identified and how you addressed them if you didn't tell us?"

He fished around in his brain for a civil answer. "I don't know. I guess I was thrown by the term, *Additional*. I didn't realize *solved* problems had to be listed." He took a brief pause. "Is there anything else?"

"Actually, there are several things."

He reached into a pocket and pulled out his pen. "Sounds like I need to take a few notes. Do you have some paper I can use?"

"You needn't bother. We'll list our concerns in *Section Twelve*. You'll find it in your email in a day or two."

"I'd be more than happy to just add the answers now and save some time."

"I appreciate your offer, Mister Redwine, but the very first sentence on the checklist clearly states that it is to be completed online and submitted for approval through our website."

"Miss Grundel, it *was* completed online. The other Cabinet members have reviewed it and approved it already."

"They approved it as written. You are changing it."

"I'm not changing the answers. I'm merely expanding them based on your input."

"Let me put it this way, Mister Redwine. I am the *Special Needs* expert on the Committee. If I say it needs reviewed again, they will defer to me."

"That's what I understood and that's why I'm here. We are sort of under the gun timewise, so since it has been approved by everyone on the Committee but you so far, I thought if I completed it to your satisfaction today, we could still get on the agenda for final approval."

"Mister Redwine, you are no longer…" she flashed finger quotes "…under the gun. The submission deadline has passed. If we had discussed this trip a-week-a-go, you would have had a chance at getting it on the agenda. Buuuut…" Her voice trailed off.

She picked up her papers again and shrugged. "T's and I's, Mister Redwine. You can't say I didn't warn you."

He took a deep breath; let it out slowly. "This trip means a lot to these children, Miss Grundel."

"Then perhaps you should have been more careful with the paperwork."

"It's a very big deal. They'll be horribly disappointed."

She shrugged. "Guess you shouldn't have told them until you got a *yes*."

Tension hung heavily in the air while Grady struggled to maintain his composure.

He looked directly into her eyes. "Please. Help us. These children deserve to go."

She glanced at the door as if reassuring herself it was closed, then leaned toward him on her forearms. "You expect my help when you're out there undermining me and my work? I don't think so."

"I'm not asking for me. I'm asking for the chil-dren... chil-dren who have done nothing to you... chil-dren who step up every Fri-day and try their best to please you by ordering their Chicken Nuggets right."

He pointed toward the door. "I saw your picture on the bulletin board Miss-Teacher-of-the-Year. You want to make a difference in the world? Well, here's a chance to do it."

She got a look on her face like she smelled something disgusting. "There you go again, Mis-ter-High-and-Mighty." She gestured across her wall of framed certificates like Vanna White revealing vowels. "I've already made a difference in the world. And I cer-tain-ly don't need any help from you and your..." He saw her jaw tighten and the word *stupid* forming on her lips, but she just said, "...field trip."

She paused, thought for a moment, then continued. "I love these kids. I *love* them. I've spent fifteen years of my life trying to help them....fif-teen years of being spit on, scratched, strangled and kicked. —her nostrils flared, and her eyes grew dark—

"...fif-teen years dealing with heartbroken parents who expect me to work miracles no one can possibly deliver.

"I've spent my entire career trying to help children fit in...to learn the skills they need to live on their own someday...to help them have a decent future."

He gestured toward the rows of college psych books on her shelves. "You are obviously an educated, experienced teacher and I respect the fact that you are being careful. Everything you've pointed out about the circumstances surrounding this trip has been accurate and important, but you are completely missing the point, Miss Grundel. I. Care. About. These. Kids. Too."

She opened her mouth to reply but he held up a hand and stopped her. "I-listened-to- you. -Now-you-listen-to-me. These aren't very healthy kids, Miss Grundel. I know you're working really hard to help them with their future, but it's just a fact that some of them may not even have one.

She sat there, scowling at him as he continued to talk.

"I'm trying to give them a *now*...a *today*...a reason to even *want* a tomorrow."

He let that soak in a minute. She said nothing and just sat there impatiently tapping her pen, as if debating her decision.

He dared to hope for a moment that he'd convinced her to change her mind, but she soon broke eye contact with him and returned to her papers as if the whole conversation had never happened.

Grady turned on his heels and stormed toward the door but turned back again before he left. "If you can live with knowing that you hurt five children just to get even with a bus driver, then, **Be. My. Guest.**"

###

Grady only had to say hello when Clara called him—for her to say... "I take it our answer is still no."

"For today, anyway."

"So, what are we going to do?"

"Oh, no doubt about it, we're still going to the game."

"And just how do you propose to do that?"

"Plan B."

"Didn't know we had one."

"We don't. But we will

Evening at Home

Grady spent the entire evening systematically studying his copy of the field trip rules— line by line and point by point— looking for an out. He could hear Grundel's voice echoing in his ears as he read: *"T's and I's! T's and I's, Mr. Redwine."* *She probably wrote the damn thing.*

It wasn't until he'd given up and tossed the papers on the TV tray beside him that he found the answer he was searching for—hiding in plain sight in the title of the very first page: *School Sponsored Field Trip Checklist.*

It didn't say: **Field Trip** *Checklist*...or *Field Trip* **Guidelines**... *Field Trip* **Rules**...or **Weekend** *Field Trip Checklist.* It clearly stated: **School Sponsored** *Field Trip Checklist.*

He couldn't help it. He was so excited, he had to call Clara again and give her the good news.

She answered immediately. "What's wrong."

"I'm happy to report that *nothing* is wrong. I just have news I couldn't wait until Monday to tell you."

"Monday? Oh! That's right! I forgot! You have that *Safety* meeting tomorrow. So, what's up?"

"We're absolutely —definitely— going to go to the game. I've got Plan B."

"What is it?"

"Have you got your printout handy?"

"Yes."

"Pull it out and read the title. What does it say?"

He heard paper rattling, then she said, *"School Sponsored Field Trip Checklist."*

"We're not going on a **School Sponsored Field Trip.** We're going to have a **Private, Bus 86, Basketball Party**. All we have to do is provide our own transportation."

"But Grady, where are we going to get a bus…with a lift?!"

"*The Hamilton Home* has one. I'm sure they'll loan it to us for this. I feel certain they'll let me drive it, so we don't have to worry about having an extra driver either."

"And if they can't or just plain won't?"

"If I have to pay for an *ambulance* and ten taxis, we're going."

"What can I say? You're a genius. I'm excited!"

"Me too. See ya Tuesday."

FRIDAY
March 15, 2019-Spring Break
&
First Day of March Madness

Grady hated it when the *District* scheduled a Safety meeting in the *Admin* auditorium. It wasn't so much the unbearable boredom and bad coffee that got him, or the fact that it was a Teacher Workday which was supposed to be a day off. It was the mid-morning breakfast break, racing against fifty other old men to a bathroom with only four urinals.

This particular morning, waiting in line wasn't an option for Grady, so he decided he'd better take his breakfast break somewhere else. He weighed possible alternatives while he walked to his truck. Unfortunately, his best option was where he and Mary met for brunch every Sunday when she got out of church.

If he had another viable choice, this restaurant would not have been where he chose to go—there were far too many memories there. But, under the current circumstances, it was truly his only choice…close by, clean bathroom, no lines, good coffee, and a great triple stack with sausage.

He'd learned over the years that the best place to park was behind a hedge in the garden right outside the rear exit, so he made a sharp left into the lot, skidded into a spot, made a mad dash up a short flight of steps and rushed down the hall to the men's room.

Just out of habit, when he finished up there and headed for the dining area, he glanced through the archway leading to the kitchen prep area, intending to wave if he saw anyone he knew.

The prep room was empty except for a thin young woman standing at a table folding napkins. She seemed vaguely familiar, but he couldn't quite place her, and she was busy, so he didn't wave.

It wasn't unusual for Grady not to recognize someone right away, especially when he didn't have on his distance glasses. He had a terrible time identifying people out of context. If he first met someone in their office and later, bumped into them at a grocery store, their face just didn't register for some reason. He found it extremely embarrassing.

It was at times like this that he missed Mary the most. She remembered everyone, so she officially became what Grady called the *Keeper of the Faces*. Now that she wasn't with him, he'd developed a habit of having someone he didn't recognize speak first if he could. He did a lot better with voices.

Just as Grady neared the farthest edge of the archway, he saw a man walk into the prep room and let his hand brush lightly along the woman's backside as he passed by and entered an office at the other end with a sign on the door that said, *Manager.*

His eyebrows shot up to his forehead. *Whoa.*

Grady saw the woman flinch when it happened but didn't hear any comments. She just tossed the guy a weak smile when he passed, then gazed forlornly back at the table as she returned to mechanically folding the napkins.

Grady paused in the hallway. *Did I just see what I thought I saw?*

He altered his route to the dining room and turned into a lower hallway so he could glance through the serving window and check in on the woman.

He stopped in his tracks. The man was back.

The woman was leaning against the table; held by the wrist. The man wasn't twisting it but there was a message in the grip. And when her hair happened to swing away from her face, Grady caught a glimmer of fright in her eyes, and he noticed a slight bruise on her cheek. He got only a fleeting glance of the room, but there was no doubt in Grady's mind about what was going on.

He also knew it was none of his business, but he wasn't about to ignore it, so he did the only thing he could think of to make the man stop. He started whistling the *War Eagle* fight song as loud as he could and headed past the archway again.

When he walked by the second time, there was no sign of the man, but Grady was able to get a longer look at the young woman…dark brown hair…deep brown eyes. Who *was* she? A former student? A friend of Mary's? Or maybe she just waited on him a few times.

When he finally reached the dining room, Grady realized he'd lost his appetite for pancakes, so he just bought a coffee and biscuit to go, then headed back to his truck.

He strode along the stone sidewalk beside the garden and made his way onto the back lot, shifting the coffee and biscuit to his left hand so he could pull his keys out of his pocket. But as he rounded the hedge, his elbow got caught on a branch and everything in his hands went flying.

Swell.

He dropped to one knee to retrieve what he could and as he struggled back to a standing position, he stopped short—completely stunned. Parked on the other side of the hedge, in a shady space clearly marked *Manager*, was a blue metallic import. Grady got a sudden sinking, hollow sensation in his stomach, and in an instant, he realized who the woman folding napkins was.

###

The jolt from seeing that car in the lot brought actual physical pain to Grady. It was as if life had given him a backhanded blow and forced him to see the reality of Sonti's situation at home.

*What must be going **on** in that **house**?*

Shaken to the core, he returned to his truck and began fusing together fragments of disjointed images in an attempt to form a full picture of what he had just witnessed—the constant cuts and bruises on Sonti's body and on his mother's; the fright in Sonti's eyes when they dropped him off at home sometimes with Chicken Nuggets saved in his cheeks; the blue metallic import parked at the house just a touch too early in the morning.

Then Grady's mind shot back to that day on the hill when Sonti spoke, and the memory knocked him down hard. *Oh, my Lord, has Sonti been taking the blame for things he didn't **do**?*

Heaven knew Sonti's condition caused him to be aggressive at times, but it also made him an easy target for blame because he had no ability to explain something or defend himself. Grady grew sick just thinking about it.

The morning they were recklessly cut off by the Junker kept flashing through his mind. Was the driver really Sonti's uncle? If he was, could it be that they were having a crisis at home and, rather than just being reckless, he was rushing to his sister's house to help her?

He remembered an import's taillights booking it over the hill when they pulled up to their house, and poor Sonti—terrified—running toward the bus screaming for what he now realized was an attempt to get someone to help his mother.

Grady clenched his jaw. *This whole situation was unjust and wrong. Just horribly wrong.*

Late Morning

Grady fidgeted around in his chair for the rest of the Safety meeting. *Nobody can take an hour of information and turn it into four hours of endless boredom better than these guys.* He had to push down on his knee the whole time to keep his heel from tapping and felt himself becoming increasingly impatient. He had things to do and people to see today. Both the field trip application and Bennie's entry form were due, and he had to touch base with Clara and Mrs. Hamilton to make sure everything was in order.

Miracle of miracles, the meeting ended on time. He was so upset and distracted by the events at the restaurant, everything else that morning was mostly a blur. Fortunately, he'd been a driver long enough to get a decent passing score on the final exam, and he could read the stuff they gave him to catch up on anything new later. Right now, for sanity's sake, he had to get out of there.

Afternoon

Grady received two texts on his way home: Clara had already received an official receipt for the application, along with a statement that they were waiting for the final approval from Miss Grundel; and Mrs. Hamilton got the entry form delivered to Mr. Walsh.

Finally. Some good news. He took a deep breath and relaxed a little. What a relief. School approval no longer mattered because they were having a private party, and Mrs. Hamilton was right on time.

When he reached the driveway at home, Grady actually managed to send a thumbs-up thingy with a flawless *thank you* text to each of them …his one and only point of pride for the day.

He flopped down in his recliner and clicked the remote. A voice from his usual sports network blasted through the television speaker, "…and what are we talking about today? *March Madness*, of course!" Grady leaned back to enjoy.

"Grab your phones, folks. Call the number displayed on the screen below and cast *your* vote for what teams you think will make *The First Four*!"

In his mind, Grady listed his picks: for the East: North Dakota State vs. Central, and Belmont vs. Temple; for the West: Fairleigh Dickinson vs. Prairie View A&M, and Arizona State vs Saint Johns.… ***had*** *to be.*

While the fans called in, the announcer and a panel chit-chatted as votes were recorded and tallied. Grady tried to focus on the rest of the program, but his mind kept wandering back to Sonti.

Everything in him wanted to report that guy to the authorities, but he had no hard evidence to prove what he was thinking was true. It would be futile and irresponsible to file a report based strictly on supposition, and he suspected there could be a logical explanation for everything…that's how the guy got away with it.

Not only that, but the School District had very strict rules about getting involved in the private lives of students. He could hear them now: *You're a bus driver, Grady, not a counselor.*

Yeah, but he was also a caring human being, and he was determined to figure out a way to help that family.

SATURDAY
March 16, 2019-Morning

Spring Break & Talent Night Rehearsal

The rehearsal slot for Bennie in the Talent Contest turned out to be mostly a logistics and technology run-through. The Hamiltons brought BennieToo down to the auditorium, and after Bennie practiced the timing of dancing him down the ramp to the stage a few times, they left him in Grady's care, while the music and lighting logistics were worked out by Mr. Walsh and J.D..

Grady checked out the satellite feed for BennieToo by calling up Bennie.

"So how are you feeling about things, Bennie?"

"Oh great, Mister Redwine. We have practiced and practiced the dance here at home and I feel really comfortable with it."

"I'm excited for you, son. I think you're going to knock everyone dead tonight."

J.D. took over from across the room. "I will have all the sound and lighting weady foh you, Bennie. It is going to be weally fun."

"Thank you for all you've done, J.D."

"I'm looking fohwuhd to watching you get you balloon too."

When he and J.D. finished up the logistics, Grady invited him to *Indy's* for lunch. They approached the counter together. After Grady ordered his usual double cheeseburger, fries and a chocolate shake, J.D. gave him a sly smile and said to the lady, "I am going to have what he is having."

They ate in the main dining area, made a bunch of small talk, then Grady took J.D. home.

"I'll pick you up again at five o'clock, J.D. Wear something nice."

"I will." Then, for the first time ever, J.D. held up his hand for a high-five. Grady touched J.D.'s palm gently with his own and they both smiled, knowing what a momentous moment that was.

Evening
Talent Contest

After the audience in the packed auditorium spent an hour watching garage bands, cheerleaders, baton twirlers, hip-hoppers and some slightly off-key singers, the house lights faded to black, and J.D. started their act.

Base drums pounded, shaking the floor.... BOOM-Boom BOOM-Boom BOOM-Boom BOOM-Boom ...

Grady felt anticipation rising in the room; reaching its peak and exploding when the announcer's voice thundered through the PA, "Laaadies and gennntlemen – Let's welcome Bennie Hamilton and The Reeeal Deeeal!"

A flourish of bugles blared through the darkness bringing a wild, swirling energy to the room. Excitement swelled and soared skyward then surged down the center aisle along the beam from J.D.'s searchlight boring a hole through the blackness. The back doors blasted open exposing BennieToo standing bathed in light, arms shot to Victory.

The kids went wild; lifted their *phones* aloft, sending screen strobes flashing and hazard lights dancing along the sea of smiling faces. Flickers of *War Eagle* blue and orange trailed along the balcony, painting shadows on the walls where proud parents watched.

BennieToo lowered his arms while strobes still fired, and started a head bob in short, sharp strokes; bumpa, ba bumpa, ba bumpa, ba bumpa...

Grady saw Bennie's eyes glow with joy on the screen when kids bobbed with him and danced in unison... bumpa ba bumpa, ba bumpa, ba bumpa, ba bumpa.

BennieToo swayed left and dipped; then swayed right and dipped; left again, right again, striding toward the stage with high-performance hydraulics singing wa-wa whoop. Head left, wa whoop, head right, wa whoop; right arm wave, left arm wave, right arm, left arm. Wa whoop, wa whoop.

Kids waved left with him; kids waved right with him, following his routine...wa whoop, wa whoop. wa whoop, wa whoop.

Base vibrations shook the floor. Girls screamed with glee.

BennieToo threw a combination left then right...wa whoop, wa whoop.

Beats intensified; vibrations shook the floor; Bennie continued his combination left then right boom ba boom ba ba boom ba boom.

BennieToo boxer-punched up; boxer-punched down...wa whoop, wa whoop.

Head-slip right; head-slip left, right, left, right left…wa whoop, wa whoop. wa whoop, wa whoop.

Shoulder-roll left, shoulder-roll right, roll left, roll right…wa whoop, wa whoop.

Three-sixty spin left; three-sixty spin right…wa whoop, wa whoop.

BennieToo reached the steps to the stage and strode up them one at a time to center stage. Moon Walk, Moon Walk, Moon Walk.

For a moment the entire room was dancing in unison— magically uniting the audience, the music and Bennie in an intimate connection that Grady had never witnessed before.

When the last note played, J.D. cut the searchlight, leaving the stage in sudden darkness.

There was a long moment of stunned silence filled with palpable feelings of deep respect, almost reverence over the miracle they had just witnessed.

The house lights came back up, breaking the spell, and the room erupted with foot stomping, cheers and unrestrained rapturous applause.

Grady's chest filled with pride as he watched the projection of Bennie's blue eyes spilling tears on BennieToo's screen.

It took Grady a long time to come down off of the high of Bennie's performance that night. It seemed like the entire world was drowning in joy when the lights turned on, and it was over.

Mrs. Hamilton had stayed home with Bennie to help him, so she watched from there, but Mr. Hamilton sat in the audience with the Milers and was obviously moved to the core as people surrounded him, praising his son.

He gave a wonderful speech when he accepted Bennie's trophy after the voting and couldn't have been more gracious when he shook Grady's hand. "Bennie told me what you said about impossible things happening every day." He then leaned closer to him and said, "You're obviously a believer in miracles, Mr. Redwine, and I think you just helped make one today. I'll cross my fingers for you April 6th."

In a moment or two, Clara approached them and handed Mr. Hamilton a sealed jar full of glitter and a dollar bill. "These are for Bennie. At first I thought maybe BennieToo could pop his balloon for him, but when I saw what all the glitter did to the air quality in the bus during J.D.'s balloon ceremony, I didn't want to risk harming his mechanics. So, would you please give these to Bennie for us? And tell him how proud we all are of him and how much he's loved."

Mr. Hamilton got a little misty-eyed. "Of course. Of course I will. Thank you all so much."

SUNDAY
March 17, 2019-Last Day of Spring Break

Grady bounded out of bed that morning, still fueled by adrenaline from the previous night. This was also an exciting day for him too—*Selection Sunday for March Madness.*

He picked up a coffee from the drive-thru on the way to the store to stock up on ingredients for what he and Mary used to call, *The Red-wine, Gen-u-ine, Madness Buffet*— a combination of dishes they served the gang every year while they watched team announcements, and everybody added their twenty dollars to a bracket pool…winner take all.

Grady had everything on his list in the cart, but on his way to the register, he noticed a sale on kids' sunglasses and on a whim, read the product description while he waited for his turn in line:

- *Polarized and 100% UV Protection-ultraviolet blocking lenses with added polarization for eliminating glare. 7-layer Triacetate TAC lens allows for added durability and impact resistance.*
- *Sized smaller specifically for active teenagers and kids during sporting activities FREE carrying pouch and microfiber cleaning cloth included.*

He glanced at the sale price: 2 for $10. *Worth a try*. Maybe, just **may**be, he'd found a way to wean Sonti off of that banket.

It was a tradition for the guys in Grady's group of friends to go home to watch the tournament after brunch so they could completely control their remote; and the women would leave for the airport to escape constant conference calls and trash-talk.

For the first time since Mary's demise, Grady felt peaceful and calm in the house because it was *normal* for her not to be home. After all the guys had moved on or away, she turned being gone for a while during *March Madness* into an annual gift to him…time alone, buried in what he loved best to do.

So, for the next week or two, in his heart Grady could rest, believing Mary was gone because she loved him…not because she had passed away.

WEEK ELEVEN

MONDAY
March 18, 2019-Morning

Grady arrived at the bus lot a little early that morning, so he passed the time sipping his latte while performing the pre-trip, then sat down in the drivers' seat and checked the schedule. He was just finishing his coffee when Clara bounded aboard with a wry smile on her face. "Didn't expect to see *you* here today."

Grady screwed up his face. *What? Why?*

"It's Miss Grundel's last day. Thought you might have the flu; you've been feeling so feverish lately."

He responded with a smirk. "Funny."

She set her things down on her seat and he continued his thoughts. "Who has a last day on a Monday? Everybody knows you're supposed to leave your job on FRIDAY."

"Guess she wanted to attend the Committee meeting. Are you sure you don't want to go with me to her luncheon?" He glared at her.

She shot him an innocent, wide-eyed glance. "Just double-checking," then she glanced at the grocery bag on the console. "Whatcha got there?"

He reached over, opened it, and pulled out Sonti's glasses. "Look what I found."

"Okaaayyyy. I see that you only bought two pair, so I know they aren't for everyone."

"I got them for Sonti."

"Annnnndddd..."

"I've been watching him lately. He's always holding his arm across his forehead or pulling his blanket out a little to shade his eyes from the sun. I'm hoping that if he has these glasses to wear, we might be able to wean him away from the blanket."

"Good luck with that one, Grady. Everyone I've talked to about it says he wears it for comfort and emotional support. Shade is merely an added benefit."

"Maybe. But let's try it and see."

"He doesn't like to be touched; you know. Be prepared for those glasses to be toothpicks in five minutes."

Afternoon

Grady mostly ran errands during his lunch hour and picked up some fast-food on his way back to the bus barn. He was just finishing when Clara came flying up the stairs after parking her car on the lot. "You're not going to believe this. **Grady!** *I* cannot believe this! We've had a miracle! Miss Grundel changed her mind. The Committee has approved our field trip!"

He was stunned. *The old bat had a conscience after all.* "That's *wonderful* news!"

Reality set in, however, about the time they arrived back at the school to pick up the kids. *Ho-ly Hell! I'm gonna need another driver for sure now...and that means another ticket.*

Grady didn't have much time to think about it right then, because Mr. Wilson was bringing Sonti out to the bus.

Grady pointed their direction. "See? See how Sonti pulls that little ledge out over his eyes?"

"Yes."

'That's what we're trying to fix."

###

When Sonti came on board and got clipped into his seat, Grady approached him holding the glasses. "I've got a surprise for you pal."

Sonti perked up a little and began rocking in his seat.

"Want to try them on?"

Grady reached for the blanket on Sonti's head. He leaned away. "You'll have to put the blanket down to try them on, son. You don't *have* to try them on. It's only if you *want to.*"

Grady got inspired. "Want to see them on me first? They're really cool." He took off his own glasses, slipped Sonti's on and hit a few poses. "Whaddaya think?"

Sonti leaned toward him. Grady backed away this time. "You'll have to take the blanket off. They won't fit with it on."

Sonti pulled off the blanket and reached out a hand—Grady placed the glasses in his palm— Sonti gently slipped them on.

"Wow, Sonti! You look great!"

Sonti looked at his reflection in the window...turned left...turned right...looked up...looked down...and just plain glowed all over.

"They're yours to keep here on the bus." — Grady showed him the plastic box and placed it on the dashboard. — "We'll keep them up here for you."

When they pulled up to his house, Sonti paused next to the mirror at the top of the stairs to admire himself and show off his gift to his mother.

She held out her arms. "Sonti! You're so *hand*some!"

Grady opened the plastic case and held it out for him. Sonti removed his glasses, folded them up carefully and placed them into the box. Then he grabbed it, leaped down the stairs and managed to dodge everyone who stood in his way to the house with the skill of a wide receiver.

His mother took off up the hill after him.

Grady smiled at Clara when he closed the doors. "Glad I bought two pair."

"Toothpicks," Clara replied. "By tomorrow."

TUESDAY
March 19, 2019-Morning

Sonti's Mom had hauled the empty trash can halfway up the driveway before Sonti's sister arrived at the bus to tell them he wasn't riding today.

Out of desperation, Grady grabbed the *District's* bright pink permission slip and trailed after her, waving it over his head. "Mrs. Smith? Mrs. Smith! Ma'am. Could I please talk with you for a minute? I have something for you to sign."

She spoke over her shoulder. "Could we talk tonight? I must be at work in one hour. As you can see, I am not dressed, and I have to walk there."

"Unfortunately, the paperwork is due today, I'll make it fast. I promise."

She kept walking. "If you will please just leave it with me. We have a fax at my work. I will look it over and if I decide to sign it, I will send it over."

He side-stepped up the hill with her. "Unfortunately, I don't have access to a fax. Please. It will only take a minute and then you won't have to worry about it anymore."

She sighed and turned his way, hand on hip.

"As you know, the program Sonti is a part of involves taking the kids on field trips."

She sounded nervous. "Yeeeessss."

"Well, we have something exciting coming up. Our group has been invited to be guests of honor at the *Comets* game next month and you know how much Sonti loves basketball."

"Yeeeessss."

"But since it's on a Saturday, we have to do some additional paperwork." He chuckled apologetically. "Always paperwork, huh?"

She sent a worried glance toward the paper in his hand. "I have signed the permission. Has it been lost? Is it not in the file?"

"Oh, don't worry about that one. It's definitely in his file. But that one only covers trips during the week. This one is on a weekend, so it's a different form."

"When is it?"

"April the sixth…it's a Saturday."

She screwed up her mouth. "Oooo, Can I get back to you? I don't know my work schedule yet and I don't always have a car."

Grady swallowed hard. "Oh, you don't have to worry about your work schedule. I can pick him up anywhere and keep him the whole day. We'll just flex around your schedule whatever it is."

She hesitated. "I am not sure. He spends most weekends with us at home…with his sisters and brother. They look forward to it."

"This is a really special occasion. I'll bring him home right after the game. He'll love it."

"Does it cost any-theeng?"

"Nope. Not-a-dime. Admission and meals are all taken care of. And like I said, they're giving prize money for baskets and he's a pretty good shot, so he might even come home with some extra money."

"Let me talk to the other kids. I can let you know on tomorrow."

"Well, unfortunately, the deadline is this afternoon, so I kind of need it today."

"If I sign, does he have to go?"

"Well, the tickets will already be paid for, so there's that."

"I would hate to waste the money." She handed him back the paper. "The schools let children study from home now when they need flexible instruction days. This game will be on television. He can participate that way, and you can do whatever activities with him later."

"It's only on cable. Do you have the sports channel? ESPN?" Grady tap-danced hard. "There is a test. We would like him to pass."

"Sonti fails most of his tests."

"This is one he can pass. This is a chance for him to be number one."

"You are make-eeng me late, Meester Bus Driver."

"I'll tell you what. Why don't you go ahead and sign, and I'll get someone on standby in case you have to cancel. That way, it wouldn't be a wasted ticket. How does that sound?"

She didn't answer. He kept talking. "I'll take him for the whole day, so you don't need to worry about work." — He handed her the paper again. — "So, if you'll sign here to give me permission, I'll arrange for everything."

She rolled her eyes while she shook her head and mumbled, "A-yi-yi," then she surrendered. "Where do I sign?"

He handed her a pen and pointed. "Here. Just here. And then over here to give permission for him to shoot."

She signed all three places and handed the paper and pen back to him. He double-checked her signature and even though he felt a wave of relief, he couldn't seem to be able to suppress a sense of foreboding growing within him.

"Thank you, Mrs. Smith. He's going to have a great time."

She turned away without saying another word, then took giant strides to the top of the hill while making sharp gestures with her hands toward the sky, clearly having a "Why me? Why now?" dialogue with God, in Spanish.

Clara was all aflutter when Grady returned to the bus. "How did it go?'

"Great! We're on. April sixth all day."

"I saw her signing the papers. Is she excited? Is she coming? Will she be riding with us?"

Grady felt a sudden jolt of remorse. He'd thought of everything but this. He'd been so intent on getting her approval for the trip and was so thoroughly convinced that what he was doing was a great thing for Sonti and his family, the unfairness of cheating his mother out of witnessing the event never crossed his mind.

"I didn't tell her about the money."

"What!" She stood in the aisle, staring at him. "Miss-ter Redwine. What-have-you-done."

He carefully tucked the paper into his folder. "I haven't *done* anything, Clara. We're still up to our ears in the paperwork, and we're not even sure yet if it's going to happen. I didn't want to get her all excited then have to disappoint her."

She mulled that over a minute. "I guess that makes sense."

The possible consequences of his actions still weighed heavily on Grady, but even though he knew that what he did was the equivalent of telling Sonti's mother a lie, he refused to feel guilty.

She'll forgive me when she gets the money, and if Sonti doesn't pull it off, no harm no foul.

J.D. stopped in his tracks at the top of the stairs and scanned around the bus when he got on that morning. "Whea's Pwissy?"

"She had a doctor's appointment, but she'll be back this afternoon."

"Oh."

Grady expected J.D. to make his usual mad dash down the aisle to his seat, but this morning, he lingered at the top of the stairs and leaned toward him. "Can you see how happy I look today, Mistow Wedwine?"

Grady tilted his head back and checked him over. "Now that you mention it, you *do* look happy today J.D., what happened to make you so happy?"

"This mohning they told me my Grandma Pahkuh died."

He heard Clara gasp a little and he reached out to console J.D., but he was already headed for his seat, rattling on with more happiness than despair in his voice. "They said she left me huh cah. They ah going to sell it and put the money in the bank fo me—eleven-thousand-dolluhs!"

Grady watched him settle in. "That's a lot of money, J.D."

"I know. I'm pwactically witch." He pulled out his computer and turned it on. "I'm going to save it and buy an electwick cah when I tuhn eighteen."

Grady and Clara exchanged amused glances. "Well, it will be nice to have something good to remember her by."

J.D. replied in a distant, matter-of-fact tone. "They isn't much to wemembuh about huh, weally. The fuhst time I evuh saw huh was when I was nine, aftuh my fahthuh wunned off with the neighbuh lady..."

Grady met Clara's sad eyes in the mirror.

"...Social Suhvices bwought huh to the house with them to tell me my mothuh had to go away foe awhile and since nobody else in the family wanted me, they wuh sending me to live at the sheltuh." He adjusted a couple of things on his lap. "But having a cah will be nice."

Clara checked J.D.'s seat belt. "Did you hear from her after that? Did she visit you?"

"I got a post-cahd once. She said she had a stwoke, so she was living at the V.A. Home foh the Age-ed in Flohida, and my fahthuh was in Califohnia living with the neighbuh lady. They ah going to have twin guhls soon."

Grady released the brake and began pulling away from the curb. "Do you have any other brothers or sisters?"

"Yes. They all live somewheah in Califohnia too. I have two weal sistuhs olduh than me, two step bwuthuhs—one olduh and one younguh—and if the new baby twins ah gulls, I will have thwee step sistuhs—all younguh."

"Did your grandma say anything about your Mom in the postcard?"

"No. Nothing."

A few minutes passed with J.D. obviously deep in thought. Then out of the blue, he said, "I wonduh how you get two babies in theyuh at the same time. Do you know how Mistoe Wedwine?"

Grady felt his eyebrows fly to his hairline. "We don't talk about things like that on the bus, J.D."

"Oh, Mistoe Wedwine. Miss Mahston told us evwything in health class alweady. Don't woowy."

"Well, I think you should probably ask Miss Marston about this too."

"I bet it weally huhts to squeeze out two babies. What do you think? It's such a small space."

"J.D., let's talk about your car."

"Is it because I am not eighteen yet?"

"No, J.D., it's because we don't talk about things like that on the bus."

"Well, Miss Mahston says it is okay to *talk about it* befoe you eighteen. You just can't *do* it until then."

"J.D., let's talk about your car."

"I am weally looking fowood to doing consummation. Do you like it?"

"Let's change the subject, okay?"

"It's just us, Mistoe Wedwine. We just *talk-ing* about it. We not *do*-ing it."

"The car, J.D., the car."

"Today in health class we ah discussing problematics."—*Prophylactics, maybe?* — "My fwiend told me last yeah in class, they put one on a banana."

Grady was starting to get a headache—*Don't ask, Redwine. You don't wanna know.*

In the mirror, Grady watched Clara stuffing down peals of laughter.

Afternoon

Miss Miller dropped Prissy off near the bus loop before the bell rang, so she wheeled aboard the bus early.

"Did you hear about J.D.'s grandma leaving him her car?"

Clara buckled her down. "Yes, we did. I'm sad his grandma passed away, but I'm happy he has the car."

"I heard Miss Miller tell someone on the phone this morning that if the old bag thought she could buy her way outa Hell with that damn Junker after the way she treated J.D.—just bringing him here and dumping him like she did—she had another thought coming."

Clara found words first. "Prissy. Don't you dare tell J.D. what Miss Miller said, or anyone else."

"But Miss Mill..."

"I don't care what Miss Miller said. It wasn't nice. J.D.'s grandmother passed away. She deserves some respect."

Prissy wasn't having it. "Miss Miller said J.D.'s grandma told him the reason he couldn't talk right was because his Mama didn't want any more babies, so she took drugs hoping he would die."

Grady and Clara gasped.

"And she *all-so* said..."

Clara quickly drew an imaginary zipper across her lips, but Prissy continued on in a mumble, "She was a mean old biddy and deserves every day in Hell she gets."

Fortunately for all parties involved, the bell rang, and the rest of the gang rushed their way, led by an exuberant J.D..

"Did you heah, Pwissie? I got a cah!"

Grady saw Clara shoot a warning glance across Prissy's bow. For some mysterious reason, Prissy paid attention. "Yes, I heard."

"They ah going to sell it and put the money in the bank foe me—eleven-thousand-dolluhs!"

"Wowwww."

"I'm going to save it up until I'm eighteen. Then I'm going to buy a bwand new cah...a fast one."

Grady hid a smile. Prissy continued. "Then what?"

"I'm going to Califohnia and find my Mom."

The bus went silent for a moment. Finally, Grady looked in the mirror and said, "California's a big place, J.D. Do you know where your mother lives?"

"No. But I dug thwough some boxes one time and found a old dwivuh's license. It has huh pick-cha on it, and I know the last foe digits of huh *Social Secuwity* nuhmbuh."

Grady prepared to leave the bus loop. "Well, it sounds like you've got a good start."

Prissy spoke up. "My Mama's in Heaven. Do you think your Mom could be there too, J.D.?"

"Well, wheah evuh she is, I'm going to find huh. No maattuh what. I'm going to see my bwuthuhs and sistuhs again. And find out why my fahthuh left us."

Grady and Clara dropped the kids off at *The Hamilton Home* then drove back to the Bus Lot in relative silence. Finally, Clara spoke up. "Poor J.D. Whatever will become of him when he learns the truth."

Grady parked the bus in the usual place then turned around to face her. "J.D. is a lot more capable than people give him credit for. I feel certain that he'll find his way through it somehow."

She gathered up her things and said, "From your mouth to God's ears."

Evening

Grady headed for home totally amped. It was Tipoff day for *March Madness*.

At six o'clock sharp, he sank into his lucky spot in the center cushion of the couch, surrounded by everything he thought he would need for the next seven hours. The recliner was a lot more comfortable, but the couch was where all the good energy accumulated last year when he correctly called both the Buffalo/Arizona and Loyola-Chicago/Tennessee upsets. It just made sense to continue to corral that karma and leverage it again this year.

He readjusted the angle of his television set, positioned his completed brackets on the cushion to his left, and the broadcasting schedule from CBS to his right. On the floor next to the couch was a fully stocked cooler, and his large pepperoni pizza with extra cheese was within close reach on a side table. He could watch the TV in the mirror of the front bathroom, so he was okay in that department, too.

He sat for a while and ran down his mental check list. One can never be over-prepared for this occasion, because you don't want to have to leave to get something after the first tip-off.

Checklist complete, he finally felt fully prepared to watch *The First Four*, and in time, watched Fairleigh Dickinson whup Prairie View A&M 82-76; then Belmont tromp Temple 81-70. He knew it and he called it. *March Madness* didn't ever get kicked off better than that.

Thirteen Weeks On The Last Mile Bus

WEDNESDAY
March 20, 2019-Morning

Grady's breath hit the air in little white clouds and hung around him as he opened up the bus in the lot that morning. It took so many cranks to get the old girl started; he was glad he came early to heat everything up.

He conducted his walk-through mentally cursing the sadist in the School District who determined that elementary schools should open at seven-thirty. Whoever it was, obviously never had to get up at four-thirty on a freezing, crummy morning like this one, and start picking up little kids in the dark.

His phone started dinging text alerts shortly after he sat down, and he was scanning through them when Clara came on board. She handed him a tall steaming coffee. "What's up?"

"This is the fourth text telling me someone's not riding this morning. J.D.'s the lone survivor."

"Wow. Four?" She settled into her seat. "Why?"

"Doctor appointments. They'll be back this afternoon."

"Ohhh. That's-not-good." She sipped at her coffee. "Hope you got your flu shot."

Grady scrunched up his mouth; settled on, "Uhhhh, not yet."

"Don't put it off, Grady. It's going to be bad this year." She gazed around the bus. "They gave us new disinfectant. I'll spray the seats when we drop off J.D."

"Good. That's good." Grady glanced at the fuel gauge, happy to have a reason to change the subject. "Today's our fuel day. I figure we can drop J.D. off and get down to the pumps early. That way, we won't have to wait in line during lunch," — He glanced at the rear of the bus, and the window in the back door streaked with dirt from recent rain. — "and I'll finally be able to clean off that back window—been trying to get to the long-handled brush at the wash station for three weeks."

He backed out, shifted to low and headed for *The Hamilton Home*. "Better take advantage of the situation every way we can. After a morning away from school, the kids will probably be wound up tighter than clocks this afternoon."

When they pulled up to J.D.'s dorm, he climbed aboard and looked around a little wide-eyed. "Wheah is evwybody?"

Grady gave him a hearty greeting. "You're a lucky guy, J.D. Everybody else is at the doctor this morning. That makes you king of the bus."

J.D. appeared to be thrilled silly at the news. "Does that mean I can eat my bweakfast on the way to school?"

Grady knew he was breaking the rules, but... hey... this was a special day. "If you don't drop any crumbs, it does."

"Oh, that's so gweat! Thank you! Miss Milluh made bluebewwy cwumble!"

Clara's jaw dropped.

"Can I dwink my juice too?"

He saw Clara scrunch up her mouth but continued anyway. "If you promise not to spill, you can."

"And my Sticky Bun? Can I eat it too?"

Clara answered before he could. "Don't push it."

Grady knew Clara well enough to keep his opinions to himself after that and headed out of the complex.

The drive to the school went along without incident until they passed Second Street. They were well on their way to the mid-town intersection at First, when the radio crackled to life and the calm, monotonal voice of a police dispatcher filled the bus.

> *Base to all drivers; attention all drivers. There is a collision with injuries at First and Main.*

J.D. jerked the hoodie off his face and said with a mouth full of Sticky Bun, "A weck!?"

> *Emergency responders are on the scene. Expect long delays. Re-route if possible.*

Grady clicked his tongue. "That would be us."

J.D.'s face appeared in the aisle, and he managed to say while still chewing, "A weck! They was a weck!"

Grady saw Clara turn around in her seat. "Don't talk with your mouth full, J.D., you might choke."

J.D. responded, still chewing, "Okay. I won't,"

Grady adjusted his seat higher to check out the situation. The only thing between them and several hours of sitting in traffic was a residential subdivision on their right. He glanced at the fuel gauge. *Got no choice.*

He quickly changed lanes—signaled to turn. "Hang on everyone."

He heard Clara plop down in the seat beside J.D. "Grady! The sign on the gate says *Dead End*!"

He checked his mirrors.

"Grady! It says, *No Thru traffic*!"

"Trust me!" He gripped the wheel and cranked a hard, fast right.

The bus swerved into the entrance of the subdivision and made it safely past an unmanned guard shack, but scraped across a half-hidden speedbump too fast, sending everything not tied down, sailing.

While personal items and cleaning supplies crashed to the floor, Clara's face appeared in Grady's mirror. "Well, that was im-pres-sive."

J.D.'s face, all saucer-eyed and covered with crumbs, popped into the mirror beside hers. "Wow! Can we do that a-gain?"

Clara pulled out a handi-wipe and cleaned off his mouth. "Ab-so-lute-ly not."

In the mirror, Grady watched her pick up a roll of paper towels, stand beside J.D.'s seat and survey the situation. "Good grief!" J.D. looked up at her. "I dwopped my cwumbs."

Clara began sweeping the crumbs off the seat into her hand. "I see that."

J.D. licked his fingers. "I spilled my juice."

She rolled her eyes. "I see that too"

J.D. let out a whine. "Now my seat's all wet."

Clara soaked up the spill while shooting daggers at Grady in the mirror. "It cer-tain-ly is."

J.D. searched around in his lap. "I can't find my stwah!"

Clara clicked her tongue with disgust and fished for a straw on the floor under the seat in front of them "We'll get another one."

Clara sent Grady a final *thanks a lot* glare in the mirror then rolled out some towels and started to straighten things up.

Grady knew he was already on thin ice with Clara for letting J.D. eat on the bus. But just *how thin* was made crystal clear the minute he heard how hard the dirty towels hit the trash.

She plunked herself down across from him and spoke through gritted teeth. "Now what."

Fully aware that he was the only one impressed with what he had just accomplished, Grady decided it was best just to take the safe approach and press on. "Wellll, I suppose we should finish taking J.D. to school."

Her nostrils flared. "Prob-bab-bly-not-a-good-time-to-get-cute, Grady." She reached for her *phone*. "Want me to request a tow?"

"Nah—we're fine. Everything's fine."

She leaned across the aisle and whispered, "I'm telling you right now, Grady Redwine. I am NOT. Pushing. This. Bus."

J.D.'s voice drifted their direction. "I'll push."

Grady turned around to him. "Thank you, J.D., but everything's fine. Nobody has to push."

Clara lowered her voice again. "Your definition of fine is cer-tain-ly different from mine."

"Honest, Clara. We're fine! Those signs on the gate are fake. They bought them at a hardware store and put them there to keep people from cutting through the complex."

She pointed at a post outside the side window. "That one too? The one that says, *No Turn Around*?"

"Well, actually, that-one's-real."

Clara's eyebrows shot to her hairline. "You mean to tell me we're tr... She caught herself and dropped to a whisper. "We're-trapped-in-here?!"

J.D.'s face appeared in the mirror, eyes bulging out of their sockets. "Twapped! I can't be twapped! I have a test this mowning."

Grady turned sideways in his seat. "Calm down. Please. Just calllllmmmm dowwwwn, you two. No-body's trapped. There aren't any turnarounds because they don't *need* them here."

He illustrated his explanation with his hands as he spoke. "Every street in this complex is just a biiig circle cut through the mid-dle by the Parkway. No matter what you do or where you drive around here, you will eventually end up back where you started, even if you didn't want to.

"All you have to do to get out of here is take the Parkway to Main Street through the east gate"—he motioned back to where they came in— "or go west to the back gate"—he motioned straight ahead — "and get on the highway."

He turned his full attention to Clara and softly said, "Since we want to get J.D. to school on time for his test this morning, and because Main Street is blocked right now, my plan is to take the Parkway to the west gate and get on the highway...unless you'd rather sit here in the cold and wait for a tow."

J.D.'s face appeared in the aisle. "Pick tow, Miss Clawa. It sounds fun."

Grady sent a bewildered look Clara's direction. "He's got the hearing of a damn hunting hound."

"I hood that."

Clara chuckled and shrugged.

Grady continued. "So, what's it gonna be? My way or the high-way."

Clara threw her arms in the air. "I give up."— Then she headed for the back of the bus— "Just do what you think is best."

Between drivers sharing traffic information on the radio and sirens speeding by, conversation on the bus became close to impossible. The incessant thwump-thwump-thwumping of helicopters hovering overhead didn't help much either.

J.D. was soon enthralled by it all. "Miss Clawa! Look! It's TeeVee news! And...and they's Med Evac! Ooo! Ooo! I see a Huey! I think that's the cops! Mistow Wedwine! I think the cops are he-uh!"

Clara corrected him. "Police, J.D., honey. We call them police."

Grady sneaked a quick glance upward. *That's gotta be one big pile-up...all the commotion out there.*

As they approached the west gate, Clara hurried to the front of the bus and focused on the highway. "Wow Grady. It's bumper-to-bumper up there. What do you think we should do?"

"Remain calm and take it a step at a time, I guess."

"Well, we better figure out the first step fast, my friend. We're less than a mile from gridlock."

He glanced in her direction. "Tell ya what. Why don't you go work on the remain calm part with J.D., while I work hard on the rest."

"OK, good. That sounds good."

When she was gone, Grady stretched up to check out the highway for himself and weighed his options. *If we go up there and sit in that traffic for hours, we're gonna run out of fuel. If we park and wait for a tow, we'll run out of fuel and be ice cubes before a truck can get here un-lesss...*

A little shortcut he used as a boy bubbled up from his memory. They might have closed it off—or moved it—or changed it so much he wouldn't recognize it. But even though it was a longshot, he believed it might be a way to get them safely out of this mess—if he could find it.

He poked along for a while, searching the streets for clues to where the road might be, but when he struck out, he spent his time trying to make peace with the possibility of being forced to join the logjam on the highway. It was when they passed a little grove of maple trees, that beams from a streetlight breaking through the branches caught his eye and literally pointed to a little road half buried by leaves, about a hundred feet off the Parkway.

Well, I'll be damned. There it is.

He double-checked the fuel gauge—slightly less than half a tank. *If you've got no fuel, you've got no heat, Redwine. Can you make it?*

He thought he could. He hoped he could.

Grady pulled over to the side of the road and glanced in the mirror at J.D. and Clara. He had to be right.

Clara's face appeared beside his reflection. "What's up? What happened?"

"I've got an idea."

He saw her looking around them, obviously bewildered and worried. "Oh-Lord."

Grady returned his attention to the road. *You're half a block from the west gate, Redwine. Make a decision.*

Finally, he gripped the wheel with firm resolve. "Hold on you two. We're gonna go on a field trip."

J.D. perked up. "I love field twips."

Clara's face disappeared from the mirror as he turned into the clearing but reappeared when he finished. "Really, Grady? Through the mud!?"

He shrugged. "What can I say? Some field trips are just muddy."

They mucked along for a while, then Clara's voice drifted his way. "How do you know this stuff?"

"What stuff?"

"How do you know so much about this place—the circles—the Parkway—this road?"

"I grew up here. Back when I was a kid, all this land belonged to a dairy. My friends and I useta ride our bikes down here, buy a cone at their ice cream stand and watch the cows. Then, when the old man who owned the place died and his kids sold the land, we rode down and watched them build houses."

Things went just fine for a mile, until they rounded a sharp curve, and the road turned into a cow path.

Oh, My Lord.

The path was neglected and narrow —a deep rutty mess full of puddles and potholes, old tires and trash. Grady checked all his mirrors. There was no backing up or turning around. The trees were too close to the road.

"Check your seatbelts, you two. It's gonna be bumpy."

He glanced at Clara. She looked shocked and alarmed, but J.D. was having a ball.

For the next several miles, not one of the six wheels seemed to be on the same level. Grady gripped the wheel—swiped the sweat away on his forehead.

Thank God for dual axels.

They rocked slowly along like a ship in a storm, with J.D. providing play-by-play and analysis.

"Whoa. Whoa. Whooooa. That-was-a-big-one. W-w-w- whoooah. Wa—whoah. Oh- my-gosh. Watch Out!"

Grady spoke over his shoulder. "J.D.! J.D.! J.D. Please! Keep it quiet!"

"I'm twying, but...Oh my gosh! That was a twee limb, Mistow Wedwine! Whoa! And a tie-uh! We just missed it!"

They tackled the climbs and curves on a couple of hills, then eventually entered a pasture planted with fescue.

"Whoooooaaaaaahhhh, Mistoe Wedwiiiiiine. Look at the gwass! It's all gween like we just went to *Hea-ven*."

Clara met his eyes in the mirror and mouthed, "Where in the *Bloody Hell* are we?"

"We're at the old Hopewell farm." He pointed right. "If I remember correctly that road down there feeds into an entrance to *First Street.*"

When they reached the intersection outside the farm, Grady pointed to eastbound traffic hemmed in by cement planters and shrubs. "Look over there."

"Oh-my-gosh, Grady. It's full stop for miles."

He eased the bus over a sidewalk and curb, made a free-wheeling turn onto an empty lane westbound, and booked it down the street to the school.

When they finally pulled into the empty bus loop, they saw Mister Wilson perched in a wheelchair in a Shelter next to the road.

Grady opened the door, and Wilson approached them obviously amazed. "You're either the luckiest driver in the world or the best one."

J.D. started to pack up. "Mistow Wedwine is the best one."

Grady smiled. "Well, thank you, J.D."

Wilson continued. "You're the only one from the south side who made it. How did you manage to get here?"

Grady shrugged. "Took a couplea back roads."

Wilson kicked some mud off the edge of a step. "I can tell."

J.D. appeared at the front of the bus. "We went on a field twip."

"That sounds like fun."

"It was! We almost got hit by a twee."

Just then, a dispatcher's voice crackled on in the bus.

Attention all drivers. Attention all drivers. Classes have been canceled today. Parents have been notified. Take every precaution to get children home safely. Check for updates tomorrow.

Clara glanced sideways at Grady. "I'd like to request a different route home."

J.D. returned to his place on the bus and slumped back in his seat. "Awww Miss Clawa. I want to go on the woe-luh coastuh woad again."

THURSDAY – FRIDAY
March 21-22, 2019

Grady had grown to appreciate the ding of an incoming text at four in the morning because it almost always meant an extra day off.

He groped around in the dark for his phone and squinted hard at the screen.

In consultation with the District Safety Committee and the Highway Department regarding street closures required to repair damage from yesterday's incident, the School District has decided that today and tomorrow will be online learning days for the students.

Grady fluffed his pillow and rolled over. *Wow. Two days of online learning for students and two days of First Round viewing for me! Thank you. Thank you-Thank you-Thank you-Thank you.*

SATURDAY
March 23, 2019-Morning

After being up until 2:30 watching post-game commentary, Grady was in such a dead sleep, he answered the phone before being fully aware it was ringing. "Huh?" he mumbled, gathering together some saliva. He swallowed. "Huh-lo?"

"Mister Redwine? Did I call too early?"

He squinted at the clock on the nightstand and guessed it said 6:30...or so. "Nuh...uh...no. That's okay. Who's this?"

"This is Hattie Miller with The *Hamilton Children's Shelter*. I'm so sorry to bother you on a weekend."

Grady stifled a yawn and stretched. "No problem, Miss Miller. No problem at all. What can I do for you?"

There was a lot of stress in her voice. "I'm calling because I promised Prissy I'd let you know she's in the hospital."

He leaped to alert in an instant. "What hap-pened?"

"I'm not sure if you knew it, but she's been having trouble with the circulation in her foot lately."

"Yes...yes. She told me she might be having some surgery. But it wasn't supposed to be until June."

"Well, she woke up in the middle of the night feeling really bad and when I pulled back the covers, her foot was all swollen and black...just covered with blisters. And the smell...uh!...don't get me started. So, we called the EMTs and rushed her to the hospital and they...they...well they had to remove it today."

Grady sank against his pillows. "Is she okay? Is everything okay?"

"She came through the surgery just fine, but she's very upset about it all as you can imagine."

"Where is she?"

"She's in the children's wing at *City Hospital*. They have her in critical care."

"Who's with her?"

"No one right now. She's sleeping. I was in the recovery room when she first woke up, but I had to come back here to fix the children a meal. The Hamiltons are out of town this week so she's alone, but the nurses take wonderful care of her. She's had to spend almost every holiday in that place having something done ever since I've known her, so she's kind of considered family around there."

"Can I go see her?"

"I know she'd love it if you could, but they only let immediate relatives in that ward. They're very strict about that."

"Oh."

"I'd wait until she's out of critical care. They think they'll be able to move her by the end of the day tomorrow or maybe Monday."

Grady felt a silent, selfish sense of relief. There were no basketball games on Monday.

"Thank you for letting me know, Miss Miller. And please keep in touch."

He hung up slowly. *Ahhh, Prissy. Poor Prissy. She must be terrified.*

Grady knew going to sleep again after hearing the news about Prissy was impossible, so he pulled on his lucky IU sweatshirt and headed for the fridge. After a brief survey of the contents, he settled on a corn beef sandwich but got stuck on what to drink.

Beer…OJ… beer… OJ…It's seven A.M., Redwine. Maybe you should have some coffee. Maybe, but this is March Madness.

He gave in and picked up the OJ, then sprawled on the couch to watch the pre-game shows and check his brackets while he casually unwrapped the sandwich so he could take a bite.

First day, Second round. Maryland vs LSU. So far so good.

He settled in and listened to the chatter of the broadcasters floating off the screen, but a single statement from his conversation with Miss Miller kept haunting him.

She's alone.

Prissy.

Redwine. Stop feeling guilty. No one will think twice if you don't go. You have no responsibility in this situation. Zero. None.

But it's Prissy.

Don't be ridiculous. Miss Miller told you only relatives are allowed to see her today. They wouldn't let you in if you tried.

He sipped at his juice.

She's just out of surgery. She'll be sedated. She probably won't even know you're there. You can go on Monday. There are no games that day. You could kill two birds with one stone.

He took a bite of his sandwich. Chewed.

Trying to get in would be a complete waste of time. It's against hospital policy. You couldn't make it past the receptionist.

He drank.

He finished his sandwich.

He threw the wrapping toward the trash basket. Missed.

Something is trying to kick Prissy's butt, Redwine. And you're just going to sit here?

You know how to get into that hospital room. You know you do.

He checked the clock over the television. If he left soon, he could get there and be back for the opening tip-off at Noon. He glanced at the clock. Eleven-thirty. Pre-game had started already. He pressed the *record* lever. He'd watch it later.

Grady hurried through the kitchen into the garage; moved a few things out of the way; opened the storage closet and pulled out the Army fatigues he wore during his stint in the National Guard. He held the hanger holding his jacket against his body.

Well, that ain't gonna happen.

He switched to Plan B and fished around for his father's old hunting gear.

They're nurses. They won't know. Camo is camo.

He found his old tactical work boots in a corner toward the back. The leather was worn and a little nappy. The laces were frayed, and the toes permanently pointed upward, but they'd do.

He dressed, threw on his *Comets* raincoat and headed for the hospital.

Grady was grateful the children's wing was separate from the adult section at City Hospital. The nurses would recognize him over there.

He found his way to the proper floor and marched down the long corridor, following signs pointing toward critical care. The hallway smelled medicinal and clean, but after the many hours he'd spent at the hospital during Mary's illness, the overwhelming odors of pine cleaner and urine made his stomach clench. To him, attempting to hide the smells of sickness that way was about as effective as someone whose clothes reeked of cigarettes chewing breath mints to convince people they hadn't been smoking.

The sound of his military boots on the tile seemed uncomfortably loud and disturbing in the empty halls. Grady tried to minimize the sound as he approached the nurse at the reception desk.

"I'm Major Milcamp. I'm here to see my daughter, Prissy...Prissy Milcamp. She had emergency surgery this morning."

The receptionist scanned him from head to foot and frowned. "Milcamp, you say?"

"Yes. Milcamp."

She gripped her mouse and began maneuvering around the computer monitor as she entered information into the system. "Major...Maa-jor."

Grady took a deep breath to calm his nerves and concentrated on maintaining a casual stance. "Milcamp."

"Milcamp. Hmmmm." She got a puzzled look on her face. "Could you spell that for me please?"

He smiled and tried to sound pleasant. "Sure. It's Milcamp...m-i-l-c-a-m-p."

"I have a Captain Milcamp."

Grady managed a chuckle. "Oh, they must not have updated her records yet. I just got a...his mind raced up the rankings...promotion. It's sort of a surprise. I'm Major, now. Major Milcamp."

"Well congratulations!"

"Thank you."

She started moving the mouse again. "If you give me a moment, I'll just update the records from here."

"I appreciate that very much."

Grady's guts churned like a perfect storm as he watched her work. He should have checked Prissy's contact information before coming. He didn't know her father's first name. He pulled the rank of Major out of thin air and couldn't give a correct address for the man if they put a gun to his head.

Please, nurse, please, please don't ask for ID.

In time, she put down the mouse and said, "You'll find gloves, a mask and a gown in the closet in the outer room. Never go into her room without them." She pointed down the hall. "Room two hundred. Second door to the right." He turned and began to leave. "Oh," she said. "I forgot to mention you are not to use a telephone or any electronic device of any kind while in the room...and sanitize your hands...there's some sanitizer on the shelf."

"Thanks for the heads up," he said over his shoulder.

I can check the scores later. I'll be back home by the pre-game.

Grady heard the respirator long before he stepped into Prissy's room, but he was still jarred when he saw her lying there attached to one. Tubes ran into and out of her little body as if she were an interstate interchange. A hanging traction device kept the stump of her tiny leg elevated.

He was doing pretty well until he heard the heart monitor.

Grady probably should have been more prepared for resurrected memories of Mary's room…the equipment beep, beep, beeping as her life slipped away…but he wasn't. The sound swept him back to those days filled with pain and anxiety and he began living it all again.

Prissy was groggy, but reached out and made a weak, muffled, happy sound when she saw him there.

He stepped carefully over and around the cords surrounding the bed and sat in the chair beside her. Forcing calmness into his voice, he stretched his arm through the bed rails, gently took her hand in his and whispered, "It's Mister Redwine, honey. Don't try to talk."

Prissy limply clung to his fingers, made some more muffled sounds, then finally relaxed and fell asleep, leaving him alone with humming machines and antiseptic smells that brought back heart-wrenching memories of endless hours spent in the hospital listening to the raspy inhalation of Mary's breathing. He was surrounded by painful reminders of her body ravaged by cancer and felt the same emptiness that consumed him when she slipped away and left him in the horrible silence that followed.

Grady began feeling the sting of helplessness along with the crushing blow of knowing that there might be nothing he could do to make Prissy's life better.

It hit him hard.

A commotion out in the hall jarred Grady back to reality, then he heard the sound of the outer door slamming against the wall as a surgeon burst into the room looking genuinely alarmed. He scanned Grady from head to toe and shot him a look as if asking, "Who in the **Hell** are you?"

Grady felt a bead of sweat trickling down his spine.

The doctor maintained a civil voice but kept his suspicious expression. "I didn't realize it was hunting season…" he referred to Prissy's chart and studied Grady's clothing. "Major, is it? Major Milcamp?"

Grady immediately knew he'd been busted.

Oh God. How can you explain to people that you've been thrown into jail for trespassing and impersonating an Officer…well actually, impersonating a convict who was impersonating an Officer.

Grady pulled his hand away from Prissy's and stood up. "Please. Let me stay, doctor. This child has no one. She shouldn't have to go through this alone. She needs to know somebody cares about her."

"I'm asking again, sir. I know you're not her father. Who are you and why are you here?"

Grady's mouth went dry. "How…?"

"When you wear a uniform as many years as I did, you know. Besides, military hasn't worn tiger stripe camo since the early eighties, and they don't use black anymore." He shifted his weight. "Are you going to answer, or should I call the police?"

"Uh…I'm sorry…what was the question?"

"Who are you and why are you here."

Grady gave in and offered a hand. "My name is Grady Redwine. I drive a school bus for the County and I'm part of a new *Special Needs* program that Prissy is part of."

The doctor finally relaxed and shook Grady's hand. "Nice to meet you, Mister Redwine. I'm Doctor Florian." He paused a moment; looked Grady straight in the eyes. "I realize It was a big sacrifice and a huge risk for you to come here today, and I respect you for that."

"She's a special little girl. She's worth it."

"Just for full disclosure, Mister Redwine, I've done all thirty-three of Prissy's surgeries and I'm one of the few people who know the truth about her parental situation, so you really didn't stand a chance of fooling me."

Prissy moaned and adjusted her position.

Grady tipped his head her direction. "Has she really gone through something like this thirty-three times?"

"I've watched her bravely face extraordinary challenges over the years. Thirty-three times she's been here, but she's a trooper. She accepts it and moves on."

"Tell me about it. She's more upset about having her balance thrown off and ruining her races than actually losing the foot."

"It hardly seems possible, does it? She's such a tiny little thing. But it's true. Thirty-three."

"How can that be? Does she have any internal organs left?"

"The combination of spina bifida and Scoliosis is cruel and heartbreaking, Mister Redwine. They're horrible diseases individually and— if you'll pardon my language— true bastards when they get together. They affect Prissy's swallowing, her bones and her circulation—mainly her heart and lungs. They don't usually require loss of organs—mostly make it hard for them to work. There *is* one redeeming factor in Prissy's situation, however."

"What's that?"

"She doesn't have much feeling in her legs, so her level of physical pain is low. Prissy's issues always come from phantom pain…she feels throbbing in the part that has been removed. Unfortunately, as beneficial as it is during the surgery, it makes recovery far more difficult. She's got some rough times ahead of her. When you amputate a limb, the presence of that limb is still felt. You're fully aware that it is gone, but in your mind, it's still there…like an itch that you just can't find to scratch."

The doctor started to leave then turned back. "By the way. 83-71 Gonzaga."

"What?"

"The game."

Oh. Oh yeah! The game.

Grady was stunned. He hadn't given the game a single thought all day. That was Earth-shattering to him. "How did you know?"

The doctor pointed at the raincoat hanging in the outer closet. *Comets.* "Big basketball fan?"

"The biggest. You?"

"Afraid so."

"*Comets?*"

"We're *Ravens* fans at our house. My son's a fanatic."

"Done your brackets?"

"Yep."

"Good luck." Come back any time. Use your own name. I'll put you into the system."

As Grady made the long walk to his truck he thought, *I'll never complain about my feet hurting again.*

SUNDAY
March 24, 2019-Morning

Grady was determined to go sit with Prissy until the Hamiltons came back into town. He threw on some clothes, brewed a quick cup of coffee, and headed straight back to the hospital.

He didn't need Prissy's room number to find her. He could hear her quietly crying down the hall. He wasn't sure how he was able to sort her voice out of the confusion in the ward, but he could.

"Are you crying because you're hurting honey? Do you want something for pain?"

"No. I'm crying because I'm going to miss my 4K."

He reached over and took her hand. "Aw, honey. Please don't worry about your 4K."

"But my balloon. I won't be able to get my balloon,"

"Remember when we first talked about goals and J.D. asked if your goals were going to be forever?" Prissy nodded. Grady pushed on. "And do you remember what I said about that?"

She didn't hesitate. "You said they don't have to be forever." He prompted her further. "Beeecauuse."

"Because they are our goals, and they belong to us."

Grady smiled. "So, can you change them?" She nodded again.

He continued. "How often can you change them?"

She smiled and answered. "Whenever we want to," then she got a pitiful look on her face and turned toward him teary-eyed again. "But I don't *want* to change my goal, Mister Redwine. I want to run my 4K for my daddy…for Father's Day."

He swallowed hard. "Well, honey, a change doesn't necessarily mean you have to quit and do something completely different. A change can just be doing the same thing in a different way."

"How can you run a 4K differently?"

"Right now, I don't know. But I guarantee you, we're going to figure it out."

Grady had grown used to nurses kicking him out of the room so they could clear Prissy's chest and make it possible for him to visit the bathroom. He tried once to just lean against the wall outside the door and wait, but hearing the sickening noise of Prissy coughing and retching as they sucked the mucus from her lungs was more than he could handle.

He headed for a nearby break room, hit the bathroom, then paid for a cup of the swill they considered coffee from the vending machine. Then he sat down at a table and spent some time contemplating Prissy's 4K issue.

He felt completely heartbroken about the whole situation, especially now that he knew the truth about Prissy's father. This might be the only local 4K, but maybe he could find another one somewhere else…maybe farther along on the calendar. Father's Day wasn't until June 16, so they had time.

He was alone in the lounge, so he picked up his *phone* and asked for help from his new best friend. "Hey Siri."

"Yeeeesssss."

"Please find 4K races on Father's Day." — There was a several second pause, then she returned. — "Here's what I found."

He clicked on the link and a list appeared: *Shreveport…no… Fairhaven…no… Dover, NH…Nope…same date for them as for here.* Then a website popped up:

Join us for our fifth annual FATHER'S DAY 5K virtual race!

*What the Hell is a **Virtual Race**?* —As if the web site had read his mind, the next sentence that appeared on the screen was an article entitled: *WHAT IS A VIRTUAL RACE?* —He read further:

> *A virtual race is a race that can be run, walked, jogged or wheeled from any location you choose. You can be on a road, a trail, a treadmill, on the track of a gym, or even at another race. You can run your own race, at your own pace, and time it yourself. When your race is completed, submitted, and approved, a certificate celebrating Father's Day, and a medal will be shipped directly to you.*
>
> o **Parameters**: *You can choose to complete a virtual 4k, 5K, 10K, half marathon— or determine a distance of your own. It's your choice.*
>
> o **Timeframe**: *Start your race whenever you wish, but you must have completed and submitted your documentation by May 15.*

- o **Medals/Certificates**: We will ship your medal and certificate by mid-May, to make sure you receive them in time to celebrate Father's Day.
- o **Tracking**: Use a spreadsheet or journal to record your runs. You must note the date, the time of the start, time of the finish, and the distance covered by each run.
- o **Registration/Submission**: Log on to this website to register for your race and submit your results. NOTE: The amount of time it took you to complete your race does not matter. What matters is that you went the full distance and completed it by the deadline.
- o **Cost**: Registration fee is $25. This includes the entry fee of $20 and cost of purchasing and mailing the medal of $5. All credit cards are accepted.

Grady almost levitated out of his chair; he was so excited. *This is perfect! PERFECT! Inside, he said, "Thank you, Lord. You've made a little girl very happy."* Grady kept tapping the screen on his phone all the way back to Prissy's room because he was afraid he'd lose it. He tiptoed back into the room, happy to find her awake, then paused beside her bed and handed her the phone. "I did some searching during the break and look what Siri found."

Prissy read for a minute and cried out with joy. "Oh, let's do it, Mr. Redwine! Can we do it?"

Two seconds later, a nurse burst into the room.

Grady and Prissy stared at her, bewildered. The nurse skidded to a stop looking bewildered too, "What are you two **do-ing** in here? The alarm just went off on her heart monitor!"

Grady left Prissy's room physically exhausted and emotionally drained. Even though everything had turned out well for her and he felt uplifted by the positive outcome, the gut-wrenching memories of Mary's suffering still stuck with him, and it took some of the glow off the day.

He was proud that he had managed to keep his feelings under control, but when he settled in behind the wheel of his truck and saw Mary's empty seat beside him, the dam finally burst and all he could manage to do was stare at it and cry, completely heartbroken.

In time, Grady managed to pull himself together; drove home in a fog of despair; and collapsed into the bed fully dressed and exhausted.

WEEK TWELVE

MONDAY
March 25, 2019-Morning

Grady was jolted out of a dead sleep by the ding of an incoming message at 3:30 a.m. He fumbled around in the dark for his phone until he found it buried in the blanket beside him, then squinted at the screen through bleary eyes and read:

Sonti has a doctor's appointment this morning.
I am going to take him.
He will ride home with you after school.

He groaned and dropped the phone back onto the bed, then rubbed his temples for a few minutes in an unsuccessful attempt to relieve what was becoming a blinding headache.
Why are you so surprised? Sonti always has issues on Monday.
Shortly after he was able to nod off again, Grady heard a second ding and rolled over to read that message too.

Attention all drivers:
Be advised that there will be mandatory fire drills and an assembly at all schools today. Students will not be available for pick-up until after fifth period.

By then, he had abandoned any hope of getting a decent night's rest and knew from experience that if no one was there to nudge him awake after he'd had a hard day, he would sleep through the alarm until Noon.
Grady decided he'd better just throw on some clothes and leave early for work. That way, he might be able to sneak in a few winks on the bus without worry before he had to start driving and have a better chance to get over his headache.

###

The sky was a patchwork of gray when Grady climbed into his truck and headed for the bus lot. The wind had a crisp edge to it that carried a hint of rain, and he began to feel a sense of change in the air—a reminder that Spring was just around the corner.

It was Clara's turn to get coffee that morning, so he drove directly to the bus lot and dragged through his pre-check, then eased into the driver's seat, leaned his head against the headrest, and conked out.

When Clara arrived, she nudged him awake, handed him a large latte and said, "Haven't you got a bed at home? You look exhausted."

He rubbed his eyes and replied, "That's because I spent the whole weekend at the hospital. Prissy had emergency surgery."

"What! Was it her foot?"

"They had to take it off early."

"Oh, my Lord. That poor child. How is she?"

"You know Prissy. She's fine about the foot but upset about maybe not getting her balloon."

Clara smiled. "That's so like her."

He glanced at the clock and took a welcome sip from the cup before he continued. "Did you get the email about the assembly today?"

"Sure did."

"Let's grab some lunch…catch up on the weekend and do some planning."

"Sounds good!"

"You got the coffee today, so lunch is on me. What do you have a taste for?"

Clara smiled, batted her eyes and said, "Steak would be nice."

Grady didn't miss a beat before he replied, "Okay! Steakburger at Indy's. Sounds good to me!"

She let out a loud cackle. "I was hoping for a medium-rare ribeye."

Grady casually peered at the sky and replied, "The coffee was *good* this morning, my friend, but it wasn't *that* good.

He cranked up the bus. "I didn't get home until midnight and Sonti's Mom woke me up with a text at 3:30."

"Good Grief!"

As he drove to the gate, Grady was able to keep an eye on the road and glance in the mirror at Clara now and then while she folded blankets. She picked up the purple one and said, "So, is Sonti riding today?"

He merged onto the highway. "Nope. No Sonti this morning. Doctor's appointment."

She set the folded blanket aside. "Wonder what happened."

Grady thought, *"The **weekend** is what happened."*

Clara kept on. "Why wouldn't his Mom take him to a doctor at *The Hamilton Home*? It's got to be free for her there." — She pondered it over a minute longer then said, "All I can think of is that Sonti is with her for weekends and it's easier to take him somewhere else on her day off."

Grady made no comment, but the blue metallic import shot through his mind and made him feel queasy.

Clara continued to rattle on. "It can't be anything too serious if she said he'd be riding with us this afternoon."

Grady brought the conversation to a conclusion when he entered the code to open the gates of the Hamilton Complex, and they entered the grounds. "Let's catch up on the details of everything else at lunch."

When they rounded the curve leading to J.D.'s dorm, he was already waiting for them on the sidewalk. Grady pulled over, opened the door and greeted him. "Good Morning!"

J.D. climbed on board, flying high. "It's a **weally** good mowning."

Grady figured he hadn't been told about Prissy.

After taking his seat, J.D. gripped the back of the seat in front of him and shouted, "I have been thinking, Mistow Wedwine."

Grady glanced at him in the mirror. "Oh? What about?"

"I have to get a luhnuh's puhmit befoe I can dwive my cah."

"Thaaat's riiight."

"So, I was think-ing. Maybe you and I could make a deal."

Oh-Lord.

"Since you ah the gweatest dwivuh in the wuhld and I am good at computuhs and stuff, maybe I could teach you moe about you phone and you could teach me how to dwive."

Grady sent a wide-eyed S.O.S. to Clara.

She got really busy doing something else.

Swell.

He shifted his focus back on J.D. who was nervously rocking with his elbows on the seatback in front of him while he waited for a response "So, whaddaya think, Mistow Wedwine? Can we make a deal?"

Grady made one last appeal to Clara who finally had mercy on him and stepped in to help. "I could be wrong, J.D., but I think you have to take *Driver's Ed* in *school*."

J.D. scrunched up his face and slumped back in his seat. "I will still have to pwactice sometimes." He pulled his hoodie over his face. "How am I going to pwac-tice?"

Grady hoped the topic would go away when they picked up BennieToo, but it took a while.

J.D. pulled the hoodie off of his head and twisted around to talk to Bennie while he took his seat. "I'm luhning to dwive, Bennie."

BennieToo's screen lit up. "That's great, J.D."

"Mistow Wedwine might help me."

Bennie's smile filled the monitor. "That's great!"

A long awkward silence fell over the bus after that, and Grady drove to the school deeply absorbed in a struggle with his conscience. *You can't say no to J.D., Grady. He didn't say no to you when you needed help.*

His guilty feelings grew even stronger when J.D.'s voice drifted to the front of the bus again. "Please help me, Mistow Wedwine. I don't have anyone else to ask."

Grady rubbed his eyes with his palms and tried to beat back his feelings but failed. His head was throbbing again, but he finally managed to pull a few thoughts together. "Let me check and see if there are any policies around this, J.D.. The school might not allow it."

"If they will, will you help me?"

"I'll do what I can to help you, J.D., as long as it's within the rules. I can't promise until I know for sure that I can.

"I've stahted luhning some stuff on my own alweady. I downloaded a navigatuh app on my computuh..."

Navigator app?

"...I can tell you how to get to any place in this town...actually any place in the whole countwy. We don't have to wemembuh diwections any mow oh wowwy about getting lost. Isn't that gweat?!"

Why am I starting to get worried.

In the mirror, Grady watched J.D. open up his computer.

"Okay, Mistow Wedwine. I'll show you. Can you heah me?"

"Yes, J.D. I hear you."

"You need to go stwaight on this stweet, then in fifty feet tuhn left onto Bwady."

Grady drove onward, mystified.

"Okay, this is Bwady. Tuhn left on this stweet."

Grady looked at Clara in the mirror and mouthed, *Save me.*

She turned around in her seat. "J.D., instead of telling Mister Redwine where to go, maybe we should just test him and if he makes a mistake, then correct him."

"But I am getting weady to luhn how to dwive so I am luhning how to navigate. Annnnd I am helping *him* not to have to wemembuh how to get places. That's what we do. We ah Miluhs. We help each othuh."

"But it is more helpful to make sure he's doing it *right*—Isn't it, Mister Redwine?"

Grady jumped at an opportunity to answer. "Yes! Yes, it is!"

Clara continued. "So, since it's more helpful, let's just give Mister Redwine a test instead."

J.D. continued to problem solve. "Okay, I won't tell him anything any moh." He appeared to push a couple of buttons and a woman's voice said, "In five feet, turn right on Central."

Grady looked around. *Who the Hell is that*?!

"Can you hear huh, Mistow Wedwine?"

"Who's talking J.D.?"

"The Map talks when I ask it to and it will tell you what to do instead of me. Do you need it to be louduh?"

Clara persisted. "J.D., we are only going to tell Mister Redwine when he makes a *mistake*, remember? He's a good driver. He knows where to go."

J.D. plugged in his headphones. "Okay."

Grady breathed a sigh of relief and concentrated on the road. As he approached the main entrance to the school, J.D. shouted, "You know what to do, Mistow Wedwine. That's wight. You got it."

When Grady entered the drop-off, J.D. struck again. "You got it, Mistow Wedwine. The Map says you did evvything wight!"

Clara spoke up again. "J.D. We are only going to tell him when he does it *wrong*, remember?"

"I only pwaised him foe what he did wight! I didn't *tell* him anything."

Grady looked at Clara. *I changed my mind. I don't want to be saved. Shoot me now.*

Afternoon

Grady was ready to drop to the ground and kiss it when they finally parked at Indy's for lunch. Silence. Heavenly silence.

They stood in line and ordered their steakburgers, then Grady asked a cashier for permission to eat in the meeting room where it was quieter.

She smiled and said, "Sure! We don't have anything scheduled today."

Grady took a seat at a table then sat back for a moment to relax. Clara sipped on her soda and said, "So catch me up on what's going on with Prissy."

Well, as I told you earlier, they had to amputate that foot and she took it well, but she was very upset about her balloon. You know how competitive she is. She doesn't want to be the only one who didn't get one this year…but thanks to you and Sonti, we were able to work it out."

Clara had a confused look on her face. "What did **we** do?"

"You taught me how to use Siri. I asked her to help find an alternative to the race Prissy was scheduled to run, and Siri found a way for us to do it virtually."

"**Grady!** I'm so **proud** of you! That's **won-der-ful**!"

He puffed up a little. "I'm sort of proud of me too."

She ate a few French fries and said, "So, what should we do this afternoon?"

He leaned back in his chair and relaxed a little. "I figured we'd just drop by the gym, let J.D. and Bennie help Sonti shoot a *few* balls; maybe run a few laps to blow off some steam; then just take them home."

Clara shrugged and said, "Sounds good to me."

After School

Grady and Clara were waiting for the kids to emerge from the building when Grady spotted Halim racing across the yard in their direction, arms pumping like mad as he sped along.

Uh oh.

As he approached, Grady opened the doors and Halim made his usual bus-rocking leap onto the stairs, looking frenzied.

Grady smiled and said, "Well, hello there, Halim! We've missed you, son. What have you been up to lately?"

Halim threw a wild-eyed glance his direction, and using a voice an octave lower than his own, hissed out, "I've been in a little town called *Vengeance*."— Grady felt goosebumps rise on his arms.

Clara stood up to handle the situation. "We're glad you stopped by, and I'm mighty glad to see you again, Halim, but you don't ride Bus Eighty-Six anymore. You need to go to bus Twenty-Seven."

Halim perked up, looked around and said, "Oh! Yeah!" Then he focused on Grady. "You said I could come back here next year; do you still mean it?"

Grady smiled. "Of course I do! We're looking forward to it."

Halim turned and hopped down to the bottom stair where he whipped back around to say, "Remember, Mister Redwine. You just made a real promise…" He jumped to the sidewalk and looked up at Grady to finish his sentence: "…so **watch** yourself." Then he beat it back around the bus loop to where bus Twenty-Seven waited.

Grady turned to Clara and shivered. "He can still get to me."

She chuckled.

Grady paused to think for a minute. "Who was that? Boris Karloff?"

"Don't have a clue where he got the voice," Clara said.

Grady continued. "I'm pretty sure Boris is no longer with us. *Vengeance* must be a town in some new TV show."

Clara peered down the sidewalk, obviously looking for Sonti and said, "J.D. will probably know. We'll ask him."

When Mr. Wilson brought Sonti out with an elastic bandage on his right hand, Grady's heart leaped to his throat. "What happened?"

Wilson helped Sonti up the first stair and answered, "Meltdown. His sister said he got it slammed in a door."

Grady studied the hand trying to determine the damage. "Is anything broken?"

Wilson shook his head no. "Just a bad bruise—scraped lots of skin off his knuckles. He can still move his fingers, but they'll be stiff for a while."

Grady and Clara exchanged nervous glances. Only twelve days until the contest.

After the other two boys came on board, Sonti gingerly stuck his hand out in the aisle and showed it to Grady.

Grady gave him a sympathetic look and said, "Yes I see it, son." He reached gently toward the hand and squeezed it a little. Sonti flinched. "Sorry, pal. Didn't mean to hurt you."

He turned his attention to Clara. "Let's go ahead and go to the gym. See what happens."

From the back of the bus, J.D.'s voice floated up to them. "Okay! To the gym! I have alweady got *the Talking Map* weady to go."

Grady punted. "I'm pretty sure I know how to get to the gym, J.D.. Why don't you help Sonti by looking up the best treatment for his hand."

J.D. eagerly replied, "Okay. I can do that. I will set the Map to talk in the backgwound and tuhn it up loud so you can heah it."

Grady pounced on that one. "Tell ya what, J.D. Let's look up treatment for Sonti when we get to the gym. You listen to the *Talking Map* using your headset and report any wrong turns, because that's more important. Okay?"

J.D. glanced down and said, "Okay."

Grady breathed a big sigh of relief.

Sonti was unusually quiet all the way to the gym. He pressed his injured hand against his chest and even though he supported it there with his other hand, he still let out a small groan when they hit a bump in the road.

Grady studied him in the mirror. *That's not good...not good at all.*

###

In the gym, the group worked like a well-oiled team getting ready to practice. J.D. quickly got everything gathered and properly arranged at the foul line for Sonti. Bennie positioned himself in a good spot on the court and prepared to chase balls. Clara pulled up chairs for everyone close by, while Grady sat Sonti down and took charge.

"How are you doing, Pal? Are you okay to try this?"

Sonti gave a slight wince when he lifted the bandaged hand off the front of his chest and flexed it a little, testing.

Grady was quick to say, "Don't do anything that will hurt your hand more, son. We don't have to do this if you don't want to."

Sonti stared at the stack of balls J.D. had gathered for him and flexed his hand a few more times.

Grady continued. "Seriously, Sonti. We don't have to do this. If you don't feel up to it, we'll find something else fun to do."

Sonti flexed the hand again and wiggled his fingers. To Grady, it appeared to be loosening up a little.

Sonti stood up and walked over to the foul line and reached out for a ball.

Grady gently placed one in Sonti's hand.

After a few breathless moments, Sonti bounced it a couple of times but lost control and dropped it. It was obviously just too painful.

J.D. sighed and started re-packing the balls, but Sonti picked up a second one.

Grady reached out. "Don't hurt yourself, son. You need to let your hand rest."

J.D. seemed somewhat panicked and added, "I looked it up, Sonti. Mistow Wedwine is wight. You need ice, heat and west but keep it limbuh."

To everyone's shock and surprise, Sonti switched the ball to his left hand.

J.D. whispered to Grady, "Do you think maybe Sonti is ambidextuwus? Some people ah you know."

Grady shushed him and said, "Let's just watch him and see."

Sonti wasn't very good with the left-handed bounce, and he missed the basket when he threw it, but he wasn't very far off when he chucked the ball.

Grady was impressed. "Wow Sonti. That was great. Want to try another?"

Bennie handed Sonti the second ball. It went better, but his level of discomfort was obvious.

Grady took charge. "Don't hurt yourself, Sonti. That's enough for today. Let's take some time to get better."

On the way back to the bus, J.D. walked beside Grady. "I looked up ah chances of winning the contest, Mistow Wedwine. The odds ah fifty-to-one."

Grady smiled. "Then at least it's not totally hopeless."

J.D. still seemed upbeat. "Nope. It's pwetty simple. We just have to make shoe Sonti's the ONE."

C.A. Caldwell

TUESDAY
March 26, 2019-Morning

After a restless night spent stewing over Sonti's situation, Grady concluded that he had no choice but to take things one step at a time today. He received another early text from Sonti's Mom saying he had a follow up doctor's appointment that morning, so he wouldn't be riding to school, but he would need a ride to *The Hamilton Home* that afternoon.

Grady decided to get ready for work early this morning, so he'd be able to flex around whatever took place the rest of the day.

Grady figured he had to plan for two situations: the one where Sonti showed up, like his Mom said he was supposed to; and the one where Sonti didn't show, which was far more likely. With Prissy still in the hospital, he was left with the challenge of how to make the experience meaningful just for J.D. and Bennie.

He didn't want to go to the gym again because it seemed to put too much pressure on Sonti. He believed Westlake might be a better environment and would give him more flexibility.

That decided, he glanced at his phone to check the time. It would be tight, but since he was only a block from the *Qwick Pick,* he figured he'd pop in to buy some snacks, a few soft drinks and bottles of water, an extra elastic bandage…just in case…and some adhesive tape to help him teach some first aid.

The stop made him run a bit late, but he felt better about being prepared.

###

Back at the bus, Clara met him at the top of the stairs.

"You're not normally late. I was beginning to worry."

He hurried up the steps. "Sorry. Running errands…traffic and stuff."

She stepped aside. "Well, next time text me and let me know what's going on!"

He set the shopping bags down on the floor. "Sorry. Normally I would have, but stopping to do it would have made me even later."

It was obvious his excuse didn't fly with Clara. She put her hands on her hips and said, "I need to know what's going on, Grady." —She turned and slid into her seat. — "So, what are the plans for this afternoon?"

Grady talked as he hurried around through his pre-check. "I picked up some snacks on my way back…thought we could have a small picnic at the park next to Westlake and turn the afternoon into a first aide lesson to teach the boys how to care for sprains, cuts and scratches, or an injury like Sonti's."

She finally smiled. "Sounds like fun! I'll text Bennie's Mom and have her take him something special so he can join us."

Relieved to be off the hook, Grady sat down too. "Great idea."

Grady continued explaining his thought process. "I figure we've got two possible scenarios to prepare for: what to do if Sonti shows up, and what to do if Sonti doesn't show." —Clara helped complete his sentence by adding, "…as usual."

Grady continued. "With Prissy still in the hospital, we have the additional challenge of making the experience meaningful just for J.D. and Bennie."

Clara nodded. "Good thinking."

Grady summed it all up with, "If Sonti shows up like his mother said in her text this morning, great. If not, we can still have a lesson then go to the tennis court if it's empty and shoot some hoops, practice J.D.'s dribble, or just toss some balls around with Bennie."

Her eyes scanned the sky. "Good plan. It's a sunshiny day. We should definitely take advantage of it."

Afternoon

Sonti turned out to be a no-show, so they headed out to implement Grady's Plan B.

At Westlake, Grady parked beside a large oak tree in the green space next to the tennis courts and they gathered around a nearby table to enjoy their snacks.

"What have *you* got today, Bennie?"

"Mom brought me a fruit smoothie and one of her homemade granola bars."

"Yum."

J.D. chewed for a while then said nonchalantly with his mouth full, "It feels stwange not to have Pwissy heah bossing evwybody awound. I miss huh."

Grady scrunched up his mouth. "I miss her too."

Bennie chimed in. "So do I."

Clara summed it up with, "We all do."

J.D. finally swallowed and asked what seemed to be on everyone's minds. "What ah we going to do if it tuhns out Sonti can't be in the contest, Mistow Wedwine?"

"We're going to do what Milers do when they fall down, J.D. Do you remember what that is?"

"They pick themselves up and keep wunning."

Bennie's face lit up on the screen. "And they never stop until they reach their goal."

Grady smiled. "Very, very good, you two! You're right! I'm impressed! We're going to let ourselves feel sad for a while and then, just like we always do, we're gonna pick ourselves up and try again."

They pondered the situation for a few more seconds, then Bennie said, "I'm pretty sure the *Comets* are going to have the contest again next year."

J.D. perked up. "So, we can twy again then!"

Grady smiled. "Youuu *got* it!"

"With all that extwa pwactice, Sonti might even have a bettuh chance then, than *this* time!"

"Good point! That's true!"

###

Grady gathered the few folks that were there around the table intending to hold the first aide lesson as planned. He pulled out his *Sports Injury and Rehab Guide*.

"Since Sonti has become injured, I thought we'd spend some time today talking about sports injuries and first aid."

Grady watched what began as a bored expression turn into frustration on J.D.'s face. —He paused. — "Is something wrong?"

J.D. shot back, "Why not just go online and watch a video about it. It's fastuh."

Grady recognized an approaching train wreck when he saw one, so he leaned toward him and said, "April Fools!" Then he picked up a basketball and threw down a challenge. "Bet I can make more shots than you."

J.D. grinned from ear-to-ear. "Mayyybeee. But you would *Eat My Dust* if we dwibbled."

Grady looked him straight in the eyes. "Let's just test it and see."— He turned Bennie's direction. — "Bennie, have you got a coin we can flip and a stopwatch?"

BennieToo's screen lit up. "Sure do!"

"Great! You'll be our official timer, and Miss Clara can be our referee."

He glanced in her direction. "You wouldn't happen to have a whistle with you, would you?"

She smiled, reached into her purse and dug around for a while, then emerged with one on a chain. "Yep!"

Grady continued. "Do you also have something we can use to mark our course?"

She pointed at a small cooler. "I've got cans of soda."

Grady grinned. "Great idea! That'll do. I now dub you, Official Referee and Field Setup Coordinator too."

He returned to J.D. "Pack up the ballbag, son, and follow me.

###

Once inside the tennis court fences, Grady pointed toward a pathway separating the courts and turned to Clara. "Why don't you set up our dribble contest on the path while we do our shot contest in this court."

She studied the area for a minute or two. "Looks good to me," she said as she took off in that direction.

J.D. called after her, "Make it a hahd one, Miss Clawa!"

"Will do!" she shouted back over her shoulder.

Grady, J.D. and BennieToo headed for the chosen foul line. Grady retrieved a ball from the ballbag and twirled it in his hands. "I think we should have a side-by-side dribble race the length of the court first, then make a few free throws...best out of five; and finish up with the obstacle course Miss Clara is making. How does that sound, J.D.?"

J.D. shouted, "Gweat with me!"

Grady continued his survey. "Bennie? Okay with you?"

BennieToo's screen lit up. "Fine with me!"

Grady rotated to Clara at the end of the pathway. "Clara? Okay with you?"

She flashed tumbs up.

He bounced the ball. "Then let's do this!"

###

Grady, J.D. and BennieToo gathered at the side of the tennis court. Grady pointed to a place a short distance from them where Bennie could see the action clearly but not be in the way. "Let's have you stand over there, Bennie.Too"

BennieToo took the position.

Grady continued his instructions. "Bennie, can you see the finish line okay and hear me?"

Bennie's voice reached him. "Yes. The sideline of the court, correct?"

Grady replied. "Correct. Got the stopwatch ready?"

Bennie responded. "Ready."

Grady waved Clara over to them. "We need our official referee. Are you ready?"

She stood nearby. "Ready."

Grady began reciting the rules. "Miss Clara, please count down from five to one, then say Go!"—She said, "I have a whistle. Couldn't I just blow the whistle?"

"Ohkaaaaay."— He focused back on the boys and continued. "When Miss Clara says Go! and blows the whistle, Bennie, you start the stopwatch and J.D., you and I will dribble across the court, touch a foot on the line then turn around and dribble back to this line. Everyone got it?"

He was met with a universal, "Yes!"

Grady retrieved a ball for himself; placed his foot on the line beside J.D.'s; took a starting position; then winked at Clara to begin counting down.

Clara raised her arm and shouted, "Five! Four! Three! Two! One! GO!"

At the whistle, Grady took off like a bat out of Hell, but soon realized he was racing alone. He stopped and whipped around. J.D. was still In starting position.

"J.D.! My man! What are you do-ing!?"

J.D. shouted back. "I am giving you a head staht."

"What head start? We didn't discuss a head start!"

"I know. It was a supwise."

"Why?!"

"You ah *old*, Mistow Wedwine. I wanted to make the race fay-uh."

"J.D.! I have longer legs than yours and more experience. The race is already fair."

Still in starting position, J.D. shouted back, "Well, I didn't want to mention it, but you ah *fat* too."

That did it. Grady sucked in his gut and took off dribbling. By the time J.D. caught up with him shortly after the turn, Grady had only a two-dribble lead. He was breathing hard, streaming with sweat, and his tank was nearing empty.

J.D. easily beat him to the finish line and after the whistle, Clara officially declared J.D. the winner.

When Grady was able to speak again, he looked at Clara and managed to croak, "Water."

J.D. slumped to the ground. "Me too."

Clara pulled some bottles out of the cooler and handed them over. "Only a sip you two. You need to hydrate, but if you drink too much, you'll get sick."

After fifteen minutes or so of rest, Grady picked up the ball again and looked at the basket, then focused back on J.D.. "Best out of five?"

J.D. dragged himself off the ground. "Go foe it."

While he approached the basket, Grady felt waves of nostalgia. It seemed like eons since he'd been involved in something like this, and he missed it.

He turned toward BennieToo. "Are you ready to flip the coin, Bennie?"

Bennie responded. "Got it right here!"

Grady turned his attention to J.D. "What do you want heads or tails?"

"Heads." J.D. said with conviction

"Heads it is," Grady replied. "That makes me tails." He turned back toward Bennie. "Okay, Bennie, flip it!"

Bennie's voice came through the speaker. "It's tails, Mister Redwine. You go first."

J.D. seemed rather relieved when he sank to the ground to watch.

When Grady was ready, he stepped up to the line, began his routine by popping his neck first left then right, still loving the familiar weight of the ball in his hands. He bounced it a few times; took a deep breath; settled into his stance and focused.

When he felt centered, he rose up, lifted the ball, and let it roll off his fingers, following through with a perfect gooseneck.

The ball struck the rim, skittered along the circumference for a while; then wobbled for what seemed to be an eternity. Gravity finally took charge in a heart-stopping moment, and as the ball dropped through the net to the floor, Grady made a fist bump and said, "Swish."

"Looks like you've still got it, Coach," Clara said with a smile.

Grady smiled back, then bounced the ball to J.D. "You're up!"

J.D. pushed himself up from the ground and replied, "They's no way I can do that. Let's just call us even."

"Want me to teach you how?"

"I'd weathuh luhn how to do a lay-up, but not today. I think I should pwesuhve some of my enuhgy."

Grady graciously accepted. "Coach one/J.D. one. So far, it's a tie."

###

The gang moved over to the pathway where Clara had set up the course. Grady asked her to explain what was expected.

"As you can see," Clara said, "I've placed soda cans to mark where turns should be made throughout the course. It's essentially a zig-zag pattern down the length of the path. You will dribble across the path, make a turn at the can, then come back across the path in the opposite direction and turn again. Does that make sense?"

Grady and J.D. both nodded.

Clara smiled. "Good. You are required to use your right hand to dribble the first half of the course, but when you reach the cooler in the center of the lane, you must switch to your left hand and dribble the rest of the way to the finish. Any questions?"

J.D. and Grady answered with a simultaneous "No."

Grady took over. "Looks great, Miss Clara. Thank you."—He turned to J.D.. —"I started first last time, so it's your turn to go first., Okay?"

J.D. nodded. "Okay."

Grady continued. "Miss Clara will count down from 5 to 1 and say, Go! like the last time, then Bennie will time you."—He looked toward BennieToo. "Bennie, can you see? Are you ready?"

Bennie's voice came over the speaker. "Yes! I can see and I am *Read-dy*!"

Grady turned back to J.D. "You're up!"

J.D. went to the line and took a deep breath, then looked back at Grady; placed his hand on his heart and patted a few times; then sent a smile Grady's direction. Grady placed his hand on his heart too and sent a smile back.

J.D. soon took the starting position and looked at Clara who said, "This is for the championship. Are you ready?"

He nodded. "Weady."

Clara raised her arm and shouted, "Five! Four! Three! Two! One! GO!' then blew the whistle.

J.D. streaked across the path, gracefully weaving in and out of the cans, eyes locked on what was ahead. He made a flawless exchange of hands at the cooler and finished without a flaw.

Grady stood there flabbergasted. ***Wow.***

When J.D. made his way back to the top of the course, Grady said, "J.D.! That was just spectacular!"

J.D. smiled and replied, "I've been pwacticing."

Grady responded, "Well, it shows." Then he continued, "And *I* haven't, so I'm going to just declare you the winner!"

Clara announced, "That's two wins out of three, J.D. You're officially the champion!"

J.D. grinned from ear-to-ear. "Wow. I'm a champion. Wow."

WEDNESDAY
March 27, 2019-Morning

J.D. usually had his computer packed away in his book bag when he boarded the bus, but this morning, he had it open and turned on.

Oh-Lord. Not the Navigator again.

Grady watched him make his way up the stairs. "Whatcha got there, my man?"

"IIII've gooooot..." He set the computer on the dashboard and backed away. "...Pwissy!"

Prissy's pale little face appeared on the screen. "Sur-priiiise!"

Everyone on board gasped with shock and Bennie went absolutely berserk. "Hey Prissy!"

Clara and Grady chimed in, "We miss you, Prissy!"

She didn't pause a second before responding, "I miss you all too!"

Grady turned toward J.D. "How did you pull this off?"

"She's doing wemote assignments while she gets bettuh, and she wanted to wide the bus with us. So, I logged into Bennie's Wi-Fi and vee-ola! He she is! Widing the bus. With us."

Grady smiled and said, "That's great, J.D. Good thinking!"

Clara bent into the aisle. "Prissy. We're so glad to see you, how are you doing?"

"I'm okay—busy healing." She pointed to her food tray. "Look what I've got."

Grady squinted at the screen. Something that looked like a huge gelatinous potato was floating around in an enormous jar. "What IS that?"

"It's my foot! Isn't it cool? I'm naming it Shirley."

Everyone on the bus let out a gasp. J.D. let out an amazed, "Cooool beeeans!"

Clara's hands flew to her mouth in disbelief. "Oh-my gosh!"

Grady shook his head slowly. "I've never heard of such a thing."

Bennie ended it all with, "Ho-leeeey cow!"

Clara leaned into view on the screen. "Prissy! What are you doing with your foot? In a jar! In your room!?"

"Doctor Florion is going to help me get a new one made out of the bones from my old one. Isn't that cool? I have to keep it here in my room because if I don't have it with me, the rules are they have to burn it up."

Grady prepared to head for the school. "We better hurry! Don't want to be late! You and Shirley have a good day! Let's talk again soon."

"Okay! Bye!"

Grady turned to the kids on the bus. "Say goodbye everyone! "Bye! Good Bye! Miss you! See you soon!" The screen went dark.

After they dropped the kids off at school, Clara turned to Grady. "That Prissy is *something,* isn't she?"

He nodded and replied, "*Verrry special.* By the way, I think we should contact the *Food Bank* about sorting cans for Citizenship this afternoon. Sonti's injured, Prissy's out, and we don't have any Wi-Fi in the building that we can use for Bennie."

She picked up her phone. "Good point. What do you think we should do instead?"

He shrugged. "I don't know. Let's have a treat—go get ice cream—ruin their dinner."

She smiled and said, "Count me in."

THURSDAY
March 28, 2019-Morning

Grady spent most of the morning stewing over the tickets. He thought the problem of being one ticket short was solved when they decided to call the trip a private party and arrange their own transportation. But now that Grundel had changed her mind and thrown a wrench into everything by approving the field trip, he was up to his ears in alligators again.

He knew it would be impossible to find a certified driver in the District who would be willing to sit in the parking lot all night and listen to the game on the radio, and although his first choice would have been to invite his buddy Charlie Carlson to drive, Grady figured that if *he* wasn't considered certified, *Charlie* wouldn't be either. That left him with one final option—persuading Jack Riley to skip having dinner with his wife on their anniversary by bribing him with an invitation for his son to come along with them. He knew Jack's wife well enough to know she wouldn't turn down their son if *he* wanted to go, even on her anniversary, so he didn't feel too guilty.

Grady also knew that if he decided to do this, he wouldn't be one ticket short, he would be short two. *Ugh.*

Even so, one thing was certain: he wasn't going back to Victor Hamilton for help again. He had already been more than generous.

What to do? What to do.

Afternoon

Sometime during lunch, Grady smacked himself on the forehead with the heel of his hand when it dawned on him that he was overlooking the obvious. The Comets were playing the Ravens that night.

The Ravens, Grady—Malik and Brandon's team—and both of them will be playing!

Grady knew members of the team always get complimentary passes. Maybe they could help.

Inspired, Grady looked up the main number of the Ravens training facility in Chicago and got an answering machine. "I would like to leave a message for Malik Perry. Would you please ask him to contact Coach Redwine. Please tell him it's important. He has my number. Thank you."

###

Grady's heart leaped when Malik's name appeared on his phone early that evening. "Well, well, well, how is the greatest *power forward* in the U.S. doing these days?"

"Doing great! How are you?"

"I'm great, too, son. How's the ankle?"

"Coming along. Coming along. I should be good as new soon."

"Have you got a few minutes to talk?"

"Rushing off to study some film. What's up?"

"I need a favor."

"Anything. You know that."

Grady crossed his fingers. "I want to bring some *Special Needs* kids to the game when you guys are here, and I need some floor seats. I'm wondering if you can help me out."

"Ohhh maaan. That's going to be tough, Coach. How many kids are you bringing?"

"Four kids and three chaperones, so seven. Victor Hamilton has given me five, but I need two more."

"Floor seats are going to be tough, Coach. They only give players seats in the stands. Can you get by with two in the stands?"

"Unfortunately, my kids are in wheelchairs. Bleachers won't work."

"I could be wrong, but I think there are only around nine on the floor in that arena. Victor Hamilton always gets dibs on those."

"Yes. He has very generously given me five of them, but I need two more and I don't want to have to ask him for them."

"Tell ya what...let me check around and see what I can do. I'll get back to you."

"It's a deal. Thanks so much, Malik. This means a lot to me."

"I'll call as soon as I can."

FRIDAY
March 29-Morning

Last Workday Before Spring Break

Grady had just completed his pre-check and was on the bus waiting for Clara that morning when he got a call on his phone.

"Who in the Hell would call me at this time of the day?" He fished around in his backpack and managed to find it, only to rejoice when he saw Malik's name on the screen as the caller.

When he answered, Grady could tell from the volume of background noise that Malik had him on speakerphone. "Hi Coach! It's Malik! Guess who I've got here with me."

"Hmmm I wonder. Who could it possibly be?"

"It's me, Coach! Brandon!"

"Not THE Brandon Baldwin, *Point Guard...First team All-NBA, Offensive-Player-of-the-Year.*"

"The one. The only."

"Looks to me like you'll bring home some serious hardware this year."

"From your mouth to God's ears, Coach."

There was an awkward pause. Finally, Malik took over. "Sooo, we're calling about your tickets."

Grady crossed his fingers. "Annnnndddddd..."

Brandon took over, sounding absolutely despondent. "And we feel just awful about this, Coach. They had already assigned the seats. We tried hard, but we were just asking too late. We feel terrible about this, but we weren't able to get you tickets..."

Grady's heart sank while Brandon continued. "...and you know how the *Half-Court* promo goes. The arena is always packed. Scalpers don't even have 'em."

Grady swallowed hard and even though he had a sick feeling of failure, he still tried hard to sound reassuring. "I know you did your best, boys...you always do. Thank you for..."

Laughter burst over the line from the other end. Together, the guys said, "We couldn't get tickets, so we got..." their voices sounded gleeful and closer to the phone. "PRESS PASSES instead! SCOOOOORE!"

Grady sank into his chair. "Wowww. Wowww." He raised his eyes to the heavens in thanks.

Malik said, "We got them from Dugger Whitmore...you remember him, don'tcha Coach?"

Grady responded, "Sure do. He announced every game in the old days...voice of the *War Eagles*. One of the best."

Malik continued, "Dugger said you can sit with the press on the floor...and...AND... you can all come in through the Press Entrance. It's a lot closer to the arena."

Grady gave a sigh of relief. "That's great, guys. A shorter walk will really help."

Malik kept on. "The only problem is that there isn't any handicapped parking back there..." Grady scrunched up his mouth. Yikes! "... so, you'll have to park the bus in the regular lot down the block."

Grady blew out his cheeks and broke into a sweat. "Thank you so much, boys. You have no idea...no idea at all, what a difference this might make in a young man's life." He hesitated for a moment, then continued. "Just between us, there's a possibility that one of my kids is going to be able to participate in the Contest."

Mayhem erupted at the other end of the phone. "WHAAT?! You're kidding! Tell us more!"

Grady went on to explain, "Victor Hamilton has said if the crowd agrees, he will let him be a last-minute contender."

There was a simultaneous, "Wowww."

Grady forged on, "And I suggested that the two of you be allowed to be his sponsors."

Malik sounded moved. "What an honor, Coach. Of course I will."

Brandon added, "And me too!"

Grady continued. "Thanks, I knew I could count on you. It's top secret and will only happen if the first contestant fails and the crowd votes to let him try. There can't be even a whisper of a fix or a scandal so tick-a-lock."

Brandon spoke first. "Not a word. I swear."

Malik followed up with, "I swear too."

Grady concluded with, "Thanks again guys. I'm so proud of you."

Grady hung up the phone on an emotional high but had to get down to business.

Afternoon

Right after lunch, Grady picked up the phone and dialed Jack Riley.

Jack answered, obviously in a hurry. "Hi Grady. What's up?"

"I'm calling to answer one of your prayers."

"J.D.'s trying out for JV?"

"No. Even better. How would you and your boy like to go to the Half-Court contest for free?"

"What brought that up?"

"I need you to drive the bus and park it for us."

"Can't. Like I told you, that's my anniversary."

"All you have to do is tell Jackie that he will get to go if his Mom says yes, and he'll start working on her. You know she can't tell *him* no."

Jack sounded sold on that solution. "Okay, now that you've put it that way. I've got a meeting right now but will get back to you soon."

"The offer can only last until tomorrow morning, Jack. If she says no, I'm going to have to find someone else."

"I understand. Thanks Grady. Gotta go. Talk to you soon. I promise."

Grady hadn't been home for more than half an hour when Hattie Miller's name appeared on his phone.

Oh maaan. What's wrong now.

Her voice sounded strained. "Mister Redwine, I'm calling to let you know that one of the toes on Prissy's other foot has turned blue."

"Oh, my Lord. What are they going to do?"

"We don't know yet, but I thought you would want to know. They're planning the procedure for tomorrow.

"She's been asking for you, Mister Redwine. She's all upset that she might miss the field trip. Do you think you could go down there for a few minutes around one o'clock? The doctor will be making his rounds then and would like to talk to you."

"Of course I can. Absolutely."

"Thank you, thank you, thank you. She'll be so glad to see you."

"I'll be glad to see her too."

"Room 217."

"Got it."

Grady didn't need to read the numbers on the doors to find Prissy's room. He wasn't sure how he was able to filter the sound of her quiet crying out of all the confusion, but, for some reason, he just could.

He lightly knocked on the door and tiptoed in.

Prissy held out her arms. "Oh Coach. I'm so glad to see you."

"Are you hurting honey? Do you want something for pain?"

"No. I'm not hurting."

"Why are you crying?"

"Because I'm afraid I won't be able to go to the game and watch Sonti on Saturday. Please. Please let me go."

The situation about broke Grady's heart. He took her hand in his and said, "If there's any way at all to do it, I promise we'll get you there, but we'll have to talk to the doctor."

As if on cue, the door opened and Doctor Florian walked in. Grady stood up and said, "Annnd here's Doctor Florian now!"

"Hello you two." Florian smiled down at Prissy. "What's this I hear about you being all upset, Missie?"

"I want to go to the big game with my friends on Saturday and Mister Redwine said we had to ask you."

"Oooo that's a big question. Today is Monday. We're doing the procedure tomorrow morning. That's Tuesday. The game is on Saturday. That's only three-and-a-half days. You're supposed to take it easy for at least a week."

Grady stepped in. "What's the possibility of putting the procedure off a week?"

"That's just too long. We have to restore circulation. She could lose the toe."

Prissy grew indignant. "I don't NEED that toe! I don't even USE it…except for picking up stuff I drop and keeping my flip-flop on."

The doctor chuckled. "I'm afraid putting it off is just not an option, honey."

Grady reset the conversation. "When are you planning on sending her home?"

"Sometime Wednesday unless something unforeseen happens."

"So, we wouldn't be taking her out of a hospital bed or anything. And she can be around people. What if she's doing really well by Saturday. Could you make an exception?"

"Going into a public setting with lots of people milling around is a lot riskier than being around family. If she bumped her foot, or if someone ran into her, it could do some major damage. She could begin hemorrhaging and still lose the toe."

Prissy rearranged her blankets. "I'll be careful. I won't bump any-thing."

Think, Redwine, Think.

Grady grasped at a straw… "We'll be going through the Press Entrance and right onto the court, so it's not quite as big a risk." Then he suddenly got inspired. "I know! What if there was someone right there who could immediately stop the bleeding…like a med tech or something."

"That would help."

"How about you? You like basketball. How about if you were there?"

Doctor Florian began thinking it over.

Grady pushed harder. "Primo seating. They're playing the *Ravens*."

"That's very tempting, but I couldn't go to a Half-Court contest where the *Ravens* were playing without my son and still live at home."

"Well…well then, both of you come. I'll…I'll get you tickets…" *Somehow.*

The doctor wrote something on Prissy's chart. "I'm scheduling a check-up for Friday afternoon. If she's healed enough. And if it's safe enough, you've got a deal."

Prissy went nuts; rocked wildly in the bed. "Yaaaaayyyyy! Yaaaayyyy! I'm go-ing to the ga-ame! I'm go-ing to the ga-ame!"

Dr. Florian pointed a finger at her. "IF…and ONLY IF" you're healed enough to go."

She plopped back on her pillow. "Noooo prob-lem. I'm starting right now."

Grady climbed into his truck and slouched behind the wheel. *Okay, big mouth. What-are-ya-gonna-do-NOW?"*

He wasn't going back to Malik or Brandon. And he wasn't going to ask Dugger Whitmore for anything more. They had all been more than generous already. It was definitely hands off for Mister Hamilton, too. That could jinx the whole thing. And there was no way he would try to take the seats away from any homeless kids living at *The Salvation Army Home*…unnnlessss…

Wait a minute! Wait. A. Min-nute!

He started up the truck and headed for the Salvation Army in the center of town.

Shortly after he entered the lobby, he was greeted by a receptionist behind a tall counter.

"Welcome to the Salvation Army, sir. How can we help you today?"

"I'm here to see Mike Patterson."

She looked somewhat startled. "Do you have an appointment with the Commander?"

"No, but please tell him Grady Redwine is here. We're old friends."

"I'm sorry, Mr. Redwine, but he's in a meeting right now, and he told me not to interrupt him. He's under deadline for an important project."

Just then, a woman began exiting an office through a door at the rear of the reception area. She stopped, turned back, and lingered there a moment, apparently waiting for last-minute instructions.

Grady quickly moved sideways so he could see past the woman. When he saw a man with a shock of gray hair sitting at a desk, reading a document through glasses low on his nose, he stretched across the reception desk and waived.

"Mike! It's me! Grady!"

The receptionist whirled toward the open door too, obviously confused. 'I...uh...I..."

When Grady maneuvered past her and headed toward the door, she started quick-stepping along behind him. "Uh...sir...uh..."

When the woman exiting the office spotted him, she froze like a deer in the headlights.

Grady continued shouting. "I need to talk to you, Mike."

The man looked up with a scowl on his face, but it soon turned to surprise, then softened into a smile as he waved Grady into the office.

Both women appeared completely confused.

"It's okay, ladies. He's harmless...just an old buddy of mine from the *Guard*."

Both women made a quick exit, then closed the door behind them.

Grady felt a little indignant. "***Harm***-*less?*"

Mike stood up and extended his hand. "They were already afraid, Grady. If I told them the truth, they would have left and called the police."

Grady smiled and extended his hand too. "Then harmless it is."

They shared a firm handshake with a solid pat on the shoulder, then Mike stepped back and gave him the once-over. "As I live and breathe, Grady Redwine! It's great to see you. How are you?"

"Doin' fine. Doin' fine, Mike."

"I was so sorry to hear about Mary. She was a wonderful woman."

"Thank you, Mike. I appreciate the thought."

"So, to what do I owe this honor?"

"Actually, I'm returning one of *your* calls."

Mike sounded mystified. "Uhhhhhh, which call might that be?"

"The one asking me to teach a basketball clinic for your kids."

"That was a couple of years ago."

"I've had kind of a long to-do list lately. Still want one?"

"Absolutely. You know we do. I would have called to follow up last time, but I didn't know you were still doing that…since…well…"

Grady interrupted. "I'll make you a deal. One two-day basketball clinic for a couple of tickets to the game this weekend."

"The Half-Court contest?" Mike laughed. "Do you know how many people have called this week and offered big money for seats? Twelve, Grady, twelve."

"Did any of them get one?"

"Hell no. You know I don't do stuff like that."

"They're wheelchair kids, Mike."

There was an awkward pause. "I guess I could ask for a couple of volunteers to give up their tickets. Let me check it out and get back to you."

"I need to know today, Mike."

"Then no. The answer has to be no, Grady. The seats have already been assigned and I'm sure as Hell not kicking someone out because you didn't get in line like everyone else… and waited until the last minute, besides."

"I didn't *know* until today. I would have been in line if I knew sooner. You know I try to follow the rules."

"When did that happen?"

"Well, there's that, but…"

"Okay listen, there are bound to be some last-minute no-shows because of illness or something. Just bring them on down to the front door and I'll give you the no-show seats."

"They're wheelchair kids, remember? We need floor seats."

"Then we've moved from *No* to **Hell No**, Grady. Floor seats are for kids who have won them as rewards for hours of hard work. I told you already. I'm not kicking anyone out."

Grady got creative. "Where are you and your wife sitting, Mike?"

"In the front…oh-Lord.…"

"Don't tell me the Commander of the Salvation Army would refuse to give up his floor seats for two kids who can't climb the stairs."

"Geez, Grady. Hit me below the belt why don't ya."

"It's for a good cause and I'm desperate."

"Then you're giving two clinics, not one. I want one for each ticket. My wife and I will take the no-shows."

"Deal! You've got a deal. You're a great man, Mike Patterson."

"And you're a sneaky pain in the ass."

"Trust me. You can see the game better from the stands. Besides, these kids are worth it, Mike. You'll both be proud you helped."

Mike seemed to relent and said, "Watching *March Madness* this weekend?"

Grady stood up and prepared to leave. "Wouldn't miss these games for the world!"

Mike walked him to the office door. They shared another firm handshake and a brotherly hug this time, then Grady walked through the lobby, smiled at the receptionist and said, "Thanks so much for everything."

She smiled too. "You're welcome. Come back any time."

Grady left the building and climbed into his truck feeling greatly relieved. *Mission accomplished.*

WEEK THIRTEEN

MONDAY
March 30-Friday April 5, 2019

Spring Break
&
Absolutely Nothing but March Madness

SATURDAY
April 6, 2019- Late Afternoon

The Half-Court Shot Contest
Getting There

Grady picked the bus up early, parked it at the Activities Center and took the shortcut to the boy's locker room. At the bottom of the stairs, he paused and took a deep breath, then entered the hall and started his walk. "Rafer Alston, Royal Ivey, Kevin Love, Lamar Odom…"

He picked up speed, "Bill Russell, Wilt the Stilt, Karl Malone…"

He moved into a trot, "Kareem, Shaquille…" hit warp speed with, "Magic, Michael, Kobe, and this day, raced to the top of the stairs, ending with raised arms and a jubilant, *Sonn-Tiii*!"

Totally pumped, he jogged back to the bus, patted his shirt pocket just to double check that he hadn't forgotten the tickets and press passes then headed back to the bus lot for Clara.

She smiled and climbed aboard. "You're half an hour early. I'm glad I was here."

"Well, I didn't want to leave anything to chance. You never know what's at the other end…traffic and parking and…stuff."

She chuckled. "Yeah…have to watch out for that stuff part. I'll text the *Shelter*. Give them a heads up—make sure everyone has on their shirt."

"Good idea."

She settled in, sent the text and smiled at him in the mirror. "I still can't believe you managed to pull this trip off, Grady. Who would ever imagine that one of our children could have a chance to do something so extraordinary."

"Better make that *might* have a chance. Someone ahead of us has to fail first."

"I can't help but have a good feeling about it all, though."

"Me to."

As they turned into the Hamilton complex, Clara began to prepare for onboarding. "So how is tonight going to work?"

"The Hamiltons are taking BennieToo to the *Shelter* and we're picking him up there."

"BennieToo's riding? I thought he'd go with the family."

"Nope. We decided he's part of the team and should *travel* with the team so both he and Bennie can have fun with us on the bus." He switched lanes. "So that's the Hamiltons. We're also picking Sonti and Prissy up here, and Doctor Florian with his son, Frankie…"

She interrupted. "Can you imagine the look on that little boy's face when he first sees BennieToo?"

"It will probably look a lot like mine the first time *I* did." He tried to regain his train of thought. "Sooo, we get those four. Coach Riley and his son, Jackie, are picking up J.D., then we're meeting up with them at *Indy's* and he's driving all of us to the arena."

"What about Sonti's Mom?"

Grady hesitated. "I think she has to work."

"On a night like this? Oh, surely, they're giving her the night off."

Grady squirmed a little. "Not sure. It's possible she got confused and thinks this is just a regular ol' field trip."

There was a long pause. "Graaady. Is there something you need to tell me?"

He pulled into the Hamilton complex and ducked the question by pointing ahead to people milling around on the drive in *Comets* gear. "Oh look! A send-off party."

He pulled into place and looked at Clara in the mirror. "Let's discuss Sonti's Mom later, okay?"

She sent him a suspicious sounding, "Ohhhhhh, Kaaaaaay."

He quickly opened the front door and glanced up the driveway. Sonti and his Aides were at the top, waiting. "There's our boy!"

Clara descended the stairs and opened the side door. "Doesn't he look nice, all dressed up in his Milers shirt waving his *Comets* pennant." She sent the lift grinding its way to the sidewalk. "I wonder if he knows tonight is his big night."

Doctor Florian emerged from the building, carefully wheeling Prissy. Her legs were covered by elastic bandages and big puffs of surgical gauze, but they didn't seem to curb her enthusiasm any. She began waving her arms and shouting the minute she spotted them.

"Coach! Coach!"

Clara clasped her hands to her chest. "Look at how excited she is! She doesn't appear to be in any pain at all…"

Frankie followed Prissy and his dad, skipping joyfully along beside BennieToo, obviously enthralled.

"And just look at that child. Is he in Heaven or what?" She turned his way. "This is so much fun, Grady...our own little parade."

Sonti came next with an Aide on each arm...big guys, looking alert and a little jumpy around all the festivities.

Prissy glanced back at the *Shelter* door and leaned forward in the chair, giving an occasional pump on the wheels as if urging the doctor to go faster. "Come out here, Coach! Really! Please come here!"

Dr. Florian placed a hand on Prissy's shoulder, obviously trying to calm her down, but she persisted. "I need to talk to you Coach!"

Clara's happy chatter halted. "Grady. I think there's something's wrong."

A moment later, Sonti's mother blasted through the door at the top of the driveway. She rushed their way, arms flapping wildly, shouting something in Spanish.

Clara spun toward him. "What's happening, Grady? What's going on."

Grady fixed on Clara's eyes and said, "Get everyone on the bus. Fast."

She froze for a moment, digesting it all, but quickly sprang into action.

When Prissy's procession reached the door, she shouted up to him, tears in her eyes, "I had to tell her, Coach. She was going to take Sonti home. I had to tell her about Sonti and the contest."

Grady took a deep breath and spoke softly to her. "It's okay, honey. Everything is going to be fine. Just do what the doctor and Miss Clara tell you to do."

Grady pulled one of the pink permission slips from a folder on the dash and waited.

Well, Hell.

Halfway down the drive, Sonti's Mom pushed the Aides aside and took firm possession of her son. The Aides trailed behind her anyway as she continued toward the bus, pulling Sonti along.

She glared at Grady. "What is this I hear, Meester Bus Driver? Just what do you theenk you are do-eeng with my son?"

"I'm taking him to a basketball game...to the *Half-Court Shot Contest*." Grady showed her the pink slip. "Remember? We talked about it when you signed this paper saying it was okay."

Sonti began to board the bus. She pulled him back; reached in; snatched the paper from Grady's hand and ripped it to shreds as she spoke. "Don't you tell more lies to me."

"I didn't lie to you, Mrs. Smith. I told you he might shoot baskets while he was there."

"You have him in a con-test. On the Tele-vision. In front of the whole United of States! That is not the same theeng.

"What were you think-eeng? What-have-you-done?" She smashed the shreds into a ball and hurled it into darkness. Sonti shrieked; shook loose and chased after it like a bat out of Hell.

Everyone on the sidewalk went bonkers.

Behind him, Grady heard Frankie's voice, "What's wrong, Daddy? Why is that lady so mad? Why is Prissy crying?"

In front of him, Grady watched chaos erupt and surge like a tsunami into the darkness of the yard. Screams followed, and shouts, and the sounds of feet pounding in the dirt.

Grady felt sick to his soul. *This is your fault, Redwine. You caused it, and you have to make it right.*

He checked the mirror and saw four deer in the headlights sitting behind him, but everyone was safely inside. He glanced at his watch. They still had some time, so he set the emergency brake, shifted into neutral and shut the bus down.

Clara leaped to attention. "Grady, no! Grady! You can't do that!"

He ignored her; stepped down the stairs.

Doctor Florian's voice drifted his way. "Should I be calling for help or something?"

Grady went military…raising a hand to head level signaling, *stop…no.*

By the time Grady reached the bottom step, Sonti's Mom was halfway back from the woods, pulling her son along with her. She whirled toward him. "You have no i-dea what you have done."

"I can explain…"

She lowered her tone. "My son is not some trained puppy who does tricks for people…poor-leetle-autistic-boy-make-eeng-baskets-Isn't-he-cute. How dare you…make a fool of heem like that. No way. No way in the world he can do this."

Grady looked her straight in the eyes. "I believe he can."

"Then you are a fool." She pulled on Sonti's hand. "Come, son. We are go-eeng home."

Sonti planted his feet and jerked at her as she took some steps toward her junky old car. "Ahhh! Ahhhh!"

Grady began to follow. "Please. Can we talk about this?"

She continued without listening, pulling Sonti along. "I have three children already bulleed at school. So now you want to shine this light on us and make it ***worse***!?"

Grady walked with them. "I know you love your son, Mrs. Smith. It shines from your eyes every time you look at him. So, what you're doing just doesn't make sense to me. I just don't understand why. Why won't you let him have this moment?"

She stopped and whirled toward him. "My son cannot speak, Señor. He cannot tie his shoes or button a shirt and he wears pull-ups all day when we can keep them on heem. It is a miracle that he can feed heemself and drink through a straw. He cannot stand noise, and he has a meltdown whenever lights flicker! And you theenk he can go to a basketball court and make baskets for thousands of people?"

Grady looked her straight in the eyes. "Yes. I believe he can…"

"Like I said. You are a fool."

"I believe your son deserves some happiness."

"So now I am *selfish*? A bad *mothe*r?!" Her voice took a bitter tone. "You cannot imagine what I have sacrificed for my children."

For the briefest moment, Grady wavered. Should he retreat? Or run toward the fire.

He chose fire.

"Actually, I believe I *can* imagine."

"Just what is that supposed to mean?"

"It means I've seen the blue sports car, Mrs. Smith."

Her eyes became saucers. A hand shot to her mouth. "You are *spy*-eeng on me?!"

"No! No! It's nothing like that."

She got in his face, voice dripping venom. "That man gives me a job so I can have the Workfare, and my babies can go see their doctors. He gives me time off whenever they're sick and still pays me for twenty hours. I get a free meal every day and he gives me leftovers to help feed my family."

"You're right. That's very generous of him." Grady glanced at the bruise marks circling her wrist. "Did he give you those too?"

She let out a small gasp of surprise, slid her hand into a pocket and took a step backward..

"I'm trying to help you, Mrs. Smith. Please. Let me help you."

She looked him straight in the eyes, defiant. "There-is-no-help-for-me."

"Then, let me help your son."

She became misty-eyed. "There-is-no-help-for-heem-either."

"The prize is a hundred-thousand-dollars a year for five years. It could be a whole new beginning for you."

"*Could* be? *Could* be! And if you fail, what then?" She clutched at a necklace hanging under her shirt that Grady assumed was a rosary. "You are chaseeng the wind with our lives, Señor, and you know it. When this is over, you will be gone, and we will be left with handfuls of dust. The State lady already warned us that they are watcheeng. The last theeng this family needs is more attention!"

Grady gathered himself and managed to mumble, "I care for your son, Mrs. Smith. I see something special in him. Please. Please. Try to trust me."

"After all this? After your lies! I am to ***trust*** you?"

Grady took a deep breath. "Yes…truly…yes."

At that moment, the horn on the bus began blowing. Clara appeared in the window and pointed at her watch.

Sonti's Mom flicked her head toward the driveway. "You are a *bus driv*er. Go. Drive your bus and…leave…all of us…alone."

Sonti dug in and started to struggle again, so she called to his sister who had stayed in the car. "Carmella! Come out here and help me."

Carmella climbed out of the car and ran toward them. "Please, Mama. Please let Sonti try."

Her mother sent daggers her way. "Don't. You. Start."

Grady knew better than to offer help, so he just stepped aside and watched while the two of them stuffed the struggling boy into the back seat.

His hand Mrs. Smith! Watch out for his hand!

She made a U-turn at the end of the road and sped past him back to the exit. Sonti was screaming—pounding the window—the picture of abject despair.

Lord, Lord, what have I done.

He lifted a hand to Sonti in farewell.

Sorry, pal. I'm so, so sorry.

To The Arena

When Grady made it back to the bus, Doctor Florian was poised at the top of the stairs looking bewildered. "Everything okay?"

Grady gave him a thumbs-up but switched his attention to Prissy who was drowning in tears, leaning against Clara's side. "I broke the tick-a-lock and now Sonti's not coming, is he, Coach?"

"No, not this time. But we won't give up, will we? There's always a next time."

"I ruined everything, didn't I?"

"Oh Miss Priss, you didn't do anything wrong. If you hadn't told Mrs. Smith, she would have taken Sonti home and he wouldn't have had any chance at all. You did what good Milers do. You tried to help your friend. It isn't your fault his mother said no."

She swallowed a couple of times and wiped her eyes. "What are we going to do Mister Redwine? Are we still going?"

"Of course we are! Milers don't let a little bump in the road keep them from having a great time, do they, Bennie."

He got no response. "Bennie?"

He turned toward Clara who explained: "Bennie has gone off-line, Grady."

"What do you mean, Bennie's off-line?"

"His screen isn't working." She checked a few dials. "No Wi-Fi. He's off-line."

Swell. What an effin' disaster.

He concentrated on maintaining his game-face and fighting off the what-ifs, if-onlys, and could-have-beens while driving to *Indy's* to pick up the rest of the crew.

This isn't the first time you worked hard, played hard and still lost a game after a bad call. Shake it off, Redwine. Don't let this ruin the night for everyone.

Traffic was fairly heavy around *Indy's*, so it took some extra time. The boys were obviously anxious while waiting on the sidewalk with Coach Riley. Predictably, J.D. stormed onboard and announced that the bus was late then noticed Sonti wasn't there.

Prissy piped up. "Sonti isn't coming."

J.D. looked bewildered. "But..."

Prissy began to explain. "His mother wouldn't let him."

J.D. was obviously very confused. "But..."

Prissy summed everything up with, "We're going anyway."

J.D. seemed relieved, then relaxed some and said, "Good."

Grady was feeling gutted and raw, but he stood and faced a bus full of forlorn faces.

"We're all sad about Sonti and we'll miss him tonight. But we're Milers and what do Milers do when they fall?"

Everyone else on the bus responded, "They pick themselves up and go for the goal again."

Grady pumped a fist their direction and said, "Right! What else?"

The gang answered, "They help each other."

Grady punched in the air, "Right again! Sooo...we are still going to the game and we're going to have a wonderful time. Let's start now."

Miss Clara stepped up and said, "Let's sing something. What should we sing?"

Prissy joined in. "I know, I know. How about *Take Me Out to the Ballgame*?"

And so, they did.

A few blocks away from the arena, BennieToo's screen flashed back on.

Grady glanced in the mirror and said, "Welcome back, Bennie! We're so glad to see you again. Where have you been?"

"Sorry, everyone. I had some family stuff to do."

At the Arena

When they pulled up to the Press Entrance, Clara shaded her eyes and gaped at two figures waiting under the overhang at the outside door. "I think that's Mrs. Hamilton..."

Grady's heart began to pound in his chest as Clara finished her sentence, "...and I *think* she's with Mrs. Smith!"

Grady panicked. Oh, my Lord what if she thinks I said something!

Clara went on with her observations, "And...And...*Grady*! I think I see Sonti!"

BennieToo lit up again and spread his arms. "Sur-pri-iise!"

From behind the wheel, Coach Riley said, "Uh...we better get going, folks. It looks like it's going to rain and those cars behind us are getting antsy. We've got five wheelchairs to unload."

While Clara got busy unloading everyone, Grady pulled out Jack's tickets and handed them to him. "I saved two courtsides for you."

Jack took them and smiled. "Thanks, buddy."

Grady gave him further instructions. "We'll take Jackie in with us. You can meet us after you park the bus—give me a call and I'll tell you where we are."

Jack pocketed his tickets and said, "Great. Will do."

Grady stepped off the bus and approached Sonti's Mom. "I..."

She held up her hand to stop him and squatted down next to her son—Grady's eyes followed. "Show Meester Bus Driver what you have for heem, Sonti."

Sonti opened his hand and revealed a big muddy wad of pink paper that Grady knew had been his permission slip.

Feeling overwhelmed, Grady pressed a hand on his chest and his throat tightened as he accepted the wad and placed it on the stack with the others. He swallowed hard and managed to say, "I'm sure glad to see you here, son."

There was a moment of silence after that while the magnitude of what just happened sank in. Grady was a little afraid to ask how all this happened, so he decided it was best just to be grateful, let it go and move on.

As if she'd read his mind, Mrs. Hamilton rushed toward them. "I know you two have a lot to catch up on, but could we please discuss details later?" She turned to Grady and began guiding him toward the door. "Bennie called and told me what happened, so I went over to get them. We had a good talk, Mom-to-Mom. I told her how wonderful you have been with Bennie, then explained what was going on a little bit better and finally convinced her to let me bring them down here.

"I assure you everything's fine now, Mr. Redwine, and everyone's here, so let's try and put this behind us and go have a good time, shall we? Mr. Hamilton and I have planned some surprises."

She led them through a short maze of hallways until they reached what appeared to be a reception area where five golf carts with drivers were waiting.

Clara grabbed his arm. "Grady! How wonderful! We won't have to walk!"

Mrs. Hamilton continued her introductory tour as they climbed in. "We've reserved one of our *Limited Mobility* suites on the second level lanai for you all. You have a great view of the court and there's a wall-size TV. It is sound-proofed and the noise from the game is piped in with volume control speakers so it can be comfortable. It has accessible bathrooms and elevators right there and we've ordered hot dogs, hamburgers and pizza."

The Milers erupted and raced for the golf carts. "Pizza!!! We get pizza!!!"

Grady felt so overcome with gratitude, he could barely get *Thank You* out of his mouth. Eventually, though, he looked over at Clara. "Got sound suppressors for Sonti?"

She perked up. "Yep! Got the tickets?"

He patted his pocket. "Yep!" Then he turned to face Prissy and J.D. behind him.

"Are we ready?"

They popped their necks left, then right, and J.D. answered for both of them, "Weady!"

Grady let loose with a howl. "Then let's go win some money!"

###

While the kids ooohed and ahhhed around in their private room, Grady, Clara, Sonti's Mom and Mrs. Hamilton had a strategy meeting out in the hall. Grady took charge.

"I think it would work best if Sonti and I still sat in the *Press Section* courtside. It will give him a chance to get acclimated and the changes in crowd level and noise won't be so impactful." He turned to Sonti's Mom. "I think you should go down with us when we first settle in, just in case."

She nodded. "I agree."

"Doctor Florian and Frankie will stay in the suite to help with Prissy, but I think Coach Riley and Jackie would still enjoy sitting down courtside with the crowd."

He pulled the bundle of tickets out of his pocket, removed his press passes and the two courtside seats he bullied out of Mike Patterson, then handed the rest of them to Mrs. Hamilton. "These are the seats Mr. Hamilton gave us. I guess you can still sell these or donate them or something."

She took them. "Thank you. I'll send them to *Will Call*."

He then held up Mike's two primo courtsides. "These belong to the Commander of the Salvation Army. Would it be possible for you to send these to *Will Call* too? His name is Mike Patterson."

"Sure! No problem. I'll take care of this now."

While she walked away, Grady pulled out his phone, looked up Mike's number and handed the phone to Clara. "Do me a favor and send a text to this number. Tell Mike he's getting his courtside tickets back and he can get them at *Will Call* under his name."

He watched as Clara's fingers flew over the keys. Soon the phone dinged, and she pulled up the text. "He says thank you, but he already scheduled the clinics."

Grady didn't hesitate. "Tell him I'll still do them, just let me know when."

She did. The phone dinged again. "He says thank you again. He'll be rooting for Sonti tonight."

###

Down at courtside, Grady parked Sonti's wheelchair in the *Press Section* in time to watch the pre-game activities and tip-off. "Look at this room, *Big Shot*, Isn't it grand?"

Happy in his sound suppressors, Sonti seemed awe struck by all the activity—until several monstrous thunderclaps shook the arena and the fluorescent lights in the first level food court flickered. Sonti took an immediate dive to the floor.

Grady turned toward Sonti's Mom. "Did you, by any chance, think to bring Sonti's shades?"

She appeared mystified. "His what?"

Grady explained, "Sunglasses. Did he bring them?"

Her eyes sort of skittered around. "I am not sure. He might have them. I weel check."

Grady stepped quickly aside so she could scoot in front of him and search through Sonti's pockets. She came up empty.

Sonti was still refusing to get up from the floor, so she reached into the pocket at the back of the wheelchair, pulled out his purple blanket and handed it to him.

Grady's heart skipped a beat. *Please. Sonti. Not on your...*Sonti sat up, unfurled the blanket, piled it on his head and shaded his eyes with his elbow. *Oh-Lord.*

Grady glanced nervously at a crowd of people starting to elbow each other and point.

Yeah-yeah-yeah—wait until half-time—see what you think then.

Sonti's Mom lifted the sound suppressors away from her son's ears and said, "Sontino Silva, you fought hard to be here, do not *dare* to ruin it now. Get up off that floor this very second and when it is your turn, you go out there and make everyone in this buildeeng wish they were you for those five minutes."

###

Even though Malik and Brandon emerged from the locker room on fire, Grady knew the *Comets* were out for blood after losing to the *Ravens* in the finals last year. And with home court advantage, the odds were in the *Comets*' favor...but you just never know. Malik looked fairly comfortable with the ankle brace and both of his guys had the ability to score thirty points or more when they clicked.

If they clicked tonight, the *Comets* might just find the *Ravens* unbeatable.

Grady knew better than to outwardly root for the *Ravens*, but he could still secretly watch his guys play great ball with pride. Brandon hit a killer sixteen-footer fall-away with three minutes in the first half remaining, giving the *Ravens* a twelve-point advantage. The *Comets* Coach called a time-out.

When the ref blew the whistle, a young woman wearing a Hamilton uniform came through the doorway behind them and held out a package. "This is from Malik for Sonti." Grady smiled. *Malik strikes again.*

She continued, "I left boxes upstairs from him and Brandon for the other kids too. They sent everyone autographed hats and t-shirts for both teams."

Grady grinned at her. "That's wonderful. Please tell them thank you for us."

She grinned back and answered, "I will." Then she hesitated for a moment and continued. "I don't know if this means anything to you, but Malik said to say, 'Tick-a-Lock.'"

Grady chuckled and replied, "Please tell Malik thank you."

When she was gone, Grady opened the bag and found some shades inside. "Wooooaaah, Sonnnntiii. Look what you've got. *Designer Aviators.* Beau-ti-ful." He opened the attached note and read it aloud. Malik says, "If you look great you play great, Sonti. These should help get you halfway there. I'll be rooting for you tonight."

He handed the glasses to Sonti who practically levitated off his chair when he slid them on.

Grady saw his reflection in the lenses when he turned to Sonti and said, "No worry here, pal. You've practically won this already."

Sonti's Competitor

An announcer's voice filled the arena. "Welcome, ladies and gentlemen, to the *Comets Half-Time, Half-Court Shot Contest*. Our contestant will have two minutes to take three shots. There will be no warm-up or practice shots."

Grady suddenly shot to attention. *Warm-up Redwine. Warm-up! What were you think-king?!* He reached into his bag, pulled out Sonti's exercise ball and gave it to him. "Gotta warm up that hand, buddy."

Sonti grinned and began squeezing.

"Let's give a hearty welcome to the contestant selected at random from the hundreds of applicants who filled out an entry blank to qualify for the contest tonight—Ollliver Luuuucas.

"Ollie is a volleyball champ who participated in the 2016 Summer Olympic Games in Rio de Janeiro. He's competing today so he can afford to train for the 2020 Summer Olympics in Tokyo."

Raucous cheers and whistles erupted as Ollie trotted onto the floor wearing black jeans and a *Comets* jersey. Anyone could tell by how Ollie moved that he was definitely a physical specimen.

Grady looked at the biceps on the guy. *Uh oh.*

Girls in the stands went wild, forming hearts with their hands over their heads, but Oliver was all business. He circled the ball around his waist, tossed it hand-to-hand and twisted side-to-side, stretching.

The shot clock was set to two minutes.

The ref took the first ball off the table; held up one finger; bent and pointed to the center court line, reminding him not to step over it. Ollie nodded, agreeing.

The ref pointed at the clock. "Two minutes."

Ollie nodded again.

The ref blew his whistle. "Go!"

Ollie licked his fingers, wiped them on his jeans and bounced the ball three feet ahead, bringing it back to his hands with spin. Finally ready, he skipped backward to the line.

Relax Redwine, it's a half-court shot, for crying out loud. Getting a ball through a hole barely big enough to hold it is not what spikers do best—they play with a net on a beach.

The big screen zoomed in on Ollie's chiseled face and laser focus on the goal, then followed him as he trotted to the line, pushed off and released the ball.

Grady followed with coaching eyes. *Good form, gonna be short.* The shot clipped the rim.

Moans of disappointment traveled through the crowd followed by shouts of encouragement.

"Come on, Ollie. You can do it!"

"Hang in there, Ollie. Relax."

"Go for it Ollie! You got this!"

The ref retrieved the second ball; held up two fingers; pointed to the center court line and the clock; blew his whistle.

Ollie repeated his ritual; let another one go. The crowd erupted; cheered it on.

"In the hole!"

Grady watched intently. *Good form, good trajectory, proper rotation. Too hard.*

The ball hit the back of the rim, bounced up…rolled off to the right.

The fans groaned with frustration.

Grady breathed a slight sigh of relief.

The ref retrieved the last ball; held up three fingers; pointed to the center court line; pointed at the clock and blew his whistle.

Ollie caught the third ball, popped his right shoulder, then his left. He went through his routine one last time; pushed off and let it go.

Frozen in position, Ollie watched it fly, mouthing, "Soft, baby. Soft. Soft. Soft."

Action in the arena stood still.

Heart in his throat, Grady studied the apex of the shot. *This is it. It could go either way.*

Ollie clenched a fist. "Come on, baby! Come on!"

The ball soared toward the goal; softly hit the back of the rim; bounced lightly to the front...

Grady held his breath. *Oh God.*

Then the ball fell harmlessly to the floor.

The crowd groaned in sympathy as Ollie crumpled into a crouch with disappointment, then cheered him as he trotted toward the circle of friends waiting to console him on the sidelines.

Sonti

Able to breathe again, Grady stood up. *Time to get to work.*

Grady looked up at the Hamilton booth. Hamilton gave him a thumbs-up and the announcer took over.

"Ladies and Gentlemen! We have some special folks with us today...the Milers Club from State Junior high school who are guests of Malik Perry and Brandon Baldwin. Give the crowd a wave, Milers."

Up in the *Mobility Suite*, Prissy, J.D. and Frankie suddenly grew shy but waved. Down in the *Press Section*, Sonti adjusted his *Aviators*.

"The Milers are here today to see the game, but Malik and Brandon say there's a member of this club who is something special, and they believe he has the stuff to sink this shot. His name is Sonti Smith.

Grady helped Sonti out of the wheelchair and the ref waved the two of them onto the floor. A murmur coursed through the crowd.

"Whaddaya say. Should we give him a chance?"

The screen again zoomed in on the *Milers*. Prissy had her eyes squeezed shut and her fingers crossed next to her lips saying, "Please-please-please-please-please." A nervous J.D. held up both hands with his fingers crossed and poked Frankie in the ribs as he pointed toward their faces on the screen.

"If you think Sonti should have a chance at the competition, say yes."

A rousing roar rose through the arena. "YESSSSS!!"

The announcer talked over the crowd. "Whoah! Whoah! Looks like you got a definite yes, Sonti."

When everyone in the arena got to their feet and cheered, the screen filled with Prissy, Frankie and J.D. going wild. Then it panned back across the crowd, hovered a moment on Sonti's teary-eyed Mom in the booth clutching a tissue with trembling fingers, then flew over to Victor Hamilton himself looking pleased.

The shot moved to Grady crossing his chest with his arms, silently addressing the crowd and bowing a little. "Thank you. Thank you so much." Then the camera shot back to Sonti's Mom; still obviously overcome.

"Sonti. You have two minutes and three balls. Please go to the center of the court."

The screen filled with cheering fans uploading photos of Sonti and the Milers to social media.

It seemed to cast a spell over the arena when Sonti adjusted those *Aviators* like he was Tom Cruise, set aside his blanket and began ambling his way to the half-court line with a slight swagger.

Grady felt a rush of nerves while he walked the twenty-two feet toward half-court with Sonti. It felt surreal to see the two of them projected on the overhead screen larger than life; with every expression and movement reflected back at them.

As a fan, Grady loved what the big screen added to his enjoyment of the game. And as a coach who had to be aware of every visual detail on the court, it was a welcome tool, sort of like having a third eye on his forehead. It was especially helpful tonight, when he was watching the first challenger—but for now, it seemed to be somewhat intrusive and distracting to see himself sandwiched between the stunned reactions of fans in the crowd and being able to lipread various versions of: "Can you believe this?"; "What's happening?"; "Are you kidding me?"; and "What the Hell?!"

Stranger still, was to be in the dead silence of that massive arena where the loudest sound streaming out of the speakers was the squeak-squeak-squeaking of Sonti's sneakers on the hardwoods.

When they reached half-court, Grady positioned Sonti in place and pointed at the basket. The minute Sonti spotted the goal, his eyes stuck there like a magnet on metal. He was obviously in his bubble again, completely alone in his own world…unaware of the growing whispers in the crowd.

Ball One

Grady spoke softly. "Here you go, *Big Shot*. You shoot from here. Forty-five feet to the center of the goal. Just like the gym and your driveway at home."

Sonti remained peaceful and relaxed as he shifted his eyes between the ball and the goal, obviously mentally measuring the arc of the ball. The screen finally cut away to the ga-ga eyes of a teen fan talking to her friend. "How could he be so han-some?"

Grady froze a moment when a close-up of Sonti's face reappeared. *Please, Lord. Don't let him think it's a mirror.*

Fortunately, the screen shifted to a fan in a muscle shirt shaking his head, shouting, "No way. Noooo waaay that guy's gonna drain a half-court."

Then it zoomed to another guy sitting nearby. "This is a joke. No-chance-in-Hell."

Soon the shot shifted left and filled the right side of the screen with a close-up of Sonti jiggling his injured hand, seeming to try to shake off the pain. The no-chance-in-Hell guy squinted and elbowed the man next to him. "I think the kid's hurt. Look. Look at his hand."

He wasn't the only one to notice. A murmur began flowing through the crowd while Sonti awkwardly began bouncing the ball.

Grady took a deep breath. *Patience, Redwine. Be patient.*

The screen shot panned back and focused on Sonti, tongue twisted through his lips, moving from side-to-side as he carefully pointed his feet in the direction of the basket.

He fiddled with his shades and tugged at the shoulder seams of his shirt. He dribbled twice in the middle then once to the side and wiped his forehead with his elbow.

Grady glanced at the clock, mercilessly ticking down from thirty seconds. He groaned. Sonti may only get two shots off on time.

At long last, Sonti glanced toward the basket; cracked his neck left and right; then readjusted the location of the seam of his sleeve on his shoulder again.

Grady's stomach started filling with acid. T*en seconds...nine seconds...eight.*

Sonti shifted the ball to his left and shook his right hand; then he made a fist and flexed his fingers a few times.

The *No-chance-in-Hell* guy was back on the screen, "See that? I told ya."

Apparently satisfied with how his hand was feeling, Sonti completed such a flawless crossover dribble to shift the ball back to his right, an audible gasp swept through the crowd. *Whoa!*

Grady would have felt thrilled with it too if he hadn't been dying a thousand deaths over the count on the clock. —*Five seconds...four seconds—Shoot, Sonti, Shoot!*

Grady forced himself to stand motionless and stare at the goal while his heart hammered hard in his chest. He knew if Sonti was distracted by him, he would stop his routine and start over.

Three seconds.

Even though he had appeared to be ready, Sonti paused once again. *Good God! This is going to kill me!* Then with no warning, Sonti sank his chin to his chest; drew back his arm and launched the ball toward the hoop like a rocket, beating the buzzer by merely two seconds.

A thunderous roar rose from the crowd as the screen shared the path of the ball with close-ups of frenzied fans spurring it on.

"In the hole!"; "Go Go **Go!**"

Grady winced as he watched. *Could be short.*

He was right. The ball started off strong but missed by a few inches. The room filled with disappointed groans and the muscle shirt fan showed up on the screen elbowing his pal. "See that? I told ya."

Grady stepped towards Sonti. "Good job, pal. We're a little short. Let's do another one."

Ball Two

Grady saw the rails on the upper levels begin filling with fans who obviously had stopped in the middle of their hot dog order to watch the ref take the second ball off the table and give it to Grady who handed the ball over to Sonti.

Supportive applause filled the auditorium as the ref put up two fingers, pointed to the clock then the line, and blew his whistle to start the count.

It took a while, but Sonti eventually turned and began fidgeting through his routine again. He looked at his feet and began circling like he was chasing his tail.

On the screen, Grady saw Mister Muscle Shirt screw up his mouth and say, "What the *Hell?*"

Grady watched Sonti circle some more. *He's confused. He can't find the nail.*

He took a clip like the one on the lead line at Sonti's home out of his pocket and carefully placed it on the mid-court line. "Shoot from here, Big Shot. Just like in the driveway back home."

After what seemed like an eternity, Sonti stopped turning and seemed somewhat buoyed by energy from the crowd, but there was a faint wince on his face…a distinct look of discomfort.

With five seconds still on the clock, Sonti shifted the ball to his left hand again; shook his right one a few times and flexed it.

Grady's guts twisted to knots while he forced himself not to speak or to move and prayed for no other distractions.

Sonti finally shifted the ball back; locked his eyes on the goal; then let loose less than a second ahead of the buzzer.

The crowd erupted. "*Go Go GO!*" Then the stadium filled with immediate silence while everyone watched the ball reach the rim…

…circle slowly…

…and teeter.

For a moment, the only sound in that cavernous space full of people holding their breath was the raw, high-pitched voice of a child making a passionate plea: "Fall in the net ball! Please! Just **fall in!**"

Grady bit his knuckles. *Oh God.*

When gravity finally took charge, the ball tipped outside the net and dropped to the floor. The entire crowd came unglued.

Couples collapsed into each other's arms.

Ball Three

Something major seemed to shift in the air when the ref reached for ball number three. Grady first noticed it in the faces of fans on the screen. Then in the increasing number of rubber-neckers lining the rails and in the eyes of the previous contestant who watched from the sidelines surrounded by his supportive buddies.

Grady didn't know what the shift was, but whatever it was, it was contagious—dead serious—and he knew it was heartfelt when peanut sellers and beer hustlers all stopped their patter and thirty-thousand people went dead silent.

There was no more trash-talking shown on the screen, only hope. Grady saw it in the eyes of the Hamiltons when the camera passed by; in Clara's eyes; and in the eyes of Sonti's mother.

The screen soon switched to the *Limited Mobility* suites, filled with whole sections of children with challenges most people don't have to face; then focused on kids in the crowd there, clutching each other's hands, rooting hard for him. *Can he do it? I don't know. Oh, I hope he can.*

Grady saw hope grow in the eyes of those kids when the camera panned by, and somehow Sonti's next shot became a cause bigger than everything surrounding the game.

It was for the homeless children at the Salvation Army, the Milers and the kids at *The Hamilton Home*. It was as if Sonti was making this shot for them all...to show them what could be done.

And Grady felt a glimmer of hope inside himself too…hope that some of the thousands of people who witnessed this moment would see how gifted in their own way these children were…how brave they could be through adversity…somehow see their potential and want to help them lead productive lives.

The cutaways to the crowd soon came to a standstill when the ref's whistle sliced through the air.

Grady saw the camera zoom to center court for a closeup of Sonti shaking his sore hand, then pan out to include him in the shot beside Sonti…obviously nervous and sweating bullets; then switch to wide shots of the arena and gradually tighten to oppressive split-screen close-ups of the jerk in the muscle shirt and his buddy, the *No-Way-in-Hell Guy*, guzzling their beer and gloating.

The shot switched to split-screen, bringing J.D. into focus. He was bobbing his head toward his left shoulder and mouthing, "Left. Mistow Wedwine. Twy the left."

Grady knew Sonti had only hit the hoop twice with his left hand, but so far, with the right one, he was at zero.

Why not. What the Hell.

Grady accepted the ball from the ref; polished it a little for luck and placed it in Sonti's left hand. "Try it this way, *Big Shot*. You can do it."

Sonti gripped it, stared at the goal and adjusted his stance somewhat.

Grady no longer had to count down with the clock because the crowd began its tradition of chanting:

"Ten!...Nine!...Eight!…Seven!..." *—Shoot-Sonti-Shoot!* —
"Six!...Five!..."—*Oh God*— "...Four! … Three!..."

Grady sucked in a breath. Sonti tossed it on "Two!..."

As the camera started tracking the arc of the ball, the moment became so stressful and emotionally charged for Grady, he had to close his eyes and just listen.

He heard the sharp, metallic clang of the ball hitting the rim hard, and in his mind, he imagined it spinning—floating high and weightless over the net—hovering there as time stood still.

He held his breath and sensed the world holding its breath with him as he re-lived the ten weeks of his journey there: the sacrifice and setbacks; the stress and anxiety from fighting the system; the sleepless nights and struggle of scrambling for tickets.

Soon Grady pictured the ball giving in to gravity and saw the legion of people who helped him flash through his mind like a shuffle of face cards: the Hamiltons who took a big risk and stood behind him; the Milers and Clara; Marie Sleidell, Malik, Brandon and Dugger Whitmore who walked the extra mile for him; Mike Patterson at the Salvation Army.

Grady heard the ball tap the rim again and after the crowd's reaction, panic set in. For the very first time, it dawned on him that it was possible Sonti could fail.

The weight of it hit him hard.

He found himself forced to face the fact that his laser focus on the short-term goal of getting Sonti a chance had blinded him to the bigger picture. He had completely overlooked the turmoil failure could unleash in Sonti's life and the impact it would have on that family.

How could I have been so irresponsible?

Grady knew deep inside that he never would have gone into an important playoff game without a contingency plan–how could he have done *this* without one?

You were playing with someone's life, Grady. This was no game.

He felt hollow inside—ashamed and guilty.

I should have waited a year and given Sonti's hand time to heal.

I should have prepared him to shoot faster.

I should have made sure he would have a soft, safe place to fall if he failed.

All Grady could see in his mind at that moment were the faces of all those kids in the crowd and their shattered hopes piled on the floor of the court when the whistle blew.

Lord, what have I done?

Grady heard a collective gasp from the crowd and his eyes flew open. Then he heard Sonti Solari—a child who had only managed to say three words in his life—say, "Ssswish."

This isn't the end of Grady's story...it's the beginning.

Grady and Clara team up on Bus 86 for the School Year of 2020.

Halim is back.

A new student arrives with a rare challenge.

Watch them make magic again.

Coming Soon!

THIRTEEN MORE WEEKS on the LAST MILE BUS

ACKNOWLEDGEMENTS

Writing this book has been a long, labor of love, and I couldn't have completed it without the unwavering support of my husband who believed in me even when I doubted myself. Thank you for patiently answering my hundreds of questions about basketball to help make this story believable. Your love and encouragement have meant the world to me.

I am deeply thankful to my daughter who spent many hours she really couldn't spare, helping me perfect my manuscript; and to the rest of my family, who encouraged and helped however they could, every step of the way.

To my editor—Clayton Jones: What an honor, education and joy it was to work with you. Your insights, suggestions and uncanny ability to push my writing to a higher level by asking simple questions were invaluable.

And to the staff at BookLocker who have created such a supportive and family-like atmosphere for their authors: thank you for believing in my vision and guiding me safely through this difficult publishing process.

ABOUT THE AUTHOR

C.A. Caldwell has an unyielding commitment to doing what she can to make the world a better place for children with *Special Needs,* because she believes that everyone has the right to thrive and reach their full potential. Her unusual career path has given her a unique 360-degree view of *Special Needs* issues…at home interacting with the *Special* kids in her family…in the classroom as a substitute teacher…and on a school bus as a monitor, helping get challenged children to school. Her background in business consulting gave her additional insight into the economic and legal conflicts that create many of the educational issues she encountered, and they are often reflected in her writing. She is hoping that this book will bring some of them to the surface, create awareness among the people who can bring about change, and present an example of effective advocacy as well.

SPEAKERS BUREAU

The Speakers Bureau for The Last Mile Bus provides professional presentations for conventions and fund-raising events for organizations interested in learning more about Special Needs issues; need some help in raising awareness; or want to learn more about effective advocacy. For more information, please contact us through our website: lastmilebus.com.

www.ingramcontent.com/pod-product-compliance
Lightning Source LLC
LaVergne TN
LVHW020341231025
824106LV00015B/903